Also by Jennifer E. Smith

ADULT

The Unsinkable Greta James

YOUNG ADULT

Field Notes on Love
Windfall
Hello, Goodbye, and Everything in Between
The Geography of You and Me
This Is What Happy Looks Like
The Statistical Probability of Love at First Sight
You Are Here
The Comeback Season

MIDDLE GRADE

The Storm Makers

PICTURE BOOK

The Creature of Habit
The Creature of Habit Tries His Best

Fun for the Whole Family

Fun for the Whole Family

A Novel

JENNIFER E. SMITH

Ballantine Books
New York

Published in the United States by Ballantine Books, an imprint of Random House, a division of Penguin Random House LLC, New York.

BALLANTINE BOOKS & colophon are registered trademarks of Penguin Random House LLC.

ISBN 978-0-593-35830-6

Printed in the United States of America

Book design by Virginia Norey

For Declan

There's no such thing as fun for the whole family.

—JERRY SEINFELD

Fun for the Whole Family

Michigan

1997

BY THE TIME THEY ACQUIRED A MAP, THEY WERE ALREADY
seventeen states in. They'd never bothered to count before—not
really, not officially—though they each had their own way of keeping
track. Gemma had a leather pouch full of rocks, one from every
place they'd been. Connor kept a journal, scribbling his observa-
tions as the country scrolled by unseen out the window. The twins,
Roddy and Jude, collected snow globes. But there had never been
any formal way of marking their progress, of ticking off states as
they saw them.

That all changed when Jude discovered the map at a yard sale,
propped up against a grim-faced old rocking horse. It was enormous, almost bigger than she was, with the world's ugliest red frame
and a tear that went from the Florida Panhandle all the way to Okla-
homa. She didn't care. She enlisted Roddy to carry it back with her,
the two of them stopping every few feet along the gravel edge of the
road to adjust their grip on the heavy frame.

At home, they burst into the kitchen, two proud fishermen hauling in their catch. Their dad was at work—was always at work—but
Gemma and Connor were there, and they looked up from their

homework to stare first at the threadbare map, then at the twins. For a moment, Jude worried she'd miscalculated. That it was a terrible idea. That nobody else would understand.

But of course they did. Connor hurried over to help them set it on the table; Gemma disappeared upstairs and returned a few minutes later with a box of colorful thumbtacks. They set to work, recalling stories, arguing over memories—that diner where Roddy spilled a milkshake, was that in Vermont or New Hampshire? was it last August or the one before that they saw that black bear in upstate New York?—and when they were done, they stood back to admire their handiwork. There was a smattering of pins along the East Coast, the rest arranged like a fist around Lake Michigan. Seventeen in all.

Proof of what they'd seen.

Proof that she'd been there too.

They stared at the map, each examining it for their own kind of evidence. Gemma's eyes ran over the blocky states in the western half of the country as she tried to guess where she might be now. Connor was remembering the time he'd gotten carsick on a highway in Kentucky and she pulled over to rub his back, whispering stories about her adventures as his brother and sisters slept. Roddy wondered if she'd show up again this August; it always felt like a magic trick when it happened, but magic wasn't all that reliable, so it seemed best to keep his expectations low.

Only Jude was looking at the box of thumbtacks.

To her, it felt like a promise.

More.

There would be more.

Gemma

Illinois

2025

It's been three years since Gemma has seen any of her siblings, three years since they've exchanged anything more than the occasional polite text, but somehow, she'd always known that when one of them finally got in touch for real, it would be to ask for something. She'd also known that—no matter how many times she'd told herself otherwise—she wouldn't be able to refuse.

The text arrives just after five A.M. in Chicago, which means it's three A.M. in Los Angeles, though Jude could be anywhere right now. Gemma is already awake; she sits up in bed, her heart beating fast. Beside her, Mateo shifts in his sleep, upsetting the dog, who gives him an indignant look. She stares at the phone, her sleep-deprived brain trying to make sense of the words: **Meet me in North Dakota this weekend?**

Behind the curtains, the night is punctuated by streetlamps, and Gemma blinks into the semidarkness, thinking: *North Dakota?* and then: *Jude.*

Jude.

She gets out of bed and walks quietly into the kitchen, phone in hand. The dog, Waffles, follows her, a mop of an animal, shaggy and smelly and not terribly smart. Gemma reaches for the coffeepot automatically, then remembers she's not allowed to have any caffeine right now. She glances over at the counter, which is crowded with vials of saline and packets of syringes, prenatal vitamins and pages of instructions from the fertility clinic. In the fridge there's more, the bottles of medication stacked neatly alongside the ketchup and the mayo and the expired jar of applesauce.

Gemma had never expected to find herself here, forty-three years old and still not totally sure she wants to be a mom, even as she waits to find out if their first round of IVF has worked. She'd always assumed she'd have figured it out by now, that she'd have enough distance from her childhood to know either way. Instead, she's continued to inch through this process with alarming ambivalence, first the months of medication to boost her numbers, then the three unsuccessful rounds of IUI, and now this: a single embryo, which will either stick or it won't, which will either turn her into a mom or not. She wishes she knew which she was hoping for.

When she looks up again, Mateo is standing in the doorway of their tiny kitchen with evident bewilderment. "What time is it?" he asks as he stoops to pet the dog, who promptly flips onto her back, gazing up at him adoringly. She might've belonged to Gemma first, but from the minute Mateo came into their lives, over a decade ago, she's had eyes only for him.

"I got a text from Jude," Gemma says, and Mateo straightens, looking surprised.

It's not as if she hasn't spoken to her siblings at all in the three years since their fight. But if anyone ever reached out, it was usually Gemma, whose job it had always been to keep them together. In spite of everything, she sent birthday cards and texts on holidays and congratulatory emails when she read something interesting about any of the other three in the news, which had been happening with increasing regularity. Sometimes she got something in return: a **thanks!** or a **you too** or simply a hollow-feeling **xo**. But usually she didn't.

"Wow," Mateo says, raising his eyebrows. "What did she say?"

"You wouldn't believe it."

"I'd believe just about anything when it comes to your sister," he says, his accent like music, her all-time favorite song. He walks over to give her a kiss, lingering for a moment in case she needs more. But she feels too fragile right now. Behind her, the sun is beginning to stream through the window above the sink, and the old man in the townhouse next door is playing the same tuneless rendition of "Heart and Soul" he does every morning. For years, Gemma had thought about complaining, but then she ran into him in the courtyard one day and he told her how his late wife used to play the other half, the two of them side by side at their old piano, and she's since grown to love it. Even if it's badly off key.

Mateo grabs his favorite mug, the one with the Brazilian football logo on it, and starts to make coffee with an apologetic look. But Gemma's mind is elsewhere.

"She wants me to meet her in North Dakota," she tells him.

He laughs, then realizes she's serious. "Oh."

"This weekend."

"Oh," he says again, setting down the mug, clearly searching for the right thing to say. "Have you ever been?"

"To North Dakota?" Gemma says with a frown. "No."

"I thought you went everywhere as kids."

"Not everywhere," she says, thinking about their childhood map, the thirty-two states they'd marked off with pushpins before everything had fallen apart so abruptly the night of the fire in Texas. It's been a while since she's bothered to tally up her official number, to count all the states she's seen in the years since those breathless road trips with their mother, on travels with friends and adventures with Mateo, summer vacations and business trips to marketing conferences in random cities. If she had to guess, she'd say that maybe she's been to forty or so by now. But mostly she's lost track. They all have. Or at least that's what she thought.

"Maybe she's filming something," Mateo says, and then—trying and failing to sound casual—he adds, "Do you think you'll go?"

His eyes flick to her stomach, and the look on his face is so hopeful it could break her heart if she let it. She shakes her head.

"No," she says. "Don't worry."

"I'm not worried," he says with a too-quick smile, but she knows that's not true, and she feels a stab of guilt because it's her fault they're here. From the moment they met, Mateo was ready to be a dad. Everything about him fits the part, from his periodic table sweatshirt to his corny jokes to the way his sixth-grade science students adore him. This had always been their plan eventually, to have kids, but it was Gemma who insisted on waiting, hoping something would tip her into feeling ready too; at first it was just a couple years, and then more, until nearly a decade had slipped by, and the question mark she'd been carrying around inside her all that time stopped mattering as much as the unforgiving fact of her biology.

Sometimes she can't help feeling jealous of Mateo's certainty. But it's easier for him. He grew up in a wealthy suburb of São Paulo, in a house with two loving parents and a protective older brother, an abundance of riches as far as Gemma is concerned. Her childhood was something different altogether. Until she was twelve, she and her younger siblings had a mom like any other. Frankie Endicott was maybe a little more scattered than most, a little less reliable, but she still managed to brush their hair and pack their lunches and give them baths before bed most nights. Then one day, she sent the four of them off to school with hugs and kisses, and when they came home that afternoon, they found a tuna casserole in the fridge with a note explaining that she would be gone for a while.

That was May. She didn't return again until August—and then, only long enough to whisk them off on the first of those summer road trips. But already, she didn't seem like their mom anymore. Already, she seemed more like a stranger.

Their dad, Paul, worked long and unusual hours as a feeder driver for UPS, and so it was Gemma who became responsible for making grilled cheese and forging permission slips and walking the twins to school, for making sure Connor didn't stay up too late reading and finding Roddy's inhaler before soccer practice and keeping tabs on Jude. It wasn't until years later, when their dad met Liz—a pediatric nurse whose best and worst quality was that she was not their mother—that their home finally regained a semblance of order. But by then, Gemma was nearly out of the house herself. Which meant she'd never really been a kid. Not when her mom was around. Not when she wasn't. Not even when she came back at the end of each summer to take them on those freewheeling adventures, crisscrossing the country in great lurching strides before depositing them back at their dad's.

Especially not then.

Across the kitchen counter, Mateo is still watching her with an anxious expression. "I know we're talking about Jude here," he says very gently. "So if you feel like you need to—"

"I'm not going," Gemma tells him, because today is Tuesday, the fourth day of February, which means that in exactly five days she's meant to take a pregnancy test—and while she has no idea which way it will go, no idea what she's even hoping for at this point, she does know that she'd rather not be in North Dakota when she finds out. She shakes her head. "This is so typical. You can't disappear for three years and then out of nowhere just . . ." She trails off, her throat suddenly thick, and blinks a few times. "I'm not going. I can't."

Mateo frowns. "Are you sure?"

"I'm sure," she says firmly.

"Okay," he says, and then he brightens. "You've got plans this weekend anyway."

"I do?"

"Yeah, it's only the biggest event of the sixth-grade academic calendar."

"Right," she says with a faint smile. "The science fair."

He runs a hand along his rapidly balding head. "We've got to see whether Beatrice W's potato ends up with more hair than I have at this point."

Gemma walks over and kisses him lightly on the cheek. "It might, but you'll still be cuter," she says, and he grins. "I'm gonna run out for some milk."

Mateo opens the fridge and points inside. "We have plenty."

"Then I'm going for a walk," she says, already disappearing into their bedroom to get dressed.

Outside, it's unseasonably warm for February in Chicago, even at this early hour. The air still smells of rain from last night's storm, and in the distance, the sunrise is reflected in the flashing silver of the skyline. Gemma feels a deep fondness for all of it: the elevated train rumbling by, the old woman watering her plants on the steps of a neighboring brownstone, the line out the door of the fancy coffee place on the corner. All those years growing up in the little A-frame house in Michigan, staring across the lake from the opposite shore, this is what she'd wished for: a city. A sense of freedom. A place where she, too, could disappear.

In the convenience store, Gemma weaves aimlessly through the aisles and arrives at the checkout with an armful of items she barely remembers grabbing. She spills them onto the counter and then hands over her credit card, which the blue-haired girl glances at before swiping.

"Endicott," she says, and Gemma follows her gaze to the magazine rack beside the cash register, unsurprised to find Jude looking back at her from the cover of *People*. She's wearing a gold sequined dress, her strawberry-blond hair—the same color as Gemma's, the same as all of theirs—sleek in a long bob and the fair skin across her nose sprinkled with freckles. It's a special Oscars preview, and the headline across the front reads: GOLDEN GIRL.

"That's not you, is it?" the girl asks with a sardonic smile as she swipes Gemma's card. "Is this one of those stars-are-just-like-us moments?" Gemma is about to assure her it's not when the machine lets out a shrill beep, and the girl looks up again. "Oh. Um . . . it's been declined."

Behind her, a mom trying to pry a candy bar out of her toddler's hands averts her eyes, clearly embarrassed by this turn of events.

Gemma had forgotten they'd put the entire cost of the IVF on this card, which amounted to thousands and thousands of dollars and had raised a fraud alert they were still trying to untangle. *See*, she'd almost said to Mateo, *even the bank thinks it's unlikely that I'd be trying to become a parent.*

"Now you know for sure I'm not a movie star," Gemma says as she fumbles through her wallet for cash, but then she realizes she doesn't really need any of this stuff. "You know what? I think I'm okay actually." She waves awkwardly as she backpedals out of the line, but even once she's outside, her words continue to ring in her ears: *I think I'm okay, I think I'm okay.*

She tips her head back to look at the sky, taking long, ragged breaths. She has a powerful urge to text Connor and Roddy and ask if they've heard from Jude as well, to see if there's some universe in which they're actually planning to go to North Dakota this weekend. But she doesn't. She's not sure if she's more afraid that they'll write back or that they won't.

Three years, she thinks. How could they have let so much time go by?

This isn't the first time their family has fractured. That happened when Frankie up and left them out of the blue, and then again years later on the night when Gemma and Connor and Roddy woke up in a Texas motel to the smell of smoke and stumbled outside to find Jude and Frankie huddled together on the grass, their faces pale behind streaks of ash, watching the old red Honda burn in the blue-black night. They'd apparently been sitting in the parked car when Frankie decided to light a joint. "It must've been a spark," she kept repeating afterward, her voice strangely robotic, her eyes a little haunted. It didn't occur to Gemma to ask why their mother thought it would be a good idea to smoke pot in an enclosed space during a heart-to-heart with her fourteen-year-old daughter; Frankie had been largely absent from their lives for years at that point, and Gemma had long since stopped asking those types of questions.

Afterward, their dad had forbidden her from seeing them, which meant it was the last summer of the road trips, the last summer the country revealed itself through the window of the ramshackle Honda, the four of them fighting over who got shotgun, the other three jammed in the backseat, their mother's hair whipping in the breeze from the open window and the Rolling Stones on repeat in the cassette player.

It was the last summer of a lot of things.

And now, all these years later, the Endicotts have managed to split themselves apart for a third time—only this is somehow even worse. Because both their parents are gone now, and they have no one to blame but themselves.

Gemma begins the walk home empty-handed. When she reaches their brownstone, she sits down on the cool of the front stoop, wrapping her jacket tightly around herself, watching an endless stream of kids hurry by on their way to school. She sees an older sister pause at the crosswalk to wait for her younger brother, a hand outstretched, and she remembers her own days shepherding the other three to school, walking along the edge of the road in a wobbly line, Gemma and then Connor and then Roddy and Jude, side by side as always.

Her phone buzzes with another text, and she looks down, expecting it to be Mateo asking if she's okay. But it's Jude again.

Please, Gem. It's important.

She was thirteen when Jude was eight and started having nightmares. Gemma knows she could've gone to Roddy, who was in the bunk right below her, or their dad, who was just down the hall, but it was her bed that Jude would climb into every night, burrowing in beside her to fall into a feverish sleep, her body blazing with heat. All night, she'd toss and turn and kick, but Gemma never minded; she just held her tighter, waiting until her little sister had drifted off before she closed her own eyes.

When she walks back into the condo, Mateo is sitting on the couch with a copy of the *Tribune*. Her suitcase, which they usually keep in the basement storage locker, is on the floor beside him. He looks at her with a tentative smile.

Gemma walks over and runs a hand lightly over the handle. "How did you know?"

"Because," he says, "I know you. And I know this is important."

She sinks down onto the couch beside him, leaning her head against his broad chest as she works her way up to her next question. "You don't mind?" she asks, motioning toward her stomach. "That I won't be here when we find out?"

He kisses the side of her head. "You'll be right where you're supposed to be."

She laughs. "In North Dakota?"

"With your family," he says, and Gemma thinks back to the last time she saw her siblings before their big fight: they'd all flown to L.A. for a premiere of Jude's, and had watched with a mixture of awe and amusement as she worked her magic on the red carpet. Afterward, they settled into the darkened theater to watch, but only ten minutes into the film, Gemma felt a tap on her shoulder and turned to see Jude motioning for them to follow her. Instead of the movie, they went out for dumplings, and instead of the after-party, they headed back to her suite at the Four Seasons to drink champagne and eat the chocolate strawberries the studio had sent her. They stayed up most of the night, laughing and talking and catching up, reminiscing about their strange childhood and the even stranger turns their lives had taken, and then the sun began to rise over downtown Los Angeles, and they stepped out onto the balcony to watch, the four of them lined up in a row, the sky a riot of pink and orange, the palm trees turning to silhouettes.

"If anyone asks," Jude told them, "you loved the film."

"It was brilliant," Gemma said with a nod.

"Best thing I've seen in ages," Roddy agreed.

"I have some notes," Connor added, and Jude swatted at him, laughing.

Gemma twists to look at Mateo now, her throat tight. "Thank you," she says, grateful that he understands. "Though I'm sorry to miss the science fair."

"That's okay," he says, and his eyes shift to her stomach again, his expression so tender it makes her a little panicky. "There's only one experiment I care about right now anyway."

She manages a smile. "Don't tell the hairy potato."

"Wouldn't matter anyway," he says. "Potatoes only have eyes. No ears."

In spite of herself, Gemma laughs. "You're such a nerd."

"Which is why you love me."

"I really do," she says, and she leans over to kiss him.

Indiana

1995

THAT SECOND AUGUST ON THE ROAD, NOT LONG AFTER they'd made their way out of Michigan, Roddy had strained forward against his seatbelt to squint at the semi-mysterious figure behind the wheel of the car.

"Where are we going this time?" he asked, and from the front seat, their mom's eyes flashed at him in the rearview mirror. She had dark brown hair, so different from their own, and one of her front teeth was chipped, just barely, but enough to make the memory of her smile feel precise when they tried to picture it the other eleven months of the year.

"You'll see," she said, pressing harder on the gas.

Roddy looked past Connor to the window, the highway markers whipping by. He was eight years old that summer, and instead of becoming clearer, the world felt more and more like a mystery to him. "Have you seen it all?" he asked his mom, and though he was talking about the country, the flat land unspooling around them, it made her laugh that deep, jangly laugh of hers.

"I've seen it all twice," she said.

Roddy

Washington, D.C.

2025

Roddy in motion: breathless and joyful. He runs through the cobbled streets of Georgetown, his muscles burning, his bad knee sending up the occasional flare. His lungs are full of the spring-like breeze, his heart thumping hard in his chest, his mind blissfully calm. He is simply running, as he's been trained to do, as he's done his whole life, moving fast through the streets of the city he loves, the city that's given him so much, not just his home and his career, but his fiancé too—all of which he might be leaving in the next few weeks.

Somewhere behind him, a distant voice: "Oi!"

Roddy glances over his shoulder, then turns, still jogging in place, to wait for Winston, who looks like he's limping through the final mile of a marathon, though they've only been running for twenty minutes. He's gasping for breath, his dark brown skin dripping with sweat, and when he reaches a mailbox, he drapes an arm over it with a groan.

"You okay?" Roddy asks, loping over to him.

Winston lifts his head and glares. "This is madness," he says, his English accent—usually so clipped and precise—punctuated by jagged breaths. "Can we not just go for brunch like a normal couple?"

Roddy grins, resuming his standstill jog. "This is more fun."

"Maybe if you're a professional athlete," Winston says, grimacing as he braces a foot against the mailbox to stretch his calf. Even sweaty and exhausted, he still manages to look handsome—*dashing*, Roddy had once called him, which made Winston laugh. But it's true.

"Come on. You're the one who got second place in that 5K for Parkinson's research!"

Winston straightens up. "Oh. Right. You should know that I lied about that."

"You did?" Roddy asks, surprised. "Why?"

"I was trying to impress you," Winston says, as if this should be obvious. "I hadn't met very many footballers."

Roddy grins at him. "And I hadn't met very many scientists," he says, leaning to give him a kiss, a hand on the small of his back, which is slightly damp.

"Well, this one needs some coffee," Winston says when they break apart again. "Will we call it?"

"I can't," Roddy says. "I need to be training in case—"

"In case of Orlando." Winston runs a hand over his close-cropped hair. "*Orlando.*" He says it very slowly. "It doesn't even sound like a real place, does it?"

"Well, it is," Roddy assures him. "And assuming I get the offer, they're probably going to expect me to be able to run for more than a few miles."

Winston sighs. "Fine. How about we do one more?"

"How about three?"

"How about you do that," Winston says, pointing across the street, "while I work on the crossword from that bench over there?"

Roddy laughs. "You've got yourself a deal."

"See, this is why we're going to ace this whole marriage thing."

"Only ten more days," Roddy says over his shoulder as he jogs off.

"Only if you bring me back a coffee!" Winston calls after him.

Roddy runs past the colorful brick shops and houses over to the park, tracing a path along the Potomac, where a single orange kayak bobs in the water. It's the kind of day that tricks you into thinking winter is over, though it's barely February. He spots a group of kids playing soccer and has a brief urge to join them, but he keeps going, head down, eyes watering from the wind off the river.

His phone buzzes in his pocket, and he pulls it out to see that it's his agent, Zack Ramos. He steps off the path to answer it, still breathing hard. "Hey."

Zack laughs. "You okay, dude?"

"I'm in the middle of a run."

"Good, because we just got the offer," he says, and Roddy's heart lifts. "It's a decent start. Room to improve, but not bad considering . . ."

Roddy grins. "I'm old as shit."

"You said it, not me," Zack says with a laugh. "What do you think? You and your knee ready for one more year?"

Roddy is suddenly back in Orlando a few weeks ago, walking out through the darkened tunnel and onto the pitch, impossibly green beneath the blazing Florida sun. It was real grass, cut so evenly it looked almost fake, and he spun in a circle, a wild jolt of nostalgia winding through him, a burst of love for the game so powerful he almost couldn't breathe.

He'd thought it was over, all of it. Last fall, D.C. United—the team where he'd been lucky enough to play his entire career—had elected not to renew his contract. It wasn't a surprise; after all, he was a thirty-eight-year-old midfielder with four knee surgeries under his belt. So he said his goodbyes, hung up his jersey, bid an emotional farewell to the players and coaches and fans. There were tributes and speeches and a standing ovation at the end of his final match. And then, just like that, it was over.

He spent the winter grieving the loss of that life, the only life he'd ever really known, trying to convince himself it was a good thing, that it made sense to move on after three decades of dragging his increasingly battered body across soccer pitches. It was time to rest, to focus on other things, Winston and their wedding and their future together. He'd been wanting to paint the spare bedroom and plant a little garden out back, mostly vegetables, but maybe some flowers too. He could go to Winston's work functions for once, all the fundraisers and galas, maybe watch some other sports in his free time. Eventually, he'd start to sort through the other opportunities Zack had been fielding for him, a speaking tour and an offer to commentate and various coaching gigs. But he wasn't in a hurry. He'd been in a hurry his whole life.

Then, a week into preseason, and several months into his retirement, Orlando City SC decided they needed a veteran midfielder to round out their lineup. And Roddy Endicott—who had managed to paint only one wall of the spare bedroom and had already given up on the idea of a garden—was available. He was more than available. He was ready.

Now he squints up at the cloudless sky, his chest fizzy and light, and presses the phone closer to his ear. "Yes," he says to Zack. "Hell yes."

"Fantastic," Zack says, sounding genuinely pleased. "They need you down there a week from tomorrow. Wednesday the twelfth."

The smile slips from Roddy's face. "I can't," he says. "I'm getting married on the fourteenth."

"Oh. Shit." There's a brief silence. "You didn't invite me?"

"It's super small. Not even family," Roddy says, and there's a catch in his throat at this. "Just the two of us, and a couple close friends as witnesses."

"Then it should be easy to move, right?"

"It's our anniversary," Roddy says uneasily. "I didn't think— We arranged it all before Orlando was a possibility. I just figured I was done."

"Well, you're not," Zack says. "Maybe have Winston come down to Orlando and you guys can do it there."

"Right," Roddy says. "Because they love a gay wedding in Florida."

"Good point," says Zack. "Is your anniversary really Valentine's Day?"

Roddy smiles sheepishly. "Neither of us realized what day it was when we scheduled our first date," he tells him. "We walked into the bar and it was wall-to-wall hearts and roses. But it makes it easy to remember."

"Okay, well, let me see what I can do about the timing," he says. "But congrats again on the new gig. A surprise second act. Not everyone gets one of those."

On the way back, Roddy runs faster than he needs to, his head buzzing. He can't bring himself to worry about the wedding yet. Zack is a fixer of problems, so if anyone can sort it out, it's him. Besides, what's a few more days? It's not like he's going to be starting for the team anyway. And the regular season doesn't even begin for another couple weeks.

When he arrives at the bench where Winston is waiting, Roddy bends over with his hands on his knees, breathing hard.

"You forgot the coffee," Winston says, his eyes bright behind his glasses, and as Roddy looks at him, the magnitude of his mistake immediately becomes clear. He'd been so excited about the offer that it didn't even occur to him to wait and talk it over with his fiancé before making a decision about what the entire next year of their lives will look like.

All the air goes out of him. He opens his mouth, then closes it again, not sure what to say or how to begin. Finally, he says, "I'm really, really sorry," and it comes out sounding so desperate and earnest that Winston is taken aback.

"It's fine," he says quickly, standing up from the bench and putting a hand on Roddy's shoulder. "It's only coffee. I've probably had too much this morning anyway."

"No, I'm—" Roddy falters. "I got the offer from Orlando."

"Oh," Winston says, his face shifting. "Wow."

"Yeah." Roddy fishes the phone from his pocket and holds it up like it's proof. "Zack just called to tell me."

"And you're sorry because . . . you want to take it?"

Roddy looks at him, pained. "I'm sorry because I already did."

"Right." Winston sits down again, clearly trying to process this. "Okay."

"It's not like this was totally unexpected," Roddy says, sinking onto the bench beside him. "We both knew it was coming. But I realize I probably should've—"

"You should've waited," Winston says flatly.

Roddy nods. "I should've waited."

"We should've talked it over. Together."

"You're right."

"It's my life too."

"I know," Roddy says, contrite.

Winston is quiet for a moment. "And you're absolutely sure this is the right thing?"

It's hard to know exactly what he's asking, whether he means for their relationship or for Roddy's career. Winston is two years younger than him, but because he's a literal genius—one of the top minds doing research into Parkinson's disease at the National Institutes of Health, and the smartest person Roddy has ever met by a mile—Roddy often feels ill-equipped for conversations like these.

"I want to keep playing," he says, which is the only thing he knows for sure. He thinks about the first time he ever shoved his feet into a pair of Connor's old soccer cleats, scoring eight goals against a bunch of kids who were mainly interested in picking dandelions. For thirty years, this has been his entire identity: the athlete, the prodigy, the hustler who never gives up even after all the injuries and surgeries, even after he blew a penalty kick in an Olympic qualifier, even after he lost his starting spot and earned it back again half a dozen different times, even after all the setbacks and misses and failures. So how can anyone expect him to quit now, when his whole life has been spent training for the opposite?

Winston nods, his face oddly blank. "When does the season start?"

For a second, Roddy doesn't answer. His mind is whirring, flipping through possible answers, weighing the outcomes. Finally, he says, "February twenty-first," which is the truth. The first match of the season is scheduled for February 21. He just fails to mention that the preseason has already started, and that they want him down there well before that, in just over a week, on February 12, two days before he and Winston are meant to be getting married right here in D.C.

Winston frowns. "I guess it's lucky we're not doing a honeymoon yet." His gaze moves down to Roddy's bare legs. "What about your knee?"

Roddy wipes his sweaty palms on his shorts, his heart jangling. "It'll hold up."

"And the distance?"

"We'll figure it out," he promises. "It's only for one season."

"And the team?" Winston asks, a flicker of annoyance passing across his face.

"It's fine," Roddy says shortly, because he can't handle this discussion on top of everything else right now. "They need a backup midfielder with experience. That's me. You don't have to read into it more than that."

Winston nods, but he doesn't look convinced. Roddy's phone buzzes in his hand, and he glances down at it distractedly, then back up at Winston. It takes a moment for what he's seen to register, and when it does, he studies the screen again, his eyes widening.

"What?" Winston asks. "Is everything okay?"

Roddy doesn't answer. He's staring uncomprehendingly at his phone, his brain like a car spinning its tires in thick mud. "It's Jude," he says, his voice full of wonder.

Winston blinks in surprise. "Really?"

Roddy glances down at his phone again. The message says: **Can you get away this weekend?** And that's it. The text above it is three months old, an article Roddy had sent her about the psychological bond between twins. He'd only half-read it himself; it was mostly an excuse to get in touch. She hadn't replied.

He leans forward on the bench, staring at the cobblestones. Winston places a hand gently on his back, and for some reason, it makes

Roddy feel like crying. They've been together for two years, engaged for one, and Winston has never met his family. If you'd told Roddy when he was younger—if you'd told him even a few years ago—that his twin sister, the most important person in his life, wouldn't know his fiancé, he would never have believed it. But it's been three years since he's seen any of them: not just Jude, but Gemma and Connor too. And now this.

He looks at the message again, and Winston leans in to read it too. Their knees touch, and the electricity of it runs through Roddy like a shock, as it always does when Winston is nearby.

"Can you get away this weekend?" Winston frowns. "Get away to where?"

"I have no idea," Roddy says. He wonders if she means Los Angeles, where she lives, or somewhere else entirely. Knowing Jude, it could be anywhere.

Though he's not all that sure he knows her anymore.

The last time he was in L.A. for a match, he'd spent most of the time on the bench, eyes scanning the crowd for her, though of course if she'd shown up, it would have been obvious. It was always obvious when Jude showed up anywhere, even before she was famous. But still, he felt like he would be the first to know, that he would be able to sense her in the stadium. When they were little, it had always felt that way, like there was a thin thread stretched between them at all times. But now that thread has more or less been cut, and he has no idea what this text is supposed to mean, no idea what he should do except to follow her lead, the same way he always has.

"Well," Winston says, sitting back again. "I suppose it doesn't matter anyway."

Roddy looks over at him. "What do you mean?"

"We have the wedding next week." Winston is staring at him like he's lost his mind. "And you've just told me you're moving to Orlando after that. I hardly think you have time to go off on a lark of a weekend with your estranged sister."

The word *estranged* hits Roddy square in the chest. He turns it over in his mind, the edges of it hard and unyielding. What he wants to say is: *That's not fair.* Winston doesn't know what it's like to have a sister like Jude. He doesn't know what it's like to have a sister at all, to have your siblings half-raise you because your mother is long gone and your father is always at work.

Winston is an only child, raised in South London by two Nigerian immigrants who adored and fussed over him, who cooked him dinner and showed up to his chess matches and tucked him in every night after they got home from the lab where they worked. They still call him every Sunday at the same time, and Roddy listens from the next room while he assures them he's eating enough vegetables and getting enough fresh air. Winston can't possibly know what it feels like to look into the stands at a soccer game and see your siblings with their homemade banners, to walk home together after the matches in the blue-cold Michigan nights because there's nobody to pick you up. They were his first team, his most important team, and even though it's been years, and even though they have their issues, he will always—always—show up when they need him. That's just how it works.

"I never said I was planning to go," he tells Winston, though his mind is still on Jude.

Winston stands up, looking at him with resignation. "You didn't have to," he says, then bends to kiss him on the cheek. "I'll see you at home."

For a long time, Roddy just sits there alone on the bench, his head in his hands. Around him, people are hurrying to catch the Metro or waiting in line for bagels or popping into red-brick shops. His phone vibrates beside him, and he grabs it up fast. But it's not Jude. It's a text from Zack: **So sorry, but they won't budge on the dates**.

Roddy tips his head back and closes his eyes, his heart dropping.

The phone buzzes again, and he lifts it hopefully, only to find a second message from Zack: **Let me know where you're registered**.

It begins to rain, the sidewalks specked with gray. Roddy walks home through the chill, hands in the pockets of his running shorts.

A block from their brownstone, he passes Winston's favorite coffee place and stands on the street for a moment—his thoughts a million miles away, his phone still heavy with Jude's unanswered message—before heading inside.

As he waits amid the smells of caramel and mocha, he listens to the two middle-aged women in front of him talk about their plans to see *Rose Gold* tonight.

"I hated her last one," one of them says, "but I'm still weirdly obsessed with her."

Her friend nods as she scans the menu. "Did you ever read that book that's supposedly about her family?"

"No!" says the other one. "Should we do it for book club next month?"

Afterward, Roddy walks in the direction of the brownstone. The rain has stopped, but it's still too cold to be out in shorts and a T-shirt, and he's grateful for the warmth of the cups. A few yards from home, he stops short. Winston is there, fumbling for his keys while balancing a tray with two paper cups of coffee on it.

"I've got it," Roddy says, hurrying over, and Winston gives him a sheepish look when he turns and sees they had the same idea.

Carefully, Roddy places one cup and then the other into the empty slots of Winston's tray, their faces close, their warm breath mixing in the cool air. Then, once his hands are free, he digs for the keys in his pocket.

"Hey," Winston says quietly as the rain falls around them, and Roddy looks up at his face, the dark eyes and the day-old stubble, the familiar curve of his nose and the small scar above one eyebrow. It's a beautiful face, his favorite face in the world. "I'm sorry for being a prick. I was just upset about you saying yes without talking to me. But it's fine. I know what football means to you. So we'll figure out a way to make it work. Because I love you. And I can't wait to marry you. Even if it means our honeymoon has to be in bloody Florida."

Roddy's heart dips at the mention of the wedding. But he can't bring himself to tell him. Not now. Not yet. "I love you too," he says instead. "And I want you to come with me."

"To Orlando?" Winston shakes his head. "I can't. You know that. My work is here, so we'll have to—"

"No, I know," Roddy says. "I meant this weekend. To wherever Jude is summoning me. I have to go. I'm sorry the timing is so terrible, but I just have to."

Winston nods. "I know."

"I have no idea what we'll be walking into," he says. "It could be anything. Literally. You don't know Jude."

"I don't know Jude," Winston repeats thoughtfully.

"But I'd like you to," Roddy says with force. "You're my family, and so is she, and whatever this weekend is, I know it would be better if you were there too." He smiles. "Everything is better when you're there too."

Winston looks pleased. "I suppose it would give us some quality time together before . . ."

"Yes," Roddy says, nodding. "Exactly."

"Okay then, as long as you're not hauling me off to some made-up place like Orlando," he teases, and Roddy thinks about their old childhood map for the first time in ages, the way Jude used to count the colorful pins again and again when she couldn't fall asleep.

"How old do you think we'll be when we get to the last one?" she'd asked him once, a million years ago, and Roddy had shrugged.

"Old," he said.

Now he unlocks the front door and holds it open for Winston. "Let's find out."

Kansas

1996

ONCE, ON A LONELY ROAD OUTSIDE OF WICHITA, THERE was a shooting star.

They had stopped on the side of the highway so that Frankie could have a cigarette. She was pacing back and forth along the edge of a cornfield when Connor spotted it.

"Look," he said, sliding off the hood of the car in his excitement.

Roddy and Jude, who had been kicking a soccer ball around, turned their faces to the sky. But it was already too late. It was gone.

"Did you see it?" he asked, wheeling around to face Gemma, who was leaning against the car door, and Frankie, who had stopped walking.

"See what?" they asked, and Connor felt a surge of despair that he'd been the only one to witness it. Eleven years on this planet, and he'd never seen anything half as astonishing as this: a star skidding across the sky.

He pointed up at the navy dome above them, which was now disappointingly still. "A shooting star," he said quietly, trying to hide his regret. "It was right there."

Frankie dropped her cigarette on the dry grass and stubbed it out with the heel of her boot. Then she looked over at Connor with a faint smile.

"Tell us about it," she said.

And so he did.

Connor

Tennessee

2025

At a country bar in the Nashville airport—the bleakest kind of country bar—Connor sits with a beer, reading the texts from Jude again while he waits for his kids to arrive. It's not their first time flying here alone; normally he goes back to New York to see them, but they've come out to Nashville a few times as well, to stay with him in the apartment he'd rented to research his new novel, the three of them doing what Connor thinks of as divorced-dad activities: playing mini golf and eating pizza and watching mildly inappropriate movies. But this time, they're not staying here. This time, as soon as their flight lands, he's going to scoop them up and hurry them over to another gate so they can get on a second plane to every kid's dream destination: North Dakota.

When he'd called his ex-wife, Nicola, to ask if it would be okay to spend his appointed weekend with them somewhere other than Brooklyn or Nashville, she'd been skeptical. "Who goes to North Dakota?"

"Jude," he said. "Apparently."

"Wow. You guys are talking again?"

"So it would seem," he said, trying to sound casual, but honestly, he doesn't really know what the hell is happening.

There's a band in the corner of the bar playing a song he doesn't know, something twangy and full of heartache, but he isn't listening. If anything, he should be writing—or pretending to write, which is at least writing-adjacent—but he can't bring himself to open his computer. Instead, he studies his phone.

Ever heard of Portree, North Dakota? Jude had written, and Connor, his interest piqued by both the oddness of the question and the unlikely appearance of the text after so much silence, had gone down a rabbit hole.

Population 2,024, he'd replied, after looking it up. **72 miles from Bismarck. Known for its flaxseed production and honey farms. Pretty much the middle of nowhere.**

Bingo, Jude had responded. **Want to check it out this weekend?**

Connor had stared at the message, trying to figure out what in the world was going on. Of the four siblings, he and Jude were never the closest. She and Roddy had always been their own separate entity, a universe of two, and Gemma was practically a surrogate mother to all of them. Connor had been the most self-contained, quiet and studious and more than happy to disappear into his books. He'd never needed his siblings quite as much as they needed one another. Which made him the least likely recipient of an out-of-the-blue text from Jude. Especially after everything that had happened with the book.

So what, then? She was summoning him to the middle of nowhere to yell at him some more? To pick up the fight where they'd left off a few years ago? To rub it in his face how much more successful she is than him, how much better her life has turned out?

I can't, he started to write back, though what he was really thinking was: *No fucking way.*

But then a new thought occurred to him: that maybe this was a pity invite. Maybe she knew—or had guessed at—how bad things had gotten for him since they'd last seen each other at their father's funeral. He'd been happily married then, at least in appearance, still living with Nicola and the kids in a brownstone in Brooklyn Heights, just weeks away from winning the National Book Award—*the National fucking Book Award!*—for that infamous third novel of his and signing a bigger-than-he-ever-could-have-imagined contract for two more.

Now, three years later, he's sitting in an airport bar in Nashville, where he's spent the last eight months trying and failing to find his way into the next book, a sad, middle-aged divorcé waiting for his kids to fly in from the city he used to call home so they can join him on what might possibly be the world's most depressing weekend getaway, to Portree, North Dakota.

He'd tried to say no to Jude that day. He really had. **Sorry,** he'd typed more than once, but he'd found he couldn't finish the thought. He'd read enough books in his life to know that people were funny and life was weird and sometimes there was no explaining your gut. Maybe it's that he was curious. Or that he had nothing better to do. Maybe he was hoping for more material, as colossally ill-advised as that would be. Or maybe he just missed his sister. It was hard to say. But even Connor had to admit that nobody sends a pity invite to spend a weekend in the upper regions of the Midwest in the middle of February—and so, in the end, he'd said yes.

His phone dings now: a flight-arrival notification. He downs the rest of his beer, feeling lightheaded at the nearness of his children, whom he hasn't seen in over a month—something that would have once been unthinkable—then leaves a few bills on the bar and hurries off through the busy terminal.

At Gate A7, he waits amid a crowd of impatient travelers. They're the first two off the plane, accompanied by a flight attendant who is gripping Hugh's little hand in a way that cracks Connor's heart. Rosie trails after them, looking disenchanted in the way only an eleven-year-old from Brooklyn can. He hasn't told her yet that they're going to see Jude, who has—in her three-year absence from their lives—attained an almost mythic status as the glamorous movie-star aunt, so different from the Jude that Connor always pictures, who is still eight years old, her knees streaked with dirt, her long hair tangled, her freckled nose pink from the sun.

He spreads his arms wide and stoops to greet them, and Hugh—looking so much like Roddy at six that it nearly takes Connor's breath away—runs headlong into him, a mess of light curls and untied shoelaces.

"Are we gonna see Mount Rushmore?" he asks, stepping back. He bounces from one foot to the other, thumbs hooked under the straps of his dinosaur backpack. "My teacher said we probably were."

"That's South Dakota, buddy," Connor says, turning to pull Rosie into a hug; she groans, already too cool for such displays of affection, but he leans down to kiss the top of her head anyway, feeling suddenly cheerful about this strange weekend excursion. "We're going to *North* Dakota."

Hugh frowns. "That's what I told her. But she said I must be wrong."

"Why?"

"Because," he says matter-of-factly, "she said there's nothing to see in North Dakota."

Rosie leans against the handle of her purple suitcase with a sigh. "Fantastic. Can't wait."

"Don't worry," Connor says. "There's at least one thing I'm pretty sure you'll want to see there."

"What?" Rosie asks, skeptical, and Connor grins.

"Your aunt Jude."

Her eyes widen. "No *way*. Are you joking? You're joking, right? Are you?"

"I'm completely serious," he says, placing a hand over his heart.

"But why? What's she doing there?"

He doesn't have those answers for her. Not yet. But it doesn't matter. Rosie's eyes are shiny as they begin to walk toward their next gate, and she's practically vibrating with excitement. Connor knows she's not thinking about the aunt who's been sending increasingly extravagant gifts on Christmas and birthdays (what eleven-year-old needs a

Gucci toiletry kit?), or even the one who once upon a time taught her how to roller-skate in Prospect Park. It's been too long since she's seen her, too long since Jude has felt like a real person. She's thinking instead of the public version of her aunt, the one she sees on Instagram and on movie screens, the one she invited her friends over to watch in that Jane Austen adaptation a couple years ago, a huddle of nine-year-old girls with bowls of popcorn and dreamy expressions.

"I can't believe you're related to her," one of them had whispered, and Rosie had smiled.

"Me neither," she'd said in a way that made Connor's throat go tight, because already it had been a year since he'd seen Jude at that point. Already, she didn't seem quite real to him either.

On the flight to Bismarck, the kids watch movies on their iPads while Connor stares at his cursor, blinking against the stark white background of a blank page. He'd come to Nashville to write an epic novel, tracing one family's history over a hundred years on a farm in rural Tennessee. But he quickly realized this was bullshit. What did he know about living on a farm in rural Tennessee? What did he know about anything, really? He'd already told the truest story he could, and in spite of its success, it had also backfired so wildly that he didn't know what to write anymore. The whole experience had felt more like setting off a bomb than publishing a book, and now he was too gun-shy to write more than fifty pages in any given direction.

Last weekend, he'd decided the answer was to get as far away from his previous work as possible. He'd spent hours at Parnassus, a local indie bookstore, picking through thrillers and mysteries and schlocky commercial novels, debating whether he could write about something like a disillusioned FBI agent sent to arrest his old mentor or a high-stakes heist set against the backdrop of the bourbon industry. When he'd carried a swaying stack of mass-market paperbacks to the register, the woman behind the counter—who had let out an audible gasp the first time he'd ever walked through the doors and now regularly asks him to come in and sign copies of *The Almost True Story of the Astonishing Atkinsons*—had winked at him. "Guilty pleasures?"

Connor had managed a nod.

His agent, Agnes, thinks the problem is the National Book Award. "Writer's block is extremely common after a success like that," she keeps reminding him. "It's a hard thing to follow up."

But it's not that. He wishes it were as simple as that.

Beside him, Hugh shifts to lean against his arm, and Connor closes the laptop gently, looking over his children's heads to the window, where in between wisps of clouds, he can see vast patches of squared-off land, flat and dull and endless. It's so typically Jude to pick a place like this, somewhere random and uncool and obscure that will somehow, he knows, be transformed by the very fact of her presence. Jude could turn a truck stop into a hot spot; she could make an empty road feel whimsical, and a run-down house seem charming and full of warmth. It's part of her magic.

It was their mother's best trick too.

"Welcome to Bismarck, folks," the pilot says as the wheels touch the runway to scattered applause. "It's one forty-two P.M., and a balmy twenty-four degrees out there. So bundle up and enjoy your stay."

Rosie sighs. "You know that Mom and Neil are in Antigua this weekend, right?"

Connor hadn't. He'd known about the boyfriend, but not the trip.

"North Dakota is way better," he says, and Rosie gives him a pitying look.

"*How?*"

"Because you get to hang out with me instead of Neil?"

Rosie just shakes her head like there's no use explaining anything to him, then turns back to the window.

"Neil gives us candy," Hugh points out, and Connor digs into his pocket, triumphantly producing a stale mint.

"Don't underestimate your old man," he says as he hands it over.

He's ordered the Uber before they're even off the plane, and they hurry out to meet their driver, Annie, who has four stars and a silver 2004 Prius. They squeeze into the backseat, Connor, then Hugh, in his booster seat, then Rosie, already shivering from the frosty North

Dakotan air, and when Annie turns around, it's with the kind of bright midwestern smile that Connor imagines everyone has here, the kind meant to prove you're not too cold or too bored or too unhappy with your life.

"Where to?" she asks, and Rosie and Hugh—city kids and thus Uber experts—both stare back at her blankly.

"It's in the app," Hugh says helpfully.

Annie grins at them, full of seemingly genuine warmth. "I know. But this is only my third ride, and I'm still trying out the whole taxi driver thing. So just humor me here."

"It's only your third time?" Connor asks, not sure if she's being serious.

"I mean, it's not like my third time *driving*," she says cheerfully, turning back around and putting both hands on the wheel. "I'm just new at the chauffeur gig. But don't worry, I already have one five-star review."

Connor frowns. "What happened to the other one?"

"I offered him some gum."

"And?"

"And he had no teeth," she says, her green eyes meeting his in the mirror. Beside him, Rosie and Hugh both look like they're deciding whether or not they're allowed to laugh.

"Only kidding," Annie tells them as she pulls out ahead of an airport shuttle. "He was just an old grump. I have a feeling we can do better."

The drive is long and empty, the sky a heavy gray over low-slung buildings and barren fields. Hugh falls asleep against his sister, who has her headphones on again, the thump of the music filling the quiet car. Connor watches the back of Annie's head, the way her auburn hair falls over a cable-knit sweater that matches her eyes. He wonders how old she is—early thirties, if he had to guess—and what made her start driving an Uber. But he feels too weary to ask, too out of practice for social niceties. So he sits quietly, watching the stark landscape roll by.

A half hour later, they pass a sign for Portree, and Annie's eyes flick to the mirror again. "First time?" she asks Connor, who sits up a little and nods.

"What about you?" he says. "Are you from around here?"

"I was," she tells him.

"And now?"

"I'm still figuring that out," she tells him with a smile.

There's not much to see as they turn onto the main drag: a few bars, a bookstore, a pharmacy with a mechanical horse out front. At the end of the street, across from a park with a gazebo, the Portree Inn looks out over the rest of it, a stately white building with ivy climbing up its three columns.

Annie gets out of the car to help them with their bags, even though Connor tries to wave her off. He can see now how tall she is, just about his height, which is nearly six feet. But she's willowy and graceful in a way that makes him feel slow and self-conscious by comparison as he drags Rosie's purple suitcase out of the trunk.

"Well," he says when the bags are assembled on the cold asphalt. Rosie is on her phone and Hugh is spinning in circles around one of the columns in front of the hotel. In the park across the street, a few crows circle for scraps.

For some reason, Connor holds out his hand. Annie looks down at it with a bemused expression. "It was nice to meet you," he says, like he's never been in an Uber before, like he has no idea how any of this is supposed to work.

Her eyes are full of laughter. "You too. And don't forget: five stars. But only if you mean it."

"I mean it," he says a little too earnestly.

"See you tomorrow," she tells him as she ducks back into the car, and it takes a beat for this to register. When it does, Connor walks back over to her window.

"Wait. You will?"

Annie shrugs. "It's a small town."

Then she grins and starts the engine, and Connor stumbles back a step, watching the Prius drive off.

When they walk inside, it's immediately clear that the hotel has seen better days. The carpets are worn, the curtains faded, the whole place a little dusty. At the desk, a young white guy with acne and a name tag that says *Martin* smiles broadly at him.

"Welcome to the Portree Inn," he says as Connor approaches. "Will you be dining with us or staying with us?"

"Both, I expect," Connor says, kicking Rosie's suitcase—which she's abandoned in favor of her phone—over to the counter. "Reservation for Connor Endicott."

"Terrific," Martin says as he begins to type. "Nonsmoking, two double beds?"

Connor nods. "Can you tell me what room Jude Endicott is in?"

Martin's smile slips. "I'm sorry, sir. I'm afraid I can't give out information about any other guests."

"It's okay," Connor says. "I'm her brother."

"I'm sorry, sir," he says again, more nervously this time. "It's just a rule."

"Look," Connor says, pointing to his driver's license, which is still sitting on the counter between them. "We have the same last name."

Martin glances at his computer. "I'm not—I'm not sure we have someone under that name." He reaches for a stack of brochures and slides one across the desk. "But can I interest you in a Segway tour? They leave every morning from the lobby at nine sharp and include—"

"We're not really here to see the town," Connor says as politely as he can. "We're here to see my sister. Can you at least tell me if she's checked in yet?"

Martin is practically sweating now. "I just don't think I can—"

"Dad," Rosie says with a hint of impatience, like he's the one holding everything up. "You just have to prove to him that she's your sister. Like, what movie did she do right before *Rose Gold*?"

"How does that prove anything?" Connor says. "Anyone could know that."

"Do you?" Hugh asks.

Connor frowns. "Was it that one about the woman who walked across—"

"*Breakers*," Rosie says. "And no. It was *Blue Note*."

"Anybody could look that up," he says, but he's distracted, trying to remember the night several years ago when Jude was in New York for a press junket and he took her to dinner at her favorite Japanese place in the Village; it was the first time he'd noticed how many people were always coming up to her, asking for photos or wanting to tell her how much they loved her in this movie or that, and she told him it had gotten to the point where she had to use an alias when she checked into hotels. He could distinctly remember teasing her about the name she'd chosen, but couldn't for the life of him recall what it was.

"Or, like how tall is she?" Rosie is saying as she types furiously on her phone.

Martin is watching this all unfold with rising anxiety.

"Five-six?" Connor guesses. "Five-five?"

"Five-seven," Rosie says. "You're not very good at this."

"What's her favorite ice cream flavor?" Hugh asks, and though Connor's mouth is already open, ready to argue that this is a silly exercise, the question stops him short. He's suddenly ten years old, sitting with Jude on the steps of the Aberfoyle Library, the two of them racing to finish their dripping cones, hands sticky with ice cream. That was the day Connor had won an award for a short story he wrote. It was about a cowboy who got outsmarted by one of his cows, and it had been chosen as the best entry from the entire school, an honor that came with a shiny gold medal. The day of the ceremony, their dad was at work and Gemma had to walk Roddy to soccer practice, so Connor wasn't expecting anyone to show up. But when they called his name and he made his way across the stage, he spotted Jude's little face in the back of the auditorium.

Afterward, they went for ice cream, and he let her try on the medal. "Wow," she said, gazing down at it, her eyes bright as a magpie's.

"It's yours," he said, full of gratitude and sugar, and later—much later—in interviews, she would tell people that of all the awards she had on her shelves, the one her big brother had given her was still her favorite.

At least, she used to.

Behind him, a grandfather clock chimes three times, the sound long and rich and full. Connor closes his eyes. "Mint chip," he says quietly, and then, as if he's summoned her, the door opens behind them, and they all turn to see Jude, framed by the glow of the afternoon light. Rosie lets out an involuntary squeal. Hugh looks with benign interest. Martin gasps. And Connor—to his surprise, Connor feels like crying.

"It's black cherry now," Jude says, taking off her sunglasses and smiling that famous smile of hers. "I guess we've got some catching up to do."

Pennsylvania

1997

FRANKIE HAD LEFT THEM TO BECOME AN ACTRESS. AND maybe because it hadn't worked out, or maybe because she was still trying to prove that it could, she had a habit of putting on a show for everyone they met on the road.

"We're just on our way to my great-aunt's wedding," she'd tell a gas station attendant in a deep southern accent, her blue eyes bright with mischief. "She's eighty-nine and marrying a forty-two-year-old. And get this . . . he's the rich one!"

At a motel, she'd explain to the clerk that they were part of a traveling circus. "The twins are acrobats," she'd say, pointing at Roddy and Jude. "Best in the Midwest."

She told a waiter she was visiting from France and a family at a rest stop that she traveled around the country selling buttons. She claimed the kids were her nieces and nephews, that they were orphans, that she'd never seen them before in her life.

She never told the truth.

Not once.

Gemma was fifteen by then, and found it completely mortifying. The boys thought it was hilarious. But Jude was transfixed.

One day in Pittsburgh, they stopped for lunch at a diner. When it was her turn to order, Jude hesitated a moment. Then, in a nearly perfect Scottish accent, she ordered the fish and chips. "A wee taste of home," she explained to the waiter, who simply nodded and headed for the kitchen.

When he was gone, Frankie turned to Jude, bemused. "Where did you learn to do that?"

"I saw it on TV," Jude said, trying and failing not to look too proud of herself.

There was something appraising in Frankie's expression. She picked up her gin and tonic and swirled the glass, her eyes steady on Jude. "Well," she said finally, "you're very good."

It didn't quite sound like a compliment. Not exactly.

But Jude beamed anyway.

Jude

California

2025

The night before she leaves for North Dakota, Jude dreams of the fire again.

When she wakes up, heart pounding, Spencer is lying on his side, watching her with a worried expression. She blinks a few times, her body still tense from the imagined heat of the flames, the memory of that too-hot Texas night, which she's been reliving since she was fourteen. Even so, it flattens her every time.

"The fire?" Spencer asks, his forehead knit.

Jude rubs her eyes and nods; she hasn't yet fully emerged, is still somewhere between asleep and awake, dream and reality.

Spencer props himself up on his elbow, his eyes traveling to the thick red scar on her upper arm, the patch that makeup artists are always having to hide when she's working. "If that happened to me, I'd be dreaming about it every night too."

"I should be used to it by now," Jude says around a yawn.

"Anything I can do to make it better?" Spencer asks with that lazy grin of his, the one that makes all the girls swoon—the one that makes *everyone* swoon. He's already moving close, his breath on her neck, and then his lips too, and for a second, she thinks about giving in. Because that's the thing about Spencer; everything is fun and easy with him. And when she's around him, so is she. But then she remembers what today is and wriggles away apologetically.

"I think I just need some coffee," she says, trying to ignore his wounded look.

Beneath the covers, he runs his fingers over her hip bone. "You sure?"

"I'm sure," she says, sitting up to give him a kiss before he gets out of bed—distractingly shirtless—to see if Estella, the housekeeper, has made their cappuccinos yet.

When he returns a few minutes later with a mug, he's wearing a blue-striped apron over his bare chest and boxers. He looks like a model, which he sometimes is, or the star of a cheesy rom-com, which he's currently in talks to be. Jude can't help laughing.

"What?" he says with a smile. "You don't think I'm capable of whipping up some pancakes?"

"You don't even eat gluten," she says, amused.

"They're for you," he says, leaning to kiss her again, this time long and slow. "I wanted to make you breakfast before you leave for . . ." He squints. "Idaho?"

"Good try."

"Minnesota?"

"Closer," she says. "North Dakota."

He sits down on the edge of the bed. "Are you sure you don't want me to come? I'd love to meet your family."

"You have your table read."

"I could fly out tomorrow."

"What about that Netflix party?"

"Fuck the party," he says, falling onto the bed beside her, so that their faces are suddenly close. "I'd rather be with you."

She puts a hand on his chest, traces the stripes of the apron. This is where she's supposed to say: *Come with me.* But she can't. Because this is serious and Spencer is not. He's nine years younger than she is, only twenty-nine, carefree and boyish and already one of the most in-demand actors in town. If Jude is a star, then Spencer is a comet; he's absolutely soaring right now, and the dizziness of that—the sheer drunken height of it—doesn't lend itself to reality.

In the six months since they met on the set of their last film, Jude has felt like a scuba diver, dazzled by all the gorgeous sights below the water but still keenly aware that she doesn't live there, that at some point, she'll have to drift back up to the surface in order to breathe. From the start, their chemistry was instant and obvious; but still, to Jude, there's no universe in which this is anything more than a phase. She's just not sure if Spencer knows that.

"I'll be back on Sunday," she tells him, a hand on his smooth jaw. Then she leans close, as if to kiss him, and whispers into his ear: "Did you say something about pancakes?"

He laughs and rolls off the bed. On the nightstand, her phone begins to buzz, and he picks it up to hand it to her. "Who's Eugene Lim?" he asks with a frown.

"My travel agent," she says quickly, reaching for the phone. "It's probably about the flight."

He gives it to her with a shrug and heads off to the kitchen. Jude stares at the phone, which is no longer ringing, her heart beating fast. She lets her thumb hover over the name—waiting, waiting—then changes her mind. Instead, she slides the phone under her pillow and goes back to sleep.

Later, after Spencer wakes her again by wafting a plate of pancakes under her nose, after she packs a suitcase that's much too big for a three-day trip and says a goodbye that's much too dramatic for one, she steps into the black town car that's waiting in front of the house. Her travel agent must have ordered it, or maybe her assistant; Jude has no idea. She's used to things just appearing when she needs them. When the driver steps out to grab her bag, his face is neutral. But she's aware that every interaction she has—no matter how small or insignificant—is a story for someone else, and so she tries to make an effort, even on days like this, when her mind is spinning and her anxiety is like an elevator moving from her stomach to her throat and back again.

She takes off her sunglasses and smiles at the driver. "What a day, huh?" she says, and he nods in agreement. Then he opens the door for her to slide in, and they wind their way out of Laurel Canyon, the window a blur of palm trees and bougainvillea, the car silent and cool.

At Van Nuys, she's driven straight onto the runway, where a private jet is waiting. Jude rarely travels this way—it's wildly expensive and feels overtly pretentious, not to mention terrible for the environment—but the logistics of getting from Los Angeles to Bismarck, North Dakota, had turned out to be too tedious for principles. Even before she gets out of the car, she can see the two flight attendants—both women in their thirties—nudging each other, their excitement clear, and she fixes her face with a broad smile before stepping out.

"Good morning, Ms. Endicott," one of them says, stepping forward to greet her.

Jude motions vaguely to the sky, so blue it almost hurts to look. "What a day, huh?" she says, and then she climbs aboard.

On the plane, she settles into one of the cushy leather seats and braves a peek at her phone. The only one of her siblings who has texted is Roddy: **At the airport,** he's written, and then later, **About to board!** He's bringing his fiancé, she knows, and the idea that Roddy— Roddy!—is getting married makes her heart swell and then immediately contract again, because she's thrilled for him, absolutely, but she's also devastated that she doesn't know this man who has taken her place as his other half. Worst of all, she knows it's her own fault. Which is why she has to figure out a way to make it right this weekend.

One of the flight attendants appears beside Jude. "Madison sent ahead your sushi order," she says, "but is there anything I can get you to drink?"

"Just some sparkling water, if you have it."

"Of course, Ms. Endicott."

"Please call me Jude," she says, and the woman beams at her.

"What's bringing you to North Dakota, Jude?" She says her name like she's trying it on for size, like it's a gift Jude has given her. "Work? Family?"

"Family," Jude says for the first time in far too long, and the word is like a tuning fork, chiming its way pleasantly through her: *Family, family, family.*

Once they're in the air, flying low over the scorched brown mountains, she reaches for her bag—which has appeared miraculously beside her—and pulls out an old notebook, then flips to the list of states she's kept since she was a kid. She glances through it, thinking back on that old childhood map, those summer trips in the too-close backseat of the Honda, until her eyelids grow heavy and she falls asleep.

When they land, there's a second voicemail from Eugene Lim, and she stares at the notification as they taxi to the private terminal under a sky crowded with clouds. Out the window, everything is bleak and empty, and Jude shivers, thinking of her mother, who died of ovarian cancer twenty years ago, and had been on a mission to see all fifty states before she did.

On the way to the hotel, the driver isn't nearly as discreet as the ones in Los Angeles. He stares at her openly in the rearview mirror for so long that Jude has to clear her throat and politely ask if he'd mind paying attention to the road.

"Sorry, hon," he says, which immediately sets her teeth on edge. "I've never had a celebrity in my car before. Especially not an Oscar nominee. Best supporting actress, eh? Tough category this year."

His eyes flick to the mirror again, and he lets out a big laugh at her look of surprise.

"Did a little research when I found out who I was picking up," he tells her. "Sounds like you're a long shot. Not a lot of screen time. You must've really knocked it out of the park when you were in there."

Jude isn't sure whether this requires a response. "Thanks?"

"Oh, I didn't watch it," he says. "Not really my cup of tea. A period picture? With accents? No thanks. Though I guess that must've helped you out with *the Academy*." He takes his hands off the wheel long enough to put air quotes around this, like there's a chance it might not be a real organization. "Have you ever seen *The Avengers*? Now, *that's* a movie . . ."

Jude is relieved when her phone begins to ring.

"Hey, babe," Spencer says when she picks up. "I miss you already."

"I miss you too," Jude says, wondering if that's true. Is it possible to miss someone when it's only been hours? Is it a sign that something's wrong if she doesn't?

"The table read has been awesome so far," he says, then launches into a story about finally meeting the beloved star who is playing his dad. But Jude's eyes are on the window, the blur of cornfields moving past. She's thinking about Gemma and Connor and Roddy, how many hours she's been away from them, how much missing she's done over the last three years.

By the time Spencer is called back to the reading, they're turning onto the town's main street, and Jude swivels to face the window more fully.

"This is it," the driver says as they pull up in front of the Portree Inn. "I'm sure it doesn't seem like that much to someone from Hollywood, but . . ."

"It's beautiful," Jude says, peering up at the old columned building as he deposits her suitcase on the sidewalk beside her. He doesn't offer to help her in, and she doesn't ask him to; instead, she stands there rubbing her cold hands until he's gone, then hefts one bag over her shoulder and grabs the handle of the other, squaring up to the green double doors like a game show contestant unsure of what she'll find.

When she steps inside, the entryway is dim, and she can hear voices coming from the lobby. The first is unfamiliar; the second she's been hearing her whole life. As her eyes adjust, she sees them: Connor, looking the same as always, except for an unkempt beard, and the kids, nearly unrecognizable from the last time she saw them. They're talking, inexplicably, about ice cream, and when she chimes in, they turn, faces etched with surprise.

Connor is staring at her the way so many other people in the world stare at her: like she's a mirage rather than a real person, like they can't quite believe she really exists. But then his face shifts, and his eyes soften, and once again, he looks like nothing so much as her big brother.

They stand there, watching each other across the lobby, and then Hugh—so big! so grown up!—tips his head back to look at his dad. "Is that Aunt Jude?"

Connor nods, but his eyes are still on Jude.

Hugh frowns. "Aren't you going to say hi?"

This makes Connor laugh, and the sound of it feels to Jude like going home again. He walks over to her a little sheepishly, then folds her into a hug. "Jude," he says, his voice gruff in her ear. "Before you say anything, I feel like I need to apologize for—"

"Later," she says, smiling as he steps back. "We've got time."

He nods, and she gives his hand a squeeze, and then there's the clattering of footsteps on the old wooden stairs, and they look up to see that Roddy has appeared, his handsome fiancé a few steps behind him. He pauses, blinking fast at them, then grins and launches himself down the rest of the steps in a single athletic bound, wrapping Jude in a fierce bear hug.

"Thought you'd forgotten about me," he says as he sets her free again.

"Never," she says solemnly.

Roddy turns to Connor then, both of them smiling a little nervously as they go in for a hug too, and when they're done, Roddy puts a hand on his fiancé's shoulder. "This is Winston," he says, beaming at them. Then he winks at Jude. "He's a big fan."

Winston doesn't even bother to pretend this isn't true. "I'm thrilled to finally meet you," he says. "And huge congrats on the nomination. You must be absolutely chuffed."

"Thanks," Jude says, her eyes darting around the lobby automatically. But there's nobody with a phone, nobody trying to take her picture; it's just her and her family and the wide-eyed hotel clerk, who is observing all this like it's the best TV show he's ever seen. She clasps Winston's hand warmly in hers. "I'm really glad to meet you too." Her eyes slide back to Roddy. "I'm sorry it took so long."

She's about to greet the kids when the door to the lobby swings open again, and Gemma is there, silhouetted in the light from the street. She stands very still for a moment, staring at the three of them—Jude and Connor and Roddy—all lined up in a row like they've been waiting for her this whole time, which maybe they have.

"You know," Gemma says, letting her bag slide off her shoulder and onto the floor with a thud, "I was practicing what to say the whole way here. In case this turned out to be awkward."

Connor laughs. "Thank goodness it's not."

"I had some pretty good opening lines," Gemma says. "Some decent jokes too."

"And?" Roddy asks.

Gemma's eyes are damp. "And now I can't remember any of them," she says, half-catching, half-hugging Jude as she hurries over to throw her arms around Gemma's neck.

"Guess we'll just have to be sincere then," Jude says, and Gemma hugs her back hard.

Later, Jude knows, she'll have to tell them the truth. She'll have to spill her secrets, all three of them, and when she does, their joy at seeing her will evaporate. She doesn't know if it'll be replaced by anger or resentment—or maybe, if she's very lucky, forgiveness. But she knows it's the right thing to do. Time, after all, is not an infinite resource. And they've lost too much of it already.

But that's all for later. For now, she's just happy to be here, one of four again.

They all are.

Kentucky

1993

THEIR LAST CHRISTMAS ALL TOGETHER BEFORE THEIR MOM left was spent in Louisville, at their great-aunt Mimi's house, an old Victorian that had once been grand but was now peeling around the edges and smelled of decades-old perfume. It was where their dad had gone for holidays as a kid, and since Mimi was dying (though from what, nobody quite knew) and the house was up for sale, it was important to him that they celebrate one last Christmas there.

Nobody believed in Santa anymore at that point; Connor's third-grade classroom had been abuzz with theories that year, and in his distress over learning that the story might not be what he thought, he'd managed to accidentally spoil it for the six-year-old twins too. So there were no illusions about how the big guy and his reindeer would find them wherever they were. Instead, they stuffed their wrapped gifts into the trunk of the minivan, and Roddy and Jude—who always had to sit in the way back—spent the trip twisting around in their seatbelts and speculating as to what the packages contained.

There was no snow in Kentucky, but Mimi lived next to a horse farm, and that first day, she tipped a few sugar cubes into each kid's palm and let them wander out to feed the sway-backed mares who spent their days idly grazing in the nearest pasture.

"Keep your hands flat," she said in her raspy smoker's voice. "Otherwise they'll mistake your fingers for carrots and bite them right off."

Alarmed, Roddy slipped his sugar cubes into Jude's hand, figuring he'd be just as happy to watch her feed the horses instead. Their parents traipsed over with them too, their dad holding an apple in each fist as he told stories about his childhood visits here.

"I used to dream that I'd wake up Christmas morning and there would be a horse under the tree," he told them, and Jude laughed and laughed.

"A horse in the house!"

"That's what I wanted," he said, pleased to have amused her. He was with them so rarely, and when he was, he seemed tired and distant, much older than his forty years. But here, in this place that reminded him of childhood, he came alive again, his cheeks rosy as they strode out across the frostbitten field. The horses sniffed their hands with velvety noses and took the treats gently, leaving a coating of slimy drool in return, which Connor tried to wipe on Roddy's jacket. Gemma leaned across the fence to hug a dappled gray horse around the neck, and Jude watched her parents in the golden light, her mom lit up by the change of scenery, her dad slipping an arm around her waist and pulling her close, whispering something in her ear that made her laugh, a sound that Jude couldn't remember hearing for weeks, maybe even months.

The next morning, they sat around the stout little tree in Aunt Mimi's living room, which was decorated so much more elegantly than their own ever was, with silver tinsel and white lights, and they exchanged gifts. Mimi gave each of the kids a stuffed horse, and though they were too old for such things, they were still under the spell of the very real horses just beyond the fence, and they hugged them to their chests, each privately glad to have one.

"What do you say?" their dad said, and they chimed their thank-yous; Jude even ventured a small hug, trying not to breathe through her nose so she didn't inhale as much perfume.

Then it was their parents' turn to hand over their gifts, and there were shouts of delight as they unwrapped them: a Gameboy for Connor and a Maradona jersey for Roddy and a necklace with a heart-shaped locket for Gemma. When it was Jude's turn, her mom passed her a small package. She tore off the paper to reveal a delicate wooden box with an elegant *J* carved into the top.

Jude ran a hand over the surface, then opened it up. The lid yawned back on its hinges, the inside smooth and empty and waiting. "What's it for?" she asked, and Frankie smiled.

"Anything you want," she said. "Pencils or baseball cards or love letters. Anything."

But later, when everyone else was crowded around Connor's video game, Frankie leaned in close to Jude again. "It's for your dreams."

Jude looked over at her, confused. "Like, at night?"

"No, like in the future." When Jude still seemed puzzled by this, Frankie went on: "I had a box like that when I was a little girl, and I filled it up with tickets from all the plays I went to. And then later, all the shows I was in. Sometimes it's nice to have a place to put your hopes. Especially if you're the kind of person who has a lot of them."

Jude leaned against her, peering into the empty box, bursting with pride to be singled out like this, already dreaming of what she'd put inside. "Like you," she said, and Frankie kissed the side of her head.

"And you."

Five months later she was gone.

Gemma

North Dakota

2025

As soon as she and Jude break apart again, there are more hugs from Roddy and Connor, and then Gemma steps back and opens her arms so that Hugh—smiling shyly—can run into them too. The last time she saw him in person, he wasn't much more than a toddler, and the Christmas card photos and video calls on birthdays haven't prepared her for how much older he looks. He's all skinny legs and sharp elbows, with a missing front tooth and a mess of curly hair.

"Dude," she says when she leans back. "You got old."

"I'm only six," he says, but he seems pleased.

Gemma glances up to see that Jude is giving Rosie a similar once-over—"You have to tell me where you got those glasses," she exclaims, and Rosie looks like she might faint from happiness—and when they're done, they switch kids—Jude tousling Hugh's hair and Gemma squeezing Rosie—and then Roddy jumps in, grabbing Hugh around the middle and heaving him into the air, legs flying, even as he bends to give Rosie a fist bump, and it's at once so wildly strange and so devastatingly normal that Gemma can't seem to get her bearings. It feels like she's somehow wandered into a memory, like all this has already happened and she's watching it from a great distance. She does her best to swallow the knot in her throat as she watches Jude pull a sheaf of papers from a bag that looks far too expensive to be making an appearance in the lobby of this particular inn.

Jude clears her throat, suddenly all business. "Right," she says, looking up at the little circle they've automatically formed around her, not because she's a celebrity, or because she planned this trip, but because she's Jude, and ever since she was very young, she's had a unique ability to command their attention. "Here we are."

"Yes," Connor says with a faint grin. "And why is that exactly?"

Jude ignores this, passing out stapled packets of paper. Gemma glances down to see the words "Endicott Family Weekend" in neat type across the cover page.

"I'm so glad you could all make it," Jude says a bit too formally. "I know it was last-minute, and I really appreciate everyone making an effort to be here. But we only have forty-eight hours, and there's a lot on the agenda, so I want to make sure we accomplish everything—"

"Why does this feel like the beginning of *Ocean's Eleven*?" Connor says, flipping through his packet. "What are we stealing? Money? Jewelry? A newly discovered Van Gogh?"

"We're not—" Jude blinks at him. "Never mind. I just meant that it's a short—and long overdue—trip, so I want to make the most of it. Which is why I put together this itinerary."

Gemma looks up at her incredulously. So do Roddy and Connor.

"Fine," Jude says. "Which is why my *assistant* put together this itinerary."

"And . . . ?" Connor asks.

"And my manager's assistant," she admits. When nobody responds, she sighs and adds: "Fine. Okay. Whatever. My travel agent helped too. The point is that we have a lot to do, so we should really get going."

Gemma is halfway through scanning page 2—a tightly packed schedule of events involving a trip to a honey farm and an old-timey train depot and a wine tasting—the word *why* thrumming through her head like a flashing red light. As far as she can tell, this itinerary holds absolutely no clues as to what in the world they're actually doing here.

"The zoo?" Connor says, glancing up from his own copy. "Um, no. Not happening."

Beside him, Hugh perks up at this. "Wait. What kind of animals do they have?"

"Probably just cows," Connor tells him, and Jude rolls her eyes.

"Don't be such a snob."

Connor gestures at her bag. "You're the one wearing Prada in North Dakota."

"I repeat," she says, giving him an exasperated look, "don't be such a snob."

Winston—who Gemma knows is Roddy's fiancé only because of his Instagram account—leans tentatively into the circle. "I was thinking," he says, shoving his hands into the pockets of his pressed khakis, "that maybe I should let you all get reacquainted on your own? I'm feeling a bit peckish anyway, and I saw there's a pub—" This gets a nod from the pimply hotel clerk, who is still watching them from behind the desk. "Right, yeah. Brilliant." He takes a hand from his pocket to give Gemma an awkward wave. "I'm Winston, by the way."

"Sorry," Roddy says, quickly putting an arm around his shoulders. "This is my—"

"I'm so happy to meet you," Gemma says, reaching out to shake Winston's hand. "I can't wait to—"

"We're all going to do everything together," Jude informs them with all the authority of a tour guide. "That's the whole point."

"Oh, *that's* the point," Connor says. "So glad you cleared things up."

"Are we really going ice fishing?" Rosie asks, leaning in to peer at her dad's itinerary, wrinkling her nose at the thought. If Hugh looks like Roddy, then Rosie is a carbon copy of young Jude, down to the freckles, and seeing the two of them together makes Gemma feel like time has bent in on itself somehow.

Hugh dances around, suddenly excited. "I've never been fishing before," he says. "Do you think there are any sharks?"

"What's the deal with this cabin?" Roddy asks, frowning at page 3, which includes a list of outdoor activities and mentions a one-night stay at a "rustic cabin." "How remote are we talking here?"

Winston grins. "He's worried there won't be a gym nearby."

"I'm worried there won't be *anything* nearby," Roddy clarifies.

"There's not," Jude says. "The idea is to spend time together."

"Right, but does it have to be in the woods?" Roddy asks.

"Of North Dakota?" adds Connor.

Gemma looks over at Jude with a trace of a smile. "The least you could've done is save Hawaii for your last state," she teases, searching Jude's face for clues. "I assume that's why we're here, right? Because this is your last one?"

Ever since Jude was a kid, there's been something preternaturally graceful about her, something intentional about her movements, and she turns to Gemma now with that same deliberateness. Nothing about her appearance should be surprising, because even in these three years of absence, she's been everywhere: on billboards and social media, on talk shows and commercials. ("If you're like me, sometimes you need to recharge. Which is why I always take the new Fizzy Water with electrolytes with me wherever I go.") But now something is different. She's older, of course—it's been three whole years, which isn't nothing—but it's more than that. Roddy and Connor look pretty much the same. A few more white hairs, maybe. And the lines around their eyes and mouths have deepened. But underneath that, they're still the same two boys Gemma has known all her life. But not Jude. Jude has changed. And Gemma feels a gut punch of sadness at the thought that, whatever it is, she's missed it. Whatever it is, she's returned too late.

"We're here," Jude says firmly, apparently determined not to give anything away, "to spend time together. Starting with a walking tour of the town."

Connor folds up his itinerary. "Is this a guided tour, or can we catch up later? I've got a few things I need to do with the kids."

"Yeah," Roddy says, "and Winston and I were really hoping to . . ."

He trails off, and the two of them exchange a glance, which evolves into a sort of smirk.

"Hoping to what?" Hugh asks.

Everyone ignores him.

"I need to run an errand too," Gemma says quickly. "Can we just meet up for dinner?"

"Fine." Jude sighs. "But you all better be on time."

"Says the girl who was an hour late to the SATs," Roddy points out, and Jude lets out a laugh—not the kind she does in the movies, but a big, genuine burst of a laugh.

"Hey," she says, "I still did okay, didn't I?"

"Only because Gem made me tutor you," Connor points out.

Jude makes a face at him. "Which is why my math score sucked."

"Who needs math in real life anyway," Connor says, and Rosie looks over at him triumphantly.

"I knew it," she says under her breath.

Roddy and Winston are the only ones who have checked in already, so they head upstairs, holding hands, heads bent close. Gemma waits, letting her other two siblings go first: Connor because of the kids, and Jude because she's in charge of this whole inexplicable thing. When it's finally her turn, she asks the clerk where the nearest drugstore is, and he looks amused.

"There's only one," he says, as if this should be obvious, and points vaguely in the right direction.

Upstairs, Gemma unlocks the door to a small, musty room. She's surprised Jude would have picked a place like this but imagines there aren't a whole lot of five-star options in Portree, North Dakota. Which is just one more reason to wonder why they're here. She sits down on the edge of the bed and calls Mateo.

"How is it?" he asks without saying hello.

"Weird," she says, picking at a loose thread on the comforter. "They're all here. Even the kids. And Winston."

"Winston?"

"Roddy's fiancé."

"Oh right," he says. "Is he nice?"

"Very."

"How's Jude?"

"I don't know how to answer that," she tells him. "She doesn't seem like herself, but who knows what that even is anymore."

"Did she say why now?"

Gemma walks over to the window and nudges back the curtain, looking out over the little town, the gunmetal sky turning silver at the edges, an unsettling mix of light and dark. "She basically just handed us itineraries for the weekend and that was it."

On the other end of the line, Mateo whistles. "How are you feeling?"

"Weird," she says again.

"Weird about your family or weird because . . . ?"

She sits back down on the bed, laid out by the hope in his voice. He's usually so good at hiding it, always more worried about her feelings than his own. But sometimes it breaks through anyway, and those are the moments when Gemma feels most guilty.

"Weird about my family," she says gently, and she can almost picture the way his mouth will have snapped back into something less cheerful. She debates whether to tell him she's been feeling a little light-headed today, but the truth is, she doesn't know if it's from the flight or the meds or the shock and strangeness of seeing her family again, and it doesn't seem fair to give him false hope. Especially when it's probably not that. It never is.

She lies back on the bed and stares at the ceiling, where there's a light brown stain in the shape of a dog's head. The silence between them lengthens, and she finally says, "I'm gonna go pick up a test if I can find one."

"But you'll wait till Sunday, right?" he asks anxiously. The first time they tried doing IUI, they were given a date to come in for the blood test that would tell them if it worked. But a few days beforehand, Gemma was sure she could feel something, and they decided it couldn't hurt to take an at-home test. Together, they stood in the bathroom, staring at the white stick like it was some sort of oracle, waiting to see what it said. When the word PREGNANT flashed onto the little digital screen, Gemma's heart stuttered and then very briefly soared before coming back down to earth again with a juddering kind of panic. But Mateo had already folded her into a hug, whispering "Obrigada" into her ear with such earnest gratitude that Gemma's throat went tight.

"We should take another," she'd said, disentangling herself from him. She felt cold and robotic, shot through with disbelief. "Just to be sure."

When it was time to check the second one, the words were much blunter: NOT PREGNANT.

"Here," Mateo had said, already handing her another stick. He looked grimly determined even as he attempted a smile. "We need a tiebreaker."

The third one was negative too. So was the fourth. And the fifth.

Gemma felt immense relief. Mateo looked crushed.

A few days later, the official blood work confirmed that they were not, in fact, pregnant.

"Must've been a faulty test," their fertility doctor told them. "It's always safer to wait if you can stand it."

And so they had. The two times after that, they'd waited almost religiously for the official test on the appointed day. But this time, it falls on a Sunday. *This* Sunday. Which means she won't be able to see the doctor until Monday, when she's back in Chicago.

So they'd agreed that it made sense to take an at-home test on the actual day.

"Not a minute earlier," she promises him now. "And I'll call you when I do it."

"I have a good feeling this time," Mateo says with a little sigh.

It's what he always says.

"Me too," Gemma tells him, trying to sound more hopeful than she feels. "How's the science fair going? Was the potato really that hairy?"

"Hairy enough to make it into round two," he says, and she can hear the smile return to his voice. "But Saoirse N's seltzer volcano is getting all the real attention. You know how it is. Spectacle over substance every time."

"Sixth graders, man."

He laughs. "I'll let you know how it turns out."

"I can't wait," she tells him.

When they've hung up, she starts to head out of her room. But she hears Connor and the kids down the hall—Hugh singing a song about frogs and Rosie asking if she can hang with Jude instead—and ducks back inside. She stands with her back against the door, feeling guilty. It's her brother, after all, and they only have forty-eight hours together after not having seen each other in years. But still, she doesn't feel quite ready for all this family togetherness. She's badly out of practice.

Once they're gone, she steps quietly into the hallway and tiptoes down the corridor to the wooden staircase, then hurries past the front desk and out into the fresh air. The sky is now laced with gold as evening comes rushing in, the way it always does during these midwestern winters, like a curtain passing over the world. She takes a few deep breaths, happy to be outside, then shoves her chilly hands into the pockets of her coat and rushes down the street toward the only drugstore in town.

It looks like something from the fifties, with a flickering neon sign that says PORTREE DRUG and an ancient mechanical horse out front that costs a nickel a ride. Inside, a man with a green apron gives her a wave as he helps an elderly woman in a thick parka, and Gemma smiles back before winding her way toward the pharmacy section, her shoes squeaking on the faded linoleum tiles.

She walks up and down a few aisles until she finds the pregnancy tests. There are only two kinds, neither of which she's tried before, and the boxes are a little dusty. She picks one up and stares at the image on the front, the two red lines that indicate a positive test and the single one that says the opposite, trying to imagine which will appear this time, which she *hopes* will appear. It's funny how you can want something and not want it at the same time, how you can love your life the way it is and also wonder if there's more.

She's still holding the box when she hears a clatter of cans, then a familiar voice.

"Hugh," Connor is whisper-yelling from the next aisle over. "I told you to stop touching things."

Gemma quickly drops the pregnancy test back into its place and spins around to the opposite shelf, grabbing the first thing she sees. She doesn't even realize what it is until they come strolling around the corner, and Connor raises his eyebrows at the package of adult diapers she's holding. "So is this what happens when you turn forty-three?"

She quickly shoves them back onto the shelf. "Shut up," she says, though she can feel herself blushing. "What are you guys doing here?"

"We need glue for Harold," Connor says, and before she can even ask, Hugh holds up a paper cutout of a penguin.

"It's my turn with him this weekend," he says. "I have to take pictures of all the cool stuff we do."

Gemma gives him a sympathetic look. "It probably would've been more exciting if you were back home in New York."

"No kidding," Rosie says flatly.

"I think I saw glue over there," she says, pointing to another aisle. "Although tape is probably better. Less messy. And you don't have to wait for it to dry."

"Yeah, let's get tape, Dad," Hugh says, already skipping off toward the next aisle.

"Yeah, Dad," Gemma echoes, giving Connor a little thump on the back as they follow him, leaving the pregnancy tests behind. "Let's get tape."

As they trail after the kids, Connor looks at Gemma sideways. "So what's your best guess?"

She doesn't have to ask what he's talking about. "I don't know. A reunion?"

"Sure, I guess. But why now?"

Gemma shrugs. "I've just been assuming it's her last state."

"Nah," he says. "She was cagey about that when you asked. Plus, who saves North Dakota for last?"

"A lot of people, actually. It's kind of a thing. They have a whole ad campaign about it. 'Save the best for last.'"

Connor looks at her, incredulous. "That's maybe the saddest thing I've ever heard."

"So what's your big theory?"

"I don't really have one," he admits, rubbing his beard, which is flecked with white. "At first, I figured it was an anniversary, but unless my math is wrong, it's not."

"What anniversary?"

He shrugs. "Take your pick. Mom's death. Or Dad's. The fire. The fight."

"Our greatest hits," Gemma says ruefully, and Connor laughs.

"You can say a lot about our family, but it's rarely been dull," he says as they continue to weave toward the front of the store. "Whatever this is, it's kind of weird. To do it now? After all this time? With the Oscars in less than a month?"

"What does that have to do with anything?"

"They campaign for those things," Connor says, as if she should already know this. "There are junkets and luncheons and interviews and all sorts of events leading up to it. It's a busy season for her. She shouldn't have time for a random weekend in North Dakota with a bunch of people she hasn't spoken to in years."

"We've spoken," Gemma says, trailing her fingers along a display of beach towels as they walk by.

Connor glances over at her sharply. "You have?"

"Well, we've texted."

He makes a harrumphing noise, as if to say, *See?* "Fine. A bunch of people she hasn't *seen* in years, then."

Gemma is quiet as they pass through the snacks aisle, the stomp of the kids' footsteps somewhere nearby, a tinny Christmas song playing from the store's speakers, though it's early February.

"You never texted *me*," Connor says, his voice uncharacteristically small, and when she looks over at him, his face is etched with hurt.

"We talked."

"When?"

"On the group chat."

He snorts. "The group chat practically has cobwebs on it."

"I wished you a happy birthday," she says. "We all did, right?"

"Lucky me," he says in a voice that reminds her of his younger self, a little bitter, a little bored, smarter than everyone else and eager to prove it. They were always paired up, the two of them, since the twins formed a natural set of their own, and though they were very different, she and Connor, they'd made a pretty good team once.

She comes to a stop in front of a display of greeting cards. "What do you expect?" she says, but she says it gently. "You started it."

"That's not fair."

"But it's true," she says, her eyes landing on a Mother's Day card with a cartoon rabbit on it. She realizes how completely unprepared she is for this conversation. "Let's not get into it now, okay? It was a long time ago."

"Three years," he muses. "Is that a long time?"

She nods. "Felt that way to me."

"Me too," he says, his voice thick.

They both fall silent for a moment, unsure what comes next. Then Hugh yells for them from across several aisles, and Gemma tears her gaze away from her brother. He falls into step beside her as they begin to walk toward the kids. "I heard about you and Nicola," she says, and his face flashes with surprise.

"She told you?"

"I'm still on the Christmas card list. But the fact that she's in Antigua with her new boyfriend this weekend instead of here with you is something of a giveaway too."

Connor sighs. "Did the kids tell you that?"

"Instagram."

"She's happier now, I think."

Gemma studies him. "Are you?"

"Who's happy, really?" he says with a self-deprecating grin, and she stops again, putting a hand on his arm.

"I'm serious. Nashville?"

"It's for a book."

"A book that actually exists?"

"Define *exist*," he says.

"Are there pages somewhere?"

He taps a finger to his head. "It's still cooking."

"Connor," she says with concern. "What are you doing? I'm assuming you can not-write in New York just about as well as you can not-write in Tennessee."

"Possibly even better," he admits.

"Then why aren't you living in the same place as your family?"

"We're not a family anymore," he says, but there's no heat to his voice. He's simply stating a fact. "I thought you read the Christmas card."

She studies his face under the harsh drugstore lighting: the fine lines around his mouth, the dark circles under his eyes. "Are you okay?"

"That feels like a trick question," he says with an attempt at a smile.

"It's not."

"I'm okay," he reassures her. "Just figuring some stuff out right now."

"I get it," Gemma says, and he looks surprised.

"Do you? You seem incredibly put together."

"Well," she says with a shrug, "you don't really know me anymore."

He looks at her for a long moment. "I'll always know you," he says in a voice so matter-of-fact that it makes her want to put her arms around him, to pin him in place somehow; it makes her want to cry because everything is different and everything is the same, and because they're both here now, unlikely as it is, after all this time.

"I'll always know you too," she says.

Oklahoma

2001

THEY'D BEEN DRIVING FOR ONLY A FEW HOURS, BUT IT FELT
like years to Gemma, who was nineteen that summer, their eighth on
the road. Out the windows of the Honda, the landscape had hardly
changed. Nothing but patchy brown fields and a horizon so big it
seemed likely to swallow them. There was something unnerving
about all that space, and about the flat white sky bearing down on
them.

The hotel that night was particularly grim. A bored clerk was
watching a conservative news station at full volume, and the breakfast buffet was still laid out at four o'clock, its only customers a
couple of flies.

"This is gross," Jude said when they unlocked the door to the
room.

"They're all gross," Connor said, tossing his bag onto the dingy
comforter of the closest bed. "What did you expect?"

"Hey, come on," Frankie said, her voice full of effort. "It's not so
bad."

They all looked at her doubtfully.

"Look," she said, pointing at the wall, which was pocked with little spots, a stain of unknown origin. "We can play connect the dots."

"Yuck," said Roddy.

Frankie forced a smile. "I saw there's a Pizza Hut just up the highway."

"We had that last night," Connor said, peeling back the comforter and flopping onto the bed with a worn copy of *The Great Gatsby*.

"When did you guys get to be so jaded?" Frankie said as she fumbled for her pack of cigarettes. Gemma flicked her eyes over to the NO SMOKING sign on the desk, but decided against mentioning it. The moment felt too fragile for that. And Frankie wouldn't care anyway. "I save up all year for this trip. Least you could do is be a little excited to spend some time with your mom."

They exchanged glances. Nobody wanted to say the unsayable thing: that they wouldn't have to be excited to spend time with their mom if she was around all the time like any sort of normal parent. Nobody had ever said anything close to that. Nobody ever would.

Frankie cupped her hand around the cigarette while she lit it, then looked around at them, almost bewildered at the shift in mood. She smiled, the cigarette dangling out of the side of her mouth. "Hey, come on. We're having fun, right? Tomorrow we'll be in Texas. We'll get some cowboy hats. How about that?"

Roddy was the only one to offer a smile. "Sure," he said, because he could always be counted on.

Later, they walked to Pizza Hut, one by one along the edge of the highway. The high grass, so dry it felt brittle, tickled their legs, and the cars that roared past smelled like rubber and exhaust. Every so often, a truck would honk at them, and they would all startle. None of them waved back.

Frankie, who was last in the line, caught up with Gemma and put an arm around her shoulders. "My girl," she said, which had once been enough to reel her back; how she used to wait for those words, how she used to crave them! But in just a few weeks, she'd finally be a freshman at Central Michigan University, completely on her own for the first time in her life. Which was to say: she'd be free.

Gemma had never been passionate about anything the way her siblings were passionate about their pursuits. She didn't love writing or acting, and she certainly didn't love soccer. Here's what Gemma loved: reading magazines in the checkout aisle of the grocery store and sewing patches onto her jean jacket; making mixes with just the right balance of fast and slow songs; and sitting with a book in the oversized bean-bag chairs at the local library. On the bulletin board in her room, she had a picture of the Manhattan skyline that she'd clipped out of a newspaper and pinned up before she even knew what city it was; she just liked the idea of it, all those people in all those buildings, the hum and buzz and anonymity of it all. If Gemma was passionate about anything, it was the future, the vast blankness of it, unknowable and full of possibility.

Last year, she'd deferred her spot in the freshman class at Central Michigan. She'd told her dad and her siblings that it was so she could save up more money first, which she'd done by working at the front desk of a veterinary clinic all year. But really, she'd decided it would be easier to leave once the twins were in high school. That way, all three of them would be together, and even without her there, they'd be able to look out for one another.

All this summer, she'd been restless and eager to move on, her hometown suddenly small and ill-fitting, like a sweater she'd out-grown. She'd thought about skipping the road trip this year, since it had always been—at least for Gemma—less of an adventure and more of an obligation anyway. But in the end, she'd decided to come—not so much for her mom, but for Connor and Roddy and Jude. And so here she was.

She narrowed her eyes at the sun, which was sinking lower in the sky ahead of them, a distant smudge of pink at the edge of the hori-zon, the highway unspooling before it like an endless gray ribbon. It was strangely beautiful. It always was.

Frankie's arm was heavy around her shoulders as they walked. In a burst of uncharacteristic affection, she turned and kissed the side of Gemma's head, the soft spot right near her temple.

"We're having a time of it," Frankie said, "aren't we?"

Gemma nodded. "I guess we are."

Connor

North Dakota

2025

Outside the drugstore, the four of them stand a little awkwardly. They'd passed a bookshop earlier, and Connor had promised the kids they could stop by before dinner. But he doesn't want Gemma to come. Going to a bookstore, any bookstore, inevitably means seeing a copy of *The Almost True Story of the Astonishing Atkinsons*. And seeing a copy of the book would mean having to talk about it. Which would mean talking about everything else. And Connor doesn't feel prepared to do that just yet.

"Are we still going to—" Hugh says helpfully as he bounces around on the sidewalk, and Connor is quick to jump in.

"Dinner later?" he says. "Yes. I checked the menu and there's pizza for you two."

"I don't eat gluten," Rosie says without looking up from her phone.

Connor frowns. "Since when?"

"Since last month," she says, in a tone that implies he's somehow fallen down on the job.

"Okay, well, I'm sure they'll have things without gluten in them too," he says, giving Gemma an apologetic look. "We'll see you there?"

"Sure," she says, glancing back at the drugstore, where the lights have just snapped off for the night. "I'll see you there."

They wave her off—Connor, Hugh, and Harold the penguin; Rosie is too consumed by TikTok to bother—and then stand there until she's crossed the street to the hotel before walking in the other direction, toward a little bookshop called Wordsmith's.

"Three," Hugh says as they push open the door to the sound of a tinkling bell.

"Two," Connor says, though he already knows he'll buy as many books as the kids want. The fact that they love to read feels like his greatest achievement, his one truly significant contribution to the people they're becoming. He's been largely absent from their lives for months now, returning to the city every few weekends to shuttle them to soccer practice and violin lessons and to eat dinner with them in his depressingly generic one-bedroom apartment just a few blocks from where they all used to live together; and at the end of it all, he returns each time to the airport with a knot in his stomach because it feels like he's chosen a book over his kids—a notion only made worse by the fact that there *isn't* a book—and it makes him think of his mother, who chose art over family, who chose art over *everything*, even when there was no art, and he wonders if the same thing might be hardwired into his own DNA, because here he is taking the exact wrong lessons from his childhood; here he is using her as a model rather than a cautionary tale.

So yes. He'll buy them a thousand books if that will make them happy.

"We're closing in ten," calls out a woman's voice from behind the register. "But we can stay open a little later if you have particularly good taste in books."

"Thanks," Connor says as the kids hurry to the back of the store, Hugh to the graphic novels and Rosie to the young adult section. He lingers near the front, studiously avoiding the fiction tables, though he can see the familiar orange cover out of the corner of his eye. Instead, he flips through a few of the biographies, more for something to do than out of any particular interest, pulling volumes off the shelf at random. Connor has no shortage of books at home, even in his temporary space in Tennessee, and every week, more of them arrive mostly from hopeful authors wanting endorsements and persistent publishers hoping he'll spread the word about some fantastic new writer on their list. The pitches are always the same: *heartfelt and humorous* or *a brilliant new voice* or *simply stunning*. Connor rarely reads them. Instead, he returns again and again to well-worn favorites: *The Great Gatsby* and *Slaughterhouse-Five*, because he's a cliché of a forty-year-old man, but also *Frankenstein* and *The Call of the Wild* and *Charlotte's Web*, which makes him cry harder than any book he's ever read.

"That one is really good," says the same voice behind him, and when Connor turns around, he's surprised to see his Uber driver from earlier.

"Annie," he says.

"Baldwin," she says in reply, and he stares at her, confused.

"No," he says, pointing at his chest. "Connor."

She laughs and gestures at the book in his hand. "I meant the James Baldwin biography. It's really good." And then, much to his delight, she adds, "And I remember who you are. Thanks for the stars."

"Do you work here too?" he asks, half-kidding, but she nods.

"Just a couple afternoons a week."

"Wow," he says. "You're busy."

"You have no idea," she tells him, her mouth tightening around the edges. But then her eyes brighten again as she turns to the shelves. "So what are you looking for?"

He gazes back at her blankly. *What a question*, he thinks, and then realizes she means it literally. "Oh, nothing for me." He motions to the back of the store. "I'm just here for the kids."

"You're not a reader?"

"I'm a writer," he says, which is not something he usually volunteers. In fact, it's something he normally goes out of his way to avoid saying out loud. When he does, it's often followed by tedious questions like *Would I have read you?* or *Anything I've heard of?*—which, how is he supposed to know?—or, worse, *I'm a bit of a writer myself; could I show you a few chapters?*

But standing here with this woman who is technically a stranger yet somehow doesn't feel like one—the warm lights of the store pushing back the darkness at the window, his children laughing in the back of the shop, the gluey smell of all these books—makes him let down his guard.

To her credit, she doesn't say any of the usual things. Instead, she simply nods. "Cool. Fiction or nonfiction?"

"Fiction," he says a little too quickly.

She sticks the Baldwin biography back on the shelf. "Then you've come to the right place," she says, walking over to the fiction section without looking back. Connor follows her reluctantly. "I know I should probably be reading about things that really happened," she confides in him, "but I mostly tend to prefer stuff that someone made up."

"You can learn just as much through fiction," Connor says stiffly, sounding every inch the former English teacher, while his eyes can't help darting over to the orange cover, still face out on a shelf, even after three years.

Annie follows his gaze. "Have you read it?" she asks, reaching for the book. "I had a signed copy. I brought it to New York for grad school and I think my roommate stole it."

"You're in grad school?" Connor asks as he grabs another book from a shelf at random, studying it like it's the most interesting thing in the world, though he's watching her intently out of the corner of his eye, hoping she doesn't turn hers over.

"I was," she says.

"For what?"

"Anthropology."

He smiles. "So you *do* read about things that really happened . . ."

"Occupational hazard," she says with a laugh.

"What did you study?"

"I was doing my thesis on the decline of small towns in America and how the resulting rural-to-urban migration affects economic prospects."

He whistles. "What did you find out?"

"That people usually have pretty good reasons for moving away from their hometowns," she says. "But, somewhat ironically, I didn't finish it."

"Why not?" he asks, dimly aware of his kids in the distance, of the people walking by outside the darkened window, of that blaring orange cover in her hands. But the rest of the world grows quiet as their eyes meet, and he thinks suddenly of his ex-wife, Nicola, and how long it's been since he felt this kind of flicker of—what? Attraction, certainly. But was it too much to hope for something more? Connection, perhaps? He doesn't know. If the past three years have taught him anything, it's that he doesn't know much. Still, he feels a brief spark of happiness, elusive and inexplicable.

She smiles wryly at him. "Turns out studying a non-money-making subject like anthropology in one of the most expensive cities in the world is not the cost-effective plan you might think it would be."

She starts to put his book back on the shelf, and Connor's chest loosens with relief.

"That," she says, "and my mom got sick."

He blinks at her. "Oh. I'm so sorry. I—"

It happens fast, too fast for him to react. The book slips from her hands, spinning twice in the air—almost gracefully—before hitting the floor with a hard, flat thud.

And suddenly there he is, smirking up at them from the back cover of the novel, two-dimensional and black-and-white and about four years younger, though it looks—Connor realizes now—like so much more.

Annie stares at it in surprise, her head tilted to one side. "That's you," she says after a moment, glancing back up at him.

"It is," he admits.

She clears her throat. "Sorry I didn't—"

"There's no reason you should have—"

"I just didn't put it together that—"

"It's an old photo—"

"I did read it, you know—"

"You don't have to—"

"I remember mostly liking it—"

"You *really* don't have to—"

"Except for that whole thing about the ghost," she says, and Connor stops abruptly.

"Wait, what?"

"I mean, you have to admit it was a little self-important."

"It was a metaphor," he tells her, his nonchalance falling away.

"Yeah, but in the middle of an otherwise completely realistic novel about a family of siblings grappling with the loss of their mother?" She holds up her hands, as if in surrender. "I will admit you made me cry during that scene with the hotel fire. And when the dad tells the mom she can't see the kids again?" She claps a hand over her heart. "That got me. But then you go and kill her off and have her ghost narrating the rest of the story?" She shakes her head. "Come on. Too much."

Connor stares at her. "Too much?"

"Way too much," she confirms with a nod.

"You know it won the National Book Award, right?"

"I did see the big gold sticker, yes," Annie says, now looking a little amused.

"*The Washington Post* called it a masterpiece," he says, hating himself even as he does.

"Then I suppose," she says, "we should pick it up off the floor."

They both look down at the book, at Connor's closed-mouth smile, his self-serious gaze, all of it designed to make him appear wise and important. Not long after the photo had been taken, he'd worn that same button-down while finger-painting with Rosie, and it's still in his closet, streaked with blue and green. But that day, he'd thought it made him seem smarter. Now, staring down at it, he realizes he just looks pompous.

He nudges the book with the toe of his shoe.

"You want the truth?" he asks, glancing over at her.

She nods. "Always."

"Sometimes I wish I'd never written it."

She gives him an appraising look, and he's suddenly desperate to hear what she has to say, desperate to talk to her about all of it, the book and the award and the whole messy affair, the writer's block and the blank pages and the move to Nashville in the hope of finding inspiration, all the sad, pathetic details of the current state of his life and career. But then the kids are there, laughing about something and shoving each other as they skip back up the aisle, their arms piled high with books, and the spell is broken.

"Hey," says Hugh. "You were our Uber driver."

"I was," Annie confirms.

"And you work here too?"

"I do."

"How many jobs do you have?"

"Oh, four or five," she says airily, then reaches for the top book on his stack, something about a spy school. "This one's good, and the sequel is even better."

Hugh turns to Connor. "Can I get the sequel too?"

"Let's talk after you've made it through that pile," Connor says. "How exactly do you think you're gonna get these all home?"

"We live in New York City," Hugh explains to Annie.

"So do I," she tells him. "Or at least I did. I'm not really sure where I live now."

"How can you not know?" Rosie asks, looking genuinely perplexed, but Connor understands. He doesn't know where he lives right now either. Not really.

It takes some time and negotiation to whittle the piles down to four books each, which he figures might have a shot at fitting into their suitcases, and then Annie locks up the store and they all step outside into the cold together. The kids walk ahead of them, swinging their new Wordsmith's tote bags, dipping in and out of the yellow glow of the streetlamps.

"So what's on the agenda for the rest of the weekend?" Annie asks, and Connor pulls the folded itinerary out of his coat pocket. She raises her eyebrows. "Oh. You have an *actual* agenda. Wow."

"Yeah. My sister is running the show."

Annie peers at the first page. "She seems very . . . organized."

"She has a lot of very organized help," Connor says.

"You're going up to Melvin Falls tomorrow?"

He squints at the line on the itinerary. "So it would seem."

"Huh," she says. "Not a lot up there."

"Yeah, well, I guess the point is to bond."

"With who?"

"My family."

"You came all the way to North Dakota to bond with your family?" she says doubtfully. "You're a famous author. Couldn't you come up with something a little more glamorous?"

"Trust me, none of this was my idea," he says, neglecting to mention that his sister is about a million times more famous and glamorous than he is. He glances down at the itinerary in his hands again. "But first, dinner. Is Piero's any good?"

"Yeah, it's been around forever," she says as she zips her coat up higher. "But avoid the pepperoni."

He laughs. "Don't tell me you work there too."

"No," she says. "There just aren't a lot of places to eat out around here."

A strand of her hair brushes against his hand as he holds the itinerary between them, and Connor's breath hitches in his chest. The kids are up ahead, waiting to cross to the hotel. Rosie is typing something on her phone, and Hugh is flipping through one of his new books. Connor turns back to Annie, suddenly reluctant to part ways with her.

"I don't suppose you'd want to—" He stops short, reconsidering. He has an inexplicable urge to invite her to dinner, but he knows what an unmitigated disaster that would be. It will be bad enough with just their family. Having a witness would only make things worse.

She's looking at him, amused, like she can't believe he's even entertaining the thought, and he feels a little ridiculous. But still, something makes him forge ahead.

"I don't suppose," he starts again, "that you'd want to go for a walk tomorrow morning? Or get coffee? We don't leave until—" He glances down at the schedule. "Eight."

She nods. "Coffee would be great."

"Here," he says, handing over his phone. "Why don't you . . ."

But she's already typing in her number. It would've been just as easy to meet her in the lobby or at the coffee place. But as she returns his phone, he feels something in him relax, knowing he's now able to reach her.

He sends her a message: **hi**.

Hi, she types back, and as his phone chimes, they smile at each other.

When he catches up with the kids, Hugh is making kissing noises at him.

"Dad's got a girlfriend," he says in a singsong voice, and Connor puts a hand on the scruff of his neck in mock annoyance.

"Who said you're allowed to make fun of your dad?"

Hugh giggles. "Me!"

"Do you like her?" Rosie asks, looking at him intently with those eyes of hers that are so like Jude's, so like their mom's. In the book, he'd made them green instead of blue, the thinnest of disguises. It hadn't fooled anybody.

Connor shrugs. "I barely know her."

"So?"

"So it's like when I start writing a new story," he explains as they cross the street to the hotel, the three of them in a row. "Sometimes

I get really excited about the beginning, but it doesn't end up going anywhere. Not everything is meant to be a whole book. Sometimes it's just a really great first sentence. Or paragraph. Or chapter. And that's okay too. It's better not to expect too much right at the start."

Rosie gives him an incredulous look. "That," she says, "seems like an extremely stupid strategy."

"For writing books or meeting people?"

"Both," she says, and as they walk back through the front door of the Portree Inn, Connor finds he can't think of anything to say in response.

New York

2018

AFTER DECADES OF PATCHING LEAKS AND DEALING WITH
frozen pipes, their dad decided it was finally time to sell the Michigan house. Everyone took the news in their own way. Gemma, who
was only six hours away and visited regularly, drove up with Mateo
to gather her childhood art projects and model horses and ratty
stuffed animals. A couple weeks later, Roddy had a layover in De-
troit on his way back from a match, and he and their dad and step-
mom, Liz, went back to the house, where they sat around the fire pit
at the edge of the bluff, trading stories and memories. Even Jude flew
in to say goodbye in spite of her busy schedule, sitting alone on the
beach for hours, watching the lake turn from gray to blue and back
again as the sun moved in and out of the clouds, the way she'd done
so often as a kid.

But Connor had no interest in a sentimental pilgrimage. He'd left
Michigan behind a long time ago. They all had. It felt dangerous to
go back, like swimming against some invisible tide. He didn't want
to take stock of his childhood. He preferred to leave it where it was:
in the past.

Instead, he promised his dad he'd come visit their new condo in

Hilton Head with the kids for spring break, and in exchange, a heavy cardboard box arrived in the mail a few weeks later. When he opened it, he found a sloping pile of journals and notebooks, all of them filled with his cramped handwriting, a feverish accounting of his long-forgotten thoughts and feelings, his dubious hopes and dreams, his boyhood memories.

He opened one of them, a logbook he kept on their summer trips.

8/8/95: Left early from Lexington. Stopped at a cow field because Jude wanted to pet one. Had peanut butter sandwiches at a rest stop for lunch. Gemma sat shotgun even though it was my turn. Almost ran out of gas near Memphis. (I told Mom but she didn't listen.) Finished Call of the Wild. Roddy's feet smell horrible. Jude says she doesn't smell it, but I think she's lying.

He pressed the book shut again.

The family documentarian, his mom had once called him, and even then, it had given Connor both a sense of purpose and a desperate, scrabbling feeling, like none of it was real, those strange, indistinguishable days on the road, like if he didn't pin them down with words, they might somehow float away. Even then, he was writing to capture them like fireflies in a jar.

He ran a hand over the cover of the journal, which looked like an old suitcase, full of travel stamps, full of stories, and then he set it back in the box with the others, closed it up, and walked it down three flights of stairs to their storage unit, where he tucked it between a dusty window fan and an old baby swing and promptly forgot about it.

Roddy

North Dakota

2025

"So," Roddy says, leaning against the headboard of the creaky hotel bed, the itinerary from Jude on his lap. "It looks like we have two hours until dinner. What do you want to do?"

Beside him, Winston props himself up on one elbow. "Well, we could do *that* again," he says with a grin, and Roddy laughs and gives him a kiss before throwing off the sheets and getting out of bed. "Why not?" Winston says, rolling onto his back. "We're on holiday."

"Does North Dakota really count as a holiday?" Roddy pulls on his boxers, then pads over to the window and peers out at the gray street below. "Want to go for a run?"

Winston gives an exaggerated sigh as he reaches for his glasses. "I do not."

"Come on," Roddy says, tossing a T-shirt at him.

"We only have two more weeks together, and you want to spend that time *running*?"

Roddy's stomach churns at the reminder. He still hasn't managed to tell Winston that, in fact, they don't even have one more week together. He'd planned to do it that night after hearing from Zack, but instead they got into a big discussion about how they'd make things work long-distance, and Winston was being so wonderfully support-ive and understanding that Roddy couldn't bring himself to break the news. A couple days later, while they packed for this trip, he promised himself that it would be done by the time they landed in Bismarck. But of course he'd chickened out again, and now here they are, one of them still oblivious, the other in a slightly sweaty panic.

"Hey," Winston says, and Roddy turns to see that he's wearing a dreamy expression. "Do you realize that exactly one week from today, we'll be husbands?"

Roddy's heart falls; he closes his eyes. "Winston . . ." he begins, try-ing to screw up his courage, but Winston is lost in his own thoughts.

"Well, maybe not *quite* yet, actually. What's the time difference here? I don't even completely understand where we are . . . is this the Midwest?"

"Hey," Roddy says, his heart still jangling in his chest. "Let's do something fun right now. While it's just the two of us." He holds up the itinerary. "I've heard the zoo is nice."

Winston looks doubtful. "How about we go for a drink?"

"Yeah," Roddy says with a nod, "your thing is better."

Out on the main street, the first bar they pass is dark and divey, filled with oversized white men drinking from bottles of beer with peeling labels, their eyes trained on the basketball game that's show-ing on an ancient-looking TV in the corner.

"Let's find a place where we aren't quite so likely to get killed by the locals," Winston suggests, and though he says it like a joke, Roddy knows he's serious. Winston came out when he was fourteen, but the bullying had started long before that. For being gay, for being Black, for being skinny and awkward and so much smarter than his classmates. The first night he and Roddy met, after finding each other on an app that had the veneer of respectability about it, they'd sat across from each other at a heart-spangled bar in Dupont Circle and Winston had told him about the time two boys from his second-ary school had pushed him off a ledge where he was eating lunch. He'd broken his elbow that day, and the neat scar from the surgery is still a reminder of all of it, the teasing and mocking and taunting, which got better—or at least subtler—as he got older, though the memory of those lonely years never went away entirely, trailing him from Oxford to MIT, where he got his PhD, and then down to the National Institutes of Health.

Even now, although Winston is a brilliant and award-winning scientist, confident and handsome and happy, Roddy can still see the anxiety in him sometimes, the way he tenses when a stranger stares at them, or when an article about Roddy mentions his sexuality before saying anything about his skills on the field. Roddy knows this isn't a particularly evolved standpoint, but it makes him want to go back and beat the living daylights out of anyone who ever teased that younger, scrawnier version of his fiancé, the one with the broken elbow and soulful eyes and sensitive heart.

His own path had been so different. He was an athlete, an exceptional one, which was a special kind of currency, one that afforded him a certain amount of insulation. He'd known he was gay since he was very young, ten or eleven, and he'd kissed a boy for the first time at twelve—behind the bleachers after a soccer game, of course. But he didn't come out until much later, when he was in college. Even then, only his close friends and family knew. To this day, Roddy isn't sure if he was a private person by nature or if this secret of his made him so, but he knows for sure he wasn't as brave as Winston. He was always single-mindedly focused on soccer, and something instinctively told him that his identity might get in the way of that, that it might change too much. Maybe he was right—maybe it would have. Or maybe he was good enough that it would have been fine either way. It's impossible to know. But it took him until he was twenty-nine—seven years into a solidly successful professional career—to say the words "I'm gay" to a journalist. And it turned out he'd been right: it *did* change everything. Just not in the ways he'd always imagined.

They pass another sports bar, and then a Mexican restaurant that for some godforsaken reason has hot dogs on the menu, and finally find a local tavern with a red-and-white striped awning. The smell of popcorn drifts out into the street, and Roddy pauses to peer inside.

"Look," he says, delighted. "They have games."

Winston laughs. "You are a child."

"One quick game of Skee Ball! Then we can go."

He hears Winston groan, but Roddy is already a few steps inside, where the bulky games are positioned shoulder to shoulder near the entrance.

"Hey," he says, pressing his face against the glass window of a claw machine, where inside there's a riot of cheap stuffed animals. "Want me to try and win you that hippo? Or, ooh . . . how about that teddy bear?"

"You do know I'm thirty-six, right?" Winston says, taking off his glasses to clean them with the tail of his shirt. But Roddy is undeterred. He digs through his pocket for a dollar and feeds it into the machine, sticking his tongue out in concentration as he maneuvers the joystick. He wrenches it back and forth a few times before jamming the red button in the middle, and it moves down until it's right above the teddy bear. But to Roddy's horror, it instead manages to snag a stuffed diamond ring.

He and Winston watch together as the claw begins to rise, the ridiculous, oversized diamond in its clutches. The ring goes up, up, up—dangling there like the world's worst metaphor—until at the last minute it slips and falls back into the pile of other escaped prizes, landing softly beside a round, beady-eyed whale.

"Damn," Winston says with a grin. "And here I thought we were finally going to get my ring."

Roddy stares into the glass case, the back of his neck flushing with guilt. They hadn't done it when they got engaged; it had been a spontaneous moment, the two of them walking back from brunch one particularly beautiful summer day, holding hands and laughing, and something had ballooned in Roddy's chest, a feeling of happiness so big he felt he might float away, so he'd turned to Winston and said, "I want to spend the rest of my life with you."

Winston's smile had been huge. "So do I," he said, then laughed. "With you, I mean."

"Will you marry me?" Roddy had asked, turning to face him, to take his other hand too, and without answering, Winston had kissed him, a kiss like a promise, like a vow.

They decided they'd wait for rings until they got married; Roddy already has the one he picked out for Winston—a simple gold band—tucked into his sock drawer at home. But now, almost a year later, he's keenly aware that he's about to make his fiancé wait even longer for it.

"Ah, well," Winston says lightly. "Soon enough."

He turns to give Roddy a peck on the cheek, then starts for the door of the bar, heading back outside. Roddy takes one more look at the ring before following him into the chilly evening air, his stomach leaden. They pull their coats tighter around themselves, walking in silence for a couple blocks until they stumble across a small alleyway. At the end of it is a bar with a green door, the word *Vino* written across the window in loopy letters.

"Can it really be true?" Winston says as they walk toward it. "Portree sells something other than Bud Light?"

"You're such a snob," Roddy says, but he says it fondly.

Inside, the place is dimly lit, with velvet banquettes and delicate brass tables. It's mostly empty, which makes it less glaringly obvious that Winston appears to be the only Black person in this entire town, and he and Roddy possibly the only gay couple. Still, they exchange looks of pleasant surprise as they take a seat at the bar and open their menus.

"They have bruschetta," Roddy says, impressed. "Who knew?"

"See?" Winston says. "If it were up to you, we'd be playing pinball right now."

"I guess I'm lucky to have you," Roddy says, his voice surprisingly gruff.

Winston laughs. "You really are."

Roddy had hoped a glass of wine might steady him, but by the time they're halfway through the first bottle, he's only more jittery and distracted.

"Remember that wine bar we went to in New York?" Winston is saying. "Where you ordered the pâté without knowing what it was?" He leans back on his stool, shoulders shaking with laughter. "You took one bite and ran straight to the loo like you were going to throw up."

Roddy smiles sheepishly. "I did throw up."

"You did not!" Winston says, gleeful.

"I was too embarrassed to tell you," Roddy admits. "That's why I let you eat the rest."

Winston shakes his head. "I thought you were just being charming," he says, filling each of their glasses again. He glances up at Roddy, eyebrows raised mischievously. "Good thing there's no pâté at our wedding then."

Roddy manages a thin smile. "Good thing."

"Speaking of the wedding," Winston says, clinking his glass against Roddy's, then taking a long sip. "I know this is a horrendously last-minute thought. But I've been feeling guilty about my parents. I didn't want to invite them in case it made you feel bad, not having family there. But now that we're here, now that you've seen yours, I wonder if . . ." He trails off at the look on Roddy's face. "I know the weekend has barely begun, and it might not go smoothly. But maybe it would help things along if you asked them to come?"

It occurs to Roddy that this would be the perfect excuse, a completely valid reason to suggest moving the wedding back. But he can't lie to Winston. Not about this. Instead, he just blinks at him, lost for words.

"No, you're right," Winston says, shaking his head. "It was a silly idea."

"It's not," Roddy says. "It's a lovely idea. And you're lovely for thinking of it."

Winston frowns. "I don't think I've ever heard you use the word *lovely* before."

"I have to tell you something," Roddy says, closing his eyes briefly, and Winston sets down his glass of wine to listen. "We have to move the wedding."

For a long moment, Winston is quiet, his face betraying nothing. He looks the way he does when he's working, or when he's trying to figure out a particularly tricky problem: resolute and calm and extremely measured. Roddy waits, his whole body tense.

"Because of Orlando," Winston says eventually.

Roddy nods miserably. "I'm so sorry," he says. "You have no idea. I tried to get out of it, but preseason has already started, and they want me down there next week, on the twelfth. I tried to push it back, I swear. But Zack couldn't get them to agree. So there's just no way—"

"To fit in our wedding," Winston says, his accent more clipped than usual. "Right."

"But that's the good thing about it being small, right?" Roddy says in a desperately sunny voice. "It's just an appointment at city hall and a reservation at a restaurant. All easily moved."

Winton's face is still alarmingly blank. "But it's our anniversary."

"I know," Roddy admits. "And it would be really nice to do it then. But it's not like . . . I mean, tons of couples get married on one of the other three hundred and sixty-four days of the year, right? And maybe this way, we could invite our families after all, give them some time to make plans, you know?"

Winston reaches for his wine glass, tips it back, and finishes in one go. "Can I ask you something?" he says, and then, without bothering to wait for an answer, he goes on: "Is this all really worth it? Missing our wedding and moving to Florida for eight months so you can sit on the bench of a team you don't care about for one final season?"

Roddy leans back, feeling off-balance. "That's not fair."

"I'm actually not trying to be a prick," Winston says. "Genuinely. I just can't understand why this is more appealing than starting our life together. Especially when we both know they mostly want you because—"

"It doesn't matter," Roddy cuts in. "I don't care why they want me. I want to play, and they're going to let me. It's as simple as that. Besides, I already accepted the offer. And made a commitment to the team. This is just part of it."

Winston's eyes flash at this. "And what about your commitment to me?"

"We're still going to get married," Roddy says, impatient now. "We just might have to do it later. Or earlier! We could do it next week, before I go. Whatever you want. But there's no sense in overreacting."

"Overreacting?"

"Yeah," Roddy says. "This just isn't the biggest deal in the world."

"Right," Winston says, looking hurt. "Right. Well. I suppose the thing is . . . it's pretty much the biggest deal in the world to me."

Roddy blinks at him, unsure what to say next. For a long time, they just sit there, the silence stretching between them. And then they hear a familiar voice.

"You two stole my idea," Jude says, practically floating over to them in an oversized black coat, her strawberry-blond hair falling across her shoulders in a way that seems impossibly careless but also entirely styled. She looks thinner than she did three years ago, more like the photos of the actress he's seen in magazines than the twin who used to hold his hand when they jumped off the rocks at the edge of the lake.

When they both stare at her blankly, she gestures to the bottle of wine between them. "Getting drunk before dinner."

"Oh," Roddy says, and then he pushes the bottle in her direction. "Yeah."

"It's the only thing for it," she says, winking at Winston as she unbuttons her coat and joins them. "So. Winston. Tell me everything. Who you are. How you two met. How annoying it is when my brother leaves his dirty socks all over the house." She stops and claps her hands. "And I hear you're engaged?"

Roddy and Winston exchange a grim look.

"We are," Roddy says finally.

"Congratulations," she says as the waiter produces another glass. Jude gives him a sparkly smile before returning her gaze to Roddy and Winston. "Let's start there. Who popped the question? How did it all go down? When's the wedding?"

Once again, their eyes meet. There's a long silence.

"Wow," Jude says, looking between them. She was about to pour herself a glass of wine, but sets the bottle down and slides it in their direction instead. "Seems like you two need this more than I do," she says; then she lifts a hand to order another.

California

2005

THE SUMMER AFTER THEIR FRESHMAN YEAR OF COLLEGE, Roddy went to visit Jude in L.A. She'd gone out there when school ended, intending to stay with her roommate's family for a week. But it turned out the roommate lived in a house big enough to barely register a guest, and she convinced her to stay. They spent their summer waitressing at her parents' golf club in Brentwood and sitting by the pool and doing dramatic readings from *Much Ado About Nothing*, making bets over which of them would get to play Beatrice and which would have to settle for Hero in their upcoming fall production at the small university in Wisconsin where they were both theater majors.

As it turned out, Jude wouldn't even make it to the audition. Two weeks into the new semester, that same roommate's dad, a hugely successful producer of soap operas and teen dramas, was sitting through an emergency casting session to find a replacement for the star of his new show about teenagers in a small town in Alaska—the actress they'd picked had disappeared right as preproduction began, then reappeared soon after in a rehab facility in Palm Springs—and as he watched actress after actress that day, his mind drifted to his daughter's roommate who had spent the summer in their guest house, who had a curious mix of naïveté and assuredness, like she was somehow both very young and very old at the same time, exactly what the part required, and so he flew her out for a wild card of an audition that would go on to change her life, not necessarily because the show itself was a huge success (though it had decent ratings and a cult following and later earned a surprise second life on streaming), but because it was enough to get her an agent and a manager and a little bit of money for a deposit on a tiny apartment above a nail salon in Studio City, and because the rest of it would all spin out from there, as these things tend to do, first the show and then the series about a young paralegal and then the indie movie that took Sundance by storm and the unlikely turn as an action star in that futuristic thriller and of course the period piece that first showed her dramatic chops, and on and on until the recent morning when the Oscar nominations were announced.

Back in Wisconsin, her roommate got the part of Beatrice in the fall play.

But before all of that, Roddy flew out to L.A. for a visit, using the money he'd saved from spending the summer at UNC—where he had both an athletic scholarship and a starting position at center midfield on the soccer team—as a camp counselor teaching young athletes how to break up an offensive attack. That summer, Connor was interning at a magazine in New York City, and Gemma was in Chicago, working a real marketing job, already a grown-up, as if she hadn't always been, though she was still living in a two-bedroom apartment with four roommates and a fridge full of beer.

It had been three months since their mother died, and they were hopelessly far-flung.

Jude took Roddy everywhere that week: they ate fish tacos at the Santa Monica Pier and stuck their feet in the Pacific Ocean; they went to Descanso Gardens and Grand Central Market and the Getty; they walked the grimy strip of stars along Hollywood Boulevard and hiked to the observatory in Griffith Park, the hazy city spreading out below them as far as they could see. On the last day, Jude drove him out to Malibu, where they collected rocks on a jagged beach. Afterward, they stayed to watch the sun drop between the enormous stone arches, an orange ball hanging above the waves, their faces awash in golden light.

"You like it here," Roddy said, and Jude smiled.

"I do," she said. "And I couldn't face going home this summer. I don't know why."

"Because of Mom," he said, his eyes on the water.

Jude nodded. "Isn't it weird? It's been so long since she was even there."

"But it's still where all our memories are."

"Most of them," she said, thinking of their summer trips.

The sun dipped lower in the sky. The waves continued to crash onto the beach. Behind them, someone brought out a guitar and began to sing.

"I wish I'd gotten to see her again," Roddy said, and Jude stared determinedly out at the thin line of horizon. "I know we're not supposed to, but I miss her."

"I do too," Jude said.

Roddy glanced at her sideways. "And I miss you."

"I'm right here," she told him.

Jude

North Dakota

2025

One hour and two bottles later, they step out of the wine bar into the frosty night. Jude shivers as she fumbles with the buttons of her coat, the wind making her eyes water. The streets of Portree are mostly quiet, except for the occasional rattle of a truck or scattered cheers from inside the nearby sports bar. Everything feels wide open and spacious but somehow also claustrophobic. Jude loops an arm through Roddy's as he falls into step beside her, Winston trailing behind them.

"So why now?" Roddy asks her, his eyes a little unfocused from the wine.

Jude shrugs. "I had a free weekend," she says, but he doesn't look convinced. It's unsettling to be with him again, the one person who could always see through her. He's like a human X-ray, a walking lie detector test built specifically for her. Maybe it wouldn't matter if she didn't have so much to hide right now, if she weren't carrying around quite so many secrets. But she is. And it's hard not to feel exposed as he gives her a searching look.

"Right," he says, but not without a hint of skepticism. "Well, I'm glad. I missed you."

He says this last part a little roughly, like he's more annoyed about it than anything else. But she's always been able to see through him too.

"Me too," she tells him.

Her phone buzzes in her coat pocket, and she pulls it out to see that Spencer is calling.

"*Spencer Nolan?*" Winston cries as he catches sight of the screen. He stops walking, his eyes wide. "No way. Is that—that's really Spencer Nolan? Sorry. Not my business. At all. But . . . is it? Are you dating him? Sorry. Not my business either. But are you?"

Roddy looks back at him, completely befuddled. "Do you know him?"

"He's a massive star," Winston says, then adds, a little sheepishly, "Plus, he's gorgeous."

"Aha," Roddy says, then turns to Jude. "I swear he's not an undercover gossip columnist."

Winston nods in agreement. "I'm a scientist."

"A scientist with a secret *Us Weekly* addiction," Roddy adds as they start to walk again, their frozen hands in their pockets, their faces lit by the orange glow of the streetlamps.

"I only pick it up every once in a while," Winston insists, but Roddy shakes his head slowly and theatrically at Jude.

"Every. Single. Week."

Jude isn't sure what to say. She and Spencer have so far managed to keep the press away, partly because she's always been fiercely private, and partly because she's still figuring out exactly what it is between them. Her team knows, and a few of her close friends, and of course her housekeeper, who blushes every time Spencer pads through the kitchen in his swimsuit, but otherwise, they've mostly existed in their own private bubble, and she's been reluctant so far to let anything pop it.

The phone has stopped ringing in her hand, and she holds it up as they come to a stop in front of the restaurant. "We worked together on a film recently," she says awkwardly. "So . . . yeah. I should probably call him back. I'll meet you guys in there."

"Right, of course," Winston says, lingering as Jude brings the phone to her ear, even as Roddy half-drags him inside. "And sorry about . . . I didn't mean to pry . . . He's just . . . well, you know. Okay. Right then. Toodles."

As they disappear into Piero's, the smell of garlic briefly drifting into the night air, Jude hears Roddy say, *"Toodles?"*

Alone on the empty street, she punches Spencer's name on her screen and brings the phone to her ear. "Hey," he says when he picks up. "Sorry to bother you when you're with your family. But I was just calling to let you know that Sergio dropped off your dress for that Oscar thing on Monday."

"The luncheon?" Jude says, turning her back to the warm lights of the restaurant and stamping her feet against the chill. "Great."

"I took a peek. You're going to look *hot.*"

She laughs. "Thanks."

"Am I supposed to come to that or just the ceremony?"

"Just the ceremony."

There's a pause, and then: "Red carpet too?"

She hesitates. They haven't discussed this yet. Though they've been together for almost six months, it would be their first public appearance and could mean the end of any privacy for a very long time. Jude has always been overly careful about things like this, but something about the wine and being so far away from Los Angeles, unmoored from her life, makes her feel reckless. The secrets she's been carrying are lined up inside her like pins she's about to knock down—*one, two, three*—and that makes it feel like she can say anything right now. Even yes. Especially yes.

And so she does.

She can practically hear the smile in his voice. "It will be an honor to escort you," he says with a kind of hammy formality, but she can tell he's genuinely pleased. She is too. More than she would have thought. "Hey, you didn't say how it's going there."

Jude glances back at the restaurant. Through the foggy windows, she can see Roddy and Winston taking off their coats. "It's awkward. Extremely awkward."

"Can I make a suggestion?"

"Sure."

"Alcohol."

Jude laughs. "Already on it. In case you couldn't tell."

When she hangs up and turns around, two young women have appeared as if from nowhere on the sidewalk behind her, and Jude immediately tenses, worried that they've overheard her conversation or taken a video. But they both look frozen in their excitement, clutching each other's arms through their thick puffy coats, eyes wide.

"Are you Jude Endicott?" the taller one asks, and then, without waiting for confirmation, adds: "Can we have a picture?"

The other one looks like she might throw up. "I can't believe you're really here."

Through the window of the restaurant, Jude can see her family being seated at a long table. "Yeah, that's fine," she says, forcing a smile, and the girls hurry over to either side of her, like bookends, one of them holding an arm out to snap a picture.

"Thanks," they say, then hurry off, bent over the phone and making little squeals of excitement as they stumble back up the street.

Inside, everyone is waiting for her: Roddy and Winston, Connor and the kids, and Gemma, sitting at the head of a table covered by a red-checked cloth and scattered with guttering candles.

"Sorry," she says. "Had to take that."

They're all quiet for a second. There was a time when their personal lives had been open books, laid bare for the others to see. But not anymore.

Jude pulls out the empty chair, feeling suddenly impatient. She wants to skip past this, past the apologies and explanations, the broken feeling that they're a bunch of puzzle pieces that no longer fit. She wants to get to the part where it's like old times again, the

Extraordinary Endicotts, better than ever. But she knows it's not that easy. She knows they have to start somewhere. And so she decides to begin.

"It was my boyfriend, actually," she tells them, testing out the word. It sounds strange and formal, but also nice. "On the phone."

Winston leans forward excitedly. "I *knew* it," he says under his breath.

"We met on the set of my next film."

"Are you talking about *Spencer Nolan*?" Rosie asks, her eyes going wide behind her glasses, and instinctively, Jude flinches, glancing around to make sure there are no phones pointed in their direction. But the restaurant is too noisy for that anyway, and so she nods, and Rosie lets out a little yelp. "Oh my god. He's so dreamy."

Roddy laughs. "You and Winston should start a fan club."

"Can I tell my friend Luna?" Rosie asks, ignoring this. "She won't *believe* it."

"Rosie," Connor says, his voice stern. "No."

Her face reddens, but Jude gives her a smile. "I'll let you tell her before it goes public. I promise. Just not yet, okay?"

"Okay," Rosie says, brightening again.

From the other end of the table, Jude can feel Gemma watching her closely, her chin cupped in her hands, her hair—so much shorter than the last time they saw each other—framing her face. "Is it serious?" she asks in that matter-of-fact way of hers, and Jude hesitates.

"I don't know. Maybe."

"Do you love him?"

"I think so."

"Why didn't you bring him this weekend?"

"Honestly?" Jude says with a grin. "Because I didn't realize he was my boyfriend until just a few minutes ago."

Roddy laughs. "That sounds right."

"Yeah," Connor chimes in. "Remember when David D'Angelo told everyone you were his girlfriend and you'd never even spoken to him?"

"That was fifth grade," Jude says dismissively.

"Or when Kyle Marsh called to ask you to prom and you had to look him up in the yearbook?"

"They're exaggerating," she says to Rosie, who is absorbing all this with an expression of great interest. "And this is different. With Spencer, I mean. So I guess I just..." She finds herself looking at Gemma. "I guess I just wanted you to know."

Their waitress weaves through the crowded arrangement of tables, arriving with a stack of menus as thick as novels and an enormous basket of bread. She sets them down and has started to flip open her notepad when her eyes land on Jude and she stops cold, her face etched with surprise. "Oh. Shit. Wow. Sorry. I just— Shit."

Jude laughs and reaches for a roll. "Hi."

"Sorry, I was not expecting that. I'll give you folks a few minutes to look at your menus," she says before scurrying off again, turning back once, as if to make sure of what she saw, then disappearing into the kitchen.

Jude rips off a piece of bread and pops it into her mouth, and Rosie, watching her, frowns. When the basket comes her way, she takes a roll too.

"I thought you were gluten-free," Connor says, and she glares at him.

"No."

He holds up his hands but looks amused as she takes a bite. "My mistake."

"Okay," Jude says, turning to Roddy. "Your turn."

"My turn for what?"

"To tell us something we don't know about you."

He sighs. "Is this an icebreaker? I hate icebreakers."

"Too bad," Jude tells him. "You're up."

"Okay," Roddy says, looking sidelong at Winston. He takes a deep breath, then gives his head a little shake. "I'm moving to Orlando next week. To play one last season there."

Winston attempts a smile, which falls flat.

"Not everyone is thrilled about this development," Roddy admits, placing a hand over Winston's. Their eyes meet. "It means putting off some other things I was really excited about. And it won't be easy to be away for so long. At all. But it's something I have to do."

"I read about it yesterday," Gemma says, and he glances over at her in surprise.

"You did? It wasn't exactly front-page news."

"I have a Google alert set for you," she says. "For all of you."

Connor laughs. "I don't know whether to be scared or flattered."

"Well, I had to keep tabs on you somehow," Gemma says, and to her surprise, Jude feels for a second like she might cry, as if for years she's been drifting, untethered, like a lost balloon, only to find out that all this time, her sister was out there holding on.

"That's nice of you, Gem," Roddy says, but she waves it away.

"It's your own faults for getting famous enough to be trackable. I, on the other hand, have chosen to remain incognito."

"Is that what we're calling it?" Connor teases her. "Then let's hear it."

"What?"

"Your fun fact."

"My fun fact," she says, "is that I live in Chicago."

"We already knew that," Roddy points out.

"With Mateo."

Connor shakes his head. "That too. Tell him we wish he were here."

"I'm still working at the same exact place," she continues, and then, looking around at their expressions, adds, "and will give five bucks to the first one who can remember where that is."

"A marketing firm?" Roddy ventures.

"Correct but unspecific."

Connor frowns. "It has three names, right?"

"No, because there was a merger, I think," Jude says, searching her memory. "It's something that starts with an *M* . . ."

"McDonald's?" Hugh suggests hopefully.

"Mitchell & Kelly," Winston says, and Gemma smiles at him.

"Thank you, Winston. I know this is the first time we've met, but you're officially my favorite sibling."

"Don't I get some credit for having told him that?" Roddy asks, and Gemma shakes her head as she passes Winston a five-dollar bill.

"Sorry, winner takes all."

Jude feels a stab of guilt. "I knew that too," she says, and when Gemma gives her the look she always dreaded as a kid, the one that would so quickly and efficiently cut through any lies she had told or was thinking of telling, she responds with a guilty shrug. "Or I did at one point."

"Connor?" Gemma says, turning to face him. "I think you're up. And please don't tell us there's another book. I'm not sure we could survive a sequel."

Jude tenses, automatically glancing over at Roddy, who looks equally nervous that they've already found themselves here. But Connor shakes his head.

"Don't worry," he says grimly. "There's definitely not another book."

"So what then?" Jude asks, eager to keep the conversation moving, and Rosie and Hugh—who are seated on either side of him—both tip their chins up to look at their dad.

He leans back in his chair and puts a hand on each of their shoulders before answering. "Nicola and I split up," he says, and when Rosie sighs and Hugh's mouth turns down at the corners, he hurries on: "It was hard at first. But it's been for the best. And we're okay now, right?" He looks at each of his kids. "We're okay."

"Sorry, man," Roddy says, looking at him with concern. "I didn't know."

"How would you?" Connor says, but there's no bitterness in his voice. Only a sad reminder of why this game is necessary.

Jude tries to think of what to say. Nicola had been around for half their lives, ever since she and Connor met during their sophomore year of college, and while she had no doubt they'd loved each other, they'd also bickered incessantly. She once told Roddy that she suspected they would either stay together until they were both a hundred, out of sheer stubbornness, or the whole thing would implode within five years. It was a good enough idea in theory, the two of them, but in practice, they just hadn't ever seemed to fit; Nicola was a hedge fund manager with very little patience and a very demanding schedule, and for most of their relationship, Connor had been a dissatisfied English teacher frantically writing novels in his spare time, eyes always on some distant dream. She wonders if what happened was that the dream came true. She knows better than anyone how much that can change things.

"I'm sorry, Con," she begins, and she's about to say more, but he waves it away.

"It's fine. Really. Just wanted you all to know." He turns to his son, who is pulling apart a breadstick. "What about you, Hughy? What's something you could tell us that we don't already know?"

Hugh taps his finger on his chin dramatically as he considers this, enjoying the attention of the table. Then he breaks into a grin. "I stole a book from that bookstore."

"Hugh!" Connor says, his mouth falling open. "That's not okay."

"You said you can never have enough books."

"*Legally obtained* books," he tells his son. "We'll have to return that tomorrow."

"We're leaving at eight," Jude reminds him.

"Good thing he's seeing the bookstore lady before then," Rosie says, and Jude raises her eyebrows at him.

"Making friends, are we?"

Connor's face has gone red. "Something like that," he says, and then, once again looking for distraction, he turns to Rosie. "You're up, kid."

Rosie bites her bottom lip, thinking for a moment. She tucks her long hair behind her ears and looks up at Jude a little shyly.

"I've watched all your movies," she tells her. "Except the ones that are rated R."

"Wow," Jude says, touched. "Thank you."

"And I really think you should win at the Oscars," she continues with a hopeful smile. "Because you're really, really good at acting. The best ever. In my opinion."

Jude grins over at Connor. "Well, who needs an Oscar when you've got that?" she says, then turns back to Rosie, whose cheeks are flushed. "Maybe you can come."

The girl's eyes get huge. "What, to the Oscars?"

"Sure," Jude says, and when she glances over at Connor again, she expects to see that smile he gets whenever someone is doing something nice for someone he loves, softer and subtler than his usual smile. She hadn't realized how much she missed it until she catches his eye and sees that, instead, he looks unexpectedly stone-faced.

"Hey," he says, turning to Rosie, who is staring at Jude with starry eyes. He fishes some coins from his jacket pocket. "Why don't you two go pick out some songs on the jukebox?"

"But I don't want to—"

"Rosie," Connor says sternly, and she sighs and pushes back her chair. When they're gone, he turns to Jude. "You can't do that with kids."

"Do what?" she asks, genuinely confused.

"Promise them stuff you don't mean."

"I do mean it. Why would you think I don't?"

"Because you never mean what you say," he says, an angry edge to his voice. "You're unreliable. Just like . . ." He stops himself there, but she knows what he was going to say. They all do. *Just like Mom.*

"Hey," Roddy says. "That's enough."

Winston scrapes back his chair and stands up. "You know, I think I'll go help them with the music," he says, excusing himself before anyone can say more, and then it's just the four of them, glaring at one another across the dimly lit table, the dripping candles making everything feel dreamy and a little surreal.

Connor picks up his menu and studies it so that his face is half-hidden. "Even if you were serious, you ask first," he says without looking up at Jude. "It's basic courtesy."

"Ask first?" Roddy snorts. "That's rich, coming from you."

The menu comes down again, and Connor's face is weary. "Can we not do this right now?"

Jude knows this is how it works, how it's always worked: Connor snaps at Jude, then Roddy snaps at Connor, and then Gemma snaps at all of them. But she decides to put a stop to it before they get to that last step.

"That's enough," she says, and they all turn to her. "The point of this weekend is to move forward, not backward. I don't have the energy to fight anymore. Not with the three of you. I just want our family back. Someone had to give it a shot, and I figured it might as well be me. So let's move on, okay? Or at least try to. Can we do that?"

"I think," Gemma says, her eyes trained on Jude, "that it's hard to move on without knowing where we're going. Or why we're here."

"We're here because it's time," Jude says with a hint of impatience. "Three years was enough. It was too much. It was never supposed to snowball like that, and we all let it happen, so now we have to fix it. Simple as that."

Gemma frowns. "I don't buy it."

"What?"

"Something isn't adding up. Why now?"

Connor nods. "You're in the middle of an Oscar campaign."

"That's not important," Jude says, but even she's not a good enough actress to sell that. It's not that it's been her dream ever since she was a kid or anything—that would suggest a single-mindedness about acting that Jude has never quite possessed. But it *had* been their mother's dream, and they all know how much weight that carries with Jude.

"And why here?" Gemma asks. "Even if you were set on coming to North Dakota, you can barely find this place on a map."

Jude looks away, her heart picking up speed. "That's what makes it interesting."

"How did you even hear about it?"

"I found it on a map," she says—an attempt at a joke that falls entirely flat. Gemma is watching her with something like disappointment, and the boys—because this is how she'll always think of them, even now—are looking back and forth between them.

Gemma leans forward over the checkered tablecloth. "I'm going to ask you one more time," she says, the words slow and measured. "Why are we here?"

Jude closes her eyes, and just like that, she's eighteen years old, standing outside this very restaurant, trying to light a cigarette in the wind.

When she opens her eyes again, all three of her siblings are watching her.

"Because," she says. "Mom came here."

"What?" Gemma asks, blinking at her. "How do you know?"

There's a beat of silence. Then another.

And then Jude says, "Because I came with her."

One, she thinks. That's one secret down.

Only two to go.

Missouri

1992

ONE DAY WHILE THEY WERE ALL AT THEIR LOCAL GROCERY store, Jude noticed her mother staring at a flyer on the bulletin board near the checkout. After a moment, she reached out and pulled off one of the little tabs at the bottom and folded it carefully before putting it in the pocket of her coat.

That night, while the other three played upstairs, Jude sat coloring at the kitchen table as her mother stirred a pot of mac and cheese, singing something under her breath.

"What's that?" Jude asked, looking up from her paper.

"It's from a musical," Frankie said. "*Hello, Dolly!*"

"Who's Dolly?"

"She's a person," Frankie told her, eyes on the pot of bright orange noodles, "who is trying to get back where she belongs."

After that, Frankie sang all the time: while she was giving them baths or driving them to school or studying herself in the mirror as she took off her earrings at night. She seemed happier, singing in the shower and humming as she put laundry away and breaking out into a little dance as she walked from the garage to the front door, her feet crunching on the gravel.

On opening night at the community theater, they were all in the audience, even their dad, and Jude sat forward in her seat, completely rapt, watching this woman who was their mom and also wasn't, who was Frankie and Dolly all at once, who practically floated across the stage and whose voice carried out into the darkened theater like magic.

Afterward, when the curtain closed, Jude was the last one out of her chair; she was too awestruck even for a standing ovation. As they waited for Frankie in the lobby, she felt unaccountably nervous, like she was about to meet someone famous, even though it was just her mom, who made her lunch and drove her to school and tucked her in at night.

"Bravo," her dad said when Frankie finally emerged, shiny-eyed and beaming. He handed her a small bouquet of yellow flowers, and the others clapped and hugged her too. But Jude hung back, suddenly shy.

"What did you think?" Frankie asked with a grin, and their dad shook his head.

"I hardly recognized you," he said, which didn't surprise Jude one bit, since he was rarely home anyway. But Jude had recognized her. Jude felt like she'd seen something nobody else had.

A group of older women walked past, and one of them touched Frankie lightly on the shoulder. "You were wonderful," she said with admiration before exiting through the glass doors of the community center into the wintry night.

Jude gazed after her in awe before turning back to her mom. "Are you famous now?" she asked, and Frankie laughed, but she looked pleased.

A few days later, they drove down to St. Louis to see their grandparents for Thanksgiving, and Frankie—who had only just been wearing a magnificent red dress on a stage in front of all those people—now stood at the kitchen sink peeling sweet potatoes in the house where she'd grown up.

"So how was the show?" Grandma Jean asked her, and Frankie shrugged.

"It was fine," she said.

Jude, who was sitting on the kitchen floor tracing her hand with a crayon to make a turkey, looked up with a fierce expression.

"It was *amazing*," she informed her grandmother, and Frankie smiled down and nudged her affectionately with one socked foot.

"What was the show?" asked Grandma Jean.

Frankie kept her eyes on the potato she was scraping. "*Hello, Dolly!*"

"Didn't you do that one in high school?" Grandma Jean asked, and then she leaned back from the sink and let out a sudden laugh. "Wow. I just had the strongest memory of standing here in this exact spot after that one. You told me you were gonna be an actress, remember?" She shook her head, her gray curls unmoving. "Talk about déjà vu."

From the floor, Jude looked up at them. "What's déjà vu?"

"It's when you get the feeling you've already been somewhere," Frankie said, her eyes on the window.

That night, Jude couldn't sleep. When she wandered out to the kitchen to get a glass of water, she found her mom sitting at the table, paging through a photo album.

"Here," Frankie said, motioning for Jude to come look. She pointed to one of the pictures, a beautiful girl in a red sequined dress standing onstage, her arms outstretched. "See?"

"That's you?" Jude asked, incredulous.

"It was," Frankie said, their faces close as they both examined the photo as if looking for clues. "There's nothing like it," she said, smiling. "Being the star. You'll see."

Later that night, Jude crept back out to swipe the photo of the girl in the red dress, and a month after that, on Frankie's fortieth birthday, she and the others presented it to her in a frame they'd bought at the local drugstore. They were practically vibrating with excitement, all four of them. Jude had told them about the way Frankie had smiled when she'd looked at it, the softness on her face. It was, she'd promised them, the perfect gift.

But when Frankie opened it, right there in the living room of the Michigan house, on a night when their dad was out carrying birthday packages for strangers, she didn't smile at all. Instead, much to Jude's horror, her eyes filled with tears.

"I thought you'd like it," Jude said in a small voice, and Frankie nodded as she gripped the frame with both hands, her gaze fixed on the photo.

"I do," she said. "I love it."

Connor

North Dakota

2025

For what feels like a long time, they all sit very still, staring at Jude. Connor steals a glance at Roddy, whose jaw is tight, and then Gemma, whose eyes are filled with hurt. He understands why they're upset and knows he should be too, but instead his chest is light with an unexpected and entirely inappropriate sort of glee. He'd come on this trip expecting to be the group punching bag, knowing everyone would still be angry with him. But now, after a revelation like that? He's pretty sure nobody will be talking about his goddamn book anymore.

The waitress returns, notepad in hand. "Right," she says cheerfully, her eyes bouncing among the other three in an effort not to look at Jude. "Can I get you all anything to drink?"

Connor laughs. "Please god, yes."

"I'll have a whiskey neat," Jude says, ignoring this. "Whatever you have."

"Absolutely," says the waitress as she jots this down, then steals a peek at her famous customer. "And I just have to say, I'm a really big fan."

"Aren't we all," Gemma mutters under her breath.

Once they've each ordered and the waitress is gone again, all eyes turn back to Jude, whose head is bowed, her hands worrying the edges of her napkin.

Connor waits for Gemma to start things off, because that's usually her role.

"When?" she asks, which would've been his first question too.

Jude doesn't look up. "Twenty years ago. Exactly."

"I knew it," Connor says. "I knew this had to be an anniversary."

Nobody else seems to care that he was right.

"I don't understand," Gemma says to Jude. "You came here with Mom? Why?"

Jude shrugs. "It was her last state."

"No, I mean . . . why *you*?" Gemma asks, her voice full of heat. "Were you in touch with her all that time? Because I thought after the fire none of us—"

"No, that was the first time we spoke," Jude says quickly. "I swear. She just called me up out of the blue and asked me to come."

"And you said yes?" Roddy asks, his usually mild face an angry red. "After she almost got you killed?"

Jude blinks at him, her mouth half open. She seems unable to speak for a moment, though her eyes dart between them. Then she swallows hard and shakes her head. "It had been four years," she says quietly. "It was enough. It was too much."

So was three, Connor thinks, because somehow they'd managed to do it all over again, to let the years between them pile up like they were nothing. Four years from the night of the fire to their mother's death. Four years when she was just out there floating around the country by herself. It seems unimaginable. Yet look how easily they'd just done it again, let three years slip by like they were nothing. Over a thousand days without seeing each other. It's hard for Connor to imagine a worse family tradition than this.

"I can't believe . . ." Gemma says, then stops, shaking her head mechanically back and forth. "How could you not tell us?"

Jude looks pained. "She made me promise not to."

"Why would you ever agree to—" Gemma begins, but Connor cuts her off. He's already done the math. And he knows the answer.

"Because she was already sick," he says to Jude. "Right?"

Jude nods miserably. "I didn't know until I got there. Until I got *here*."

At a nearby table, someone finishes a story about a snowplow and a deer, and there's a great burst of laughter. But the four of them are in their own small and fragile bubble, the noise of the restaurant barely touching them, their eyes on the melting wax from the candles, the flickering light on the table.

"And then . . ." Roddy says eventually, and when he looks up, his eyes are shiny.

"That was the last time I saw her," Jude says. "The only time."

In the pocket of quiet that follows, the waitress arrives with their drinks. Jude's glass is almost comically full. "I had them give you a little extra," she says with a wink, and Jude manages a grateful smile as she takes a careful sip.

Connor watches the tiny bubbles from his beer rise to the top of the mug, the stained-glass light fixture above them making everything feel warmer. In the back of the restaurant, he can see Winston playing pinball with Rosie and Hugh. They're all laughing as they try to jostle the machine.

"So I'm assuming you guys came here," Connor finds himself saying to Jude, who sets her glass down and turns to meet his gaze. "To this restaurant."

"Yes," she says quietly.

"And the hotel."

She nods. "And the lake we're going to tomorrow."

They're all silent for a moment as this information settles over them.

"So," Connor says, "we're on a ghost tour."

Nobody argues with him. Nobody says a word. But after a moment, the kids come running back over. Hugh is starving, and Rosie is bored, and Winston gives Roddy a searching look as he slides back into his chair. They all pick up their menus. Connor reads the description of the specials three times without anything registering. He orders the lasagna and sits through the rest of dinner in a daze, the same as Roddy and Gemma, the same as Jude, who barely says another word, her eyes far away. But he knows there will be more later. He knows, for better and worse, that they're not finished.

In the morning, he leaves the kids with Gemma—Rosie watching YouTube on her phone, Hugh still snoring softly—and slips out into the chilly North Dakotan morning. He feels a pang of guilt as he crosses the street at a half jog, because he knows he should be spending time with them rather than hurrying toward a coffee shop to meet some woman he'll probably never see again. And that, once again, he's choosing wrong. But still he goes.

Outside, the air smells like the promise of snow. As he passes the restaurant from last night, he remembers what Jude told them, and tries to picture his mother there. She would've ordered an old-fashioned, her go-to, and the chicken Parmesan, her favorite. She would've run the tip of her finger through the flame of the candle, because she could never help herself. She would've leaned across the table and taken Jude's hands in hers.

All these years, Connor had convinced himself that he didn't miss her. That she'd done something unforgivable, and thus he wasn't *supposed* to forgive her, even if he wanted to. But he had. Of course he had. He'd forgiven her long ago. He still didn't completely understand what had happened in the car that night; whenever he'd asked Jude, she'd told him it was all a blur, that she didn't like to think about it. But Connor had a storyteller's brain, which means he'd come up with a million different versions of it, a million different excuses for his mother.

And now he can't help wondering why she hadn't called *him* all those years later.

He can't help wondering whether he would've picked up if she had.

(He would have.)

When he arrives at the coffee shop, Annie is sitting at a table with a copy of his book. She's wearing sneakers and jeans and a Fair Isle sweater, her long auburn hair tucked behind her ears, and he has to remind himself that this isn't a date. At least he doesn't think it's a date.

"I swear," she says, placing a hand on the book with a sheepish smile, "this is not a fangirl moment."

"So you're here to tell me all the other things you *didn't* like about it?" he teases as he takes off his coat and sits down across from her.

"It's for my mom," she says, resting a palm on the front cover. "She's a huge fan."

He leans back in his chair and gives her his best humble smile. "Can't imagine why."

"Me neither," she says, but she's grinning. "Only joking. I liked it a lot. I swear."

"You just didn't love it."

"*Love* is not a word I use lightly."

"When it comes to books?"

"When it comes to anything," she says, then pushes the novel in his direction and fishes a marker out of her bag.

"Should I make it out to Annie's mom?"

"Mary," she says. "Write something good."

"I'm starting to doubt I know how."

She tilts her head to read as he scribbles out an inscription: *Dear Mary—My very best to you. Connor.* And then, with a grin, he adds: *P.S. Your daughter has terrible taste.*

She laughs as he scrawls his signature across the bottom of the title page. "In books or in general?"

"Hopefully just in books," he says, and he realizes at once that they're flirting.

In the two years since he and Nicola broke up, Connor has slept with exactly two women, and he doesn't know which is more of a cliché. The first was an ex-girlfriend in New York who he called on the night he signed his divorce papers. The second is a bartender in

Nashville who doesn't know about his life in New York, or his kids, or even that he's a writer, and he doesn't know much about her other than that she makes a mean whiskey sour and has a Dolly Parton tattoo on her shoulder. This is exactly what he's needed these last couple years, during the blur of writer's block and anxiety and big life changes. He hasn't been looking for commitment or attachments. He hasn't wanted anything real. But now, sitting across the table from Annie, he's having a hard time remembering why.

A waiter arrives to take their orders—a latte for him, a green tea for her—and when he's gone, Annie slips the book into her bag.

"Hang on," Connor says. "I've got another one for you."

He hands over the novel Hugh stole, a blue paperback with a rhino on the cover. Annie raises her eyebrows. "If this is your way of asking me to join your book club, you should know I've already read this one."

"My son took it. It's possible I might have pushed my literary agenda on him a little too hard," he says. "Or he might just be having a tougher time than I realized ever since . . ."

"Ever since?"

"The divorce," he tells her, feeling suddenly very old.

Annie slides the book into her bag. "Ah."

"It's been a couple years now, but you never know with these things. And it probably doesn't help that I moved away."

"You don't live in New York?"

"Sometimes. But mostly Nashville. At least lately. It was supposed to be for a book. But now it feels like more of a midlife crisis."

She nods. "It must be hard, following up a novel like that."

"It is," he says. "But nobody wants to hear that."

The waiter returns, setting their steaming drinks on the table, and they both fall quiet for a moment. When he's gone, Annie glances down at the orange cover of his book, which is still peeking out of her bag. "What did you love most about writing it?"

"It was personal," he says right away, though he feels oddly exposed. He's reminded again of how dating is not unlike writing; how, to have any chance at success, you have to lay yourself bare. It's been a long time since he's done that in either pursuit. "It wasn't true. Not exactly. But it was personal. Very personal. And I'm not sure I can do that again."

"Because it's too hard to be that vulnerable?" she asks, her hands cupped around her mug.

"Because it hurt some of the people I love the most."

"Ah," she says with a little nod. "I guess that's the downside of writing honestly."

"So it would seem," he says, leaning back in his chair. Snow is pinging against the window now, making this corner of the coffee shop feel cozy and warm. He twines his fingers through the handle of his mug. "I got offered a job teaching a grad school workshop recently, and I keep wondering what I'd even say to the students. I'd feel like such a hypocrite, telling them to write what they know, to be truthful and honest, when I've wasted years trying to come up with all these bullshit ideas because I'm too scared to do that myself anymore."

Annie raises her eyebrows. "So you turned it down?"

"I'm going to, but not because of that." He shrugs. "It just feels like going backward."

"How come?"

"I started out teaching high school English, and all I wanted that whole time was to be a writer. And now I'm a writer for real, and I go back to teaching?"

"Grad school isn't high school," Annie says. "Trust me."

He nods. "I know that. It's a great opportunity in a great program. Just one semester each year. Teaching really talented writers. Good benefits, et cetera. And it would probably help take the pressure off the book. But it's also the University of Michigan."

Annie gives him a blank look. "So?"

"So that's my home state."

Her eyes drift back to the book in her bag. "Not Minnesota?"

Connor smiles. "Like I said: it's personal, not true."

"Well," she says, then takes a sip of her drink, "as someone who is currently taking a break from their career, I will tell you that it can definitely be clarifying. Though I wouldn't recommend doing it the way I am."

Connor sits forward again. "How's that?"

"I put a pin in grad school when my mom got sick last fall and moved home to take care of her." She doesn't look at him when she says this, but instead trains her eyes on the napkin holder in the middle of the table, which is shaped like a cow.

"What about your dad?"

"He's older. It was too hard on his own."

"I'm so sorry," Connor says. "That must be really tough."

"We're managing. But I miss school. Especially since it took me forever to get there. And my friends. And New York. I *really* miss New York." She shrugs. "Luckily, my parents are wonderful. They just have one fatal flaw."

"What's that?"

She leans forward, as if about to tell him a great secret. He can smell her perfume, the faint scent of lavender, can see the delicate chain of a gold necklace hanging under her sweater, the fleck of gold in one of her green irises. "They live in Portree, North Dakota."

"Hard to get over that one," he says with a smile. "Though it must be nice, getting to spend some time with them as an adult."

She gives him an incredulous look. "I'm living in my childhood bedroom, which is still covered in horse posters, and when I'm not working one of my literal five jobs in an effort to make enough money to get back to New York, I'm spending most of my time helping my mom to the bathroom and watching CNN on an endless loop with my dad. I wouldn't exactly call it fun."

"No, no," he says, feeling terrible. "You're right. That sounds really hard. And it must be hell, having a front row seat to your parents' decline like that. But I sort of wish I'd had the chance. My dad and I weren't very close, but he died a few years ago of a heart attack that was so sudden there was no time to say goodbye."

"And your mom?" she asks, her eyes full of sympathy.

He puffs his cheeks out. "I wasn't speaking to her when she died. None of us were. Or at least, that's what I thought."

"Why?" she says. "What happened?"

"She never really understood how to be a mom, I guess. She left when we were young, and then came back every summer to take us on these road trips across the country. They were always the best part of the year," he says, smiling for a moment at the thought of her, at the thought of all those days in the car. "Until she screwed that up too."

Annie's face shifts abruptly. "Oh," she says with something like alarm, and he can see the pieces clicking into place as her gaze drops to the book. Her eyes fill with recognition. She says it again: "Oh."

Connor nods. "Yeah. It's not exactly like it was in the novel, but you get the idea."

"Wow," Annie says. "I'm so sorry."

"Thanks," Connor says. "And I'm sorry things are rough with your mom."

She nods, and for a few seconds they both sit there, looking at each other across the table. Then, for some inexplicable reason, Connor claps his hands.

"Well, I better get going," he says. "The great reconciliation with my siblings calls."

Annie smiles. "At least nobody's ever killed anybody up at Melvin Falls."

"Really?"

"No. It's basically the murder capital of North Dakota."

Connor frowns. "I can't tell if you're kidding or not."

"I am," she says without cracking a smile. "But if I were you, I'd watch your back just in case."

"Very reassuring." He downs the rest of his latte. "So which of your many jobs is on the docket for today?"

"Uber," she says, looking over to the window, where the snow is coming down harder, thick flakes that settle heavily over the flowerpots outside the café. "This is why I invested in snow chains. Even out here, people don't want to drive themselves in this kind of weather."

"And you don't mind it?"

"I'm a very good driver," she says, and he smiles.

"I remember. Five stars."

They walk outside together in companionable silence, their faces tipped against the wind. The streets are caked in snow, crisscrossed with shallow tire tracks, and the sky is a dull white. Connor can already feel this turning into a memory, a story he tells himself later, possibly even the beginning of a book—not the kind he writes, necessarily, but you never know. In that version, the imaginary version, this is the start of some great romance, which crisscrosses the country and defies the odds. It all begins here, in this snow globe of a town, with a woman he met only yesterday but who is making him unaccountably happy all the same.

In the real version, Connor knows better than anyone that most stories don't go anywhere. But still. He doesn't feel quite ready to break the spell.

Outside the hotel, they turn to face each other, cheeks pink from the cold.

"If you're ever back in New York—" they both say at the exact same time, and then they laugh.

"I've got your number," Annie says with a smile.

Connor nods. "And I've got yours."

He's not sure whether a hug is too much, so he holds out a hand, and she takes it, and they stand there like that, their cold fingers clasped between them, their hair specked with snow, their eyes locked for a few beats too long.

Then Winston comes ambling out of the hotel.

"Oi!" he yells when he spots Connor. "New crisis."

"What?"

"The people carrier just canceled."

Connor drops Annie's hand and frowns. "The what?"

"The van," Winston says in an exaggerated American accent, making the *a* long and flat. "Because of the snow."

"Oh."

"Gemma is sorting a rental car, but it's the last one."

"Oh," Connor says again, still catching up.

"So we can't all fit."

"Right," he says, looking over at Annie, realizing with a strange mixture of joy and panic that this story might have another chapter after all. She smiles tentatively, then gives a little nod.

"Crisis averted," he calls back to Winston. "Lucky for us, I happen to know a very good driver."

New Hampshire

2019

WHEN YOU PUBLISH A BOOK THAT DOESN'T SELL ANY COPies, you have a few options. One, you open up a blank document with enough hope and delusion to think that this time will be different. Two, you give up entirely. Or three, you take whatever shitty offers you can get while you figure out which of the first two options makes more sense.

That's how Connor found himself teaching at a writers' conference the summer after his second novel tiptoed out into the world and, just as the first had, promptly disappeared without a trace. For one week in rural New Hampshire, he read the mostly mediocre pages his students turned in and gave talks about how to write good dialogue. In between, he went for long runs on the country roads around the liberal arts university where the conference was held, and thought about his own career, and his own mediocre pages, and felt despondent at the thought of returning to his job teaching English literature to bored high school students that fall as if he'd never published any books at all, as if there hadn't been a glowing review of his debut in the *San Jose Mercury News,* as if none of it had ever even happened.

He had lunch one day with two of his fellow visiting writers in the dining hall, and over limp salads, they talked about their work and their lives. It gave Connor a frisson of pride, sitting there jawing about agents and publishers, like he was a real writer. Back then, it still felt like he was trying it on for size, pretending at something he'd wanted his whole life, something that now—the minute he'd caught it—already seemed to be slipping away.

"Where are you from, Connor?" asked one of them, a mystery writer with a cult following who would later go on to have fantastic success running a TV show about a series of murders at a university not unlike this one.

"Michigan," Connor said, setting down his fork. "But we're scattered now. Me and my siblings."

The mystery writer took a swig from a plastic cup filled with lemonade. "What do they do?"

"My sister is an actress, actually," he said. "And my brother plays soccer."

"Like, for fun?" asked the other writer, who had just published a well-reviewed memoir about his time walking the Camino de Santiago.

"Like, for real," Connor told them, and then there were more questions about both Roddy and Jude, and by the time he realized he hadn't even gotten around to mentioning Gemma, it was already too late.

"That's pretty cool," the mystery writer said, "to have so much talent in one family."

"You should write a memoir," suggested the memoirist.

"They'd kill me," Connor said with a laugh, but as he walked back to the dorm later under a cloudless blue sky, he realized that it *was* pretty cool, and he went to bed that night dreaming about a fictional version of it all, his mind busy reworking the truth, bending and stretching it like taffy, and in the morning, he woke up feeling sure of it.

Which was the moment he should have told them.

Gemma

North Dakota

2025

By the time they make it out of town—in a rental car that smells faintly of cheese—the roads are covered in snow. Gemma grips the wheel tightly, her shoulders tense as she navigates on tires that are far too bald for this sort of weather.

"This is wild," Jude says from the passenger seat, as if she didn't grow up in the Midwest too, as if she's never seen this sort of thing before.

"You've been in California too long," Gemma says without looking at her.

In the back, Rosie is leaning forward between the seats, eager to be part of the adult conversation. She'd wanted to ride with Jude, which of course meant that Hugh insisted on coming too, though now, ten minutes into the drive, he's already asleep in his booster seat, his head tipped back and his mouth wide open.

Jude's phone rings, and she brings it to her ear. "Hey." There's a pause and then: "No, I'm sure. I liked it a lot— Yeah, I know." Another pause. "The script is great. I just can't— Is it okay if we take a beat— Right, I just need to— Yeah, okay." More silence. "Okay, thanks, Sascha. Yeah, I'll see you on Monday. Oh, wait, did you hear back on the seat for— Sascha? Hello?"

She lowers the phone with a frown. "Bad reception."

"What are you passing on?" Gemma asks, her eyes on the road. In the backseat, she can feel Rosie lean forward a few inches more.

Jude shrugs. "A movie."

"But you liked the script?"

She punches a button and raises the phone to her ear again. "Yeah, it was good."

"So why aren't you doing it?"

"There's just a lot going on right now," she says, moving the phone in front of her face and glaring at the screen. "I don't know. It's hard to commit to anything."

Gemma frowns over at her. "You mean because of the Oscar stuff?"

Jude doesn't answer; she's too busy jabbing at the call button. A few seconds later, without warning, she lets out a groan and flings her phone at the dashboard, where there's a sharp crack before it clatters to the floor. "Shit," she says, turning around to look at Rosie. "Sorry about that. I just— There's a lot going on right now."

Rosie gives her a sympathetic smile. "It must be stressful. All that publicity and campaigning and the junkets—"

"How do you know about junkets?" Gemma asks, glancing at her in the rearview, and Rosie shrugs.

"TikTok."

Jude fishes around for her phone, then examines the spiderweb-thin crack across the screen, which is miraculously still aglow. "Sorry," she says again. "It's just not a great weekend to have spotty service."

"You're the one who picked it," Gemma says, her voice light. But there's a strain in it that she knows Jude hears, because she immediately starts biting her fingernails, a nervous habit Jude's had since childhood. Gemma can't help feeling a little amused that she still does it now, even with her presumably fancy manicures, even with her big Oscar luncheon on Monday.

She hadn't wanted to drive with Jude. Not after last night. But Connor seemed to have heart eyes for Annie the Uber driver, and Roddy was clearly reluctant to let Winston fend for himself with the rest of the family just yet, which left her and Jude to drive the kids up to this cabin in the middle of nowhere on these worsening roads.

Gemma tries to relax her shoulders as the snow comes thickly at the windshield. The road out of Portree is almost entirely empty, and Annie's car—which had been ahead of them—is no longer visible. On the center console, there are printed directions from Jude's assistant, which Gemma is grateful for now. She flicks on the radio, skips around until she finds an oldies station that's more music than static. Rosie sits forward again, holding out her phone.

"I've got a lot of good playlists, if we want something a little more..."

"No thanks," Gemma and Jude say at the same time, and it's such an echo of their mother—who ruled over the cassette player with absolute power on all those road trips, refusing anything but her collection of classic rock—that Gemma wants to laugh. She can see that Jude does too. But they both manage to swallow it down, the memory of last night's dinner conversation still in the air between them.

In the backseat, Rosie slips on her headphones with a shrug, and Gemma glances over at Jude. Her hair is swept back into a loose braid, her jacket zipped up all the way, even though the heat is blasting. She keeps her eyes trained on the road ahead, but her mouth twists to one side under Gemma's gaze.

"I know you're pissed at me," she says over the squeak and groan of the windshield wipers. "I'm sorry I never told you about coming here."

"But not sorry that you did it," Gemma says, her voice matter-of-fact.

Jude shakes her head. "She called. I answered. You would've done the same."

Would she have? Gemma isn't sure. "You should've at least told us she was sick."

Jude turns her head to look out the passenger window, which is fogged up from the inside. "I promised her I wouldn't," she says. "I think she wanted to do it herself."

To her surprise, Gemma's eyes prick with tears. "Yeah, but she never did. And we never got to say goodbye."

"I know," Jude says quietly. "It wasn't fair of her."

"It wasn't fair of *you* either."

"I know," she says again. "I'm sorry. I thought there'd be more time."

Neither of them says the obvious: that Gemma could've gotten in touch with their mother anytime she wanted. That for four years, Frankie was roaming around the country, sending postcards every time she landed at a new address: Los Angeles and then Santa Fe and then Tacoma and finally Sacramento. One Christmas, when they were all together at the house, they'd gotten one from Maui, and when they flipped it over, it simply said: *Love you.* Gemma had shoved it into the garbage bin, but later that night, Jude had dug it out again, which Gemma knew only because she found it on her desk a few days later, crumpled and stained with ketchup.

They pass a car pulled over to the side of the two-lane highway, waiting out the worst of the storm. But Gemma presses on, moving steadfastly over the slippery road. The snow is so heavy it feels like they're drifting through space, the car shuddering as the wind buffets it.

"How was she?" Gemma asks after a moment, once she's managed to shake the emotion from her voice.

Jude sighs. "She was in a lot of pain."

Gemma isn't sure if she means physical or emotional pain, whether it was the cancer or the fact that they had all stopped speaking to her by then. "Did she . . ." Gemma trails off, not sure what she wants to ask.

"She missed you guys," Jude tells her. "A lot. She wasn't angry. She'd made peace with everything, I think. She just wanted to finish what she started."

Gemma nods. "Why Portree?"

"You know Mom," Jude says, her voice filled with sudden warmth. "She knew nothing about North Dakota, so she closed her eyes and pointed at the map, and that's where we went."

In spite of herself, Gemma laughs. "That sounds right."

"She was still herself."

"Did you talk to her again? After that?"

"Only once," Jude says. "At the very end."

A flare of anger—or maybe it's grief disguised as something sharper—sparks in Gemma's chest. "God, Jude. You should've told us. We deserved to know."

Jude looks at her with haunted eyes. "I was eighteen. And scared. And—I never wanted to let her go. I never signed up for that. I was a kid when it happened, and everyone was so angry, but I never wanted to cut her out—"

"You should've been angriest of all," Gemma says, squinting into the snow.

Jude rests her forehead against the window. "I wasn't," she says quietly, her breath making a cloud on the glass. "I'm not."

For a few miles, they ride in silence, just the scrape of the tires and the bellowing of the wind and the occasional humming from Rosie in the backseat.

After a while, Gemma shakes her head. "I thought this was *your* last state. I thought that's why we were here."

"It's not," Jude says.

Two hours later, they pull off the highway and into the town of Melvin Falls. The snow is letting up, but huge drifts bank the sides of the roads, which are slick with ice. Gemma wishes their mother hadn't saved a place like this—windswept and cold and forlorn—for last.

In the backseat, Hugh wakes up and immediately begins to cry. Rosie slips off her headphones and Jude swivels around in her seat with a look of alarm. "What's wrong?"

Hugh squeezes his eyes shut and whimpers. "Where's my dad?"

"He's in the other car, remember?"

"I want my dad!" he cries, and Rosie shakes her head with the weariness of someone who has dealt with this sort of thing too many times before.

"He always does this when he's overtired," she says, putting her headphones back on to drown out the noise.

"What should we do?" Jude asks Gemma, who shrugs.

"Do I look like someone who has kids?" she says, trying to keep her voice neutral. Up ahead, she spots a small grocery store, and she pulls into the parking lot so suddenly the car fishtails a little. "Let's get him a snack?"

"We're almost there," Jude says, studying the directions.

"We need food anyway, don't we?"

Jude shakes her head. "I hired a chef. The place should be fully stocked."

"Well, I'm gonna run in," Gemma says, thinking about the pregnancy tests she still needs to buy. "Just give me two minutes."

"I can go," Jude says as she starts to unbuckle her belt, probably in an effort to escape her wailing nephew. But Gemma beats her to it, throwing the car into park and opening her door before Jude even has a chance.

"I'll be right back," she says, and then she's gone, skidding out into the snowy parking lot, the wind stinging her face as she picks her way across. But when she gets there, the sliding doors of the grocery store stay stubbornly shut. She cups her hands to peer through the window at the quiet, darkened interior, then turns and stands there for a long moment, deflated.

She wants to call Mateo, but there's still no reception. She wants to yell at Jude for bringing them here, for coming all those years ago in the first place. She wants to buy a pregnancy test so she can prepare herself either way. She wants to go home.

She has a sudden memory of falling off her bike as a kid. It was before the twins were born, and her mom was still—if you didn't look too closely—a regular mom who did regular mom things like bake them birthday cakes and push them on the swings at the park. Gemma had just been getting the hang of the bike, and she'd fallen off when she'd hit a rut in the driveway. One of her knees was badly torn up, and a trickle of blood was already running down her bony shin when she banged through the screen door, fighting back tears.

"It's okay to cry, you know," her mom said as she perched Gemma on the kitchen counter and pulled the first aid kit from a drawer. "It's brave either way."

When she went to dab at the scrapes with antiseptic, Gemma squirmed away. "Will it hurt?" she asked, and Frankie examined the gravel mixed in with the blood, the ribbons of skin around the wounds, and looked up at Gemma gravely.

"It won't be fun," she said. "But the only way out is through."

Gemma didn't know what that meant, but by then, it didn't matter. Her mom was already at work on her knee, and the tears—which she'd tried so hard to prevent—had come anyway.

Now the wind howls at her back as she takes one last look at the store, then turns and walks across the snowy parking lot to the car. When she opens the door, it's warm and quiet; Hugh's crying has stopped. He grins at her from the backseat.

"Aunt Jude gave me a piece of gum," he says triumphantly.

"I have zero recollection of buying it," Jude mumbles, "so who knows how old it is."

"Well, that's good because the store is closed."

"Because of the weather?"

"Who the hell knows," Gemma says as she starts the car. The snow has picked up again, but it's lighter this time, almost gentle, dusting the windshield in swirling patterns before getting swept away by the wipers. "Let's just get to the cabin."

"It'll be fun," Jude says hopefully, and Gemma shakes her head.

"It won't," she says. "But the only way out is through."

From the backseat, Hugh laughs as if she's made some sort of joke, and Jude gives her a quizzical look, but none of them say anything more as they pull back out onto the too-quiet road and turn in the direction of the cabin.

Maine

2019

ONE SUMMER, GEMMA AND MATEO RENTED A HOUSE IN Maine with another couple, a work friend of Mateo's and her wife. The house was perched on the edge of the ocean, salt-slicked and weather-beaten, and the constant roar of the water reminded Gemma of her childhood home, which she didn't say, because talking about the house would mean talking about her family, which would mean answering questions about her increasingly illustrious siblings, which was something she didn't feel like doing while she was on vacation.

But it did remind her of home, and every morning she woke up before everyone else and stepped out onto the deck and breathed in the heavy air and the moody sky and the ever-changing water.

It was a week of board games and homemade cocktails, blueberry picking and hikes along rocky beaches. On the last day, they went for lunch at a place that was supposed to have the best lobster rolls in southern Maine, and as they sat overlooking the ocean, a little girl—probably no more than three or four—was weaving in figure-eights around the tables with an ice cream cone. Her family was sitting nearby, keeping a vague eye on her as they ate. But Gemma was watching in the way you watch when you know exactly what's about to happen, and when it did—when the ice cream went flying and the girl began to wail—she was the first to hop out of her seat and help her up.

"Hey," she said to the little tearstained face, "I have a question for you. Why do ice cream cones always carry umbrellas?"

"Why?" she asked, screwing up her face, still deciding whether she was willing to be distracted from the tragedy that had befallen her.

Gemma grinned. "In case of sprinkles."

It took a beat, and then another, but then the girl let out a laugh, high and bright and surprisingly full, and pointed to her ruined cone.

"Just like mine."

"Just like yours," Gemma said, and then the girl's parents were there with a grateful smile to take over, and Gemma sat back down next to Mateo, who patted her hand and leaned in close and, with a voice full of warmth, full of certainty, full of hope, whispered, "You're going to be such a great mom."

I already was, she thought.

Roddy

North Dakota

2025

Though Winston spends the entire car ride clutching Roddy's hand and whispering that they're surely going to die, Roddy has to admit that Connor was right about Annie. She's steady and unflappable behind the wheel as she guides the car over the snowy terrain, and when—after nearly three hours of punishing weather and white-knuckled vigilance—they pull up in front of a literal log cabin, he sees that they're the first to arrive.

"Five stars," he says, opening his door and stepping out into the snow. "As advertised."

Winston doesn't move. "I think I'm going to vomit," he says, sitting with his forehead pressed against the passenger seat.

If Roddy were going to vomit, it wouldn't be from the roads or Annie's work behind the wheel. It would be from having to witness Connor's halting attempts at flirting for the last couple hours. But he can't even muster up the will to tease his brother right now. He lifts his arms in a stretch, suddenly happy to be in the middle of nowhere, the ash trees bending around them, laden with icicles. Down a steep bank from the cabin, there's a gray and churning lake, and everything is covered in deep drifts of snow.

"It's beautiful," he says, half-bending to look at Winston, who is still in the backseat. "Come see."

"Honestly, I'd rather be in Florida," he says morosely.

Inside, the cabin is enormous, with a massive fireplace at one end and an open kitchen at the other. But it still has a cozy feel to it, with metal fishing signs on the broad wooden support beams and tartan blankets draped over the scarred leather couches. Everything smells of wood and pine, and Roddy nods as he looks around.

"I'm starting to think Jude actually knows what she's doing," he says, and Connor grunts as he brushes past him with a couple of their bags.

"Jude never knows what she's doing," he says. "She just does stuff and figures it out later."

Roddy feels a prickle of annoyance, an urge to defend his twin. But the truth is, Connor is right. Still, he refuses to give up his good cheer at the thought of spending a night here. "Well, sometimes it works out."

"It's probably a little early to declare victory," Connor says. He opens the massive refrigerator, which is full of food—plastic-wrapped steaks and overflowing bags of vegetables and thick hunks of cheese—then closes it. Behind them, Winston and Annie drop the last few bags near the door and brush the snow off their coats.

"Nice place," she says, scanning the cabin. She stops when her gaze reaches Connor, and they smile at each other across the room. Roddy glances between them, amused. He knows that Connor is working up the nerve to ask her to stay. And he knows that Annie wants to. He's known it since they first set out on the drive, when she plugged her phone into the stereo and began to play "Shelter from the Storm," and Connor said "I love Bob Dylan," and she said "So do I," and then they grinned at each other dopily for a few seconds before she threw the car into gear.

"Yeah, it's cozy," Connor says, flushing a little. "And luckily, no signs of any murders."

Winston coughs. "Excuse me?"

"He's kidding," Annie tells him, then winks at Connor. "Probably."

"Hey, you should stay," he says to her, the words coming out in a rush. "At least for a little while. Until the roads get plowed. Or, you know, till we head back tomorrow. We'll need a ride anyway, so—"

"No, I should let you guys have family time," Annie insists. "I can still come get you in the morning."

Connor looks newly determined. "You can't drive back in this."

"You forget I grew up here," she tells him. "I'll be fine."

"Annie."

"Connor."

Roddy glances over at Winston, eyebrows raised. Winston shrugs back at him.

"It'll be fun," Roddy says to Annie, and Connor shoots him a grateful look. "Or at least interesting. We've got a whole agenda."

She smiles. "So I've heard."

"And you haven't met my twin sister yet, but she always brings too many clothes. So I'm sure she'll have some pajamas or something for you."

Annie walks over to the window, a tall, lean silhouette against all the white. She stands there for what seems like a long time, but when she turns around again, she says, "Okay."

"Okay?" Connor says.

"As long as you really don't mind."

He beams. "We don't."

"I'm a little shaky after that drive, to be honest," she admits. "So pretty much anything beats going back out there."

"I wouldn't speak too soon," Winston says, flopping down on the couch. He kicks his shoes off and props his feet up on a pillow in the shape of a trout. "I think their agenda includes *outdoor activities*."

Roddy rolls his eyes. "Consider it payback for the time your family made us go to six museums in London in three days." He turns to the others for backup. "Six museums!"

Winston shrugs. "That's at least five more than you'd ever been to before that."

"Possibly even six," Roddy confirms.

A phone rings from somewhere in the room, and they all startle. Annie points at the desk near where she's standing. "A landline," she says. "How quaint."

They all watch as it rings several more times, then goes silent. But a moment later, it starts again. Roddy glances at Connor, unsure of the protocol. They wait for it to go quiet once more, but when it rings a third time, Annie looks at them with raised eyebrows, and they nod.

She lifts the receiver. "Hello?" There's a long pause. "Right." Another pause. "Got it. Okay, thanks. Bye." She turns back to them. "You hired a private chef?"

Connor shrugs. "Our sister hired a private chef."

"Well, he canceled because of the snow. But he said the fridge is full."

"Great—Connor can make his famous burnt grilled cheese sandwiches," Roddy says with a grin, and from across the room, Connor throws a pillow that says *Gone Fishing* at him.

"You should talk," he says. "Mr. Peanut-Butter-No-Jelly."

Annie looks around. "Maybe we should see if there's any wood for the fireplace."

"Why?" Roddy asks. "Are there marshmallows?"

"No, in case we lose power."

Connor frowns. "Do you think we should be worried?"

"You never know," she says, already zipping up her jacket. When she opens the door, there's a blast of cold air. Connor hurries to grab his coat and follow her outside, clearly eager to be helpful. When the door shuts behind them, Winston shivers.

"If we ever do end up getting married," he says, "let's make sure our honeymoon is someplace warm."

Roddy looks at him in alarm. "If?"

They haven't talked about any of it since last night, the wedding conversation lost to the whirlwind of Jude and her revelation. After dinner, they'd walked back to the hotel as a group, and Winston had wordlessly reached for Roddy's hand, as if he could sense his sadness. Roddy ached at the thought of those years between the fire and his mom's death, the thought of her drifting around the country on her own to places like this. He hadn't forgiven her for what she'd done—after all, she'd very nearly killed Jude, his twin, his other half—but over the years his heart had softened toward her, and he likes to think that if he'd been the one she'd called all those years ago, he would've come too. But honestly, he doesn't know.

When he and Winston had returned to their room, they'd both been quiet as they got ready for bed. But as Roddy was brushing his teeth, Winston came up and put his arms around his waist, resting his forehead against his back. "I love you," he said softly, and Roddy squeezed the knot of his hands gratefully.

Now he gives him a searching look. "Winston, we're still getting married. You know that, right? We can do it whenever you want."

"Right," says Winston grimly. "Just not on our wedding day."

"I'm sorry," Roddy says with a sigh. "I know I screwed this up. I know I should've talked to you, but I promise—"

"Let's not make any more promises right now," Winston says, sounding weary.

Roddy walks over and takes both of his hands. "Come on," he says with a little smile. "It's snowing out there. Everything looks magical. We hardly ever get away. Let's not waste this weekend arguing."

In spite of himself, Winston's face softens. "What's with you and the snow?"

Roddy shrugs. "I don't know. It makes me happy."

"I like seeing you happy," Winston says quietly, and Roddy kisses him there beside a poster of a largemouth bass. Outside, the snow continues to fall, making everything muffled and hazy, and it isn't until he feels the brisk chill of the open door and Connor clears his throat that Roddy realizes they're no longer alone.

"Oops," he says as they break apart. "Forgot where we were for a second."

Annie is standing behind them with an armful of firewood. "You know what they say about North Dakota in the winter."

"What do they say?" Winston asks, adjusting his glasses.

She shrugs. "That it's romantic? Or maybe just that it's cold? I don't really know. The motto needs a little work. But I'm glad you're taking advantage so far."

"Any word from Gem?" Roddy asks, and Connor shakes his head.

"But I still have no service. Find anything that says what the Wi-Fi password is?"

"Murderhouse666?" Winston suggests, and everyone ignores him.

Roddy watches Connor set his batch of wood down in front of the fireplace with a little grunt. "Still have that bad back?" he asks his brother, rising from the couch to help stack it.

"We can't all be professional athletes," Connor says wryly, and Annie, who had been standing at the kitchen counter leafing through the house guide, looks over at Roddy.

"You're a professional athlete?" she asks. "What kind?"

"The aging kind," he tells her with a self-deprecating grin. He's tempted to add that she'd probably already know this if she hadn't spent the entire car ride flirting with his brother. But then he sees her face change, and he realizes she must have read the book.

"Wait," she says, clearly searching her memory. "Hockey, right? No . . . skiing?"

Roddy's eyes drift over to Connor, who clears his throat, looking deeply embarrassed. "He plays soccer, actually," he says in a stiff voice, and Annie nods.

"Right," she says, almost to herself. "Personal but not true."

"The truth," Roddy says, and he can almost see Connor holding his breath, "is that I'd be stuck for days if you set me on top of a mountain on a pair of wooden sticks. I'm much better on a flat pitch."

Annie smiles at him. "Well, it's pretty cool that you both get to do what you love at such a high level. Could you already tell when you were younger?" ·

"You mean, that one was a jock and one was a nerd?" Winston asks with a grin, and Connor says "No" at the exact same time that Roddy says "Pretty much."

Outside, they hear the rumbling of tires on snow, and Roddy walks over to the window, relieved to see the blue rental car. As he watches, Jude throws open the door, stepping out impatiently, and Gemma sits for a moment with her hands still on the steering wheel, her face hard to read from afar, as the kids tumble out of the back. It takes only about twenty seconds for Hugh to make a snowball and throw it at his sister, who pelts him right back.

Connor sticks his head out the front door. "I was starting to get worried."

"Gemma was great," Jude says, glancing over at her. "The car, not so much."

He steps aside to let her in, and Roddy can see him remember a moment too late about Annie. "Oh, this is my sister—"

"Jude," Annie says with wide eyes. For a moment, she looks like she might not be able to say anything else, but then she recovers herself, rearranging her face into an approximation of a normal smile. "So nice to meet you."

"You too," Jude says, dropping her bag on the floor beside the others. "You know, it's pretty awful out there. You should probably stay the night."

"We're one step ahead of you," Roddy tells her.

"Good," says Jude, winking at Annie. "I've got extra pajamas. I always travel with extra pajamas."

The kids come flying in then, with Hugh in the lead. "Are we still gonna go fishing? Do fish ever get cold? Do they go somewhere else in the winter?"

"Florida," Roddy and Winston say at the exact same time, and then the power goes out, the lights switching off and the hum of the room falling silent around them. They all stand there for a few beats in the pulsing quiet, the snow bright at the windows, pushing in against the sudden darkness.

Hugh looks up at them. "Can we go to Florida too?"

Michigan

1992

THE WILDEST THING ABOUT RODDY'S FIRST-EVER SOCCER
game wasn't the fact that he scored eight goals. It was that he did it
while playing goalie.

After the first one—a spontaneous drive from one end of the field
to the other—an ecstatic five-year-old Roddy glanced over at his
mom as he jogged back to his spot in the goal. She pumped a fist in
the air and mouthed *Yes!*

Farther down the sideline, the coach crooked his finger and beck-
oned Roddy over. "Nice work, but don't forget you're the goalie, so
your job is to stay in the goal, okay?"

Roddy nodded. He understood. But the next time the ball came
to him, instinct took over, and once again, he shot down the field,
evading the chaotic scrum of kids trying to catch him, and sent another ball into the plastic goal, this time with such force that it toppled over.

"That's my boy!" Frankie yelled, jumping up and down, and
Roddy, who had always had to compete with his siblings for her attention, was suddenly hungry for more.

"Good job," said the coach. "But let's pass to your teammates, okay?"

Roddy nodded, and then scored six more goals.

Afterward, Frankie put an arm around his shoulders as they walked to the car. "Don't listen to that coach," she said, handing him a juice box. "He doesn't know what he's talking about. Tell me this: Did you love it?"

Roddy poked the straw into the circle of foil. "Love what?"

"Scoring all those goals," she said, and he nodded. She stooped down in front of him so they were at eye level. "Listen, if you're good at something—really good at it—it doesn't matter what anyone else says. You have a responsibility to shine. You understand me?"

Roddy nodded. He didn't entirely know what she meant. But the juice was sweet and cool, and the sun was warm on his shoulders, and he'd just scored eight goals in his very first game, and as his mom took his hand in hers, he couldn't imagine ever feeling shinier.

Jude

North Dakota

2025

This isn't the cabin she'd stayed at with her mom all those years ago. That's on the other side of the lake, tucked behind a bigger house that blocks the view, because they hadn't been able to afford anything else at the time. When Jude had asked her assistant, Madison, to find out about renting it again, she'd made a face.

"Honestly?" she'd said, turning her phone around for Jude to take a look. "It's kind of gross."

Jude had squinted at the screen, trying to see past the dimly lit rooms and outdated carpets. "That's okay," she'd said with more confidence than she felt.

"Well, it's too small for a group your size anyway."

"Is it?" Jude had asked. In her memory, the cabin was huge, with only the two of them to fill up the space. They'd spent only one night there, but it had been a long one. Frankie had stopped treatment by then, and she barely had any energy. When she'd called to pitch the idea of the trip to Jude, she'd been full of big plans, as she always was. They'd go snowmobiling and bird-watching and take a sleigh ride on a farm a few miles away. They'd have their coffee out by the lake in the morning and roast marshmallows by the fireplace in the evening.

But when Jude met her at the airport, it became clear that it would be a very different sort of weekend. And so would this one, she supposes, frowning out at the snow.

Roddy returns from outside, where he'd gone to check the fuse box. "No dice," he says, shoving his hands into the pockets of his D.C. United sweatpants. "The power lines must be down."

Gemma lifts the receiver on the red telephone and listens for a moment, then jabs a few buttons before hanging up. "Phone is dead too."

Connor's new friend, Annie—who is entirely lovely and extremely out of his league—rifles through the kitchen pantry. "It's fine," she says. "Hopefully we'll get the power back soon, but in the meantime, there are candles. And flashlights. And blankets. And plenty of firewood. And the food will stay cold as long as we don't open the fridge too much."

"We could put it out in the snow too," Rosie suggests from where she's perched on the back of the couch, and Annie smiles at her from across the room.

"A survivalist in the making."

Rosie beams.

"I think fishing is probably out," Jude says, and Hugh sighs dramatically. "But according to the listing—"

Connor clears his throat.

"According to my assistant's summary of the listing," she says, rolling her eyes at him, "they've got sleds here somewhere."

"You want to go sledding?" Gemma says doubtfully.

"Not bloody likely," Winston chimes in.

"I think we should do it," Jude says, determined to press on with the family fun. "Who's with me? Rosie? Hugh?"

"Can I bring Harold?" Hugh asks, already digging through his backpack, which is resting by the door. He emerges with the slightly crinkled paper penguin.

Jude laughs. "Okay, sure. Yeah. What's Harold's deal?"

"I'm supposed to take him everywhere this weekend and then

show my class pictures of all the fun things we did," he says brightly. "Like sledding. And being with my aunts and uncles. Stuff like that."

Connor puts a hand on Hugh's head. "Then let's grab a plastic bag so he doesn't get wet."

"It's okay," Hugh tells him. "He's a penguin, so he's used to the snow."

They bundle up and walk outside together, making their way carefully down the icy front steps of the porch. When they heave open the doors of the shed, they find a treasure trove of ancient skis and faded kayaks, paddles and decades-old life jackets, knotty hiking sticks and a few spindly bicycles speckled with rust.

"This looks like the garage back home," Gemma says. "Remember when Jude got her foot stuck in that plastic car and we didn't find her for hours?"

Jude tugs her winter cap lower on her head. "I remember," she says darkly.

"In fairness," says Connor, "you were always off collecting rocks or playing on the beach or whatever it was you used to do. Nobody ever knew where you were."

"And we rescued you eventually," Roddy says with a guilty shrug. "We always rescue you eventually."

Jude smiles, though her chest feels tight. "True."

They find an assortment of sleds in the back corner, some of them old-fashioned, with wooden slats on metal skis, and others cheaper and more modern, bright orange disks and plastic toboggans. Roddy gathers up as many as he can carry and lugs them outside into the snow, and the others stand around them in a circle.

"Did you do this with Mom while you were here?" Gemma asks. There's no rancor to the question, just a quiet wish to know. Her hands are tucked up inside the sleeves of her coat, and she's wearing a pair of earmuffs she found in the cabin, and her cheeks are rosy from the cold. All of it makes her look very young.

"It wasn't snowy then," Jude says as everyone turns to look at her, "but she had all these big plans to be outdoors."

"So what did you do?" Gemma asks.

Jude shakes her head. "She was too sick for much of anything."

They're all silent for a moment, the snow falling around them. Then Roddy bends to pick up a sled.

"Let's get going," he says, and so they do, heading around the back of the house, where the land slopes up enough to constitute a hill, at least by midwestern standards. The kids run ahead with their sleds, slipping as they start up the incline, and the others follow, with Jude and Connor in the rear, moving slowly through the deep drifts.

Beside her, Connor is already breathing hard, his cheeks ruddy. "This is the worst."

Jude laughs. "Didn't you have to do this sort of stuff for your book?"

"What do you mean?"

"You had all those ski scenes, right? So didn't you have to do, like, winter stuff for research?"

"I mostly concerned myself with the après part of skiing."

"What, drinks by the fire?"

He shrugs. "Sure beats the snow."

"I still can't believe you made Roddy a slalom skier," she says. "He's terrified of heights."

Connor gives her a sideways look. "It wasn't Roddy."

"Right," Jude says. "And I'm not the famous model."

"Don't flatter yourself," he teases, and she gives him a little shove.

"And the successful journalist brother? And the sister who lives in a midwestern city with three famous siblings and a boring job?"

Connor's eyebrows shoot up beneath his wool hat. "You said it, not me."

"You know what I mean," Jude says. "I suppose it was all just a metaphorical interpretation of—"

"Jude."

She comes to a stop halfway up the hill, the wind whistling straight through her jacket. Connor's eyes are pleading, his beard flecked with snow.

"Let's not do this again."

She forces a laugh. "Why, because it ended so well the last time?"

"Because," he says, "I don't know if my heart can take it."

Jude regards him thoughtfully, then nods. "Mine either. It's a little fragile these days."

They look toward where the others are trudging up the hill. Hugh loses his footing and falls, sliding down a few feet on his belly. Roddy helps him up.

"It makes more sense to me now," Connor says, turning back to Jude. There's snow in his eyelashes, so fine it looks like powdered sugar. "That fight. Knowing you were here with Mom. You were the most upset that I wrote about her."

"I thought you said it was fiction," Jude says, but he's clearly done with that argument; he doesn't bite. The rest of the group is at the top now. Roddy is holding Hugh's sled while he climbs on. Annie is helping Rosie find a good spot. It's just Jude and Connor down below, the world muffled by the snow. She's had so much practice at hiding her feelings—is, in fact, quite literally a pro at it—that she has no problem keeping her face neutral. But underneath all her many layers, her heart is hammering in her chest as she considers what comes next.

"My relationship with her was different than yours," she says after a moment, choosing her words carefully. "My *memory* of her is different than yours. She wasn't— I didn't— It was never—" She stops, feeling dangerously close to spilling her second secret right here on the slope as they stand with their feet sunk deep in the snow.

But Connor is looking at her with interest. "See, this is what I've been saying," he tells her. "Personal, not true. Because everyone's truths are different, aren't they?"

Jude manages a nod.

"Everyone's memories are different, their experiences, all of it," he continues. "*Life* is subjective, so how can someone's telling of it not also be? And fiction has always been a tool to reflect back on these experiences and find meaning in them, to try to process all the ways—"

But Jude isn't listening. She's bent to scoop up a handful of snow, mashing it between her gloved hands.

"—we move through the world, which is why I think there's something almost more diplomatic about a novel, especially when the true things you're trying to write about are not *literally* true, but *emotionally* true, which is why I get that it must've been difficult for you guys to—"

Jude throws the snowball at him, and it hits his chest with a solid thump.

His mouth falls open in surprise. "What was that for?"

Jude shrugs. "It just felt right."

"I was trying to apologize."

"By making me sit through an essay on fiction versus memory?"

He laughs. "We are who we are."

"Well, you," she says, and they're both grinning now, "are a little bit annoying."

Connor leans forward to grab a handful of snow, then whips it at her. She laughs as she brushes it off her shoulder. "I'm too cold to fight with you right now," she says.

"Same." He glances down at his boots. "I'm pretty sure I've lost all feeling in my right foot."

"Better you than Roddy," she says, and he pretends to reach for more snow. She shakes her head, dodging away. "Only kidding."

When Connor straightens again, his face is more serious. "I'm sorry the book upset you so much. I can't apologize for writing it, not completely, but I didn't think enough about how it might affect the rest of you. And I should have."

"Thanks," Jude says. "And I'm sorry I overreacted a little."

Connor looks like he's biting back the words *a little* with great effort. Instead he says, "I'm sorry you felt like you had to keep that trip with Mom to yourself all this time. It must've been hard to carry that around with you."

Jude nods. "And I'm sorry things haven't been great for you lately."

"Thanks," he says with a grin. "I'm sorry your career is going so badly too."

She laughs at this, but then her smile fades. "I'm sorry I waited three whole years."

"Yeah, that was a pretty boneheaded thing to do," he agrees, and she makes a face at him.

"Because you ran out of material without us?"

He bends as if to grab more snow, and she holds up her hands in surrender. "Because we've always been better together," he says as he stands up again, and there's something so earnest about the way he says it, something so vulnerable, that she almost feels like crying. Instead, she reaches out to give his shoulder a little pat, and then they trudge on through the snow together, the stillness of the woods broken only by the sound of Hugh's excited screams as he careens down the hill on a neon-orange saucer.

The rest of them end up trying it out too, all except Gemma, who insists they need someone to take photos. Even Winston agrees, holding on tight to Roddy as their rickety wooden contraption bobbles its way down the slope, laughing in spite of himself as he wipes snow from his glasses. Annie impresses them by attempting to snowboard using a blue plastic sled—she falls almost immediately, but it gives Connor an excuse to help her up—and Jude is more pleased than she has a right to be when she wins the sibling race, though it's only because Connor and Roddy crash into each other halfway down, leaving them both in a fit of helpless laughter as they roll the rest of the way to the bottom.

When they arrive back at the cabin, the power is still out. They shed their coats and hats and mittens, all of them damp and smelling like snow, then grab every candle and blanket they can find. Outside, dusk is already settling over the lake, the sky lavender behind the still-falling snow. But the moment Annie manages to light the wood in the oversized fireplace, the dimly lit cabin brightens, and they huddle around the fire for warmth.

"Thank god you stayed," Connor says admiringly, and she laughs as she blows out the match.

"It's not like I rubbed two sticks together or anything."

"But I bet you could."

She grins at him. "Yeah, I could."

In the kitchen, Winston scans the refrigerator, trying to figure out what they can still make, and the kids watch him from the barstools, awaiting jobs because their devices are nearly out of batteries and there's no service anyway and the TV doesn't work and it's freezing inside and out, which means there's nothing to do but spend time with one another. He digs a wire rack out of the back of the pantry and sends Roddy out to the shed to find a couple of bricks to stand it on in the fireplace, and much to their amazement, he sets to work cooking their steaks right there over the open flame, the smell filling the house, making it feel warmer than it is, as the others pull bread and cheese and fruit from the fridge and assemble it all on plates, a hodgepodge of a meal, the best they can do under the circumstances, and better than any of them could've imagined.

"Look what I found," Gemma says, coming down the stairs with a battery-powered radio tucked under her arm. She sets it on the counter and switches it on, then turns the dial a few times. At first there's only static, but then, just like that, there's a burst of music, and they all cheer.

"What *is* this?" Hugh asks.

"It's Elvis," Gemma says, lifting him from the chair and spinning him around the room, his socked feet dangling. Roddy tries to make Winston dance too, but he's busy flipping the steaks, so instead Roddy grabs Connor, who looks embarrassed in front of Annie before giving in to it, and Jude watches them all with such fondness that it feels like her heart might burst, thinking that maybe they should make this a yearly thing, come back to this very same cabin again, start a new family tradition.

And then she remembers her other two secrets.

Winston walks by and hands her a knife. "Here," he says, sliding over a cutting board and a few tomatoes. But she just stands there, watching Annie and Connor flirt as they feed more wood into the fire, watching Gemma twirl Hugh, and Rosie bob her head to the music.

Jude looks back down at the tomatoes, perfectly ripe, and adjusts her grip on the knife. Then she slices into the first one, staring as the red juice spills out onto the wooden cutting board.

Hugh wanders over, still shimmying to the music. He squints up at her. "Are you crying?"

She blinks at him, realizing that there are tears in her eyes. "It's the onions," she says automatically, and he gives her a funny look.

"Those are tomatoes."

Jude shrugs. "I guess they make me cry too."

New Jersey

2020

CONNOR WAS AT A FARM IN NEW JERSEY, SURROUNDED BY goats, when he got the call from his agent. He'd agreed, at Nicola's persuasion, to chaperone Rosie's class field trip, which—as far as he could tell—seemed to have very little educational value. It mostly consisted of a bunch of city kids being chased around a muddy pen by a pack of wild-eyed goats.

"You're a genius," said Agnes, who was fiercely intimidating and generally sparse with praise. "It's brilliant."

"It is?" Connor said, hating himself for asking. But he'd sent her the first draft of *The Almost True Story of the Astonishing Atkinsons* weeks ago and had since been losing sleep over what she might say about it. His first two novels had sold poorly, and there were no guarantees that this new one would even find a publisher. He understood that it had to be great. He'd tried his best. And now his heart soared at this brief assessment.

"It's the best thing you've ever written," she told him. "Hands down. It's just missing one big moment."

"It is?" Connor asked, because apparently that was all he could say on this call. A goat wandered over and began rubbing its head against his leg with great intensity. "What?"

"The mom can't just stop showing up," she said matter-of-factly. "Especially since she dies pretty soon afterward. I don't understand why she'd disappear from their lives like that. It's like you've got this great big hole in the middle of the book."

"Oh," Connor said as he swatted away the goat. "Well . . ."

"Something needs to happen to make her stop seeing them," she told him. "Something dramatic. Something big. Do you think you could figure out a scene that would work?"

Connor swallowed hard. "I'll try."

Connor

North Dakota

2025

In his novels, dinner is where it always happens. The big fight. The yelling, the tears, the accusations, the storming off. But tonight's meal feels more like a scene from a sitcom, the kind where everyone laughs and passes plates and smiles at one another across the table.

It's nice. So nice that Connor doesn't totally trust it.

They're all wearing winter hats, with plaid blankets wrapped around them like superhero capes, and the table is filled with every candle they could find in the house, their faces glowing behind them. There are half-drunk bottles of red wine and steaks that taste like firewood, charred on the outside but cooked perfectly inside, and a basket with thick slices of crusty bread beside plates overflowing with cheese and fruit. Outside, the wind is roaring, rattling at the windows, but they can still hear the snapping of the fire over it and the creaking of the rafters, which makes the house feel like an old ship on some great journey, and in spite of the cold and the lack of power—in spite of everything, really—the night feels somehow warm and bright all the same.

Across the table from Connor, Rosie is busy peppering Jude with questions about the Oscars. "Have you ever been before?"

"Yes," Jude says. "But not as a nominee."

"Do you know what you're wearing yet?"

"We've got some good possibilities."

"Are you taking Spencer?"

"I am," Jude says, and Rosie clasps her hands together and lets out a happy little squeal before continuing on with all the intensity of an entertainment journalist.

"Do you think you'll win?"

Jude laughs. "Probably not. But it's pretty cool anyway."

"It's *amazing,*" Winston says, waving his fork in the air. "It's unbelievable, really. I feel like you're all playing this way too cool. It's a monumental achievement to even be nominated. Just absolutely world-class."

"He made me wake up early to watch when they announced it," Roddy says, jabbing a thumb at Winston. "We were pretty excited when we heard your name."

Gemma nods. "And I know I texted you this, but you were incredible in the movie. I cried so much at the end. Mateo too. We basically wept through the last twenty minutes."

"Same," Connor says, hating how much they all sound like polite acquaintances right now. There was a time when they would've gone to the premiere together. Or if they couldn't make it, they would've coordinated watching on opening night, then surprised Jude with a group video call afterward to tell her how much they loved it. She'd released four movies during their three-year absence from one another, and Connor had of course seen all of them. This last one, *Rose Gold,* was something special, wildly inventive and incredibly moving. He'd known right away it would be big for her, and the night he saw it, he stayed up late crafting an email about how impressed he was. But it felt too formal somehow, so it sat unsent in his drafts folder. Now he looks at Jude across the faltering light with a tentative smile. "I really loved it."

"Me too," Annie chimes in a little nervously.

"So did I," Winston says. "It was completely brilliant."

Roddy turns to him in surprise. "You saw it?"

"You didn't?" says Jude, looking hurt.

"I was going to," he says quickly, but then he shakes his head. "Actually, that's not true. Winston wanted to go the night it opened, but it just felt too sad to me, like this big reminder that we weren't in touch. Usually, I'd have been talking to you about it all before it came out, or I would've come to visit you on set—"

"You got to do that?" Rosie says, her eyes wide.

Jude's gaze is still fixed on Roddy. "Yeah," she says. "Remember when you came to Scotland for *Breakers*? And I had a late call time one day, so we drove up to that whiskey distillery and got stuck on the road with all those sheep and I was almost late to set?"

Roddy nods. "And remember that spy-dog movie you did really early on?"

"Oh god," Jude says with a groan. "*Snoop.*"

"I had a match in Seattle and then took the ferry up to Vancouver," he says. "That stupid dog ate my soccer ball."

She grins, then looks around at the others. "I tried to get him to be an extra in that one. They needed a barista. No lines. Just handing over a cup of coffee. He wouldn't do it."

Roddy waves this away. "I'm not an actor."

"This is true," Winston confirms.

"But *you* are," Roddy says forcefully, his eyes still on Jude. "You're so good. And I'm so proud of you. I just couldn't picture watching you do your thing and then sending a text about it. It didn't seem like enough. So I didn't do anything, and now . . ."

"I know," Jude says from across the table. "It's okay."

Everyone is quiet for a moment. The wind roars outside, tree branches scratching at the windows. Hugh sets his fork down and swallows a too-big bite of steak.

"What's an Oscar anyway?" he asks, which makes the rest of them laugh.

"It's an award for being a good actor," Connor tells him.

"How many people get it?"

"Just one," Connor says. "But there are five people nominated."

"So even if you don't win, you're still one of the best actors in the world?"

They all look to Jude, who starts to shake her head but then changes her mind. "I guess that's true," she says with a little smile, and Hugh nods.

"That's cool," he says, resuming his work on the steak.

"It's very cool," Connor agrees, looping an arm around Hugh's shoulders. He catches Annie watching him and smiles, surprised to feel that same flutter he felt this morning—was it only this morning?—when they met for coffee, a kind of unfamiliar happiness.

Afterward, they discover that the chef did indeed stock marshmallows and graham crackers and chocolate bars, so they make s'mores over the fireplace, trying to catch the drips with a paper plate as the chocolate melts, the flames hot against their faces. Hugh insists that Rosie take a picture of Harold the penguin roasting their marshmallow, and from the couch, Connor watches Gemma, who is sitting on the edge of the stone fireplace, guide Hugh's hand so that he doesn't get too close with the skewer. Something about the sight of it makes his chest ache.

"We used to do this back in Michigan," he says to no one in particular, but Annie is the one who turns to him.

"With your parents?" she asks, and Connor shakes his head.

"With Gemma," he says, remembering the way she'd help the twins with theirs before eating any herself, knowing that Roddy liked his marshmallows burnt and Jude wanted hers barely near the flames. Gemma would get it right every single time, night after night, summer after summer. She looks back at him now with a smile, and it feels like the weight of the years has dissolved away, like they're right back home again, their fingers sticky as they sit perched on the edge of the lake, left to run wild all summer long.

Later, as they're cleaning up from dinner, Hugh begins to yawn. Connor grabs a flashlight and peers up the darkened steps. "What do we think? Too cold to sleep upstairs?"

"We're midwesterners," Gemma tells him as she walks by with a dirty plate in each hand. "We'll be fine."

Annie nods. "Heat rises. But I'd bring some extra blankets."

So he leads the kids upstairs through the chilly halls, arms full of the thermal sleeping bags Roddy found in the shed. "It'll be like camping," he tells them, throwing open the door to their room. He gets them settled, fitting their hats on their heads and zipping up their sleeping bags and kissing their cold cheeks.

"Tomorrow we'll figure something else out," he promises, but already they're giggling, the strangeness of it all turning them giddy. "Get some sleep. I'll be back up soon."

On the way down, he passes Roddy and Winston on the darkened stairs, and they all say good night. In the kitchen, Gemma is blowing out the candles and Jude is digging through her bag for an extra pair of pajamas for Annie. "Here," she says, handing over a few things. "I've got some toothpaste too. And if there's anything else you need, let me know. I'm always well stocked."

"I'll be fine." Annie nods at the fireplace. "Are you sure you guys don't want to sleep down here? It's the warmest spot in the house."

"We'll come back down if it's unbearable upstairs," Jude promises, then glances around. "This isn't exactly what I had in mind when I booked this place."

"Not much to be done," Annie says. "I bet nobody has power for miles."

Because the last thing he wants is for this to turn into a group hang, Connor is quick to hurry things along. "It's getting late," he says, giving his sisters a pointed look. He nods at the staircase. "We left you guys the best rooms."

"You did?" Jude asks, looking touched.

"No," Connor says, rolling his eyes. "We couldn't see a thing. You get what you get . . ."

". . . and you don't get upset," they both say on cue.

"Our dad," Jude says to Annie, as if that explains everything.

"Okay, good night," Connor says, and they grab their bags and some blankets and head up, nudging each other and glancing back at him on the way. He doesn't mind. He's had years of practice ignoring them.

When they're gone, he turns back to Annie. "I can't believe you're stuck here with us," he says. "I mean, I'm glad you are. Well—not glad. That sounds creepy. Like we lured you up to some freezing-cold cabin in the woods to kill you or something." She raises her eyebrows and he hurries on: "Not that we—we're not—we would never do that. Obviously. Though you did say it happens a lot up here. But that's not— My point is just that it's nice having you here. Even though it must be kind of weird for you. Not that it should be. I mean, I want you to feel welcome. We all do. It's just that my family is a lot. And this is the first time we've seen each other in a while. And here you are. So I'm sorry if it's a little—"

"Connor?" Annie says, interrupting him.

"Yeah?" he asks, relieved.

She swings the beam of her flashlight over to a cabinet that's stacked with old boxes of board games. "Do you have any interest in a game of checkers?"

He smiles. "Yes."

There are two missing pieces, so they borrow the hat and the thimble from a Monopoly game that looks like it's seen better days, then set up on the floor in front of the fireplace. Connor hasn't played in years, but once Annie makes the first move, his hand slides his red disk forward automatically, and they go back and forth like that, inching their way closer to each other from the outer edges of the board.

"So," she says. "It seems like the great reconciliation is going pretty well."

He nudges his piece ahead one square. "The other shoe will drop at some point. It's inevitable."

"What happened? It can't just be about the book."

"It's not," he says, shaking his head. "But the book didn't help."

There's a pause, and Connor can feel the place in the conversation where he has a choice to plow ahead or to bail on it completely. He's so used to bailing that it feels almost automatic. But for once, he finds himself wanting to say more. To be honest. To open up. So he decides to try.

"We got into this big fight about it a few years ago, right after our dad's funeral," he says. "I should've talked to them before the book came out. I know that now. But at the time, I thought they were being overly sensitive about it. So we argued. And it spiraled from there. And then we all left. I thought it would blow over. Which it might have."

Annie sits back on her heels, understanding passing over her face. "But then you won the National Book Award."

He nods. "Exactly. So the book got huge. Very unexpectedly. And then everyone knew our story. Or a version of it. Jude was just hitting that next level at the time, and they started asking her about it in interviews. Me. The book. Our mom. How much of it really happened."

Annie winces. "Yikes."

"She's always been really private. Keeps things close to the vest. So it wasn't great."

"It must've been hard for you too," Annie says, leapfrogging one of his pieces on the checkerboard.

"It was," he says. "It really messed me up, having those two things happen at once. My career taking off and my family drifting away. One day I'd feel terrible for having written it, and the next I'd be thinking, *Fuck them for not getting it.* I was angry and full of guilt and not writing for the first time in my life, and it turns out when I'm not doing that I become a completely miserable person to live with, which is when the trouble really started with my wife, though I'd argue that it had been one of those staying-together-for-the-kids things for a while before that anyway, and . . . how appealing is this all sounding right now? Am I doing a good job of selling myself?"

Annie smiles. "I guess I'd say that honesty counts for a lot."

"My siblings would probably disagree."

"I'm sorry that all happened," she says, giving him a long look.

He shrugs. "Some days I am too. Some days I'm not."

"You know, when I first read the book, I didn't even bother to google you. It was just such a wild story, I assumed it wasn't real. Your mom and those road trips. Not to mention having that many extraordinary kids in one family? No way."

"Yeah, well," he says, shuffling a few of the loose checkers in his hand. "Extraordinary might be overstating it."

"Are you kidding?" she says, the light from the fire making shadows across her face. "To have that much talent between you? It's incredible. I'm amazed by it, honestly. That you've all excelled so much at the things you love."

"Except for Gemma," he says without really thinking about it, and she gives him an incredulous look.

"From what I heard today, Gemma sounds like the most extraordinary of all. She practically raised you three. And look how that turned out."

Connor nods, feeling like a jerk. "No. Yeah. I guess you're right."

Annie studies him for a moment. "I can see why you wanted to write about it all."

He almost repeats his usual caveats. He almost says: *Personal, but not true.* But he doesn't. Instead, he looks at her across the mostly forgotten checkers board and says, "Thanks."

She smiles. "You know, the only thing I ever wanted was not to be ordinary. Which is something very different from being extraordinary. Everyone who grew up in Portree moved back, if they ever even left at all. I mean, *everyone.* Some went to UND or other colleges in state. Maybe a few ventured out to Minnesota or Wisconsin just long enough to find partners. But they always came back. And I swore I never would."

"You didn't," Connor says. "Not really. You're just here to help your parents. That's different. It's temporary."

"Is it? I don't know." Her eyes drift to the fireplace. "Four months in, it doesn't feel temporary. I was always the one who got out. It was basically my whole identity. You have no idea how long it took me to do it. But I did. I managed to make it all the way to New York City, for godsakes. And then I got reeled back, and now I'm scared I won't get out a second time."

"You will," Connor tells her, but it sounds hollow. Because what does he know? They met only yesterday in an Uber she was driving to pay off her loans while her life is on hold. What does he know about anything?

"I dream about it all the time," she says. "Flying into LaGuardia. You know the way the skyline comes up right underneath you if you sit on the left side of the plane? First Staten Island, then the Statue of Liberty, then downtown Manhattan, all of it looking so miniature that it doesn't even seem real? I love that part."

"Especially at night," Connor says, closing his eyes for a moment, thinking about the many book tours and speeches he traveled for over the years, the many times he came home to the city, knowing his family was somewhere far below in that cozy brownstone in Brooklyn, and that as long as the traffic wasn't too bad, he'd be home in time to tuck the kids into bed.

Home, he thinks, but to his surprise, the word melts the city in his mind, and just like that, he's picturing the little A-frame house on the edge of Lake Michigan. For years after he and Nicola were married, even after the kids were born, it took him a moment to adjust when someone asked him about his family. For so long, family to him was Gemma and Roddy and Jude. Even sometimes, when he was feeling generous, his mom and dad. Later, when they had all receded from his life, he found himself clinging—maybe too hard—to the updated definition of the word: Nicola and Rosie and Hugh. But then they began to slip away too, and he drifted from New York to Nashville, and even though it had been in the service of his work, he hadn't realized what that dislocation had cost him until now, how completely separate he is from everyone and everything, how utterly lonely.

Annie tucks her knees up to her chest and circles her arms around them. "My apartment was right above this place called the Moon-rock Diner. Pink-and-green booths, old-fashioned soda counter, the whole thing. If I ever make it back, that's the first place I'll go. I'll sit there with a grilled cheese and a book that I won't read because I'll be too busy watching people walk by on the street, and it'll seem like a completely ordinary thing to do, but because it's New York, it won't be. Because it's New York—"

"It'll feel extraordinary," he says, and she smiles at him.

"Exactly."

He watches her for a moment in the light of the fire, weighing something, and then, before he can overthink it, he leans toward her, and suddenly their faces are only inches apart, so close that he sees the flames reflected in her eyes, and his heart beats fast as he closes his own eyes, their lips about to touch when—

"Dad?" Hugh's voice comes from the top of the stairs, and Connor jerks back abruptly, blinking like he's trying to wake himself up. "Dad! I had a nightmare."

"Me too," he mumbles, which makes Annie laugh. He rises unsteadily to his feet and looks down at her, and for a slow and clumsy moment, he considers ignoring his son, in the hope that he'll go back to bed on his own. But he doesn't do this. Of course he doesn't. He snaps back, giving his head a shake, and smiles apologetically at Annie. "I'm so sorry. But I should probably—"

"Go," she says, smiling at him.

Another beat passes. And another. And still he just stands there.

"I'll see you in the morning?" he says eventually, and she nods.

"I'll be here," she tells him, and the thought is enough to carry him all the way up the chilly staircase, into the surprising warmth of the bed with his small and restless son, and through the remainder of the deepening night.

Wisconsin

2022

GEMMA WAS THE FIRST TO READ THE REVIEW.

She and Mateo were on their way to Door County for a romantic weekend, and though neither of them had said it outright, they both knew it was a last-ditch attempt to help things along before going to a fertility clinic.

They drove up from Chicago through freezing rain. At a gas station, Gemma grabbed a newspaper and a few magazines, since it looked like they'd be stuck inside for most of the weekend. Back in the car, she'd just begun idly leafing through the arts pages of *The New York Times* when she let out a giddy yelp.

Mateo glanced over at her. "What?"

"Connor," she said, already scanning the review.

"His book?" he asked. "It's out?"

"It comes out on Tuesday," she said, but already her face was darkening as she read.

"What's this one about?"

Gemma didn't answer him. She was still reading.

"Gem?" Mateo said, trying again. "What's it about?"

She looked over at him, eyes wide. "I think . . ." she said, then shook her head and started again: "I think it's about us."

North Carolina

2022

Roddy picked up a copy of the *Times* in the Charlotte airport. He'd gotten a series of frantic texts from Gemma telling him to read the review and then call her immediately, but he'd been warming up for their match against Charlotte FC—which they'd lost, though Roddy wasn't too put out as he'd had two assists—and it had slipped his mind until he saw the news kiosk.

He felt a little guilty as he set the paper down on the counter alongside a bottle of purple Gatorade and a giant bag of Combos; he'd forgotten Connor had a book coming out at all. Roddy wasn't much of a reader, and though he'd bought copies of the first two novels, they were still sitting unopened on his bookshelf at home. A review, though—that he could manage.

He flipped through the pages to find it, smiling reflexively when he spotted the orange cover of the book with Connor's name along the bottom edge. His eyes roamed over the neat blocks of print, his heart picking up speed as he caught the words "road trips" and "fire," but then the woman at the checkout was handing back his credit card and one of his teammates had appeared, snatching the bag of Combos away before Roddy could grab it, and there was an announcement on the loudspeaker for Flight 824 to BWI, and Roddy stuffed the newspaper into his bag and hurried off to his gate, a sliver of worry threading its way through him.

New Mexico

2022

JUDE HAD SEEN THE REVIEW LONG BEFORE THE RAMBLING voicemail from Roddy, but she'd decided to reserve judgment until she'd read the book. She was on the set of a time-travel thriller she'd been filming for the past several weeks in the windswept Albuquerque desert, and so she asked her assistant, Madison, to pick up a copy. But when Jude returned to her trailer between setups, still in wardrobe—head-to-toe black, with tiny fake cuts and bruises all over her face, since she was playing a high-level CIA operative who had just crashed through a skylight—Madison was empty-handed.

"They didn't have it," she told Jude, passing her a nonfat vanilla chai latte instead. "It's a small store. They said they only carry big bestsellers and name-brand authors."

Jude rolled her eyes, irritated on Connor's behalf, even as she was preparing to be furious with him. "Is there a library anywhere around here?"

"Why don't I just download it on your phone?" Madison said, already typing away, and so that's how Jude read the book, on a screen the size of a credit card, in fits and starts between takes, the familiar story unspooling in an unfamiliar way, the back of her neck tingling as she read.

When she got to the part about the fire, she sat up on the couch in her trailer, heart racing. But she forced herself to take a few deep breaths, to steady herself. Soon she'd be a CIA agent, facing down gunmen and high-speed cars and a hired assassin. She couldn't let herself be rattled by something as small as a book.

Still, as she walked back out for the next scene, her hands were shaking.

Roddy

North Dakota

2025

It's not quite five A.M., and the house is freezing, and Roddy and Winston have been fighting ever since Winston woke up from a dream in which Roddy had apparently agreed to move to Monaco (?) to play baseball (?) on a ten-year contract (?) without consulting him, and somehow—somehow!—this had been considered urgent enough to wake Roddy and make him answer for it in the middle of an extremely cold night in an extremely dark cabin, after which things had escalated quickly. And now, well over an hour later, here they are.

"We need to go to bed," Winston moans. He's pacing around the room with a flannel blanket wrapped around him like a cape and two pairs of socks on. He breathes out and points indignantly. "I can see my breath."

From where he's burrowed under the covers in bed, Roddy tugs his winter hat down farther on his head. "You started it."

"I think any reasonable jury of our peers would agree that *you* started it."

Roddy sighs. "Let's not go backward. We need to figure this out."

"We're never going to figure it out," Winston says, "because I'm never going to understand why you'd want to move to another city to play for a football team you don't even care about—and that doesn't care about you either, aside from sticking your name all over the press release—rather than admitting you're getting too old for this, and that your knee is *already* too old for it, and making the decision to retire with dignity and get on with the rest of your life."

"You don't actually care about any of that," Roddy says flatly. "You're just pissed about the wedding."

The only light in the room is from a single candle on the nightstand, which makes it hard for them to see each other in the shadows. Even so, Roddy can tell that there's more than just anger on Winston's face. There's hurt too.

"Of *course* I'm pissed about the bloody wedding," he says. "But it's so much more than that. You didn't even consider me in the equation. You just decided! Like your life doesn't have any effect on mine whatsoever."

Roddy rubs his cold hands together. "You knew I wanted to do it. You knew I was just waiting for the offer. So I don't understand why this is such—"

"Because this isn't how it works when you have a partner," Winston says with a groan. "Why do I feel like I'm explaining what a relationship is to a five-year-old?"

"I get it," Roddy snaps at him. "I screwed up. But this is about my career. You can keep staring at microscopes and mixing potions till you're eighty-five—"

"Is that what you think I do all day?" Winston says, looking like he wants to laugh in spite of himself.

"But I might only have this one year left," Roddy continues, his voice pleading. "We could get married anytime. But this might be my last chance to play. I'm sorry the timing isn't ideal. I really am. But I'm a hundred years old and my knee could give out at any moment and this is the only club that still wants me. So it's just something I have to do."

Winston sits down gingerly on the edge of the bed, turning sideways to face Roddy, their eyes meeting in the near dark. "And why," he says quietly, "do you think they want you?"

The question hangs there for a moment between them. Outside, the wind moves through the branches, and the flame from the candle makes a little pop. Roddy breathes in and out, in and out, the way he does when he's pulled a muscle or been tackled the wrong way.

Winston is right; he can see his breath.

"You don't know what you're talking about," he says after a moment, his voice low.

"I know that Orlando had a PR problem last year because their manager used a homophobic slur," Winston says evenly. "And I know that when Chicago came to play against them a few months ago, their fans bullied the only other gay player in the whole league, and it was a huge story."

Roddy clenches his jaw. "What are you saying?"

"I think you know."

"Fuck you," he says, throwing aside the covers and getting out of bed. He walks over to the window and stares out at the inky-black night, feeling suddenly claustrophobic. He wants to yell and he wants to stomp around and he wants to storm out. But they're stuck in this cabin in the woods with the rest of his family in the middle of nowhere and he can't do any of those things.

A memory surfaces: a long-ago loss to the Colorado Rapids in which an own goal by Roddy had been the deciding factor. It was the very worst way to lose a match, and as he slid behind the mic at the press conference afterward, his shoulders were already tense. For a few minutes, he answered the usual questions about his performance and his efforts to clear the ball and his botched pass, itchy to get back to the locker room and take a shower and head home.

Finally, one last reporter stood up. "Yeah," he said, glancing down at a notepad. "Can I ask whether you think your sexual orientation might've been a factor?"

Roddy blinked at him, his heart beating much too fast. The room had gone very quiet. "Was my sexual orientation a factor," he said slowly, "in my scoring a goal against my own team?"

The reporter shrugged, unbothered. "You only came out a few weeks ago, so . . ."

"To you," Roddy said, his voice cold even as his insides were burning up. "I only came out a few weeks ago to all of *you*."

"Right, but all the media attention that ensued, the reaction of your teammates—"

"Was Joaquin Ramirez's sexual orientation a factor in his misses tonight?"

The reporter looked confused. "Joaquin Ramirez isn't gay."

"Fucking exactly," Roddy said, pushing back from the table, and then he stalked out of the room, cameras clicking behind him.

Sometimes—too often—it was like that. Especially early on, in the weeks and months after Roddy made a spontaneous public announcement the day after seeing a news story about a ten-year-old soccer player who was bullied for being gay. Before then, he'd never felt the need to say it out loud to a bunch of people he didn't know and who didn't know him. He knew who he was, and so did his friends and family, and he'd always thought that was enough. But watching that story, he'd realized there might be others who needed to hear it too.

When he'd woken up that morning, even when he'd approached the on-field reporter after the match with trembling fingers and a clanging heart, he'd already imagined all the ways going public could hurt his career. What hadn't occurred to him was that there might be an upside too. But it wasn't long before a very specific brand of publicity kicked in: there were morning show appearances and interviews in men's health magazines and new endorsement deals for various personal grooming products and a protein powder that briefly turned his pee an odd shade of green. But none of that had anything to do with him as a player. Surely, he figured, the two were separate: the person he was on the field and off it. Surely a team like Orlando— with only so many spots on their roster, with only so much money in their salary cap—wouldn't waste this opportunity on someone exclusively for the optics?

He looks at Winston, feeling off-balance. "It's not about that," he says, but there's a waver in his voice that wasn't there a minute ago.

"I'm not saying you're not brilliant," Winston says quickly. "Because you are. I just hate the thought of you going down there for the wrong reasons and—"

"Missing the wedding," Roddy says, riding a sudden swell of anger. "Right? Because it always comes back to the wedding."

Winston twists from where he's sitting on the bed to look at him more fully. "Why shouldn't it? It's a big deal."

"It's a party."

"It's a promise."

"I've already made the promise. The wedding doesn't mean anything. Not really."

"It does to me."

"Well, I guess maybe I don't care about all this as much as you do then," Roddy says, waving a hand around, and Winston stares at him, stricken. In the long silence that follows, Roddy can hear the howling of the wind, the snapping of branches, the *thump thump thump* of his heart.

Winston shakes his head. "I should've known better," he says. "I should've—" He stops and starts again. "Do you know that when we first started dating I read your brother's book?"

Roddy looks at him warily but says nothing.

"It obviously wasn't football in that version," he continues. "It was skiing. But it was the exact same thing. No matter what else, no matter *who* else, it always comes first, doesn't it?"

"That's just a book, Winston."

Winston stands up, momentarily unsteady. "At the time I thought it was a metaphor," he says. "That football wouldn't really be your first love. But maybe there's something to it. Because that's how your mum was too, wasn't she?"

Roddy swallows hard but can't bring himself to say anything. Winston looks back at him, the disappointment all over his face.

"Well, I guess better to know now," he says eventually, "before we do anything we both might regret."

"Winston—" Roddy says, but Winston just shakes his head and walks into the bathroom, shutting the door behind himself.

For a while, Roddy waits there in the darkness. He watches the door, hoping it might swing open, that the knob might turn. When it doesn't, he moves toward the bathroom door, the hardwood floor cold through his socks, and knocks softly.

"Don't," comes Winston's muffled voice from the other side, and Roddy's heart sinks at the starkness of the word: "I just want to be alone."

He knows he should apologize. Or stay at the door until Winston comes out again. Or break it down and insist they keep talking. But he feels too mixed up for any of that right now, too unsure of what he might say or have to hear.

Instead, he pulls on his jacket and an extra pair of socks, then hovers there for another moment as he stuffs his feet into the pair of duck boots he'd found in a closet earlier. "I'm going for a walk," he says to the blankness of the door. "Let's keep talking when I get back."

There's no answer.

He tiptoes down the stairs and through the warmth of the living room, where the fire is still smoldering and Annie is asleep on one of the big couches. He's so muddled from what just happened with Winston, and so focused on not waking their houseguest, that he doesn't even notice Gemma standing on the front porch until he makes it outside, closing the door gently behind himself.

She twists around, looking at him in surprise. "What are you doing up?"

"I thought I'd go for a walk," he says, as his eyes rake the snow-covered landscape. It's still dark, but the moon is bright and he can see the deep drifts piled up against the house, the way everything beyond the overhang of the porch is socked in. "But I guess that's not happening. You?"

"Couldn't sleep."

Like him, she's fully dressed in a hat and coat and boots, as if she'd been about to make some sort of escape, and she's holding her phone in one gloved hand. He nods at it. "Still nothing?"

"Still no power," she says with a sigh, "and still no service."

"Are you worried about Mateo?"

"I'm worried that Mateo will be worried about me."

"That's sweet," Roddy says, leaning against the railing, which looks out over the lake below, now frozen around the edges. "You guys have it all figured out, huh?"

Gemma looks away. "I don't know about that."

"Ten years," he says with a little whistle, thinking back on her wedding; he still remembers the expression on her face as she said her vows, remembers wondering whether he'd ever stand up at an altar and look at someone that way too, like the focus had narrowed so that the rest of the world was blurry, like all that mattered was right in front of you.

"Eleven, actually," Gemma says.

"What's the secret?" he asks in a way that's meant to sound casual, even a little jokey. But the pitch of his voice gives him away. He squints out into the darkness to avoid her eyes.

She doesn't answer. Instead, she says, "I'll go with you."

"For a walk?" Roddy asks, surveying the glowing blanket of white, the eerie shadows of the trees, the stars in the sky, which has finally cleared. "In this?"

Gemma laughs. "You've all been away from the Midwest too long," she says, moving around him and picking her way carefully down the porch steps, sinking almost to her knees as she descends. "It'll be fun."

Roddy hesitates a moment, glancing back at the door, the hush of the cabin beyond it. Then he follows Gemma down the steps and into the snow.

By the time they've made it down the drive, they're already pink-cheeked and sweating. "Maybe we should've taken the snowshoes," Roddy says, but Gemma doesn't answer. They cut over to the lake, its surface silver in the moonlight.

Gemma forges a path with the kind of resolve that makes Roddy wonder whether she's in a hurry to get somewhere or, like him, is trying to outrun something. But he doesn't mind it, the brisk pace that makes every step a battle. His quads are aching and his ears are cold and his knee feels a little fragile, but the drifts around them are untouched except by the occasional squirrel, and the world is still quiet, and he's happy to be out here instead of back in the room with Winston, a thought that makes him feel guilty and elated all at once.

"We had a fight," Roddy says, and Gemma—who is walking a few feet in front of him, too determined for someone without a destination in mind—half-turns to listen. "Me and Winston."

"About what?" she asks, slowing to let him catch up.

"He's not thrilled I'm going to Orlando," Roddy says. "And missing our wedding."

Gemma turns to him with her eyebrows raised. "Well, that's understandable."

Roddy frowns at her. "Whose side are you on?"

"You already know the answer to that," she says, her breath emerging in crystalline puffs. "But it doesn't mean I don't feel for Winston. It's hard to be the one left behind."

Roddy is quiet for a while. "When you saw the news about me going to Orlando," he says eventually, "did it say anything about them revamping their image?"

She stops walking and turns to him in surprise. "You're wondering if they only want you because you're gay?"

Roddy swallows hard. Somehow, it sounds even worse when Gemma says it. He nods, unable to say the word *yes*.

"I mean, you know more about it than I do," she says, "so if that's what you think, it's probably true."

His heart dips, because there have only ever been two people in his life who are always right: Gemma and Winston.

"That's not necessarily a reason not to play, though," she continues. "Not if you really want it."

"I really want it," Roddy says, his voice a little gravelly.

"Can I ask why?" She says it without judgment, but when she sees the look of surprise on his face, she goes on: "I get tired just from going to the gym. Not, like, working out there. Like, actually just walking the twelve blocks to get there."

He laughs. "We're old."

"We're old," she agrees. "Doesn't your knee hurt?"

He glances down at his sweatpants, as if the pain might be visible, and realizes that it does hurt. He's grown so used to the dull throb, the near constant creak of it, that he hardly notices anymore. "I'm just not ready to let it go."

"Because you love the game?"

"Yes," he says. "And because it's all I really know."

"Aren't you curious about what else is out there?"

He shrugs. "What if there isn't anything?"

The wind picks up, the snow swirling around them in a fine dust. Gemma smiles at him. "What if there is?"

Roddy feels suddenly impatient. He forces himself to pick up one cold foot and put it down in front of the other, to begin tramping through the snow again, not sure whether his sister is following until he hears the crunch of her boots and then her voice beside him.

"You know," she says, "people always think it's a gift, you guys being so good at what you do. But it's also meant you've missed out on a lot."

"Like what?" Roddy asks.

"Like being ordinary."

He laughs, the sound bright and unexpected. "Who wants to be ordinary?"

"Happy people," she says, and he can't tell if she's kidding or not as they turn past a blue clapboard house and begin to cut away from the lake. They walk in silence for a few more minutes, and then she says, so quietly he almost misses it under the rush of the wind, "I can't believe I won't be there."

It takes him a moment to realize what she's talking about. "It was going to be tiny. Just the two of us, really."

Gemma nods, but when he looks over, her eyes are very bright.

"It made me sad too," he admits. "I don't know if it'll even happen now, but if it does . . ."

She waves this away. "You don't have to do that."

"I want to," he says, and she smiles back at him. He glances around as they continue to walk. "Where are we even going?" he asks. "And don't say nowhere."

She points up ahead as they follow a barely discernible path through the trees. "Annie said there's a little grocery store up here."

"A grocery store?" Roddy asks, baffled. "It's not even six. And it's Sunday. And it's . . ." He gestures around them at the snow. "There's no way it'll be open."

"No," she agrees. "It won't."

"So what's the point?"

She's still walking with purpose. "I need you not to ask any questions when I tell you this," she says without looking at him.

Roddy hurries to keep up with her, intrigued. "Okay."

"I'm going to break into the store."

"You're . . . what?"

A little white building comes into view. Its red awning is sagging under the weight of the snow, and the window says MELVIN'S across it in peeling blue letters. Inside it's dark, and the parking lot is empty, just a neat rectangle of sparkling snow.

"Gem," Roddy says, but she turns and shakes her head.

"I said no questions."

"Okay. But . . . just one."

She sighs impatiently. "Fine."

"Can I help?"

South Carolina

2022

THEIR DAD DIED ON A TUESDAY IN APRIL. IT HAPPENED peacefully in his sleep, the way you hope it will happen if you have to hope for this sort of thing at all. When they arrived in Hilton Head, Liz told them the story: how she'd tried to wake him in the morning only to find he was gone, the whole thing matter-of-fact and free of fuss, as Paul himself had been.

The funeral, too, was a simple affair, a fitting tribute to the generally decent if emotionally distant man who had been on the road through much of their childhood and parented them only in occasional guilty bursts. The four of them sat in the front row of the church, flanked by Mateo and Nicola and the kids. Jude's eyes were full of tears; the others listened numbly during the service, thinking about how they'd never really known him, but missing him all the same.

Gemma read a Mary Oliver poem. Connor gave a eulogy about the importance of family, while the other three rolled their eyes, thinking of the recently published book. Roddy recited a Bible verse at Liz's request, because none of the rest of them would. And Jude gave an impromptu speech about the time they had a picnic on the bluff and their watermelon rolled off the edge and their dad went crashing down the steep incline after it, which made everyone laugh until they cried.

Everyone agreed that the service was lovely.

It wasn't until hours later that things started to devolve.

Gemma

North Dakota

2025

Gemma has never broken into anyplace before—has never committed any sort of crime at all—but it turns out to be far easier than expected. The back door to the market is old, the handle a little wobbly, and it takes only a few tries with a bobby pin to jimmy it open.

For a few seconds, she and Roddy stand in the doorway, both tense as they wait for an alarm to sound. But it's not that kind of store. It might not even be that kind of town.

There's no noise. No distant sirens. No manager with a baseball bat. There's just the cool dark of an empty market on a Sunday morning.

When she woke up, she definitely hadn't been planning on something like this. Last night, she'd asked Annie—who wasn't exactly an expert on Melvin Falls but was the closest thing they had, and the next best thing to the internet, which was still down, along with the power—if there were any drugstores or grocery stores in the area.

"There's a big one the next town over," she'd said, glancing out the window. "But that depends on whether we can get the car out. Which is definitely a question mark."

"Nothing walking distance?"

"There used to be a little mom-and-pop place on the other side of the lake," Annie said. "Just past the blue cottage with that giant flag out front. I don't even know if it's still in business, but I doubt they'd be open on a Sunday anyway. Especially in this."

The night had passed fitfully. When Gemma managed to sleep, she had strange dreams about Mateo: that they were seated next to each other on a plane but turned out to be divorced and still had to pass the time together. When she woke up, she lay in bed worrying about the snow, about being trapped, about another day of not knowing whether or not she was pregnant, not knowing whether or not she wanted to be. And about not being in touch with Mateo, who must be worried by now.

Early this morning, so early that the world was still a deep black, she tiptoed out into the hallway and down to the bathroom at the end of the hall. Her eyes were bleary as she stood in front of the bathroom mirror, and on a whim, she opened the medicine cabinet. It was clean and empty except for a single black bobby pin, and without thinking, Gemma picked it up and held it between two fingers, a wild and uncharacteristic plan forming in her mind.

And now here they are.

"Shall we?" Roddy asks, motioning to the empty store ahead of them, but Gemma remains frozen at the door.

"We're going to leave money," she says. "For anything we take."

Roddy nods. "Sounds fair."

They stand there another moment.

"So were you looking for anything in particular," he asks, "or just in the mood for some light burglary?"

Gemma lifts a hand to steady herself and realizes it's shaking. It's not that she's worried about getting caught. The world outside the shop is quiet and still. She peers inside, her toes at the edge of the door, scanning the shelves of chips and crackers, trying to see past the cooler filled with ice cream bars and Popsicles. But she knows she'll have to go in, and she doesn't know which will be worse: if they have the tests or if they don't.

"Or were you craving a wine cooler or something?" Roddy asks.

"How old do you think I am?" she says. Then she turns to him, her expression more serious, and says, "I need a pregnancy test."

Roddy's face rearranges itself into a look of awkward surprise. "Oh. Wow."

"Yeah."

"Is this a hopeful thing or a panicky thing?"

"Honestly, I don't really know yet."

He raises his eyebrows. "You don't know if you want a baby?" he asks, which is a fair question for someone who is forty-three and has been married for eleven years, not to mention has recently gone through several rounds of fertility treatments.

But it all feels like too much to explain to him at the moment. So she says, "The only thing I want for sure right now is a test. I just need to know either way."

"Fair enough," he says. "Let's go see what we can find."

They walk into the empty shop together before splitting up. The power is out here too, and there's an eerie silence to the place. As she walks toward the drugstore items on the back wall, she hears the crinkling of a bag and turns around.

"What?" Roddy asks around a mouthful of potato chips. "You said we could leave money."

Gemma rolls her eyes and keeps going, already scanning the wall as she approaches. Before long, her eyes land on a pink box, and her face prickles with an odd sort of heat as she walks toward it. She picks it up delicately, like it's something fragile, and stares at the words on the package: OVER 99% ACCURATE.

"Oh good," Roddy says, coming up behind her, crunching on the chips. "You found some."

Gemma nods, but she's still staring at the package in her hands. She closes her eyes and pictures one of the white sticks with two red lines on the end, imagines telling Mateo, the way his face would break into that exuberant smile of his, the way he'd spin her around the kitchen and then set her down with a worried look and pat her stomach and say, "Sorry, little baby. Didn't mean to make you dizzy."

She tries to think about how she would feel, but her mind is curiously blank.

A baby.

When she thinks of babies, she thinks of the twins being born—harder to picture now with all six-foot-two of Roddy standing right in front of her—and the way their mom had positioned five-year-old Gemma on the couch when they got home from the hospital, handing her first Jude and then Roddy, until her arms were completely full. She tried to smile for the picture, but she couldn't tear her eyes away from their busy mouths and waving arms, the soft crowns of hair on each of their heads. She looked back and forth, back and forth between them, feeling something powerful and immediate that she would only later be able to classify as love. She didn't yet know how much of their lives she'd be responsible for; if she had, maybe she wouldn't have given her heart to them so freely; maybe she would've tried to protect herself more. But that day, as Connor craned his neck to get a closer look, and her parents smiled down at her, she knew only that she was theirs and they were hers, and nothing could ever change that.

Now she stuffs the box into her coat and slides two twenty-dollar bills out of the pocket of her jeans. Near the counter, she spots a rack filled with folded maps, and she takes one that says UNITED STATES on the outside. Roddy catches her eye and smiles.

"For the kids," she says, and he gives her a knowing nod.

After Gemma leaves the money, they glance around the store one last time.

"There's something kind of cool about this," Roddy says, "isn't there?"

"What, breaking and entering?" she says, and he shakes his head.

"Being in here alone. It's like that book you used to read us, the one about the kids stuck in the museum at night. It's like anything is possible."

"It's a grocery store," Gemma says, amused. "Not the Met."

"Yeah, but stuff like this makes me feel like I'm still twelve years old, you know?"

"I'm not sure I was ever really twelve years old," Gemma says as she heads toward the door, swiping a pack of gum on her way out.

As they walk back, the world begins to wake up around them. The sun rises through the trees in orange and pink slices, and a few intrepid ducks cut through the thin layer of ice at the edge of the lake. People start to emerge from the houses with shovels and snowblowers and giant bags of salt, trying to carve a path from their front doors to their cars, though there's nowhere to go even once they do, the roads still sunk deep beneath the snow.

"Are we still in a no-questions zone?" Roddy asks as he trudges along beside her. He nods to her coat, where the box of tests is tucked safely inside.

Gemma gives him an apologetic look. "For now, yes."

"But you'll let me know when the embargo has been lifted?"

"I promise," she says, linking her arm through his, and they walk the rest of the way like that, clumsier than they were on their own, but warmer too.

When they make it back to the cabin, the house is still quiet and the power is still out. Annie is no longer on the couch, her blanket and pillow in a neat pile at one end of it. But otherwise, everyone must still be asleep. Roddy casts a nervous glance at the staircase as he tugs off his boots.

"You going up there?" Gemma asks, hanging up her coat.

"I might just hang out here for a bit," he says. "Give him some space."

"Are you sure space is what you guys need right now?"

"I don't know what we need," he admits, walking over to one of the leather armchairs near the fireplace and sitting down heavily.

"Okay, well . . ." She gestures at the stairs.

"Good luck," Roddy says, then adds: "Whatever that means for you."

Upstairs, she goes straight to the hall bathroom and stands on the other side of the door once she's closed it, trying to steady her breathing. Then she opens the box carefully and pulls out a white stick. She sits on the toilet, shivering a little from the cold on her bare skin, and holds the stick under herself while she pees, shifting to adjust her aim; then—when she's done—she wipes it gently, puts it on the edge of the sink, and stares at it.

Three minutes, she thinks, setting the timer on her phone. *Here we go.*

She unwinds the scarf from around her neck and sits on the edge of the bathtub, her leg bobbing nervously. She glances at her phone. Then away. Then back at it again, her stomach churning.

She's taken dozens of these things, and aside from that very first one, they've all been negative.

But what if this one is different?

She's just stood up, too jittery to sit still for very long, when the door—which she thought she'd locked—swings open.

"Occupied," Gemma says in a quick, strangled voice, throwing out a hand, but Jude is suddenly there anyway, wearing an expensive-looking cardigan over her pajamas, her hair tousled and her eyes still puffy from sleep.

"Oops, sorry," she says, but Gemma can see that it's too late. Already, Jude's gaze has landed on the little white stick at the edge of the sink. Her eyes widen. "Holy shit."

"Jude—"

She shuts the door behind herself, then walks over to the sink. "No fucking way."

"Can I please have some privacy?"

"How much more time?"

Gemma sighs and glances down at her phone. "Two minutes."

"Dude," Jude says, walking over to the toilet. She closes the lid and sits down on it, crossing one leg onto her other knee and pulling down her wool sock to scratch at her ankle. "Tell me everything. What are you hoping for? How do you feel?"

How does she feel? Gemma feels as if she's vibrating, though with what, she doesn't know: Nerves? Fear? Annoyance at Jude? She checks her phone again, slightly panicky. Mateo is the one who should be here right now. Or more to the point, she should be home with Mateo right now.

"I don't know," she says finally, and Jude looks up at her with a frown.

"But you want it, right?"

"I don't know. Maybe."

Jude looks pleased. "You'd be a great mom. You were for us, anyway. And if I'm being honest—"

"You really don't have to be."

"I always assumed you two would have gotten around to it by now."

Gemma scrubs at her face with her hands. "You can't say that to people, Jude."

"You're not people. You're my sister."

"Right, but for all you know, we've been trying for the past ten years, so you can't—"

"Have you?"

"No," Gemma says, suddenly frustrated. "No, we haven't. And do you want to know why? Because of you guys. Because I spent so much of my life taking care of you and worrying about you and making sure you were okay and cutting the stupid crusts off your stupid sandwiches—"

"That was only Roddy," Jude points out.

"—and it got to the point where all I wanted when I grew up was *quiet*, honestly. And freedom. I didn't want any more responsibility. And then I met Mateo, and he's like this super dad in the making who everyone agrees should have a family of eight by now, and I love him, and he loves me, and it's impossible to explain to people why we took so long to even start trying, but I couldn't bring myself to do it at first, and he was so good about it, and so patient with me, and so we just kept waiting and saying, *We'll try in the spring* or *Maybe next year,* and then all this time went by, and I got older, and by the time we actually did start, it was so much harder than we expected, and now we've tried all this fertility stuff, and none of it has worked, and we finally did IVF and only ended up with this one good embryo, and I don't know if I'm more scared of it sticking or not sticking, I just know that Mateo wants it so badly, and he's so goddamn hopeful about stuff like this even when it doesn't make any sense to be—not just about the possibility of having a baby, but also about the world in general—and sometimes I wish I were more like that too, but I'm just not; I'm way too pragmatic, and way too practical, and that makes it hard to take a leap like this and just—what?—hope it all works out for the best, because what kind of plan is that? It's not even like I have a career like yours, or Roddy's, or Connor's, where I can chalk it up to being consumed with that; all I do is help brands with their marketing strategies and live a sort of alarmingly normal life—but I love that job, boring as it sounds, and I love my life, ordinary as it is, and I'm afraid that bringing a baby into it might blow it all up, or make me feel resentful, because it'll change everything, and at the same time I'm worried that if this doesn't work, and I finally feel ready at some point down the road, it'll be too late, and I'll always regret not trying sooner. But most of all I'm terrified that this will actually happen for me and I'll realize I'm just like her, and not meant to be a mom, which is something she didn't figure out until it was way too late, and I can't imagine anything more unfair than repeating that same pattern with a kid of my own, so I just don't know if I can—"

The alarm on her phone rings, startling them both.

They look over at the screen, then at each other, then at the white stick.

Gemma begins to reach for it, but Jude holds up a hand.

"Wait," she says quietly. "Before you look, I just feel like I need to say that I know it wasn't fair, how much you had to do for us when we were kids."

"Jude, you don't have to—"

"But also, I don't know how we would've survived without you. Genuinely. You're the bravest, scrappiest, most levelheaded person I've ever known, and whatever happens with this"—she gestures toward the sink—"you'll be okay. I know it."

Gemma has tears in her eyes. "What if I'm not?"

"Then maybe it's our turn to hold *you* up for a change," Jude says with a shrug. "I know we haven't been there lately, but we're here now. No matter what."

Her voice cracks on the last word, and Gemma reaches out to squeeze her hand. "Thank you."

"And you're not Mom," she says, her eyes fixed on Gemma's. "Not even a little bit. You're better than she was in pretty much every possible way."

Gemma smiles. "So are you."

"Okay," Jude says, letting out a shaky breath. "You ready?"

But Gemma has already picked it up, the stick trembling a little in her grip. She looks over at Jude, who raises her eyebrows.

"Well?"

Gemma is almost afraid to say it out loud. "It's positive," she finally manages, and then immediately begins to cry.

Jude touches her lightly on the back. "Are you happy? I can't tell if you're happy. But Gem? I'm so happy for you."

When Gemma looks over again, she sees that Jude has tears in her eyes too. "Why are *you* crying?" she asks, laughing a little, and Jude shrugs and swipes at her face with the sleeve of her cardigan.

"Because nine months from now, you're going to have a baby," she says with a bleary smile. "What could be more hopeful than that?"

Georgia

2022

A<small>FTER THE FUNERAL AT A SEASIDE CHAPEL IN</small> H<small>ILTON</small> H<small>EAD</small>, Connor watched the rest of his siblings pile into a rental car with Mateo and tried not to feel left out. It was silly. They were adults, for one thing. And coming from their father's funeral, for another. Plus, he had his family with him, or else he was sure they'd have included him. But still, as soon as he got into his car, he loosened his tie and unfastened the top button of his dress shirt, feeling itchy with worry.

They hadn't said anything about the book. Not today, and not on any of the days since its publication six weeks ago. Until now, Connor had been assuming they hadn't read it, that they each had busy lives and things to do and didn't have time to bother with a small literary novel that had garnered exactly one (glowing) newspaper review and sold a grand total of 1,687 copies. Even if it had been written by their brother.

But now he wasn't so sure.

He yanked loose another button on his shirt, and Nicola gave him an odd look from the passenger seat. "Are you okay?"

"Completely," he said a little too enthusiastically, and then, because they'd just been at his father's funeral, he quickly revised it: "About what you would expect."

In the backseat, three-year-old Hugh was drumming his little legs against the car seat. "Where did he go anyway?"

"Who?" Connor asked as he merged onto the highway, heading across the state border toward Savannah. It had been Jude's idea to stay the night there; she had an early flight back to L.A. in the morning and wanted to be close to the airport. Plus, they'd hoped to avoid ending up back at the condo in Hilton Head, eating crab cakes and making small talk with their father's pickleball friends.

"Grandpa," Hugh said, and before anyone else could answer, Rosie said, "Heaven. He went to heaven."

In the front seat, Connor and Nicola exchanged a glance. They were not quite atheists, but they would probably classify themselves as aggressively unreligious.

"His soul flew away," Connor said, feeling satisfied with the poetic image, but when he snuck a peek at Hugh in the rearview mirror, he only looked more confused.

"Like a bird?"

"Yes."

Hugh twisted to look out the window. "So his soul is in a tree?"

"No."

"In the sky?"

"Yes."

"Like a cloud?"

"Sure."

When they arrived at the hotel, his siblings were still in the lobby. The kids went running over, and Roddy swept them up effortlessly, one in each arm, while Gemma gave Nicola a hug and Jude began chatting with the two of them. Connor hauled their bags toward the front desk, kicking Rosie's unicorn backpack ahead of him, until Mateo came jogging over to help.

"Hey," he said, and the others smiled at him. But their smiles were polite, which was somehow worse than no smiles at all. There hadn't been time to talk before the service, and at the reception afterward, they were each pulled in different directions. So now, here in the nondescript lobby of this nondescript hotel, was their first chance. Only nobody would meet his eye. Which was how he knew without any doubt whatsoever that they'd all read the book.

Fuck, he thought, but what he said was: "Anyone want to get a drink after we check in?"

The others exchanged glances. When nobody else spoke up, Mateo cleared his throat. "I've got some papers to grade," he said apologetically, but he looked relieved to have the excuse.

"Yeah, I think I'm gonna head up," Jude said. "It's been a long day."

Gemma nodded. "Me too."

"But you'll be at the bar?" Roddy asked. "Maybe we'll come down and meet you later if we get a second wind."

"Yeah," Jude said. "Maybe."

"Great," Connor said, trying to sound cheerful. He watched them head to the elevator before giving Nicola a kiss on the cheek and saying goodbye to the kids. Then he walked over to the empty hotel bar and ordered a drink by himself.

One hour, three beers, and a bowl of cashews later, none of his siblings had shown up. Which wasn't a surprise—but he still couldn't help glancing over his shoulder at the elevators every time they dinged. It was definitely about the book, he decided. Why else would they be acting so distant? He took another long swig, and when he set the bottle down, it almost toppled over. For a moment, Connor was inordinately pleased with himself for having caught it; then he realized he was the one to knock it over in the first place and plunked his credit card down on the bar. He'd had enough.

On the way upstairs, he stared at his bleary-eyed reflection in the grim elevator mirror. He looked older than he was, and just about as tired. On the eighth floor, he began the long walk to his room at the far end of the hallway. But about halfway down, he heard familiar voices coming from behind another door and paused, his face suddenly burning.

It was his siblings. They were all hanging out together.

Without him.

He lifted a hand to knock on the door, then changed his mind and pressed his ear against it, not even caring what anyone walking through the hall might think.

"Did you get to the part about the fire yet?" Gemma asked, her voice a little blurry, the way it always was when she'd been drinking. "It's going to make your head explode."

Jude was the one to answer: "The part where he makes it sound like a bar mitzvah?"

"What do you mean?" Roddy asked with a nervous laugh.

"Here," Jude said, and Connor realized with a shock that she was about to read from his book. He steeled himself. *"That night,"* she read, sounding like someone recording the audio version, *"the whole world changed, and so did he. Before the fire, he was a boy. But afterward? Somewhere between those nighttime flames and the arrival of dawn, he became a man."*

"Wow," Roddy said.

Connor felt hot all over, the back of his neck prickling with a mixture of anger and embarrassment. Behind him, there was the clatter of a room service cart, and he stepped away from the door, his stomach leaden. But the guy wheeling it paused right in front of him with an awkward expression.

"Sorry, sir," he said, pointing at the door, where the sound of voices could still be heard. He watched in a daze as the guy knocked once, then twice, and called, "Room service!"

On the cart, there was an ice bucket with a bottle of champagne and three glasses. The door opened and Roddy poked his head out to grab it. It took him a second to clock Connor standing behind the room service guy, and when he did, his polite smile wobbled and then fell entirely, before he managed to find it again.

"Con," he said a little too brightly. "Hey! What are you doing here?"

"I was just headed back from the bar," Connor said. "Guess you didn't make it down."

Roddy shook his head, his ears pink. "No, sorry. We were just—" He stopped abruptly and cast a guilty glance back into the room.

The room service guy scuttled down the hall toward the elevators. Connor reached out and pushed the door open the rest of the way to reveal Gemma, whose face was bright red, and Jude, who was busy shoving the copy of his book behind the couch cushions.

"Let me save you the trouble of attempting any more bad acting," Connor said, pushing in past Roddy. "I could hear you guys from the hall."

They all simply stared back at him like a bunch of kids in trouble at school. He could almost see their minds whirring, slowed by the empty bottles of wine and champagne that were littered around the hotel suite.

"Hear what?" Jude asked, and Connor—emboldened by his righteous outrage, plus one too many bottles of beer—thrust a finger at her.

"See?" he said. "Bad acting."

Gemma sank down into a gray armchair, looking upset, while Jude fished his book out from the couch cushions, the orange cover garish against the room's beige tones. "Takes one to know one," she said, pointing at it.

"Fuck you," Connor said, his blood loud in his ears.

"Fuck *you*," Jude shot back so quickly that Connor almost took a step backward. But he didn't. He stood where he was, arms folded across his chest, while she waved the book at him like an angry lawyer at a trial. "How could you?"

"How could I what?" he asked, indignant.

"Write about us."

"It's fiction."

"It's our lives."

"It's a metaphorical interpretation of some of the events of—"

Jude groaned. "Please spare us the writing-workshop nonsense."

"You know this is different, Connor," Gemma said in a placating tone. "It's not exactly like writing about a World War II soldier—"

"World War I," Connor corrected.

"Or a guy who gets lost in the Mayan ruins—"

"Aztec ruins," he said, exasperated. He grabbed the bottle of champagne from the ice bucket and tucked it under his arm. When he pulled the cork out, the release sounded like a gunshot. He was the only one who didn't flinch. "This is such bullshit," he said as he poured himself a too-full glass. "I'm an artist. This is how I process things, through my books."

Jude rolled her eyes in an exaggerated fashion. Roddy held out his half-empty glass for Connor to top up. Gemma rubbed her temples as if she was already exhausted by this conversation.

"I'm allowed to write about my life," he said, then glanced over at Jude, who was now leaning against the desk at the back of the room, one leg crossed over the other, looking annoyingly calm and cool in an elegant jumpsuit. "You should understand that better than anyone. You tell stories for a living too."

Her face was stony. "Not about us."

"I told you," Connor said, "it's fiction."

Gemma sat forward in the chair. They were all still wearing black from the funeral, and it made everything feel somber. "Connor," she said sternly, the way she used to talk to him sometimes when they were kids. "You should've asked."

He stared at her, the sheer unfairness of it all welling up inside him. "You would've said no."

"Well, if you thought that," Jude said with a kind of smug satisfaction, "then you should understand why we're so upset about it now."

"I was just trying to tell a story," he insisted. "And maybe make some sense out of our fucking mess of a childhood. That's not exactly a crime. Haven't you ever heard the expression 'write what you know'?"

"You don't know anything," Jude said, steely-eyed. "A *hotel* fire? Honestly, Connor."

"It wasn't supposed to be—"

"You wrote about Mom! And you managed to bring up the most traumatic event of our childhood as a way to make some money," she said, clapping her hands a few times very slowly, the sound surprisingly loud in the otherwise quiet room. "Well done. Good for you. I hope you're happy."

"Don't worry," he said, walking over to the other armchair and sitting down heavily, his champagne sloshing. "It's not making any money anyway."

Jude gave him a pitying look. "That just makes it worse. You sold us out for nothing."

There was a knock on the door. "Turndown service," someone called.

All four of them answered at once: "No thanks."

"I'm sorry if I'm the only one brave enough to take a hard look at our childhood," Connor said after a moment, regarding each of them in turn. "But you're not angry with me. You're angry with her. For leaving us. For the fire. For being so stupid as to—"

"Stop," Jude said. "You don't know what you're talking about."

But Connor wasn't finished. "For only showing up once a year even before all that. And for pretty much never acting like a real mom. You're angry with her, but you can never admit it because she's gone now. And because you put her on such a pedestal when she was here."

He addressed this last part to Jude, who shook her head. "I did not," she said. "I never—"

"It's true," Gemma said, looking at her sadly. "You were always so starry-eyed about her. She didn't deserve it."

"She didn't care about us," Connor agreed. "All she cared about was following some wildly unrealistic dream."

Jude's eyes flashed. "She cared about me. I know for a fact she did."

"She was jealous of you," Roddy said quietly from where he was still standing in the corner of the room nearest the door, looking like he wished he were anywhere else. "Your career—it was what she always wanted. It's the whole reason she left."

Jude stared at him. "I didn't have a career then. I was just a kid."

"A really talented kid," Roddy said.

"She knew you were better than her," Connor agreed. "She knew you were going to be great."

Jude shook her head. "It would be crazy to be jealous of your own daughter," she said in a small voice, and Gemma made a face that clearly said, *Uh-huh.*

"You were the only one who could never see through her," Connor went on. "She had you completely under her spell. The rest of us, we all saw it. But you never wanted to believe what she really—"

"That's enough," Roddy said, and an uneasy silence fell, the air in the room going sour. "Why are we even making this about Mom?"

Connor shrugged. "Isn't everything?"

Roddy walked past them to the back of the room, where he slid open the glass door to the balcony and stepped outside. For a long moment, he stood there with his back to them, his elbows on the railing, the sky laced with gold, the Savannah River twinkling below. "We just buried Dad," he said eventually. "Seems like the least we can do is focus on him for once."

"Like he focused on us?" Gemma said, then clapped a hand over her mouth, looking surprised. "God, sorry. I didn't mean that."

Roddy turned around. "Obviously you did. You were always the hardest on him."

"Can you blame me?"

"We all know it wasn't always ideal," Roddy said from the balcony, "the way things were. But it wasn't like—"

"It's easy to think fondly of them," Gemma said, her voice suddenly full of heat, "when you were protected from the worst of it. But being here today, saying goodbye to Dad, remembering it all . . . I feel like a soldier who comes back from war and never wants to talk about it again."

Connor made a face. "Don't you think that's a little dramatic?"

"Sometimes I don't know if it's dramatic enough," Gemma said evenly.

"We had fun," Jude insisted, her face full of longing. "All those trips . . ."

"Those weren't fun," Gemma said. "They were scary. You guys know that, right? She had absolutely no interest in being a parent even when she was pretending to be one."

Jude's face was flushed now. "That's not fair."

"She left us," Gemma said. "Repeatedly! And she almost got you killed. And somehow you're still defending her after all this time?" She looked out at the open balcony doors, where Roddy was still leaning against the railing. "And don't get me started on Dad. He knew how irresponsible she was, and he still just waved goodbye and let us drive off with her again and again. It wasn't *fun*. It was fucked up. And clearly you don't get that if you two are still defending them, and you"—she turned her angry gaze on Connor—"are milking it for entertainment value."

"Gemma," Connor began, but she shook her head.

"No," she said with force. She pointed at his book, which was still sitting on the couch. "It wasn't your story to tell. *I* was the one who kept the wheels from coming off that whole time. Did it ever even occur to you guys that maybe the reason it all seemed fun is because I was there, making sure nothing bad happened? That the reason you all got to grow up to be so fucking extraordinary was because I was the one worrying about all the ordinary things for you?"

They were silent for a moment, her words ringing in the quiet room.

"We know, Gem," Roddy said softly, and as he walked in from the balcony, he briefly rested a hand on her shoulder. "But we also didn't ask you to do that."

She twisted to look at him. "I didn't exactly have a choice."

"It's not that we're not grateful," Jude said carefully. "Because we are. Obviously. But you also can't use it as an excuse forever."

Gemma frowned at her. "An excuse for what?"

Jude glanced at Connor and Roddy, as if for backup. When they both remained silent, she turned back to Gemma and said, "For playing it safe."

"Oh, fuck you, Jude," Gemma said, eyes flashing. "It's so unbelievably condescending to assume that just because I'm not famous I'm not happy. Because I am. And I know this might come as a shock to you, but I wouldn't trade my life for any of yours. Not for a second."

Roddy looked aggrieved by this. "What's so wrong with our lives? We're doing what we love."

"Great," Gemma said. "Good for you guys. But this idea of the Extraordinary Endicotts—you must realize how toxic it is. How toxic *she* was for only caring about—"

Jude shook her head. "Just because you never understood her, that doesn't mean—"

"Wake up, Jude," Gemma said, her voice harsh. "There was nothing to understand. She was an irresponsible narcissist who decided she had better things to do than be our mom. You're never going to be able to move on until you can admit that to yourself."

"Move on from what?" Jude asked, picking up her glass with a trembling hand.

"From pretending she was this magical being who flitted in and out of your life and left all her dreams in your care," Gemma said. And then, a bit more gently, she added, "I have no illusions about the kind of person she was. What I don't understand is what kind of person looks up to someone like that."

Jude blinked a few times, as if trying not to cry, and Connor saw Roddy clock this, then square his shoulders and turn to Gemma.

"Hey," he said. "I think that's enough."

But Gemma was in no mood for this. "Stay out of it, Roddy."

He shook his head, undeterred. "Don't you think we've all—"

"I'm talking to Jude," she said, then glanced over at Connor with a knowing look. "This is just like in the book."

Roddy frowned. "What?"

"Your character," Gemma told him, "is always swooping in to defend Jude's character."

Connor cleared his throat. "They're not characters, actually. I mean . . . they are. But they're not technically you guys."

Nobody was listening.

Jude's eyes were fixed on Roddy, a curious expression on her face. "She's right," she finally said to him. "We're not kids anymore. I can fight my own battles now."

He seemed to visibly deflate. "I know that."

"I could fight them then too."

"I know," he said, sinking down onto a chair. "Of course. It's just . . . we've always been a team."

"Yeah, a two-headed monster," Gemma said, and when they looked at her, she shrugged. "That's what Connor called you guys in the book."

"I stole it from you," he said with amusement. "You said that once about them."

Gemma seemed surprised. "Did I?"

"I thought it was fiction," Roddy said, glaring at him.

"Forget about the book," Jude said. "It's not true anyway."

Connor sighed. "Can we please move on from this? I get it. You didn't like the book. If you kept the receipt, I bet you can still return it."

Jude took a long swig of her champagne, draining the glass, then stared at him evenly from across the room. "You didn't even get it right."

"Jude, come on," he said, impatient now. "You were just saying it was too true. Now it's not true enough?"

"You weren't there that night," she said, her voice oddly void of emotion. "None of you were. You don't know what it was really—" She stopped and stared down at her empty glass. When she looked up at him again, her eyes were blazing. "You put our story out into the world like it was the truth, and you didn't even get it right."

Connor felt a great weariness pass over him. "I don't know what you want from me, Jude."

"I want you to take it back."

He glanced over at Gemma, forever the referee, but she only shrugged.

"Obviously," Connor told Jude, "I can't do that."

Her face was hard and set. "Then I want an apology."

"Sure," he said. "Yeah. Fine. I'm sorry if you feel like—"

"Nope," Jude said, cutting him off. She twirled the stem of the glass between her fingers. "A real apology. No *I'm sorry if*s. That's actually worse than not apologizing at all."

"Fine. I'm sorry *that*—" he began, in a weak attempt at lightening the mood, and before he realized what was happening, something went whizzing by his ear. He ducked just as Jude's champagne glass shattered against the wall behind him in a bright-sounding, confetti-like burst of glass.

"Jesus," he said, touching the side of his head where he'd felt it whoosh past. "What the hell?"

"Grow up, Connor," Jude said, already pushing past him to the door. When it slammed behind her, Connor's heart juddered in his chest. For a few seconds, the three of them sat there in stunned silence, the only sound the rush of wind from the open door of the balcony.

Finally, Connor said, "Now I see why Mom needed a break from us."

He'd meant it as a joke, but Gemma looked over at him, her eyes rimmed with red. "Maybe we need a break from each other," she said quietly, so quietly he might have missed it. But he didn't. He heard every word.

"Maybe we do," he said.

Jude

North Dakota

2025

A baby, Jude thinks as she hurries to pull on a pair of jeans. The hardwood floor is icy against her bare feet, and she hops around for a second before sitting to put on a clean pair of socks. When she looks up, she can see herself in the mirror above the wooden dresser, her face pale. She shivers and thinks it again: *A baby.*

Jude has never imagined herself with kids of her own. It's hard to know how much of that stems from the obvious—that her life is unpredictable and she values her freedom—and how much is tied up in having watched her mother stumble so badly at the job. But Aunt Jude? That she can do. It will be different with Gemma's baby. Not like with Rosie and Hugh, who drifted away from her in the messiness of a family drama that wasn't their fault. She'll find a way to make it up to them. But this time—with Gemma's baby—Jude will do better. This time, she'll be there. Or at least she'll try.

She tugs on a thick cashmere sweater and then pads over to the window and nudges back the curtain. The sun is fully up now, glinting off the snow, and it's all so bright she has to blink a few times. Her eyes travel from the lake—indistinguishable from the rest of the world except for its blankness, a sprawling canvas of uninterrupted white—to the driveway below, then out to the road, and she realizes there's no way they're going to be getting out of here today.

She should be panicking. Her team certainly will be. Tomorrow is the Oscar Nominees Luncheon, a major event in the lead-up to the big night, full of press, members of the Academy, and studio reps. It's a chance to hobnob and mingle and schmooze, and she knows that missing it will come at a price. Her agent will be in full catastrophe mode. Her manager will be trying to figure out if there's a way to airlift her out of the middle of nowhere. And her publicist will be making calls all day, trying to manage the optics and mitigate the damage.

But what can she do? Snow is snow is snow.

The truth is that she's a bit relieved. She woke up this morning with a racing heart, knowing it was her last chance to do what she came here to do. Her last chance to tell her siblings the truth. This delay gives her more time to work up the nerve.

When she walks downstairs, everyone is up and dressed. Gemma is floating around the kitchen as she fixes herself breakfast, her face flushed, and when she meets Jude's eyes across the room, they both smile, the secret between them buoyant as a balloon. Jude is seized by a sudden, unexpected burst of happiness. The fire is blazing and the cabin feels cozy and she's here with her family, a bonus day, valuable and unexpected. What matters is that they're all together. Her secrets can wait a little longer.

"Hugh," she says, clapping her hands, and he whirls around from where he's pretending to pick the nose of a metal buffalo sculpture. "What's the plan, dude?"

He looks mystified. "Uh, we do something fun?"

"Great call right there," she says, and then she glances around at the others, trying to figure out what comes next. Winston and Roddy are sitting glumly on opposite ends of the room, avoiding each other's eyes; Connor and Annie also seem to be avoiding each other, but with a very different sort of energy. Rosie is flopped over the side of an armchair, looking massively over it all. Only Gemma, who is peeling a banana with a dreamy expression, looks happy enough to be here.

Jude's eyes land on the wooden cabinet near the window. "How about a board game?" she says, moving around the couch to pick one out. "Yahtzee? Candy Land? Connect Four?"

"You must be joking," Roddy says. "You broke my finger playing that game."

"It wasn't broken," Jude says lightly. "Just a little jammed."

He holds up his hand. "It's *still* crooked."

"Hey," Connor says, and they all look over at him. "You know we're stuck here, right?"

Jude shrugs. "Not forever."

"But at least an extra day," Connor points out. "An extra day in a cabin in the middle of the woods with no electricity."

Roddy groans. "Terrific," he says at the same time Winston mutters, "Bloody brilliant."

Annie has walked over to the window, her hair in two neat braids. "I bet it'll start to burn off soon," she says, peering at the flat gray sky. "And the plows will probably make it out later in the day. What time are your flights?"

"Earlier than that," Gemma says, a hand moving unconsciously to her stomach. Jude knows she must be eager to get home to Mateo, to share the news in person, and she feels a stubborn burst of loyalty to her new game plan.

"Come on," she says. "It's not that bad."

"Don't you have the Oscar luncheon tomorrow?" Winston asks, and they all look sideways at him. "What? I enjoy pop culture."

"It's fine," Jude says. "There's nothing we can do anyway, so we might as well make the best of it. Think of it as some extra time to enjoy each other's company."

Winston snorts. Roddy rolls his eyes. Gemma gazes worriedly out the window.

"Come on, you guys," Jude says, suddenly impatient. "It's not like I dragged you out here."

"Uh," says Connor, "it's exactly like you dragged us out here."

Jude makes a face at him. "You came of your own free will. And we've had fun, right?" She looks around at them. "Remember when we went sledding?"

Hugh is tossing a balding tennis ball up and down, up and down. He catches it with a satisfying *thwack* and frowns over at her. "Yeah. That was only yesterday."

"I know, I just—" She sighs and starts again: "What about dinner last night? That was good, right? All of us together again."

"Jude—" Connor says, but then Hugh throws the ball again, this time a little too high, and it bounces off one of the huge wooden rafters, ricocheting with surprising speed toward the coffee table, where the candles they relit earlier this morning are sunk deep in pools of wax. In a flash, one of them tips over onto the pile of magazines beside it, and the one on top—a tattered edition of *Anglers Journal*—immediately goes up in flames.

Jude is the farthest away from it but the fastest to move, hurrying backward and away, her heart hammering and her eyes wide as the pages begin to burn. The others respond with wildly varying degrees of bravery and usefulness: Roddy and Winston yelp and dart away, Rosie stares at the fire with fascination, Connor grabs Hugh, who immediately begins to cry, and Annie and Gemma—clearly the most levelheaded of the bunch—both have the wherewithal to run over and fill glasses with water, then hurry back to douse the flames, leaving only a smoldering pile of ash.

The stillness that follows is so sudden it doesn't even feel like quiet. It's more of a pause, a break in time, like a skipping record or a glitch in the system, like the whole world has been momentarily frozen in place. Jude stands there, motionless, one hand wrapped around her other arm, where, underneath her sweater, she can almost swear her scar begins to throb.

"Well," Connor says, still holding Hugh to his chest. "That could've been worse."

Rosie laughs shakily, then looks over at her brother. "You almost burned the whole place down," she says, and the others exchange uneasy glances. "What?" she says. "He did."

"Rosie." Connor shakes his head, his gaze sliding over to Jude, who moves her flattened palm to her heart, as if checking to make sure it's still working. "Let's not . . ."

"Are you okay?" Gemma says to her, from where she's standing beside the burnt pile of magazines, and Jude manages a nod.

"What?" Rosie asks, surveying the room. "Why is everyone being so weird?"

Gemma looks at Connor in surprise. "They don't know?"

"Know what?" Rosie asks.

All three of Jude's siblings are staring at her now; she can feel the heat of it on her face, though her eyes are on the window, all that dazzling snow. She rubs her hands together, though she's not cold, not right now; she's just waiting for the moment to pass, wondering if she should let it.

Connor tugs at the collar of his shirt. "I don't know," he says, then stops. "I just never— It didn't seem like something—" He looks uncharacteristically lost. "It didn't seem important for them to know."

"Know what?" Rosie demands again. When her dad fails to answer, she turns to Gemma. "Tell us."

But Gemma is still watching Connor with a baffled expression. "You wrote about it in your book."

From across the room, where she's been leaning quietly against a wall, as if trying her best to recede from the scene, Annie looks over at Connor in surprise. "There was really a fire?"

"It wasn't—" Connor says to her; then his gaze shifts to Gemma. "That was fiction. It wasn't . . ." He starts to protest again, then shakes his head. "It wasn't a hotel."

"What wasn't?" Rosie wants to know.

Roddy glances over at Jude, whose thoughts are so loud she can barely follow what's happening. *Now,* her brain is telling her, but still she remains frozen, as if she's watching it all from a great distance.

"It was a car," Roddy says, his eyes still on hers. She blinks at him a few times, and then he turns back to the others. "In real life, it was a car."

Connor nods once, then twice, and then he turns to Rosie with a serious expression. "When we were kids, there was an accident. Our mom, your grandmother—something happened." He casts a glance around the room, waiting for one of the others to jump in, and when they don't—when everyone remains silent—he continues: "There was a fire. She accidentally set a car on fire."

"What?" Rosie asks, shocked. "How?"

"It was an accident," Connor repeats, lifting his eyes to meet Jude's. "And everyone was okay. But Jude was in there when it happened, which was obviously a very scary thing, and afterward, our mom—"

"No," Jude says, and they all look at her. She shakes her head back and forth a few times, because the right words haven't worked their way to the surface yet. But she knows they're close. She knows it's time.

"It's okay," Connor says gently, pulling Hugh closer to him. "They're old enough to hear the story."

There's a feeling Jude sometimes gets right before they call "Action" on set, where her insides and outsides stop matching up. Inside, her heart is bounding. But outside, she feels a sudden, preternatural calm.

"No," she says, her voice alarmingly measured, "I mean it wasn't Mom who did it. She wasn't the one who started the fire."

They all stare at her, uncomprehending.

Jude steels herself. "It was me."

Texas

2001

JUDE COULDN'T SLEEP THAT NIGHT. IT WAS COLD FOR
Texas, the air bristling with a chill she could feel even beneath the
thin motel blanket. Beside her, Gemma was snoring softly, making a
sound like a whistle, and on the other side of the room, the boys had
their own double bed. In past years, this had been plenty of space
for the two of them, but now their feet hung off the end of it, their
arms splayed out over the sides. At the foot of their bed, wedged
into a corner beneath the window, their mom was curled up on a
cot, the light from the moon peeking between the curtains to make
shadows across her face.

The red numbers of the alarm clock switched over from 2:07 to
2:08, and Jude rolled onto her back with a sigh. Nobody else stirred.
She stared at the ceiling, restless.

Earlier, they'd gone for dinner at a barbecue place up the road—
nothing fancy, just a few scattered tables behind a smoke-filled
shack. But there were fairy lights strung through the trees, and the
air smelled tangy and sweet.

"A toast," Frankie said as soon as their food arrived, with a clatter
of metal trays. She lifted her bottle of beer. "To Jude."

Jude squirmed as the others raised their glasses. "Thanks," she said, wishing she'd never told her mom about the letter, which had arrived the week before the trip. "But it's not really that big of a—"

"It is," Frankie insisted. "It's a very big deal."

"It's an acting class," Connor said, picking up his sandwich. He looked at Jude over the bun, then said through a mouthful of brisket, "What? It is."

Frankie shook her head. "It's an intensive workshop. At one of the most prestigious art schools in the world. And she got a scholarship." She turned back in Jude's direction. "It's an extremely big deal."

Jude ducked her head, torn between pride and embarrassment. She'd applied to the program at the suggestion of her drama teacher, who'd cast her as the lead in the spring performance of *The Sound of Music,* even though she wasn't much of a singer and could rarely hit the high notes. He'd mentioned the workshop so casually and matter-of-factly that Jude felt the need to pretend that she already knew all about it, that she'd always been aware of the world-class arts institution just twenty minutes up the road, apparently a reliable feeder to summer stock programs and theater schools alike, and that—like every other drama kid her age—she'd always dreamed of getting a chance to attend.

She'd enlisted Roddy to film her monologue from *Macbeth—Out, damned spot! Out, I say!*—and in spite of his shaky camera work and her obvious inexperience, a letter had arrived a month later informing her that she'd gotten in. For weeks, she'd walked around with that single sheet of paper tucked into the back pocket of her jeans, like it was a ticket for a flight she didn't want to miss. Her drama teacher told her it would change her life, and when he said it, Jude felt like a Christmas tree whose lights had just switched on for the very first time. She thought it would be the same with Frankie, that surely her own excitement would be magnified by her mom's, but they'd been on the road a week now, and somehow, it didn't quite feel that way.

There were summers when Jude would've reveled in Frankie's stories of playing "The Woman" in a Minneapolis production of *Death of a Salesman,* about how an ice storm nearly ruined opening night, and how the guy playing Willy Loman once showed up drunk during a matinee and slurred his way through the entire first act. But Jude was fourteen now and starting to see the cracks in her mother's stories, particularly the main one, the one that had dictated all of their lives: about the brilliant actress who simply hadn't caught a break, yet was still determined to chase her dreams, at the cost of everything else.

She just wasn't so sure it was a story she wanted for herself anymore.

"People who get this scholarship, who do this workshop," Frankie said as they sat around a table made out of a barrel, "they go on to be *famous.*" She spoke the word with a reverence that made the back of Jude's neck prickle. "I'm serious. They get picked from all over the country, and they go on to do big things. Broadway, Hollywood, you name it." She turned to Jude again. "It's a big fucking deal, kid. Don't let anyone tell you otherwise."

Now Jude stared through the darkness at the pocked ceiling of the motel, realizing that this was what she'd been waiting for the whole time, from the moment she first got the scholarship letter. This was the whole reason she'd been carrying it around in her pocket. Maybe even the whole reason she'd auditioned in the first place. To see her mom look at her that way.

It was what she thought she'd always wanted. Yet somehow now it felt like too much.

Jude placed a hand over her heart, felt its steady drumbeat, then sat up in bed. She glanced over to see if this had woken Gemma or anyone else, but the room remained still, so she kicked off the blanket and stepped onto the dingy carpet. Quietly, she crept over to the jumble of bags near the closet, dug around for a hoodie and a pair of flip-flops.

Then—almost as an afterthought—she grabbed the car keys from where her mom had left them on the desk, the metal flashing in the light of the moon.

Jude

North Dakota

2025

G emma is the first to speak. "What do you mean?" she asks, and
when there's no answer, she asks it again, her voice more insis-
tent: "Jude. What do you mean it was you?"

Jude swallows hard, already wishing she could take it back. But it's
too late for that now. This is what she came here to do.

They're all staring at her, not just her siblings but the others too,
Winston and Annie and Rosie and Hugh.

Jude remembers something she learned from her high school drama
teacher, a trick to calm the nerves. Take deep breaths, and exhale for
twice as long as you inhale.

She tries it now.

A short, jagged breath in, then a long, steady one out.

Right, she thinks, looking around at all those faces. *Now or never.*

Texas

2001

BEYOND THE POOLS OF YELLOW LIGHT FROM THE MOTEL, the world was almost shockingly dark. Their car was parked at the very edge of the lot, beside a field with tall grass, which rustled in the wind. Above, the moon was tucked into the pocket of the clouds, the sky blank-faced and starless. Jude could just barely hear the low hoot of an owl over the sound of her heart.

When she found the old Honda, she unlocked the door and slipped into the driver's seat, then fit the key into the ignition and turned it. She was still two years away from getting her license, but as the engine hummed to life, the thought came into her head anyway: *Go.* It would be so easy to drive off down one of those endless roads, the way she'd watched her mom do again and again. Instead, she flicked on the interior light and reached into the backseat for her notebook. The letter was pressed inside, the page soft and worn, with wrinkles that felt more like seams at this point. She unfolded it and stared at the words: *Congratulations! We're delighted to offer you a scholarship for our autumn theater workshop . . .*

There was an orange lighter in the cup holder, and Jude glanced at it, then at the letter in her hands, wondering what it would feel like to watch the opportunity go up in smoke, to simply not go.

She knew that being good at something and loving it were not the same thing. She enjoyed acting, but it was hard to imagine ever caring about it so much—caring about anything so much!—that she'd leave her family for it, sling coffee in random cities to make it work. But what did she know? Talent, she already understood, was like a drug. So were dreams. She could see it in the way her mom spoke about the dinky productions she was in, the way Roddy lived and breathed soccer and Connor disappeared into his stories. Sometimes it seemed simpler to be someone like her dad or like Gemma, to love many things instead of one, to be content enough with just that. But there was a thrill that came with dazzling people, with doing something so well that nobody could look away.

Jude stared once more at the paper: *Congratulations!*

She picked up the lighter, then glanced at the door of the car, where in the little pocket between the lock and the handle, two neatly rolled joints lay side by side like an old couple in bed. Jude didn't know if her mom had ever smoked pot before she left them, but she knew Frankie did now—not because she'd ever seen her do it, but because the earthy smell of it was everywhere: in the car, in her hair, in her clothes. Jude picked up one of the joints and pressed it to her nose for a moment before slipping it into the pocket of her hoodie. Then, before she could think better of it, she reached for the other one and flicked at the lighter.

Jude

North Dakota

2025

"I was the only one in the car when it happened," Jude says, covering her face with her hands. "I was the one who fell asleep."

Roddy stares at her, open-mouthed. "No."

"It was my fault," she says miserably. "All of it."

Texas

2001

WHEN JUDE WOKE, IT WAS TO THE SMELL OF SMOKE AND the sound of knocking. She felt the heat before she understood the source of it, a tingly feeling that went up her spine and choked her lungs. Her eyelids were heavy; it took a few long seconds for her to come to, and when she did, she registered first that the car was on fire, then that it had filled with smoke, and, finally, the frantic face in the window beside her, the hands pounding hard on the glass.

She was still sluggish and confused, slow-moving even as the flames grew around her and the smoke thickened. Something bit her upper arm, and it took her a moment to realize it wasn't a bite at all, but a burn. She huddled against the window and felt the pounding, the vibration of her mom's shapeless screams in one ear. She twisted to open the door, her hands slipping as she tried to yank the handle. But that door—famous for getting jammed—refused to budge.

Her mom pointed to the back, her face still etched with fear, her hands still scrabbling at the glass, and Jude pushed herself up, trying to avoid the worst of the flames as she started to climb into the backseat, her knee slipping on the console, coughing as she hurtled herself over.

She heard a pop in the front and wondered vaguely if the car could explode—it couldn't, right?—but there was no time to consider this further. The plastic of the lock was starting to melt, and for a brief, terrifying moment, she thought it wouldn't work. But she clawed at it frantically until it finally sprang up, and when she managed to shove the door open, the cool night air came flooding in like a salve, like a benediction, like a second chance.

Jude

North Dakota

2025

Nobody says anything. The silence is unbearable.

"I don't understand," Gemma finally manages. "Mom said—"

"She lied," Jude tells her. "She didn't want me to get in trouble. Or lose that scholarship. She wanted to—"

"Protect you," Gemma says, her face hard. Because, of course, she'd failed to protect the rest of them in the bargain. She couldn't have known, when she told the police she was the one who'd fallen asleep with a joint in her hand, that it would mean the end of her relationship with her kids. Or at least three out of the four of them.

Connor sinks onto the couch, absentmindedly pulling Hugh down along with him, his eyes faraway. Roddy twists his mouth up to one side and turns toward the snowy window. Winston and Annie each seem to be trying their best to melt into the furniture.

"You should've told us," Gemma says, her face flushed with anger. "We had a right to know."

"Gem," Jude says, a plea in her voice. "I was only fourteen."

"But later," Connor says. "I get that you were probably in shock that night. But what about later? After Dad wouldn't let us see her anymore? Or after we stopped taking her calls? How could you not tell us then?"

Because of this, Jude wants to say. *Because you'd all look at me this way. Even Roddy. And it would be unbearable. Because I'm a coward. Because I wish it had been different. Because nothing I can say will make it better.*

"Because," she says after a moment, "she made me promise."

Roddy's eyes flash with disappointment. "We thought she'd nearly killed you."

"No," Jude says, and it comes out as a whisper. She says it again: "No."

"If we'd known the truth," Gemma says, "everything would've been different. We wouldn't have lost her. At least not then. You should've told us. You owed us that much."

Jude feels like she's underwater, like the air is filled with pressure, like it's all bearing down on her. She closes her eyes. "I'm telling you now."

"Now?" Gemma says, the word heavy with an unfamiliar scorn. Her eyes are hard and flinty. "What good does it do us now?"

Texas

2001

AFTERWARD, JUDE WOULD WONDER HOW HER MOM KNEW where to find her.

But she never asked.

She was just there, half-dragging Jude away from the burning car, Jude's legs scrambling through the grass, her chest heaving and her mouth gritty with ash. When they were far enough away, they collapsed on the ground, both of them still breathing hard, still too shocked for tears. Frankie kept her arms around Jude, and the weight of it felt like the only thing pinning her down, the only thing that was real. It wasn't until later that she realized her mom had taken the other joint out of her pocket and slipped it into her own.

By the time the others got there, the car was already a bonfire in the night.

Together, the five of them watched it burn.

Roddy

North Dakota

2025

If there were a way to walk out the door without it feeling quite so dramatic, Roddy would do it. But it turns out that when you're in the middle of a conversation like this—the room charged and tense, half the family in tears and the other half staring blankly at the floor—there's no good manner of exit.

He doesn't look at Jude as he heads for the door, because he knows that the expression on her face will break his heart. Roddy's role has always been to stand by her no matter what. That time she got caught shoplifting a horse figurine from their local toy store and he covered for her. The many times she forgot it was her night to do the dishes and he did them without anyone asking. The time she got a part in an off-Broadway production of *Twelfth Night* and he took a bus from D.C. after a match to catch the last thirty minutes of opening night.

He's always been there for her. Automatically. Without question. That's just how it works with them.

But right now, it all feels like too much.

He avoids Jude's eyes, and Winston's too. He avoids looking at anyone, because he's not trying to make a statement or cause a scene. He just needs to get out of this cabin.

When he stumbles out onto the porch, letting the door swing shut behind him, he takes a few deep, gulping breaths, like he's just stepped off a spaceship, like he hasn't breathed in far too long. His face stings from the cold, but it makes him feel immediately sharper. He stands there, staring down at the lake spread before him, the apron of snow dotted with animal tracks, and then he hurries down the icy steps, grabbing the banister to keep from slipping.

As he trudges over to the shed, Roddy tries to imagine a version of the fire where the secret had been his, where he'd been the one to fuck up, and he knows for sure that even if he'd managed to keep it from the others, he never would've been able to keep it from Jude. The fact that she never told him hurts almost as much as the rest of it.

When he reaches the shed, he realizes that while he'd grabbed his coat from the hook as he was leaving the house, he'd forgotten a hat and gloves, and his fingers burn with cold as he jiggles the metal handle. It takes his eyes a few seconds to adjust once he gets it open, and then he steps over piles of old equipment to reach the cross-country skis in the back. He finds some poles on the wooden floor in front of them, scattered like pick-up sticks, and grabs a couple, then spots a pair of puffy ski mittens on a shelf and takes them too.

He's still gathering everything, his fingers numb, when he hears a voice behind him.

"Oh, sorry," Annie says as he turns around. She's dressed in snow gear too, a winter hat pulled down low over her forehead. "I didn't realize you were . . . I was just gonna give you all some space." She points to the snowshoes. "Thought I'd get out of everyone's way for a bit."

Roddy steps aside to make room. "You're welcome to it."

"No," she says with a wave. "I'll go take a walk or something."

"Is there anywhere to go around here?" Roddy asks, motioning at the skis. "I really need to clear my head."

She nods. "There's a bar. O'Brien's. Nothing fancy, and I have no idea if it'll have power, but it's probably your best bet. Maybe three or four miles up along the main road," she says, pointing; then she takes off her hat, which is pink with a silvery puff at the top. "You'll need one of these."

In spite of himself, Roddy laughs. "Just my style," he says, but he smiles as he takes it. "Thank you."

She nods. "Figured you might not be ready to go back inside yet."

"You figured right," he says, letting the skis fall onto the snow with a thud. "Tell them I'll be back later."

"Hope it helps," she says.

"The bar or the skiing?"

She smiles. "Both."

As soon as Roddy is in motion, he feels better. His body, unreliable though it is these days, slips into gear. His legs glide forward and back, the skis cutting a clean path through the snow. His arms move rhythmically with each stride, his heart pumping wildly under his layers, the sweat frozen on his face. His eyes are watering, and his bad knee is grinding, but his mind is blissfully clear. He isn't thinking about Jude's pronouncement or his fight with Winston or anything else. He's just skiing.

Along the main road, there are tire tracks from a few bold vehicles, the grooves already slick with ice, but the plows haven't reached it yet, so it's mostly unusable. On the side opposite the lake, there are endless blank fields, the snow broken only by the occasional cluster of miserable-looking cows. But above him, the clouds are starting to burn off; there are small glimpses of blue in between them, like a mirage, and Roddy is feeling almost giddy by the time he comes to an empty intersection with a lonely gas station on one corner and a squat brick building beside it. Above the window, it says O'BRIEN'S in neon-green letters, and to his relief, it's lit up like a lantern, bright against the monochromatic landscape, an oasis in the middle of all that white.

"Civilization," Roddy mutters under his breath.

Even from outside, he can hear the music, lively after so much quiet. He leaves his equipment leaning up against the brick wall, then heaves open the door, surprised by how elated he is to be met with the smell of beer and too many warm bodies. The bar is huge, so open you can see clear across to the row of video games in the very back, and the tin beer signs and wood-paneled walls give the feeling of being in someone's suburban basement. But the power is on and the place is packed; Bruce Springsteen is playing on the jukebox, and people are jammed into booths with plates of hot food in front of them, happy to be somewhere warm and bright after the big storm.

As far as Roddy is concerned, it's heaven.

He threads his way over to the bar, then grabs an empty stool, trying to catch the bartender's eye.

"What," says the guy sitting next to him, his voice filled with amusement, "did you ski here or something?"

Roddy wipes a hand absently across his damp forehead, but he's having a hard time caring what he looks like right now. He scans the labels on the bottles of whiskey behind the bar. "Yup."

"Wow," the guy says, evidently impressed. "I was only kidding. But I guess you must be used to this kind of snow."

"Not really," Roddy says, lifting a hand to the bartender, who doesn't see him. "I'm not from around here."

"Me neither," the guy says, then lets out a laugh. "We don't get a lot of this in L.A."

Roddy glances over at him. He's wearing a plain gray sweatshirt and jeans, a Dodgers cap pulled low over his eyes, which are a startling shade of blue. Roddy squints, trying to place him, to figure out why he looks so familiar, but his mind feels too slow and too muddy to process this. "You look . . ." he begins, turning to face the man more fully. Then he shakes his head, as if trying to clear it. "Are you . . . I mean, you're not . . ."

The guy gives him a slightly weary smile. "Yeah. I am. But let's not . . ." He looks over his shoulder, then back at Roddy. "I mean, I'm happy to, like, sign a napkin or something, if you want, but if we could just keep this—"

Roddy blinks at him. "You're Spencer Nolan."

The actor flinches at the sound of the name, then grabs his beer. "You know, it's been kind of a long day, so maybe it would be better if—"

"No way," Roddy says, letting out a surprised laugh. "What are you doing here?"

Spencer now has his coat in one hand and his beer in the other. "It's a long story," he says, starting to push the stool back, clearly having decided it was a terrible idea to strike up a conversation with a sweaty stranger in an unfamiliar bar in the middle of North Dakota. "I think I'll just—"

"No, no," Roddy says, grabbing his arm, then immediately letting it go as the other man shakes him off. "Sorry. I should've— I'm Roddy. Jude's brother?"

Instantly, Spencer's face shifts. The strained look disappears, replaced by something more genuine, and Roddy understands what Jude sees in him, what the whole world does, really. His smile lights up his entire face, making him appear suddenly boyish, his blue eyes brightening. It's like there's a spotlight on him, like he's somehow shinier and more sparkly than all the rest of them. He sets his pint glass down so hard that beer sloshes out of it, looking for a moment like he might go in for a hug. Then he changes his mind and claps a hand on Roddy's shoulder.

"Dude!" he cries. "Roddy. I'm so sorry I didn't recognize you. I'm a big fan."

"You are?" Roddy asks, incredulous.

"Of course," he says with a grin. "Jude and I watch all your matches on TV. And she's shown me some of your highlights on YouTube too. I must've seen that one clip—you know that goal you scored against Chicago? the bicycle kick?—I bet I've watched it a hundred times."

"Wow," Roddy says, caught off guard by the image of Jude flipping through channels to find his matches. It's so unexpected that he feels his heart softening toward her at the very idea of it.

He's nothing if not easily won over.

"You were great," Spencer says, then he catches himself. "Still are."

Roddy smiles. "*Were* is probably more accurate," he admits. "But I'm still trucking along." He's about to make a joke about being old, but Spencer looks far too youthful and sunshiny for that sort of thing. "And hey, I'm a big fan of yours too."

This isn't quite true—he's only seen that one really popular movie of Spencer's, the one where he plays a knight. Still, it feels like the right thing to say. And he knows the next right thing too: *Jude's told me so much about you.* But he can't say it. Because she hasn't. Because she more or less disappeared from his life for three years and then turned up again armed with enough secrets to ruin everything in an entirely new way. Because she's unreliable and frustrating and careless. Because he's always needed her more than she's needed him. Because having Jude in your life is like trying to grab the tail of a comet and hoping for the best. Just like it was with their mother.

Roddy turns back to the bar, suddenly desperate for a drink. They're both silent as, for the second time, he tries unsuccessfully to flag down the bartender—a cute guy in a flannel shirt—and it takes Spencer lifting a hand for him to finally come over.

"Is he a fan too?" Roddy asks once he's got his whiskey and they're alone again.

Spencer laughs. "No, I'm a big tipper."

The jukebox switches over to Billy Joel, and behind them, a group of women begin to sing along. Roddy takes a long sip of his drink before turning back to Spencer. "I assume you're here for Jude?"

He nods. "She wasn't picking up her phone, and I got worried."

"So you flew here? In the middle of a storm?"

"Pretty much," he says, jabbing his thumb toward the door. "My car is stuck about a half mile up the road."

"Wow," Roddy says.

"Yeah. It was worse than I thought it'd be."

"No, I mean—you came all this way? For Jude?"

He nods. "Of course."

"So it's for real then, the two of you?"

If Spencer is surprised, he doesn't show it. "It is for me," he says sincerely. "But you'd have to ask Jude for herself."

Roddy takes another swig of whiskey as he absorbs this. "She's back at the cabin with the others," he says when he sets the glass down. "I just needed some time alone."

"Is she okay?"

"Who, Jude?" Roddy says with a little laugh. "She's fine. She's always fine."

Spencer's handsome face looks troubled, but he doesn't say anything. He just spins his beer glass on the scarred wooden bar.

"I'll tell you this much," Roddy says. "If she's half as good at acting as she is at keeping secrets, she'll be a shoo-in for this Oscar."

"I think she's a shoo-in either way, but I'm biased," Spencer says; then he flicks those blue eyes of his in Roddy's direction. "Can I ask you something?"

Roddy nods.

"Has she always been this way?"

"What," he says grimly, "reckless and self-centered?"

Spencer seems surprised by this. "No. I mean, has she always kept things so close to the vest?"

"Honestly," Roddy says, rattling the ice in his glass, "I used to think I knew her better than anyone in the world. But now? I have no idea. She's a total fucking mystery to me."

Spencer lifts his glass, then lowers it again, looking solemn and a little bit lost. "I'm having a similar experience at the moment," he says eventually, his brow creased beneath the brim of his hat. "I don't know if I'm handling it the right way. I wish I had a better idea of what to do. How to help. How to be there. How not to fuck things up. You know?"

Roddy shakes his head. "There's no guidebook when it comes to dealing with Jude."

"I suppose there isn't," Spencer says, looking thoughtful, then adds: "I guess that's one of the things I love about her."

Me too, Roddy thinks, but he doesn't say it.

Idaho

2022

THREE YEARS SOUNDS LIKE A LONG TIME. BUT YEARS ARE made up of days, and days go by with alarming speed.

They didn't plan not to see one another. At least not for very long. For a while, they simply retreated to their own corners of the map, each needing silence and space. A few weeks after the funeral, it was Roddy and Jude's birthday, and the group chat flickered back to life with a few perfunctory texts. There were other points of contact too. A FaceTime from Gemma to Rosie, where Connor popped on to say a brief and awkward hello. A congratulatory email when Connor won the National Book Award, and another when it was announced that Jude had landed a high-profile new role. But as time went on, the group chain fell mostly silent, and the individual texts slowed down, and the days continued to pile up as they all went on with their own lives.

Without their dad to anchor them at the holidays, those passed them by too, and eventually—like anything—it became a habit, the *not seeing* one another, and the weeks slipped by and then so did the years, and soon they had become four separate people in the world rather than a unit.

But they still thought of one another all the time.

That first Christmas, Jude sat around the fire with friends at the extravagant Sun Valley home of a director, nodding along to a story about an agent everyone knew, but really she was remembering the time Connor sat in front of the fire pit in their backyard with his feet propped up for so long that the soles of his shoes melted. When he stood up, they stuck to the ground like the gooey insides of the marshmallows they'd been roasting, and they laughed and laughed until the next morning, when their dad made them go out and scrape the rubber off the wooden deck, which only made them laugh some more.

Oregon

HOURS BEFORE A MATCH AGAINST THE TIMBERS, RODDY went for a walk to loosen up his knee and calm his nerves. It was something he did when they were playing in other cities, an old instinct—probably inherited from his mom—to see as much of a place as possible. As he made his way toward the river, he found himself staring up at the sign for Powell's, a rambling, block-long bookshop. He paused for a moment, thinking, then pushed open the door and walked inside.

"Morning," said a guy wearing thick-rimmed glasses and a button that read, *I like big books and I cannot lie.* "Can I help you find anything?"

"The children's section?" Roddy said, and if the bookseller was surprised by the request, he didn't show it. He just pointed in the right direction, and Roddy wound his way through stacks of books until he found it.

Gemma had loved *The Secret Garden* ever since she was a little girl, and though Roddy wasn't much of a reader himself, he had always made it a habit to check for new editions whenever he came across a bookstore. He knew which ones she already had, and had in fact been the one to buy many of them for her. The first time he'd been to her condo in Chicago, he'd blushed at the sight of them lined up on the shelf in her living room, shoulder to shoulder like old friends.

Every once in a while, he found something new, a beautiful cloth-bound edition or a fresh modern take on the jacket. But this time, all the covers were familiar.

He couldn't help buying one anyway.

Massachusetts

2022

AT A LECTURE IN BOSTON, ON THE HEELS OF WINNING THE National Book Award, Connor was surprised to look up during the signing and see his old college roommate, Brian.

"Dude," Connor said, standing up and moving around the table to give him a hug. Behind him, a line of fans—more than had come to all of his previous readings combined—shifted restlessly as they waited to meet him. "What are you doing here?"

"I came to see my old roommate now that he's famous," Brian said, clapping Connor on the back. "Though it seems you're not even the most famous member of your family these days."

Connor's smile froze. "Right. Yeah. She's doing really well."

"Any chance she's single at the moment?" Brian asked, half joking, half hopeful.

"No idea," Connor said flatly, and his old friend looked surprised.

"But you guys were so close."

"Yeah, she's just private about that stuff. You know how it is."

"Sure," Brian said, his face relaxing again. "Big Hollywood star now. I get it. But still, feel free to pass along my number, okay?"

"Sure," Connor said as he scribbled a note in the book. "Thanks for coming, man."

"Yeah, congrats on all your success. Your family must be really proud."

Connor nodded.

Ohio

2022

AFTER A LONG DAY OF MEETINGS IN COLUMBUS, GEMMA agreed to go to a sports bar with her co-workers. She would've much rather headed back to her hotel room—the only good thing about these kinds of business trips was ordering room service in her bathrobe—but the clients insisted on taking them out, and so they all settled into a corner booth and someone ordered a round of beers. Above them, there were rows of TVs tuned to every sport imaginable, and one of their clients—a twenty-something bald guy with a deep midwestern accent—kept flicking his eyes up to the one behind Gemma.

"Sorry," he said. "I'm being so rude. But I'm a huge soccer nerd."

Even before Gemma twisted to look at the screen, she knew. There was a tingling in the back of her neck, an almost supernatural awareness of him behind her, a small dot amid the many other small dots running across the green field. Still, she was surprised by the slight ache in her chest when she turned and spotted him sprinting for the ball.

"This is a big match," the guy said to her back as she watched, her eyes glued to the screen. "D.C. is in—"

"First place, but just barely," Gemma said, and when she turned around again, the guy looked pleasantly surprised.

"You follow soccer?"

"A little," she told him.

Louisiana

2023

ON A SHOOT IN NEW ORLEANS, JUDE NOTICED THAT ONE of the extras looked just like Roddy. He was wearing a jaunty page-boy cap that Roddy would never be caught dead in, and he had a scruffy reddish beard, but for a brief, impossible second, she thought it was him, and her heart quickened. All day, her eyes kept drifting in his direction. All day long, she stared.

Vermont

ON HIS FIRST EVER WEEKEND AWAY WITH WINSTON, Roddy noticed a woman reading Connor's book on the front porch of their bed-and-breakfast. She was sitting in a rocking chair, turning the pages with an expression of mild amusement, and as he stood there, he was surprised to see her laugh out loud at something. He reached for his phone automatically, wanting to snap a photo for Connor, but then—like a bolt slipping into a lock—the memory of that night in Savannah came thudding back, and he remembered the state of things. Still, he lingered there for a while longer, watching her turn the pages, studying her face, thinking of his brother.

Alaska

2023

ON A FAMILY CRUISE TO ALASKA—A LAST-DITCH EFFORT TO save his crumbling marriage—Connor stooped to pick up the itinerary that was slipped under the door of their cabin each morning. He carried it out to the verandah, where he sat looking out over the swirling gray water and misty spruce trees, breathing in the intoxicatingly fresh air, before glancing down to see that the film that would be playing in the ship's movie theater that night was one of Jude's.

He'd seen every single one of her films on opening night. They all had, no matter where they were, no matter what they were doing. Often, they'd gone to the premieres, but sometimes they were scattered around the country, so they'd each go on their own and chat afterward, or take selfies in the theater, sending them to the group with a frenzy of celebratory emojis.

That night, he left Nicola and the kids playing cards in one of the lounges and took the elevator down to the ship's theater, where he collected his free bag of popcorn and found a seat on the aisle.

As the movie started, he took a selfie with Jude's name on the screen behind him. But he couldn't bring himself to send it.

Iowa/South Dakota/Nebraska/ Wyoming/Colorado

2023

THAT SUMMER, GEMMA AND MATEO TOOK A ROAD TRIP out west, pushing their Subaru to its limits as it rattled through the big middle states. They visited the Iowa State Fair, gazed in awe at Mount Rushmore, got lost in a corn maze near Omaha, took fly-fishing lessons in Jackson Hole, then spent a few days hiking and white-water rafting in the wild landscape around Aspen, as it had been Mateo's dream to see the Rocky Mountains ever since he'd moved to America from Brazil as a college student.

It was a big trip for them, one they'd spent a long time planning for, and Gemma felt a powerful urge to capture it in some way that didn't include her phone. So for the first time since she was a kid, she bought a journal. It was different from the ones her mother had given each of them on that first road trip—those had colorful luggage stamps all over them and big spaces between each line, perfect for little-kid handwriting. This one was more elegant, a beautiful shade of turquoise with simple gold lettering, and when she first opened it, the spine gave way with a satisfying crack.

When she was younger, it had felt like a chore, writing down what they did on those trips. Connor was the only one who really kept up with it. But during this trip Gemma found it a pleasure, a way of reliving each day after it was done. She was already excited to read through it next year and the year after, to time-travel back to these moments in that way. It was almost enough to make her wish she hadn't thrown out her childhood journal after that night in Texas.

She wondered if the others still had theirs.

She wondered what they were doing this summer.

She wondered when she'd see them again.

All that month, she wrote, and she looked out the window of the car, and she wondered.

Nevada

2023

A MONTH AFTER HIS DIVORCE, CONNOR WENT TO LAS Vegas. By himself. Which was just about as depressing as it sounded. On the last day, after losing more money than he cared to admit, he sat down at the roulette table and put a chip on each of his family members' birthdays. He'd already tried everything else.

Watch this be the thing that works, he thought, and his eyes widened as the ball clattered to a stop on the number 24.

Gemma's birthday.

He laughed. He laughed so hard that the people around him started giving him funny looks. Then he collected his chips and called it quits.

Florida

2024

AFTER HER BRIEF APPEARANCE AT A DEMOCRATIC FUND-raiser in Palm Beach, Jude walked past the silent auction table and saw a signed copy of *The Almost True Story of the Astonishing Atkinsons.* She paused, then picked up a pen and wrote down a bid.

She lowballed it, because she was stubborn.

But still, she bid.

Minnesota

2024

THERE WAS A MAP ON THE WALL OF THE LAKE HOUSE WHERE Gemma was staying for a girls' weekend, and she stood staring at it—a glass of wine in hand—for so long that her friends came over to stand beside her.

"Are you lost?" one of them joked, tilting her head.

Gemma smiled vaguely at her.

But really what she was thinking was: *Yes.*

Utah

2024

WHILE SITTING ON THE RUNWAY WAITING FOR HIS PLANE to take off, Roddy pulled out his phone and started absently scrolling through his contacts. He paused at Jude's name, wanting so badly to press it, to reach out, to hear her voice on the other end of the phone. But then the engines began to whir, and the plane picked up speed as it hurried down the runway, and the view out the window flipped from land to sky, the clouds pressing close all around them, and just like that, the moment was over.

Connecticut

2024

ACROSS THE COUNTRY, IN A BLACK CAR ON HER WAY TO A
gala, Jude was staring at Roddy's name too. But just as she made up
her mind to send a text, the car came to a stop, and her publicist,
who was sitting beside her, looked over.

"Ready?" she asked, and Jude slipped her phone into her purse
with a sigh.

"Ready," she said.

Maryland

2024

AT THE BALTIMORE AIRPORT, GEMMA HURRIED TO HER gate, more than ready to be home after a weeklong conference. But when she arrived, the screen above the counter said NEW YORK JFK.

"If you're looking for Chicago," said a woman nearby, having clearly registered her confusion, "they just changed the gate. It's now B14."

"Thanks," Gemma said, though still she stood there for several more seconds, thinking of Connor, wondering whether this was a sign, perhaps, or a trick of fate, wondering whether she should be listening to it.

But she didn't.
She couldn't.

Delaware

2024

ONLY ONE STATE AWAY, CONNOR SAT AT A RAMSHACKLE bookstore in a seaside town, making small talk as the line inched forward.

"We're on vacation," said a woman with a huge straw hat, "and I was so excited when I saw you'd be signing here. We *love* your book."

Her husband gave a noncommittal shrug.

"We do," she said, ignoring him.

"Thanks," Connor said as he scrawled his name across the title page. "Where are you from?"

"Chicago," she said, pointing at her husband's Cubs shirt. "Have you ever been?"

Connor nodded. "I love Chicago," he said, though what he really meant was *Gemma*.

What he really meant was that he loved his sister.

Rhode Island

2024

AT THE WEDDING OF TWO OF WINSTON'S CO-WORKERS IN Newport, Roddy wandered through a sea of seersucker suits and across the windswept lawn to where the land sloped down to the ocean in a tumble of black rocks and punishing waves. He stood looking out at the frothy water, shifting and moody beneath a cloud-strewn sky, and if it weren't for the taste of salt on his tongue, he could swear he was back home again.

Connor

North Dakota

2025

When the door to the cabin swings open again, Connor is expecting to see Roddy. But it's Annie instead, her cheeks pink from the cold. She glances around at them as she kicks the snow off her boots. They're still in the same places she left them ten minutes ago—all except Jude, who fled upstairs the moment the conversation was over, making a hasty, tearful retreat that in its wake left a dark cloud hanging over the cabin.

Connor catches Annie's eye as she takes her jacket off. "I thought you were going snowshoeing," he says, and she shakes her head.

"Roddy was heading off for a ski. I didn't want to crowd him."

From where he's still sitting on the leather armchair in the corner, absently flipping through a magazine about bass fishing, Winston looks up with a frown. "Where was he going?"

"I told him about a bar up the road," Annie says, and Winston shakes his head as he returns to the magazine, turning the pages more aggressively now.

"Typical," he grumbles under his breath. "He's never quicker than when he's running from a conflict."

This is met with silence from the rest of the room. Nobody has the energy to be annoyed with Roddy just now. Not when Jude is right upstairs, secrets and all.

On the couch, Connor is still hugging Hugh with one arm like he's a human security blanket, but he feels him start to wriggle away. "Can we go too?" Hugh asks, suddenly full of enthusiasm.

"What, skiing?" Connor asks, as—from the other end of the couch—Rosie shifts her attention from one of the YA books they bought the other day. She'd pulled it out the moment Jude went upstairs and it was clear the show was over. "Or to the bar?"

"Either," Hugh suggests. "It's so cold here."

"And so boring," Rosie adds.

Across the room, where she's poking around the dark kitchen, Gemma laughs a humorless laugh. Connor knows what she's thinking because he's thinking the same thing: that this morning has been anything but boring.

"Mom says only boring people get bored," Hugh tells his sister.

Rosie glares at him across the couch, then turns to Connor. "Hugh called me boring."

"No, I didn't," he says, then sticks out his tongue at her. "Even though you are."

"Stop," Rosie says, and Connor lets out an exaggerated groan.

"Is this the world's worst weekend away?" Connor says, tipping his head back to the ceiling. "It's not even ten A.M. and it feels like midnight. We need to get the hell out of here."

"Yes," Hugh says, springing up from the couch and darting over to the row of hooks by the door. He tugs at his coat, and three others tumble down onto the floor along with it.

But nobody else moves. For a few seconds, the unspoken question hangs in the air. And then Gemma finally asks it: "What about Jude?"

All eyes drift toward the wood-beamed ceiling.

"What about her?" Connor asks, but even after all that's happened this morning, the words sound small and mean. "She's a grown-up. She can do whatever she wants."

"We can't leave her behind," Gemma says, and Connor feels a bright flare of frustration.

"Why not? This was her plan, right? To bring us here and blow up everything we thought we knew about our lives." He gestures roughly toward the stairs. "Well, mission accomplished. I think she'll under-stand if we need a little time to absorb it all." He stands up from the couch and starts for the pile of coats with an air of determination. He scoops his up from the floor and grabs a hat and a pair of gloves at random. "Come on. Who's with me?"

"I am," Hugh says from the floor beside him, where he's yanking on his boots.

Winston sets the magazine aside and sits forward in the chair, his head tilted to one side. Annie is watching Connor with an unread-able expression. Gemma folds her arms across her chest, like she's happy to wait for him to make the right call. But Rosie's the one to chime in.

"Dad," she says, and when he glances over at her, he's struck by how much she looks like Jude right now, her chin high and her eyes intent on his. "She was just a kid."

He stares at her. "What?"

"Aunt Jude," she says quietly. "She must've been really scared."

"Rosie . . ."

"I would've been," she says, and he wants to tell her that it's not about what happened that night. Not really. It's about the twenty-four years' worth of chances Jude has had to correct the record since then. It's about what this did to their family, what it did to him. It's about the last three years, how everyone was angry with him for ruin-ing everything when it should've been Jude. It should've been Jude all along. It's about how none of this is fair and all of it is horrible and how he needs to get out of this godforsaken cabin in order to even begin to grapple with it.

But he can't say any of that. Because Rosie is looking at him with all the infinite wisdom and necessary naïveté of an eleven-year-old who is unfortunately used to seeing the adults she loves argue with each other, and who has learned much sooner than she should have had to that families are complicated and not always all that reliable.

He turns to Gemma, feeling lost, and she gives him a small smile. "No Endicott left behind, right?" she says, and the words hit him square in the chest.

After a moment, he simply nods and turns toward the stairs.

The door to Jude's room is closed. He knocks once, then twice, but there's only silence. "Jude," he says, leaning close to the door. There's a small carved bird etched into the wood, and he keeps his eyes on it as he waits. "We're going out."

He listens for a moment. But there's still nothing.

"We want you to come with us."

"It's fine," she says, her voice faint. "You guys go ahead."

Connor traces the bird with one finger. "There's apparently a bar nearby. Roddy already went ahead."

"Just go, Connor," she says, the words muffled, and he very nearly does. He wants to. But then he thinks about what Gemma said—*No Endicott left behind*—and he's suddenly back in Lake Michigan on a blazing summer day, the lake doing a perfect imitation of the deep blue sky, the four of them bobbing in the water like so many buoys. Connor had been floating on his back, and he barely looked over as Jude began to flail; she was always pretending to be drowning, a too-convincing performance that the rest of them hated. Over and over again, she would slip under the water, and then a hand would break the surface, followed by her face, gasping and sputtering. Sometimes Roddy played along and went through the motions of rescuing her. But today the sky was too clear and the lake was too warm and they were all happy enough to float uninterrupted, the sun baking their faces, the water loud in their ears as they rose and fell on the waves. When Jude surfaced, she glared at them accusingly. She was ten that summer, and there was already a fierceness to her, a determination that scared the rest of them a little.

"Nobody saved me," she said, looking outraged as she wiped the water from her eyes. Her nose was freckled and her hair was slicked back and she splashed at Roddy, who had been floating with his eyes closed.

He sputtered and came upright, shaking his hair like a wet dog. "You weren't really in danger," he pointed out.

"How could you know for sure?" Jude demanded, and Roddy laughed as if this were a ridiculous question. But they all knew what he was thinking: What else could he possibly know as well as he knew Jude? What other subject would he ever be such an expert in?

"You don't have to worry about drowning around us," Gemma said from where she was treading water nearby. "If it ever *really* happened, we'd be fighting to be the one to save you."

This seemed to mollify Jude. "Yeah?"

"No man left behind," Connor agreed, and got a face full of water for his trouble. He blinked at Jude, who had been so quick to splash him. "What? I was trying to be nice."

"That's sexist," Jude said. "No woman should be left behind either."

He rolled his eyes. "You know what I meant," he said at the same time Gemma said, "Okay, maybe Connor wouldn't save you."

A flock of sandpipers took off from the beach, startled into flight by something unknown, and they all paused to watch them for a moment, the birds' wings flapping in perfect unison as they glided along the shoreline.

"How about 'No Endicott left behind,'" Connor proposed, his eyes still on the birds, and when he looked back at Jude, she was smiling.

"No Endicott left behind," she repeated, as if testing out the words. "I like that."

"No Endicott left behind," the others repeated, and it had the solemnity of a pact. But not the kind that kids make, not the kind that gets forgotten as you get older. There was something about the words, something about the moment, that made it feel weightier than that. It was something, they knew, that would last.

Now Connor leans his forehead against the door and closes his eyes for a moment. "Look," he says softly. "You fucked up."

From inside the room, everything is still. He stares down at the hardwood floor, knotted and gnarled, and suddenly feels like crying.

"I wish you'd told us sooner," he continues. "I wish I'd known all these years. I wish I'd gotten to see Mom again." He wipes roughly at his eyes. "And I know she could've told us too. She could've come to see us. She could've explained. It's not fair that she made the decision and you had to carry it. I'm sure it was hard." His voice breaks. "You were just a kid," he says, thinking about his daughter downstairs. "Not much older than Rosie."

He waits a moment, but still, there's nothing. The silence swells.

"Anyway," he says, clearing his throat and straightening up. "This doesn't mean I'm not mad at you. Because I am. But as someone who has also done his fair share of fucking up in this family, I can tell you that keeping your distance is not the best way to handle it. You clearly know that, which is why you brought us all here in the first place. So come out. There's a bar up the road that I have no idea how we're planning to get to, and even if we make it there, I have no idea if there's power, but I do know that I could really use a drink, not to mention a few hours outside of this fucking cabin in the middle of fucking North Dakota, which by the way is just another thing I'm mad at you about, because who the hell picks North Dakota in the middle of the fucking—"

The door swings open and Jude is suddenly there, her eyes red and puffy. She looks small and pale in her oversized sweater and jeans.

"North Dakota," she says, "was actually Mom's fault."

"Stop blaming things on Mom," Connor says without missing a beat, and they stare at each other for a few seconds before they both burst into laughter. "Come on," he says. "Let's get out of here."

Alabama/Mississippi/Arkansas

2025

NOBODY IN HER LIFE COULD UNDERSTAND HOW THIS TRIP
had made its way onto her very busy calendar—and none of the people who *would* understand knew she was even going. But it was important to Jude, who had been stuck at forty-seven states for several
years now and was anxious for some sense of forward motion, or
maybe of closure.

Spencer wanted to come too. He claimed it would be fun to get
away together, though they'd only just returned from Hawaii, which
made Jude pretty sure he didn't think she could do it on her own.
Neither did her agent or manager or publicist when she cleared the
dates with them. And they were probably right. Jude was like a wild
animal whose instincts for survival had been bred out of her after
years in captivity. So she took her twenty-four-year-old assistant,
Madison, who was alarmingly cool and hyperefficient and would
leave her alone when she needed to be.

They started in Alabama, where they went on a walking tour of
Birmingham, the site of so many important moments, both horrify-
ing and inspiring, in the history of the civil rights movement. Jude
wore a baseball cap and sunglasses and nobody was the wiser. The

next day they drove to Tupelo, the birthplace of Elvis, where practically every store window had a plaque to commemorate that one time he bought a candy bar there. And lastly they arrived in Little Rock, where they wandered around museums and art galleries and had lunch at a seafood shack, where the waitress asked Jude if anyone had ever told her she looked like Jude Endicott. ("Never!" she said, then ordered the fried catfish.)

Afterward, she left Madison at the hotel and went for a walk along the river, where she stumbled across a little outdoor bar selling pretzels and hot dogs and cold drinks. She bought a beer in a plastic cup and found a bench right near the water's edge. It was evening, and already the river was flecked with orange from the sunset. She pulled out her notebook and flipped to the list she'd been keeping all these years and wrote the number 50 near the bottom. Then, with a little flourish, she added the final state to the list.

But it didn't feel the way she'd thought it would, coming to the end. Sitting there beside the river, alone, it didn't feel like anything at all.

Gemma

North Dakota

2025

In the shed, there are another few sets of cross-country skis leaning against the back wall, but the snowshoes that are hanging nearby strike Gemma as far more approachable. She carries them out into the cold and sits down on the wooden bench that overlooks the lake, fiddling with the buckles and clasps. Behind her, the others mill around, picking out their own equipment, a flurry of activity, and when someone joins her on the bench, it takes a moment for Gemma, who is still bent over, to realize who it is.

Jude lets her own pair of snowshoes—first one, then the other—drop into the snow, then stares down at them wearily, as if they're now at too great a distance to possibly be useful. There's a part of Gemma that wants to put a hand on her back, to pull her into a hug. She looks so small sitting there on the very edge of the bench, a blue woolen hat pulled low over her ears. She looks like a kid again. But then Gemma remembers all those postcards from her mother, arriving at her little box in the college mailroom. Some of them had addresses or phone numbers where Gemma could reach her if she wanted to. But she always threw the cards away without writing the information down.

There were nearly four years between the night of the fire and the day of Frankie's death in a small hospital somewhere in the very center of California. Four years.

Mateo had once told her that when a branch is cut from a tree, it doesn't ever grow back. That once it's gone, it's gone forever.

But you could grow a whole new tree in four years.

You could do a lot in four years.

As Gemma stands up from the bench, she presses a hand lightly against her stomach. It's automatic, purely a reflex. But she sees Jude notice, sees her fight back a smile at the memory of this piece of good news. Their eyes meet, and just as quickly, Jude's expression rearranges itself into something more somber, and Gemma is reminded of what a good actress she is. She must be, to have lied to them all those years.

As Gemma walks over to join the others, staggering in the snowshoes, she pulls her cellphone—which had died sometime in the night—from the pocket of her winter coat, as if checking it one more time might be the thing that brings it back to life.

"Hopefully they'll have service at the bar," Annie says as she sets her skis down. Gemma is a born and raised midwesterner, but something about Annie—who is the only one on skis and looks like she's about to compete in a biathlon—makes her feel like an impostor. "Or at least a working landline."

"Thanks," Gemma says, pocketing the phone. "It would be great if I could get in touch with my husband."

Annie nods. "He couldn't make it this weekend?"

"Science fair," Gemma says. "He's a middle school teacher."

Hugh appears beside them, leaning on his poles. "We made a cloud in a bottle in science."

"A cloud?" Gemma glances up at the sky. "Like, a real cloud?"

He nods enthusiastically. "All you need is ice. And a match. Oh, and a grown-up to help." He pauses. "And a bottle. Obviously."

"Obviously," Gemma says, looking at Hugh, with his messy hair and freckled nose and blue eyes that look just like his dad's, and thinking of all the trillions of possible ways this cluster of cells inside her could turn out. The thought of it fills her with an unexpected sense of wonder. She hasn't yet landed on any feelings beyond that, hasn't let herself hurtle ahead to the next obvious worry: that it's far too early in this process to count on anything, that there are still endless ways for this to all go wrong. She's too shocked to dwell on any of that. Right now, at this very moment, and against all odds, a tiny embryo has made its home inside her, and the idea that, with any luck, it will one day become a new little person to love makes her want to laugh and cry all at once. A baby. Imagine that!

When everyone is ready, they begin a slow trudge from the house like explorers from a previous time, awkward and lumbering except for Annie and the kids, who are surprisingly quick, light over the hard-packed snow. Gemma falls in beside Winston, aware of Jude somewhere behind her. The woods are quiet except for the sound of their breathing and the occasional *whoosh* of falling ice. She unzips her coat, already too warm, as Annie leads them parallel to the road, which is still unplowed and empty of cars. Most of the houses they pass are silent and dark, the world eerily deserted.

"Do you kind of feel like we're about to get eaten by zombies?" she asks Winston, who is puffing hard at her side, flinging his poles forward and back again, his snowshoes crunching loudly with each step.

"We should be so lucky," he says morosely, and then he picks up his pace, moving ahead of her with grim resolve.

Gemma drops back to join Rosie, who is just behind her, humming an unrecognizable tune. She's wearing a hat with earflaps, like some kind of homesteader, and Gemma wonders if it's earnest or ironic. It's always hard to tell with kids her age. "They're in a fight," Rosie says knowledgeably, nodding at Winston's back. Gemma doesn't ask any follow-up questions, but Rosie is happy to supply the answers anyway. "It's because Winston thinks Roddy only got asked to play for Orlando because he's gay and they need him for publicity, and he's mad that Roddy didn't ask him about going when they were supposed to be getting married, and Roddy isn't sure he cares about getting married at all anymore."

Gemma stares at her. "How in the world do you know all that?"

"Our room is right next to theirs," Rosie says with a shrug. "But don't worry. They'll be okay."

"How do you know?"

"Because they love each other. Even when they don't."

Gemma shakes her head. "You're very wise, you know that?"

"I know," Rosie says with a grin.

There's a break in the clouds, and the sudden abundance of sunlight feels warm on their frozen faces. After a while, it becomes too hard to keep up with Rosie, so Gemma falls back beside Connor, who is bent forward and moving with great effort, plowing his way ahead like he's trying to prove something to someone. She wonders if it's Annie—who is way out ahead of the pack now, followed by Winston—or Rosie, who is easily outpacing him. Just behind them, Hugh stomps his way gamely through the deep snow, and farther back, Jude is keeping her distance, a small, blurry figure amid all the white.

"Snowshoeing?" Connor says, giving her a withering look, like she'd been the one to invent it. "Really?"

Gemma's nose is frozen and her legs are burning and she'd pretty much rather be anywhere else. But she grins at him anyway. "It could be worse."

"What," he says darkly, "we could've just found out our mother abandoned us so that our kid sister could go to drama school?"

Gemma laughs. "At least she was nominated for an Oscar?"

"Eh," Connor says, "it will only have been worth it if she wins."

"God," Gemma says, pausing for a moment to look up at the sky, little wedges of blue between the spindly tree branches. "What a mess."

"It's not all bad," Connor says, and Gemma drops her gaze to meet his, wondering if he somehow knows her news. But he just shrugs. "At least I've got something else to write about now."

Without thinking, she reaches over to punch his arm, hard, the way she used to when they were kids, and he winces.

"Jeez. You haven't lost your touch."

"You deserved it," she says.

"I usually do," he agrees, then glances over his shoulder at Hugh, who is pink-faced and sweating but decidedly cheerful, swinging his poles as he walks. "Hey, what do you say we pick up the pace, bud? Maybe try and catch Rosie?"

"Good luck," Gemma tells him, because up ahead, Rosie has managed to pass even Winston now. As they move ahead of her, Gemma pauses to catch her breath. Every part of her feels overheated except for her face, which is windburned, and her fingers, which are numb. She's tempted to turn back for the cabin, but they've come too far for that now. And somewhere up ahead, there might be a landline, a way to reach Mateo.

She drops her poles, then pulls off one glove, tucking it under her arm, and holds the other in her teeth while she rubs her stiff fingers together. She's so dazed, so completely bone-tired, that she almost forgets Jude is behind her, or maybe not entirely that she's there, because she's always aware of Jude's presence—a strange kind of radar—but she's momentarily forgotten that she doesn't want Jude to catch up, that she's been avoiding whatever the next conversation might be, and by the time she hears the *thump-thump-thump* of her snowshoes behind her, it's too late.

Jude is wheezing as she draws up beside Gemma. She's always prioritized keeping in shape, not just because it was part of the gig, but because it made her feel better. But this trek has very clearly knocked her out, and Gemma is a little alarmed at how winded she looks and how white her face is, in spite of the exertion.

"You okay?" she asks, and Jude plants her poles in the snow and leans on them heavily, still trying to catch her breath.

"I'm fine," she says. Then her face clouds over, and she looks up at Gemma with frustration. "Except I'm not. I hate this."

Gemma knows she isn't talking about snowshoeing. "I do too," she says honestly. The wind rustles the trees, and a thin layer of snow is shaken loose, raining down on them in a fine, cold dust. "But what did you expect?"

The others are drawing away from them, tiny figures in the distance. Jude pushes against her poles, straightening again. Across the road to their right is a sloping fence and an endless field. The rolled-up bales of hay are all draped in white, like hulking, misshapen snowmen. Jude drops her eyes to the ground, where the snow has been flattened and sliced by everyone ahead of them.

"I don't get it," Gemma says, addressing the top of her sister's blue hat. "You used to tell me everything back then."

Jude rocks back and forth a couple times on her poles but doesn't look up. "It would've made it feel more real, I think. What happened that night. What she did. I don't know. I wish I could say I thought it through more. But I didn't. It was a thing that happened, and then it was over, and that was the story of it. The summer ended. I went to the theater program. I tried to be good enough to make it all okay. I always have."

"But later," Gemma says. "When you knew she was dying."

Jude scans the trees above Gemma's head. "I tried. Once."

"When?"

"Right after that weekend here," she says, finally meeting Gemma's eyes. "When I got back to school. I was doing this play about an heiress, and I'd left my script at the theater the week before—I'd been so flustered when she called me. On the walk over, it was raining, and there was this little girl playing in a puddle, stomping her rain boots, you know, just laughing and splashing around. I stopped to watch for a minute, and the mom caught my eye and gave me this look like 'What can you do?' And I don't know why, but it made me so sad, how ordinary it was. We never had that. Not with her. But we did with you."

"Jude," Gemma says wearily, because that's not really true. They didn't have it with her either. She was just a kid too. They were all kids.

But Jude goes on. "I really wanted to tell you right then. I needed to. It was like"—she waves a hand in front of her chest—"I had to talk to you. Even though I'd promised her I wouldn't. I figured if I told you and not the boys, maybe it would be like a compromise. So I called."

Gemma waits for her to continue, but she's fallen silent. "Did I pick up?"

"No," Jude says, like that was that. And it probably was. Gemma doesn't need to ask the rest of the story. She probably went to the theater and got her script, and when she came out again, it was no longer pouring, and she walked back to her dorm on the rain-slicked sidewalks, flipping through the pages, and already she was somewhere else, in a different story entirely, and then, not so long after that, their mother died, and it was over.

Gemma puts her gloves back on and bends to pick up her fallen poles. They can barely see the others now. "I don't know what I would've done if you'd told me," she says as they begin to trudge forward again, their steps slow and labored. "I'd like to think I would've jumped on a plane to see her. But probably not. Probably I would've called, though. I would've liked to hear her voice one more time. Say what needed to be said." She blinks a few times. "Say good-bye."

Beside her, Jude's voice is small. "I'm sorry."

"I know," Gemma says.

"I can't go back in time."

"I know that too."

They both keep walking, moving heavily through the snow.

They both keep going.

"Hey, Gem?" Jude asks after a moment, her voice a little wobbly. "There's something . . ." she begins, then trails off, giving her head a shake. "I just—I wanted to ask if you ended up taking a second pregnancy test."

Gemma nods.

"And?"

"And it was positive."

Jude makes a gleeful noise. "So it's real."

"I'm pretty sure it's real."

"How do you feel?"

"I don't know," she says. "I think I might be happy. It's hard to tell."

Their steps are loud in the snow. Up ahead, they can see a gas station and a traffic light that's blinking yellow. Somewhere beyond that, the rest of them must be waiting.

"Do you think we'll ever be okay again?" Jude asks as they pick up their tired legs and put them down in the snow, again and again, inching their way closer.

"You and me?" Gemma asks, considering this for a moment. "Yes."

"Okay, good."

"But not today."

"I can live with that," Jude says happily.

Michigan

1992

When Jude was five, she stole a Snickers bar from the local drugstore. By the time she got home, she was already feeling too guilty to eat it. So she hid it in a shoebox under her bed. But in the middle of the night, she woke up in a panic and moved it to the back of a desk drawer. In the morning, she shifted it one last time, sticking it in the pocket of one of Roddy's coats, not so much as an attempt to frame him as to be rid of it altogether.

Later, while they were getting ready for school, she kept a nervous eye on him as he pulled on the coat. Absently, he shoved his hands in his pockets, and when he emerged with the candy bar, he looked at it quizzically for a moment, then shrugged and tore it open.

He didn't ask where it came from. That wouldn't have occurred to him.

To him, it was just a piece of good luck.

But across the kitchen, Gemma was watching, her gaze flicking back and forth between her and Roddy.

And somehow, Jude could tell that she knew.

Jude

North Dakota

2025

Jude leans against the brick wall of the bar, wishing desperately that she had a cigarette, though it's been a hundred years since she gave up smoking. She can hear the thrum of music playing inside, and every time the door opens and someone stumbles out into the blinding white, they bring with them the smell of a frat house: sticky beer and too-close bodies and sweat.

The rest of her siblings are inside; Jude had lingered behind, eager for a moment alone. As angry and disappointed as they are with her, it's still a relief—because now they know. She'd spent so long thinking about this moment, worrying and stressing and agonizing. How could it ever have been worse than what was in her imagination all those years? Things are definitely not good. But it's still not quite as bad as that. Which is something.

The wind picks up, the snow skittering across the parking lot, and the Pabst Blue Ribbon sign dangling directly above her creaks as it sways. Across the street, there's a feed store, low-slung and shuttered, and the gas station next door still has a Christmas wreath on one of the pumps, though it's February. Jude pushes off from the wall.

There's a man in a flannel shirt standing outside the heavy wooden door at the entrance, and he gives her a long look as he steps aside to let her past. Jude almost laughs, because she knows it's not for the usual reasons—her fame or her beauty, the two most unremarkable facts of her life—but because she's a sweaty mess, too bundled up to be distinguishable from most other people here. Still, she's not two steps through the door, her eyes working to adjust to the dim lighting, when she sees a crowd of people turn to stare at her.

It takes her a moment to realize it's her family.

"What?" she says, her stomach dropping. Because they're all regarding her with odd expressions. Not just Gemma, whose eyes are round, or Connor, who looks baffled, or Roddy, who is clearly trying to hide a grin. But the others too, Winston and Annie and Hugh and Rosie, who is actually bouncing on her toes a little in her excitement.

"What?" she says again, when nobody answers her.

And then she shifts her gaze to the bar, and there he is.

In the literal last place on earth she'd ever expect to see him.

Spencer.

He's sitting on a stool in that gray sweatshirt they had to buy during a weekend in Santa Barbara, when the weather had been so much colder than expected, and those impossibly soft jeans that she's always loved best on him. His faded Dodgers cap is pulled low over his eyes, and his thick brown hair is curling a bit around the edges. He could be almost anyone—almost—but somehow it's clear that he isn't; somehow he stands out amid all the locals, and seeing him there—the shock of it, the sheer unlikeliness—makes Jude feel like crying.

He's looking at her with such a mix of love and relief and amusement that she's not sure what to say. She opens her mouth, then closes it, completely flummoxed by this turn of events. He laughs, and she shakes her head.

"What in the actual hell?" she says finally, and then she hurries over to him on her aching, rubbery legs and throws her arms around his neck, overwhelmed by the nearness of him.

"It's just like in the movies," Rosie says with a sigh as Jude leans back and runs a hand over his slightly stubbled jaw, shaking her head in wonder.

"Is this even real?" she asks, and Spencer's eyes dart over her shoulder.

"Maybe we should..."

When she turns, Jude realizes they have a growing audience, not just her family, but a handful of squinting bar patrons, and so she grabs Spencer's hand and tugs him off the stool, and they weave blindly through the crowd toward the back of the bar, past the jukebox and the line for the bathrooms and the window to the kitchen, which is lined with red wicker baskets full of fried foods. She's not sure where she's headed until she sees a door marked STORAGE and pushes it open. Inside, it's nothing more than a closet with a few kegs and cases of beer, boxes overflowing with ketchup packets and neat rows of cans. There's a mop and bucket propped up in one corner, and a small stack of faded T-shirts with the name of the bar—O'Brien's—written across them in green.

She drags Spencer inside and shuts the door behind them; then—in the muffled quiet that follows—she spins around and kisses him. She can feel him hesitate a second before giving in, wrapping his arms around her tightly and kissing her back, and she lets herself disappear into him, the last two endless days melting away.

"I missed you," she says as they break apart, both catching their breath. And she means it. How could she have ever thought otherwise? Without him, the edges of the world feel sharper; he's like a drug she can't get enough of, and she reaches her hands up under his sweatshirt, eager for more.

"Wait, wait," he says, pulling it back down. "We should talk."

"Yes," she says, laughing. "Very sensible. Let's talk. What the hell are you doing here?"

"My car got stuck," he says. "This was the first place I found."

She shakes her head, still giddy. "Okay, but what are you doing in North Dakota?"

"I wanted to see you."

She steps up close to him, pulling on the collar of his sweatshirt until he lowers his head, and then she kisses him again, more slowly this time. He lets out a little moan, kissing her back, then stops, panting as he pulls away.

"Wait. Sorry. Just . . . hang on a sec."

"Right," she says with a grin. "Talking."

His blue eyes are intent on hers as he backs up a few steps. "Listen, I came because I was worried about you."

"Because of the snow?" she asks, confused. They're standing with their backs pressed against opposite shelves now, a kind of electricity between them, and Jude feels suddenly impatient. "It's fine. We're fine. It's only snow."

But Spencer's face is solemn. "Jude, I know."

Outside the door, a new song comes on—something loud and full of bass—and the bright sound of voices rises and falls all around it. Jude stands very still.

"Know what?" she asks, still smiling. But her heart has begun to thud.

Spencer looks pained now. "Dr. Lim—he called the house phone."

"Why were you picking up—"

"I don't know," he says. "I was walking through the kitchen and I just grabbed it. I hadn't heard from you, and I just—"

Jude puts one hand over the other to steady the shaking. "That's private. There's no way he—"

"He didn't," he says, holding up his hands. "I swear. But I couldn't reach you and I got worried and looked him up and found out he's an oncologist, and I just . . . Jude, talk to me, will you? Please. What's going on? You're scaring me."

Jude turns around and finds herself staring at a can of tomato soup. She runs a finger over the label, trying to think, her mind muddled and her face hot. The strange thing is that she'd very nearly told Gemma on the way here. Trekking through the snow, her lungs aching from the effort, she'd wanted nothing more than to hand over this last unbearably heavy secret, to give it to Gemma, who always knew what to do, who always figured out how to make things better. But she couldn't. In the midst of everything else, it had felt too much like a cheap ploy, a plot twist in a melodramatic TV show: just when everyone is angry with our hero, she reveals that she has cancer and is going to die and they all fall into a tearful hug, everything else forgiven. It had seemed too much like a cheat code, a fast pass out of the fight they were having. And she didn't want to take any shortcuts. Not with this.

But now this piece of information—which had belonged to her alone, something hot and scalding she'd been carrying in her closed fist—has been pried away and thrown back at her, and the shock of it throws her off-balance. She's not sure whether to be angry or upset, defeated or defiant. All she knows is that she doesn't want to be talking about this. Not right now. Not in this supply closet in a bar in North Dakota. And not with Spencer.

"This has nothing to do with you," she says plainly, and his eyes flash with hurt.

"Right," he says, "but it has to do with you. And I love you. So I need more information."

She shakes her head. "We're not serious enough for this."

"You mean *I'm* not serious enough for this," he says, clearly wounded.

"That's not what I said."

"I flew here right away," he says, his voice pleading. "I came here to be with you. To help."

"You can't help," she says, but she says it gently.

He looks stricken. "Jude. Come on. You need to tell me what's going on."

Outside the closet, there's a steady hum of voices and laughter, and underneath it all, the too-quick beat of a pop song, making this whole thing feel even more incongruous.

"Have you told them?" he asks, nodding in the direction of the bar, in the direction of her family.

She shakes her head. "Not yet."

"But that's what you came here to do."

"That's part of it."

"Listen," he says, crossing the space between them. He takes both her hands in his, and she can't shake the feeling that they're in one of his movies, or maybe one of hers, that this is happening in some alternate storyline. She can't shake the feeling that they're getting close to the end.

"I love you," he says. "And I'm here for you no matter what, okay?"

Jude thinks of her mother, who had died alone in a small hospital in a nondescript town in California of the very same thing. She thinks about how the code must've been written long ago for her too, well before the bleeding, well before the sharp pain in her lower abdomen. *Ovarian cancer*, Dr. Lim had said as Jude sat across from his desk in an uncomfortable chair, and she'd listened to the diagnosis without tears—without feeling, really—because in a way it felt like she'd already known. She'd followed her mother down every other ill-fated path in life, so why not this one too?

She looks at Spencer now, his wide-open face and kind eyes, and she drops his hands.

"You're supposed to be my happy thing," she says, shaking her head. "This is supposed to be separate from all that."

"That's not how a real relationship works," he says, and when he moves toward her again, she steps to the side. She can see the hurt in his eyes, but she feels like if he were to touch her right now, she might fall apart entirely. She stares down at the concrete floor, riddled with cracks and dotted with stains, trying not to say the thing she's thinking.

But she can't help herself. She says it anyway.

"Maybe this isn't a real relationship then."

He stares at her. "You don't mean that."

She looks up at him once more, sees the pain scrawled across his face. "I think I do," she says, and then she opens the door and walks back out into the crowded bar.

Hawaii

2025

THE ENTIRE HOUSE WAS MADE OF GLASS, AND AS THE PARTY
carried on behind her, Jude stood watching the waves pummel the
black rocks on the shore below. Up until now, she and Spencer had
spent pretty much their entire vacation alternating between the
enormous king-sized bed in their rental house and the private beach
just outside it. But yesterday, they'd made the mistake of venturing
out for fish tacos, where they'd run into a producer she'd worked
with on a recent film—which is what happened when you came to
Kona: you ran into everyone you knew from Los Angeles, only, mor-
tifyingly, they were all in swimsuits and flip-flops—and before she'd
had a chance to say no, Spencer was saying yes to the invite.

Below, the ocean was frothy and churning, white on blue, and
standing there at the window, Jude couldn't help thinking of her
mom, that final weekend they'd spent together in North Dakota so
many years ago. On the last morning, she'd gone for a walk and
discovered Frankie standing at the edge of the lake, her back to the
cabin, a silhouette against the rising sun. She was just staring, her
thin arms wrapped around herself, braced against the cold. She'd

stayed there like that for a long time, completely still, almost like she was saying goodbye to the world.

Jude closed her eyes, the waves loud in her ears.

She wasn't sure why her mother had been on her mind so much lately.

Actually, that was a lie. She knew.

She just didn't want to think about it.

Spencer placed a hand lightly on her back, and she spun around so fast she nearly knocked a drink out of his hand. He looked tanned and boyish in a blue linen shirt that matched his eyes, and he handed her a glass of something alarmingly pink. Beside him was a bespectacled man in his forties who was nervously chipping away at the damp label on his beer bottle.

"Jude, this is Michael," Spencer said, clapping a hand on his shoulder. "He wrote that screenplay they sent you about the free solo climber."

Jude smiled and shook his hand. "I thought it was very good."

"Thanks," he said, blushing. "We're still trying to get it set up."

"It's based on a true story, right?" Spencer asked, and Michael nodded.

"Yeah. She was pretty extraordinary."

"What ever happened to her? After that big climb?"

The guy's expression became sober. "It's really sad, actually. She died of cancer just a few months ago." He shook his head. "So young—and in the prime of her career. A real tragedy."

Spencer, who had not read the script, still managed to make a face that conveyed the exact right amount of sympathy. "I'm so sorry to hear that." He put an arm around Jude's shoulders. "I remember Jude saying how impressive she was when she read your script."

The screenwriter nodded. "Yeah. Life is really unfair sometimes, isn't it?"

Jude's heart was a hummingbird in her chest. She shrugged Spencer's arm off and handed him her drink. "Excuse me just a minute, will you?" she said, ignoring his baffled look, and then she walked straight through the living room and into the bathroom.

She stood with her back against the door for a moment before sitting down on the edge of the black marble tub, forcing herself to take deep breaths. The words were still circling her head, moving around and around: *A real tragedy.*

Her stomach was queasy as she imagined all the strangers at parties who might say that about her one day. *So young. In the prime of her career.*

And that would be it. The whole of her story. As if that's all there was to her life.

She thought of her siblings, whom she hadn't seen in far too long, and of her mom on the edge of that lake, just a few months away from her death. She thought of the free solo climber from the script, who'd survived avalanches and dizzying heights and heart-stopping falls only to succumb to something as ordinary as her own rogue cells. She thought of getting the Oscar nomination just a few days after the news from the doctor, how she'd cried and cried as Spencer took her into his arms, alarmed, and said, "Isn't this what you've always wanted?"

Jude had never known what she wanted. She'd never really needed to want anything, because everything had always just happened to her. She'd started acting because it was something her mom loved, and then continued because she felt like she owed her that much, like her sacrifice the night of the fire needed to somehow be worth it. But if she was being honest with herself, it was more than that too: it was that enough people told her she was good at it, and because her career had unfolded in a way that was far easier than it had any right to be. It was because all the doors that had remained stubbornly closed for Frankie had opened easily for Jude, which meant she'd never had to try that hard, never had to take anything that seriously. In a way, her whole life felt like a lark. Until now.

Almost without thinking about it, she opened the app on her phone where she'd hastily tried to type everything the doctor had said when he'd called with her results. Her transcription skills weren't great, and it read like a bad internet poem, a collection of scattered words and phrases: *stage three spread from fallopian tubes suggest chemo to start call doctor lim specialist.*

Jude had done nothing with this information in the ten days since she'd received it.

She'd made no calls, done no research, told not a soul.

All that would make it real. And she hadn't felt ready for that yet.

But now, she opened up a new search and typed: Dr. Eugene Lim.

Then she took a shaky breath and began to read.

Roddy

North Dakota

2025

Roddy steps outside the bar and into the cold, then stands blowing on his hands for a moment. The sun is blazing now, the sky a brilliant blue, and he can see that the snow is already starting to melt, the footprints across the parking lot filling with little pools of water. Even so, his breath emerges in clouds, and he shivers as he stands there in just a hoodie, thinking about the look on Jude's face when she saw Spencer, that powerful cocktail of love and joy and relief. Then he thinks of the way Winston had looked at him last night, in the midst of their fight, and his stomach churns.

The door opens again, and Gemma steps out, along with a blast of warmth and music. Her eyes are on the gas station next door; it takes her a moment to even notice him.

"Hey," she says, her boots crunching on the snow as she walks over. "Got some charge, but still no service. I heard a rumor that there's a pay phone over there." She studies him more closely. "You okay?"

"What a question," he says. "How about you?"

She smiles. "I'm pregnant."

"You are?" he says, laughing, and then, without even thinking about it, he wraps her in a bear hug, lifting her off her feet. "Gem!

That's amazing." He quickly sets her back down, looking at her stomach with concern. "Sorry. I didn't mean to— Wow. I'm so happy for you."

"You know what? I'm happy too," she tells him, her eyes bright. "Which is honestly a relief. It took me a while to figure out what I wanted."

He nods. "Yeah, that can be hard."

"It can," she agrees, giving his arm a little squeeze. "But I think when it arrives, you usually know it."

He manages a smile. "Go call Mateo," he says, nodding at the gas station, and she grins at him once more before hurrying off, skidding over the snow in her haste.

Roddy leans against the brick wall and closes his eyes. He and Winston have talked about kids. For Winston, it's a no-brainer. He doesn't care if they adopt or use a surrogate, doesn't mind how much it costs or how long it might take or what sorts of obstacles or setbacks or heartaches there might be along the way. He wants a family more than he wants anything. He wants kids climbing into bed with them before the sun is up, family vacations with sunburns and lost goggles and sandy feet. He wants what he had as a kid.

For Roddy, it's more complicated. Whatever he got out of his childhood, it wasn't exactly a road map for this sort of thing. He worries that he might turn out like his mom, who picked a hopeless dream over her own children. He worries that he's built the same way, that maybe he's already choosing wrong. On a good day, he'll tell himself he's already achieved so much more in his sport than his mom ever did in her pursuit of acting. That it's been worth it because of that alone. But how different is it, really?

The door behind him opens again, and a group of women spill outside. They pass around a pack of cigarettes, laughing and talking about the cute bartender in deep midwestern accents. Roddy's fingers are numb now, and he knows he can't hide out here all day. He turns toward the door, and just as he reaches for it, Spencer rushes out so fast he nearly runs Roddy over.

"Hey," Roddy says. "Everything okay?"

Spencer turns for half a second, his eyes shiny. He shakes his head as he pulls on his coat. "Your sister—she's completely maddening."

Roddy laughs. "If it helps, you're definitely not alone in feeling that way."

Spencer doesn't seem particularly cheered by this. He fishes his keys out of his pocket and looks over at the gas station. "Do you think they sell shovels?" he asks. "I need to dig my car out." But he doesn't wait for an answer; he just claps a hand on Roddy's shoulder. "Nice to finally meet you, man," he says, and then he's hurrying off, half-jogging, half-sliding toward the mini-mart.

Inside, Roddy scans the room for Jude, but he doesn't see her. He spots Winston instead, and squares his shoulders before walking over to where he's spinning an empty glass in circles on the bar, his shoulders hunched and his eyes as tired as Roddy's.

The bartender sets a coaster down in front of Roddy and raps his knuckles on it. "Get you anything?"

He points at the bottles behind the bar. "Macallan," he says. "Neat."

When the bartender is gone, Winston turns to him. "So it's a whiskey-level conversation then."

"Feels like it's been a whiskey-level weekend," Roddy says with a weak smile.

Winston nods. "Shall I start?"

Roddy's drink arrives, and he grips the glass. "Go for it," he says with more confidence than he feels.

Winston shifts on his stool so they're facing each other more fully. "I suppose . . ." he begins, then shakes his head. "Well, I suppose I've been sitting here wondering if we should take a break."

Roddy stares at him, a sudden scrabbling in his chest. "What?"

"While you're down in Orlando," Winston says, adjusting his glasses. "It's not— Obviously it's not because I don't love you. Because I do. Very much. But I'm getting the feeling we might not want the same things right now."

"Because you want a wedding?" Roddy says, unable to keep the petulant note out of his voice.

"Because I want a marriage," Winston says calmly. "And even more than that, I want a partner."

"We're already partners."

"This," he says, pointing between them, "is a team sport. Which is something you know more about than most people. But that's not how you've been acting lately."

"You can't be serious."

"I am."

"I mean about the break."

Winston nods, his face entirely void of emotion. Roddy has seen him cry watching a video about the friendship between a chicken and a cat, or seeing a pair of gay dads push a stroller through the park. Yet now, as things unravel mind-bendingly quickly, he is shockingly dry-eyed and even-keeled, like he's talking about another couple entirely.

"I was just thinking," he says, "maybe it would help if we had a bit of breathing room."

Roddy frowns. "When has that ever helped anything?"

"It might take the pressure off while you're busy with the team," Winston says with a shrug. "This is something you clearly need to do, and I don't want you to be worrying about me while you're—"

Roddy shakes his head. "I'm not worrying about you."

"Well," Winston says. He clinks his glass against the bar. "There you go."

"That's not what I—"

"Roddy, we never even got rings," he says, looking down at their hands, which are inches apart from each other on the bar. "Maybe that was a sign."

Roddy closes his eyes for a moment, his chest tight. "But I love you."

"And I love you."

"So you just want to throw that all away?"

"No," Winston says with seemingly infinite patience. "I simply want to take a moment to make sure we're on the same page." He brightens. "Think of it like the scientific method. We're establishing the facts of who we are and what we want, gathering empirical evidence about our relationship. Just think of this as a big experiment."

Roddy stares at him, not entirely sure how they got to this place. "And what if we accidentally blow it up in the process?"

"Then something about the equation was wrong," Winston says gently. He slides down from his stool, gives Roddy a kiss on the cheek, and turns and walks off through the bar. Roddy watches him weave through the crowd, his heart like a fist in his throat, until he no can no longer see him. He turns around again, feeling like he might be sick, and downs his whiskey in one go.

Jude slides into Winston's empty seat, seemingly out of nowhere.

"Did you guys just . . . ?" she asks, looking at him intently, and he shakes his head.

"I don't know. Maybe."

She sucks in a breath. "Wow."

"Yeah."

The bartender returns, and Roddy orders another whiskey.

"I'll have one too," Jude says, then turns to him with a shrug. "Welcome to the club."

"What, the day-drinking club?"

"The just-broke-up-with-my-boyfriend club."

"He's my fiancé," Roddy corrects her. "And we didn't break up. We're just taking a break. I think."

"Sorry to be the one to tell you," Jude says with a grimace, "but that's basically the same thing."

Roddy groans and drops his head on the bar, then looks up at her. "Wait, you and Spencer broke up?"

She nods. "Yeah, I messed that up pretty good."

"Same," Roddy says miserably.

Jude kicks at the bar with her boots. "Do you remember when we were little, we always said we'd never get married?"

In spite of himself, Roddy smiles. "We were going to be room-mates instead."

"In a beach house."

"In Australia."

"Do you think that's why we can't make relationships work?"

"Why," he says, "because we only really understand each other?"

She shakes her head. "Because we're both screwed up, but in the same way."

The bartender returns with two more drams of whiskey. Jude lifts hers and turns to Roddy. "To . . ." She pauses, thinking. "New beginnings?"

Roddy sighs. "I don't think I want a new beginning."

They both sit there, glasses held aloft, for another few seconds.

"Me neither," she says finally. "But I can't think of anything better."

"Then let's just drink," he says, and so they do.

Virginia

2023

ON THEIR THIRD DATE, AS THEY WALKED FROM DRINKS TO dinner along the cobbled streets of Old Town Alexandria, Roddy and Winston passed a fancy hotel where a wedding reception was taking place. They stood on the sidewalk and watched as the bride and groom spilled out of a black town car, laughing. Before they walked in, the groom straightened the train of her dress, and the bride reached up and adjusted his bow tie, and then they smiled at each other and headed inside, hands clasped between them.

Winston had let out a happy sigh. "I want that."

"You want to marry a woman?" Roddy teased him.

"I want a partner," he said earnestly. "A husband. A life."

Roddy nodded. "So do I."

"There's something you should know," Winston said, turning to face Roddy, his expression very serious, and Roddy's stomach gave a little lurch, because he liked this guy—*really* liked him—and this was the part where things usually went off the rails, where some red flag appeared and stopped the whole thing in its tracks. He'd been here before. Many times. There was the guy who collected pro athletes like baseball cards. The guy who was obsessed with unicycling. The guy who gave creepy hugs. The guy with the hidden racist tattoo. The guy who talked about nothing but his mother. And on and on.

"I want four kids," Winston said, his eyes intent behind his glasses, and Roddy raised his eyebrows in surprise.

"Four?"

"I've always dreamed of a big family," Winston said in a rush. "Growing up, it was just me. I used to wish for a house full of kids and laughter and built-in friends."

Roddy made a face. "As someone who has some experience with this, it's possible you might be somewhat romanticizing it. Gemma was always bossing me around and making me do chores. And Connor used to sit on me. Not for any reason. Just because he could. And Jude . . ." He trailed off, then admitted: "Jude was a built-in friend. But she could still be a pain in the ass."

"See?" Winston said as they started to walk again. "That all sounds brilliant."

"I guess it wasn't the worst," Roddy said grudgingly.

"Besides, you know what you can do with a family of six?"

"Lose your mind? Go broke? Never sleep again?"

Winston grinned. "Play three-on-three football."

"Soccer," Roddy said, but he was smiling too.

Connor

North Dakota

2025

At a small, cluttered table in the back of the bar, Connor reaches over the red plastic baskets of burgers and fries to move the thimble ahead several spaces on the Monopoly board.

Hugh lets out a groan. "Park Place?" he says, dropping his head into his hands dramatically. "Not fair. I always lose."

Rosie rolls her eyes. "Except when you cheat."

"I don't cheat," Hugh says. "Dad, tell her I don't cheat."

"You totally cheat," Connor says as he counts out his colorful money. He looks up at Rosie with a grin. "But you used to do it too. Don't you remember when you got obsessed with this game and made me and Mom play every single weekend? You'd always steal our money when we weren't looking."

"Where was I?" Hugh asks, putting a protective arm around Harold the penguin, who has aged almost as much as the rest of them over the last twenty-four hours; one of his wings has basically disintegrated from the snow, and the rest of his body is wrinkled and tattered.

"You were still a baby," Connor says, reaching over to steal one of Rosie's fries. "You hadn't learned how to cheat yet."

"It's so weird you used to live with us," Rosie says, looking up at him with her round eyes, her serious face.

Connor frowns. "Why is that weird?"

"It just feels like a million years ago."

"I don't remember," Hugh says, and all at once, Connor feels desperately sad. He spins his little silver thimble on the board, trying to collect himself, and when he looks up again, they're both watching him with mystified expressions.

"Are you crying?" Hugh asks, his eyes very wide.

Connor shakes his head. "I just really miss you guys sometimes."

"We're right here," Hugh says.

"I mean in general."

"We see you all the time," Rosie says.

"You see me once a month."

She shrugs. "It feels like more."

It's impossible to tell whether this is a compliment or an insult.

Connor decides not to ask.

It's Hugh's turn to roll the dice, and one of them goes pinwheeling off the table. Connor sits back as the kids duck down to find it, thinking about what Jude had told them this morning. He knows he should find it depressing, that his mom had given up her relationship with the rest of them in order to help Jude. But in a strange way, it's comforting. All his life, he'd assumed she cared more about her art than her kids. But in the end, it turned out she made her biggest sacrifice of all for Jude. In the end, she cared more about her than anything.

Hugh pops up from underneath the table and sets the rogue die back on the board. "Can we go play Pac-Man now?"

"Hey," Connor says, pulling a few bills from his wallet and handing them to Rosie. "You guys know I love you, right?"

"We know," Hugh says with a grin, then grabs Harold the penguin and runs off toward the ancient-looking video games in the back.

Rosie shakes her head. "You're being so embarrassing today."

"I can't help it," Connor says solemnly. "It's my job."

She rolls her eyes and starts to follow her brother, but a moment later she returns, and to Connor's surprise, she wraps her arms around his neck in the briefest of hugs. Then, just as quickly, she's off again.

Connor is still looking after her with a faint smile when Annie appears with a beer in each hand. "Mind if I join you?"

He gestures at the remnants of the board game. "As long as you promise not to cheat."

"Oh, I don't need to cheat," she says, sitting in the chair beside him. "I could beat you fair and square." She nudges one of the beers in his direction. "Thought you could use this. That was a big morning."

Connor takes a long sip, then sets the glass down. "Just another day in the life of the Extraordinary Endicotts."

"Who coined that?" Annie asks, eyebrows raised.

"My mom," he says, grabbing the stubby pencil they'd found rolling around in the Monopoly box and beginning to doodle on a green paper napkin. "It was when we were little. None of us were actually extraordinary yet. It's like she willed it into being." He lifts his head and looks off toward where the kids are huddled around the Pac-Man console. "She couldn't see it."

"See what?"

"The real extraordinary part," Connor says, returning to the napkin. "If she had, she never would've left." He pauses for a moment, then looks up again. "I shouldn't have either." He shakes his head. "All that time away, and you should see how terrible it is."

"What?"

"The stuff I wrote in Nashville. It's humiliating."

"I'm sure it's not as bad as you think."

"Trust me," he says. "It's worse."

He remembers a letter he got from Frankie a few months after Texas, after the car and the fire and the whole messy parting. *Sometimes I think about how one day I'll walk into a bookshop and see a novel of yours on the shelves,* she'd written, *and how unbelievably proud I'll be.*

Had he done it only for her?

No. But that had been a part of it.

"The problem is," he tells Annie, "I already wrote the truest book I could."

"I thought it was personal," she says. "Not true."

"Okay, you caught me," he says, lifting his pencil with a smile. "It's both. Although I guess it's not really that true anymore. I thought our mom set that fire. So that's how I wrote it."

"Well," Annie says, "you could always work it out in a sequel. You'll have enough material from this weekend alone."

He laughs. "Maybe one day. Or maybe not. Maybe I'll write some sort of heist book after all. Or a mystery about a bourbon distillery. Or maybe a story about a wealthy man who spends his nights watching a green light at the end of a dock because—"

Annie shakes her head. "I think that one's been done before."

"Has it? Okay, not that then. But something."

"Something," she agrees.

He resumes sketching on the napkin. "I think," he says after a moment, "that I've been a little stuck."

She smiles. "Admitting it is the first step to getting unstuck."

"Let's hope so."

"Can I tell you something?" she says, and Connor looks up at her. Her eyes are full of warmth. "Being with your family for the last twenty-four hours was way better than any anthropology class I've ever taken."

"We should definitely be studied," he agrees with a nod.

"Can I ask you something else?" She points to the napkin. "Why are you drawing the state of Michigan?"

Connor glances down to see that she's right. It's a doodle he perfected as a kid, that oversized mitten of a state, sketching it in the margins of his notebooks when he was supposed to be paying attention in his math classes, first the thumb, then the hand, then the more ragged Upper Peninsula, which trails off it like a skein of yarn.

"Huh," he says, staring at it. "Old habit."

She points to the Monopoly board with its scattered cards. "You know, sometimes when you get lost, the best thing you can do is go back to the beginning."

"Actually, that's not a great strategy for this one, but I take your point," he says with a grin. "You're very smart, you know that?"

She smiles. "I do."

"And very pretty," he says, before he can think better of it, and she leans forward and does what he's been wanting to do since the very first moment he saw her at the airport: she kisses him. And even in the midst of the noisy bar, the music and laughter, the rise and fall of voices around them, he can hear his heart beating as he closes his eyes and kisses her back.

They're still oblivious to the rest of the world when the air is split by a sharp, blaring noise. Connor sits back so abruptly he almost tips his chair over, and Annie laughs, bewildered, her cheeks flushed as she looks around the bar, which is steeped in confusion. Half the people are standing stock-still, and the other half are still drinking and dancing, carrying on as if it's just background noise.

"False alarm?" Annie suggests, which is when Connor smells it: the acrid tang of smoke.

"No," he says, bolting up from his chair. "Come on."

He grabs her hand and drags her through the crowd, which is beginning to shuffle toward the door, until he reaches the row of video games on the rear wall.

Rosie flicks her eyes up to him, then back to the game, where Pac-Man is running from a series of colorful ghosts. "Is that real? Should we—"

"Yes," Connor says, dropping Annie's hand to lift Hugh—who is clutching a crumpled Harold—into his arms. Rosie yanks her phone from where it's been charging against the wall, the only one of them to talk her way into a much-sought-after outlet. Then Connor leads them toward the exit amid a press of people, the smell of smoke burning his nostrils, his heart hammering in his chest. All he wants is to get outside and into the snow and fresh air and sunshine, to leave behind not just the sense of danger, but the memory that's chasing him out of this bar.

There's scattered shouting and a gathering sense of heat as he pushes toward the door. Hugh's arms are tight around his neck, his heart beating fast against Connor's chest. Rosie and Annie are just in front of him, and he wills them to move faster as the smell of smoke gets stronger.

When they finally reach the door, the clean blue air is like a knife in his lungs, but he's grateful for it, all of it, and he stumbles forward, moving around a knot of people and into an open patch of the parking lot, a bead of sweat dripping down the side of his face.

He sets Hugh down on the snow and puts his hands on his knees.

"Dad, are you okay?" Rosie asks as he gulps in air.

He lifts a hand. "I'm fine."

But when he straightens again, they're all three looking at him with concern.

He glances at the snowy road, then at the building, where the alarm is still going off. "Can the fire trucks even get through the snow?" he asks with urgency, and Annie gives him a sympathetic look.

"I think it's just a grease fire," she says. "I'm sure they got it out already."

"How do you know?"

"I don't," she says. "But I've worked in kitchens, and this happens—"

"We should get back farther," Connor says, grabbing each of the kids by the shoulder and steering them toward the road. They follow him, cowed by his overpowering panic, skidding around on the ice until they reach the outer edges of the crowd, where they stand with their backs against a half-buried car.

Annie puts a hand on Connor's shoulder, and he flinches. "Are you sure you're okay?"

"Can you stay here with them?" he asks, scanning the crowd for Roddy and Winston and Gemma and Jude.

Jude.

He hurries off without waiting to hear her answer.

As he weaves through the assembled crowd, he realizes that nobody else seems worried. People are standing with their beers, stomping their feet against the cold, laughing and joking as others continue
to file out of the building. The party has simply moved to the parking lot.

"Remember that one time Manny put tinfoil in the microwave
and almost torched the place?" one man says, and another shakes his
head and grins.

"There's no way that only happened *one* time!"

Connor spots Winston standing against the brick wall of the
building, punching uselessly at his long-dead phone. But what he's
really looking for are his siblings.

What he's really looking for is Jude.

He's on his tiptoes, still searching, when a female voice yells, "All
clear," and a cheer goes up.

"Next round on me," says a guy near the door, and everyone starts
to clap him on the back, before he adds, "Just kidding! Cindy would
murder me!"

There's a jovial feel to the proceedings, not a sense of narrow escape but more of a festive interruption to an already unusual day. To
everyone else, it's a lark, this brief brush with danger, but Connor
can't help feeling deeply shaken, and as he pushes his way past a
group of women in colorful ski jackets, he sees that he's not the only
one.

There, near the edge of the gas station that sits beside the bar, are
his three siblings. And they look as rattled as he does.

He makes his way over, moving against the stream of people
headed back inside. Above him, the clouds have returned, blocking
the sun and giving everything a silvery feel, the sweep of snow and the
ice at the edges of it, the footprint-shaped puddles, soupy and gray.

Connor picks his way over, a leaden feeling in his stomach, though
he isn't sure why. The fire is out. The danger is over. Everything is
okay.

But he knows that's not quite true. At least not for the four of them. It hasn't been true since that night in Texas. And it's definitely not true now.

When he walks over, they turn to him, faces drawn.

"Fire's out," he says.

"Good," Roddy says. "That's good."

The wind picks up, stinging their cheeks. They shuffle their feet, stick their hands in their pockets, avoid one another's eyes even as they huddle a bit closer together.

"It's hard to shake," Gemma says, "isn't it?"

Roddy nods. "Every time I smell smoke . . ."

"Me too," Connor admits.

They all look at Jude, who is trembling, her face drawn. She shakes out her hands as if they've fallen asleep and paces in a small circle.

"You okay?" Connor asks, which strikes him as a ridiculous question. Her eyes shine almost feverishly, and her breathing is ragged. She nods anyway.

"Hey," Gemma begins, putting a hand on her arm, but Jude shrugs it off.

"I'm sorry," she says, stepping back from them. Her eyes fill with tears. "You have no idea how sorry I am. I wish I could fix it. I wish I could change it." She claws at the collar of her sweater. "That night was— I still think about it all the time. I still dream about it. The heat. That taste." Gemma tries to reach for her again, but Jude dodges away. "I can't. Please. Don't touch me. I feel like I might . . ." Gemma steps back, worried. "It was awful, being in that car. And then she was there, at the window, and I . . . I didn't mean to ruin everything. I just needed you all to know." She looks tiny inside her oversized sweater, her face haunted. "I've thought so many times about what I'd do if you never forgave me—"

"Jude," Roddy says quietly, keeping her steady with his eyes. "We forgive you."

Connor nods. "You can't carry it around with you like this."

Gemma reaches out again, putting a hand on Jude's arm; this time, she lets her. "You have to let it go," she says. "We all do."

"You all lost her because of me," Jude says in a small voice, and Connor shakes his head.

"We lost her because of her," he says. "She made that choice. More than once."

"It's shitty," Roddy says with a nod. "It will never not be shitty. But at least we had each other, right? And we still do."

"Breathe, Jude," Gemma says, and she does: in and out, in and out. "You're okay."

Jude flicks her eyes up to meet Gemma's, and when she does, her face changes. "Are *you*?" she asks with alarm, and Connor looks over to see that there are beads of sweat on Gemma's forehead, her face suddenly very pale.

"I'm fine," Gemma says in that same calm voice, but then something shifts in her expression. She winces, a hand going to her stomach. Connor is already turning to call for help, his own stomach churning, when—behind him—he hears Gemma say softly, "I think I might need to go to the hospital."

Arizona

1998

ONCE, IN ARIZONA, THEY RAN OVER A LIZARD.

They didn't know it until they stopped and got out, until Jude wandered over and let out a bloodcurdling scream. The others rushed over, gathering around the poor creature in a tight circle. The tire had somehow split him clean in half, and both parts—the head and tail—were still twitching. It was horrible to watch.

"We have to do something," Jude sobbed, and Frankie shook her head.

"There's nothing to be done," she said. "Come on. Let's go."

The others started to follow, but Gemma wouldn't budge. She glanced around the parking lot until she spotted a rock big enough to do the job. Before she brought it down on his head, she took one deep breath and closed her eyes. The others looked on, half relieved and half horrified.

The first blow wasn't enough.

Neither was the second.

She hit him again and again, crying the whole time, until finally, he lay still.

Months later, in science class, she read about how lizards can re-generate their tails, how—impossibly, incredibly—they can live even once such an essential part of them has been cut off, and she put her head down on her textbook and cried and cried until the baffled teacher sent her to the nurse's office.

Gemma

North Dakota

2025

Everything happens fast after that.

Around her, there's a flurry of movement: Roddy with a hand on her back, asking if she needs water, and Connor calling around frantically to see if anyone in the crowd is a doctor, and Jude—Jude is flagging down a silver SUV that's pulled into the parking lot, the tires groaning over the ice and snow.

And in the middle of it all, Gemma crouches, one hand on the snow, her eyes closed, the pain rippling through her, a sudden cramping, first icy, then hot.

She doesn't know what it is.

But she knows that something isn't right.

She tries going very still, breathing in and then out, in and then out. But it does nothing to stop the panic rising inside her.

Mateo. She hasn't even talked to Mateo yet.

When she'd tried him from the pay phone, it rang several times before going to voicemail, and she'd hung up, feeling not so much deflated as impatient. It wasn't just that she wanted to tell him the news. Or to share the moment with him. Though she did. It was that now—suddenly, finally—she understood how much she wanted this baby. Maybe she'd always wanted it but had never let herself hope. Or maybe she'd needed all those years in between caring for her siblings and now to get here. Or maybe it was this weekend, this strange roller coaster of a weekend, that woke something inside her.

She didn't know.

All she knew was that she felt happy.

And she wanted to share that.

But Mateo hadn't been there. It felt like it had been years since they'd last spoken, since he rode with her on the train to the airport, their knees pressed together in the rattling car. When they said goodbye at O'Hare, he took both her hands in his and looked at her for a long time, oblivious to the people rushing around them, the two of them standing very still.

"Either way," he said, and Gemma smiled.

"Either way," she said, which was just their way of saying *no matter what.*

We'll be fine no matter what.

I will love you no matter what.

Now she tucks her chin against her chest, still trying to measure her breathing. She's afraid to check if there's blood, afraid to find out if the worst is happening.

Briefly, she allows herself to think, *Of course.* Of course the moment she decides she's happy is the moment it would be taken away. But then she closes her eyes and forces the thought from her mind. These things happen all the time, don't they? The cramping and the pain and the waves of worry. Still, tears spring to her eyes as another twinge moves through her, and she looks up at Roddy, who is bent over, a hand on her back.

"What's happening?" she asks, and he looks momentarily panicked, like she's asking him to explain the medical implications, rather than the logistical ones. But then his eyes dart over to the other side of the parking lot.

"I think Jude is working on a ride," he says. "What can I do? Do you want to go sit inside? Do you want a glass of water? Are you . . ."

He wants to ask if she's okay. She can tell. But they both know she has no way of answering that. Not yet.

She turns her head and sees Jude jogging back over to them, slipping a little on the ice. Behind her, Spencer Nolan stands beside the open door of the SUV, looking at them with concern. Gemma squints, trying to make sense of it.

"Is that . . . ?"

"Our ride," Roddy says with a faint smile. It's like a magic trick, Spencer showing up with a car. Roddy helps Gemma to her feet as Jude skids to a stop in front of them.

"The bartender said there's a hospital about ten miles up the road," she says in a hurry. "He doesn't know if they have power, but there must at least be a generator, right?"

"Let's go," Roddy says firmly.

Jude takes Gemma's other arm, and she winces as they help her straighten. Spencer has his hands in the pockets of his expensive-looking coat, but as they approach, he rushes over.

"We've got it," Jude says as they help Gemma into the back of the car. For a second, it seems like Roddy's going to climb in too. But then she tips down on the seat, curling onto her side, pulling up her knees, and he straightens again.

"It's okay," he says to Jude from where he's still standing outside. "You guys take her. I'll meet you there with the others."

"But you don't have a car," Jude says as she ducks into the passenger seat.

Roddy taps the hood twice. "We'll figure it out."

As soon as Spencer shuts the door, he twists in his seat. "Gemma, we didn't officially meet, but I'm Spencer, and I just wanted to say—"

"Not the time," Jude says, but she says it fondly, gazing at him with gratitude across the front seat. "Let's just go."

"Right," Spencer says, pressing the button for the ignition. "Of course."

Gemma sits up a little and stares at the dashboard as it lights up. "Your GPS works?"

"It does," he says.

"Does your phone?"

"I think so," he says, grabbing it from where it's sitting in one of the cup holders. He hands it to her. "Call whoever you need to."

Jude flashes her a little smile, then turns to face the front, as if trying to give her some privacy. Mateo's is the only number Gemma knows by heart, and she dials it quickly, hoping, hoping as she listens to it ring. But he never picks up unknown numbers. She tries him again. Then again. Then again.

Finally, he answers, sounding deeply suspicious. "Hello?"

"Mateo," Gemma says, her eyes filling with tears at the sound of his voice. "Thank god."

"Gem?" he says, the word flooded with relief. "I've been so worried. Where have you been? Are you okay?"

"I'm okay," she says automatically, but then the car fishtails and it sends another jolt up her abdomen and she shakes her head. "I don't know. I'm—I'm pregnant."

There's a pause. And then: "Are you serious?"

Gemma nods; then, realizing he can't see her, she whispers, "Yes. But Mateo? I think something's wrong."

"Where are you?" he says with urgency. "I'll come. As soon as I can."

"There was a storm, and we're in the middle of nowhere," she says, the words tumbling out. "But Jude is taking me to the hospital."

"Are you bleeding?" he asks, and when she looks down at her jeans, she realizes that she is. She begins to cry again, this time in earnest.

"Yes," she says softly.

"Okay," he says. "What can I do?"

In the front seat, Jude reaches over and takes Spencer's free hand, and they look at each other for a moment before he turns back to the road.

"Just talk to me," Gemma says into the phone. "Please. Tell me about the science fair. Who won? The volcano or the hairy potato?"

"Well," Mateo says, and she can hear the smile in his voice, "you'll never believe this, but it was actually the pinhole camera. Nobody saw it coming. Silas S took this shoebox, and poked a hole in one side, and cut a square in the other, and then he put it in front of a lamp, and . . ."

Beneath Gemma, the leather seat is soft and cool, and it cushions the bumps as Spencer makes his way carefully over the unplowed roads. She listens to the hum of the engine in one ear and the soothing sound of Mateo's voice in the other, her eyelids growing heavy.

When she wakes, the car has stopped. There's a blast of chilly air as Jude opens the door and taps her gently on the foot. Gemma lifts her head to see Jude peering into the car at her with a worried expression. "Are you okay?"

"I think the pain is gone," Gemma says, sitting up, but Jude's mouth remains grim around the edges. It's hard to know if this is a good sign or a bad one.

"Come on," Jude says, helping her out of the car, which Spencer has pulled up under the awning of an emergency room.

Inside, the few people in the waiting area gape at Jude as she fills out paperwork. Gemma sits on a chair beside a plastic plant, her leg bobbing nervously. When Spencer comes in, stamping snow off his feet and eliciting a whole new round of shocked looks, the three of them find a place where they can sit together in a row, none of them talking. But once again, Gemma sees Jude reach for Spencer's hand.

When her name is called, she and Jude stand up. Spencer digs into his pocket and hands over his phone, looking anxious. "In case you want to call Mateo again."

"Thank you," she tells him, grateful.

There was no discussion about whether she would go alone or Jude would come back with her. If you'd told Gemma about this moment days ago, she would've found it odd for them to go together. But now, after everything that's happened, she wants nothing more than her sister's presence. And so they follow the nurse, Jude's arm slung loosely around Gemma's waist.

They're led to a room that could be called that only in the loosest sense of the word: a curtain surrounds a small area with a bed and a chair and a few machines. The nurse takes Gemma's vitals and promises that the doctor will come by soon, and then they both wait there, listening to the sounds of beeping and whirring all around them. Jude's eyes dart around anxiously, one knee bouncing.

"You okay?" Gemma asks from the bed, and Jude forces a smile.

"I should be the one asking you that."

"It'll all be fine," Gemma says, trying to talk herself into it. "Even if . . ."

Jude nods, though she looks worried.

"But I really hope . . ."

"I know," Jude says.

The doctor comes in, and from where she's lying on the bed, Gemma explains what's been happening, her voice wobbling only a little. Jude stands near her head and runs a hand over her hair, the way their mom used to when any of them were sick, as the doctor talks about the possibilities of an ectopic pregnancy or a miscarriage, and all the while, Gemma is thinking that this is the reason she never let herself care this much, because there's too much room for heartbreak with something so fragile.

"You ready?" asks the doctor, a Black woman about her own age, as she readies the ultrasound equipment, and Gemma manages a nod. She and Jude tip their heads to the screen at their side, searching for something, anything, without quite knowing what they're looking for.

"Would there be a heartbeat?" Jude asks, her voice a little too high, and the doctor shakes her head.

"It's too early for that," she explains. "But we're looking for—" She pauses, moving closer to the screen. "There." She points at a spot on the fuzzy black-and-white image that resembles the yolk of an egg, and smiles. "It's in the right place, which is a good thing. And there's no bleeding that I can see."

Gemma is staring wide-eyed at the monitor. "But what about . . . ?"

The doctor hits a few buttons, then removes the ultrasound wand.

"Might've been your cervix. Might've been something else. But everything looks okay."

"But the pain . . . ?"

"It happens to some women. The bleeding too. A higher percentage than you would think." She tears off a small black-and-white photo of Gemma's uterus, the white circle in the middle of it all, a tiny bright spot amid all that darkness. "Everything looks okay. I would just take it easy the next few days and see your regular doctor as soon as you can."

Gemma's mind is slow and fumbling, a delicate sort of relief starting to work its way around the edges. "So I'm definitely . . . ?"

"You're having a baby, yes," the doctor confirms with a smile, and beside her, Jude beams down at Gemma.

"We're having a baby," she says.

Illinois

2014

WHEN ROSIE WAS BORN, THEY ALL FLEW IN TO MEET HER.
Their dad and Liz were supposed to be there too, but there was a hurricane coming up the coast, so their flight from Savannah was delayed. Which meant it was only Gemma, Roddy, and Jude who tumbled into the hospital room, their arms filled with flowers and balloons and bags full of tiny outfits and stuffed animals and rattles and books.

"Thank god she looks like Nicola," Jude said, but it wasn't true, not at all; they could see right away that she was all Endicott, from her blue eyes to the shape of her nose to her perfect little chin.

They hugged Connor and congratulated Nicola, and they each took turns holding Rosie, who was swaddled up like the world's most adorable burrito. The nurses bustled in and out as Nicola told them all the story: how her water had broken in a cab on the way to work, how Connor had gotten the call during class and had told his students to write five hundred words about a time in their lives when they'd felt wildly unprepared for something; then he bolted from the room.

"He missed the part where I had to pay the cab driver a cleaning fee for the mess," Nicola said, "but at least he was here in time for the birth."

"Wouldn't have missed it," Connor said, leaning over to give her a kiss.

Eventually, Nicola's eyelids began to flutter, and then—right in the middle of a conversation about how neither of them really knew how to change a diaper yet—she nodded off, so the rest of them moved over to the couch in the corner of the room, which overlooked the East River. It wasn't long before Rosie followed suit; they all watched her fall into an enviably deep sleep right there in Connor's arms.

"It must be exhausting to suddenly be in the world," Gemma whispered, peering down at her. She looked up at Connor and shook her head. "I can't believe you're a dad."

"I can't believe you were the first one of us to procreate," Roddy said with a grin.

Connor tore his eyes away from his daughter to look around at the three of them. "I'm so glad you're all here."

Gemma laughed. "Where else would we be?"

Rosie made a creaking noise and shifted in his arms, and they all went quiet, holding their breath until she settled back into sleep.

"A whole new Endicott," Jude said in wonder. She stared down at the baby, her face full of tenderness. "Welcome to the family, kid."

"It's quite a place to have landed," Gemma said with a smile.

"It's not so bad," Connor said, beaming at them. "In fact, it's pretty great."

Connor

North Dakota

2025

Once Gemma and Jude are gone—whisked off to the hospital in a car driven by Spencer Nolan, of all things—the rest of them stand inside the bar, discussing what to do next.

"Remember," Connor says to the assembled group, trying to project an air of confidence, though it feels like everything about this weekend has spun wildly out of control, "there are no bad ideas."

"We could hitchhike," Rosie suggests.

"Okay, that's a bad idea."

The bar still has a faint tang of smoke, but Connor barely notices. Already, the alarm seems like a distant memory. He's reeling from the shock of Gemma's possible miscarriage.

"Was I the only one who didn't know she was pregnant?" he'd asked Roddy after the car was gone.

"She only just found out herself," he said with a helpless shrug.

Now, as they try to figure out what comes next, Roddy and Winston have positioned themselves as far apart as possible, their bodies angled away from each other, their faces stoic, as if each is trying to outdo the other in an imaginary contest of who can be the most mature during whatever is going on with them right now. Between them, Hugh is trying to reattach one of the penguin's orange feet using a piece of gum, Rosie is taking a selfie against a wooden post with a sign that says ALCOHOL: CHEAPER THAN THERAPY, and Annie is standing distractingly close to Connor, her expression hard to read. He can't tell if she's worried about Gemma or wondering how she ended up so deep in a family drama that isn't hers. Either way, he's glad she's here.

"We could steal a car from the parking lot," Hugh suggests, and Connor groans.

In the end, they decide that the only real option is to go back the way they came: on foot. Or snowshoes. Or skis. And so once again, they bundle up and gather their equipment and make the long trek back to the cabin, their tired legs splattered with mud and snow, their faces beaded with sweat.

"Will she be okay?" Rosie asks Connor as they trudge along the edge of a field. In the distance, a few cows mill around in the dirt-streaked snow, and a crow takes off from a fence rail with a clatter of noise.

"I think so," Connor says through a lump in his throat.

"Will the baby?"

He looks over at her. "I don't know."

"It would be nice to have a cousin," she says, glancing off toward the cows, and Connor reaches over to give her shoulder a squeeze.

When the cabin comes into view, they can see that the porch lights are on.

"Power!" Hugh says, pumping his arms and running up the stairs as if he's just leveled up in a video game.

Rosie holds up her phone, the only one that's charged. "And bars!"

"Thank god," Roddy says, dropping his skis and vaulting up after him.

Inside, they turn on the lights in the living room, laughing as they scramble for plugs and chargers and dead phones. Jude had given them Spencer's number before they parted ways, and Connor tries it now on Rosie's phone. But it rings and rings with no answer.

"Right," he says. "Let's pack up, load the cars, and meet them at the hospital. It's time to get the hell out of here."

The kids head upstairs, and Annie goes outside to close up the shed. As Connor picks up the living room, he can't help observing Roddy, who is emptying the fridge, and Winston, who is wiping down the counters, as they start to inch closer to each other.

"Did you know?" Winston asks Roddy, who shrugs as he tips a container of wilting lettuce into a garbage bag.

"I went with her to get a pregnancy test this morning," he admits. "But I only just found out it was positive."

Winston nods. "She'll be a great mom."

"She already was," Roddy says a little fiercely.

Connor is trying to act like he's not listening as he folds one of Hugh's sweatshirts. There's a long silence while Roddy continues to dig through the fridge and Winston continues to look for an excuse to talk more.

"So when we get back," he says eventually, his voice a little stiff, "I was thinking I could go stay with Gavin and James until you have to leave."

Roddy leans back from the fridge to look at him, his face etched with surprise. "On their couch?"

"They have a guest room now, remember? They moved to a bigger place because of the baby."

"Right," Roddy says, then shakes his head. "No, I should go. I'm the one leaving anyway."

"Yeah, but you need to pack and get ready. You should be in the house."

Connor, who is now pretending to be busy fluffing couch cushions, can't bear to keep quiet any longer. The display of polite solicitousness is too much for him. He turns toward the kitchen, hands on his hips. "Please tell me you two clowns didn't actually break up."

Roddy and Winston both look over, as if surprised to discover that they haven't been alone this whole time. Then they glance back at each other, weighing something.

"I think we're taking a break." Roddy says this like he's testing the words, like it's a language he doesn't know how to speak just yet.

Winston nods. "Right," he says. "A break."

"That's the most ridiculous thing I've ever heard," Connor says flatly. "You love each other, right?"

Once again, they exchange a look. Then they both nod.

"Then for godsakes," he says, exasperated, "figure it out."

"Since when are you the expert on relationships?" Roddy says, and Connor cuts his eyes to the window, where Annie is walking back toward the house.

"There's no such thing as an expert," he says. "There's only people who try and people who don't. And I promise you the first one is better."

Before they can say anything more, he bounds over to the door. Annie is still crossing the yard from the shed, and she looks up when she hears his footsteps on the wooden porch, her face breaking into a smile.

"Hey," he says, hurrying down the stairs. "I was just thinking that the rest of today is going to be a mess with my family and the hospital and the drive back and the kids and then we're probably gonna try to fly out in the morning and—"

"Connor?" Annie says, as she closes the space between them.

"Yeah?"

She puts her hands on his shoulders and kisses him, and he closes his arms around her waist before pulling back, a moment later, with a grin.

"That was gonna be my move."

"You were taking too long," she tells him. "And talking too much."

"Occupational hazard," he says; then he kisses her again.

When he goes back upstairs afterward, the kids aren't remotely packed. They're sitting on the bed, scrolling through Rosie's phone. When Connor walks over, Hugh shoves Harold, the much-battered penguin, next to his face and snaps a picture.

Hugh nods, satisfied, then hands the phone back to his sister. "I have everyone now."

"Great," Connor says, peering over Rosie's shoulder as she scrolls through the photos on her smudged phone: Harold and Hugh roasting marshmallows, Harold with Roddy in the snow, Jude giving Harold a kiss, Gemma pretending to shake his wing, Winston with his arm around the little piece of construction paper, Harold and Rosie playing Pac-Man at O'Brien's. "Though it doesn't really look like we're on vacation."

Hugh squints at one of the photos. "Well, we are."

"Sure, it's just . . . these are all of Harold with our family. We could be anywhere."

"But we're not," Hugh says simply. "We're here."

For some reason, this makes Connor's throat go thick.

We're here, he thinks, pulling his son into a hug.

"Dad, you're squishing Harold," Hugh says, and Connor laughs and lets go.

"Okay, you two have five minutes," he tells them; then he steps back out into the hallway, where he runs into Roddy. "Hey, will you get Jude packed up and I'll do Gemma?"

Roddy groans. "Jude has at least twice as much stuff."

"She's your twin," Connor says with a grin, and they part ways again.

Connor moves quickly around Gemma's room, tossing her things haphazardly into her suitcase, knowing she'll give him a hard time about it later. In the bathroom, he finds the positive pregnancy test on the counter and makes a small wish—the closest thing he has to a prayer—that everything is okay.

He remembers the night he and Nicola found out about Rosie, how they sat beside each other on the bed, jittery and nervous, waiting for the timer to go off, waiting to see if their whole lives would change. It was Nicola who'd pushed them to try. Not that Connor didn't want kids—he did, but in some vague, far-off way. Even then, he worried that he wouldn't be able to step up in the ways that mattered, that his upbringing hadn't prepared him for such a serious endeavor, that he'd be the one to fuck them up. Which he did, of course. But he understood now that it was just part of the deal, a pattern that repeated itself through time, endless and inevitable. He should've been paying closer attention that time Rosie fell off the couch. He was on the phone with his agent when he bumped Hugh's head against a beam in his office. He didn't realize the chicken was expired until after he fed them lunch that one time. He returned with the wrong brands when he was sent to the drugstore. He said no when he should've said yes and yes when he should've said no. He gave too much praise or too little. He shouted at them out of frustration. He fell asleep on the job too many times to count. But wasn't that all parents?

Maybe. But not all parents leave.

He looks back down at the pregnancy test, wondering if it'll turn out to be something Gemma never wants to see again or something she wants to keep forever. In a burst of optimism, he wraps it carefully in a tissue and slips it into her bag of toiletries, willing it to be the latter.

When everyone is packed, they drag the suitcases outside, and Connor pauses on the front porch for a moment. "Is it weird that I'm a little sad to leave?" he asks Annie, who nods.

"Yes," she says, but she takes his hand and squeezes it, and he knows she understands.

It's late afternoon by the time they get everything loaded and split up into two cars, and the midday sun has done its job, melting much of the snow on the roads. Connor is desperate to drive with Annie, but he knows that Winston and Roddy need space, so he volunteers to go with his brother instead, and the kids come with them.

As Roddy eases the car down the long, snow-packed drive toward the lake, slate gray in the late afternoon light, Rosie lets out a little yelp from the backseat.

"What?" Connor asks, twisting around. "Did you forget something?"

"No, I just got a text from *Spencer freaking Nolan.*"

"What? How do you—"

She squeals again. "He says everything is fine!"

"With Gemma?" Roddy asks.

Rosie nods. "Yes!"

"And the baby?"

"Yes!"

Connor feels his muscles relax as he and Roddy exchange a look of relief. "Thank god," he says, and then turns back to Rosie with a grin. "Tell Spencer freaking Nolan that we'll see them in Portree."

From the backseat, there's one more squeal, and then the click of her typing.

Texas

2001

LATER THAT NIGHT, AFTER THE POLICE HAD SHOWN UP AND
taken Frankie away, the smoldering husk of the car was towed off
too, leaving nothing but a burnt smudge on the asphalt where everything had happened. Once the paramedics finished dressing the
burn on Jude's arm, she and Roddy and Connor were entrusted to
Gemma's care. Back in their room, Jude took a long shower—so long
that the others started to worry—and when she finally emerged in a
cloud of steam, her face clean of soot, she refused to talk, crawling
into bed and turning her back to the rest of them as they exchanged
worried glances.

Frankie returned sometime in the night, but by then they were all
asleep. She'd been charged with misdemeanor possession of mari-
juana, which came with a fine large enough that she wouldn't be
able to pay it herself. Their dad agreed to cover it, and then he and
Liz—who had been in his life for only about six months at that point—
booked the next flight to Dallas. When they arrived, Connor took
one look at his dad's face and understood that he was supposed to
feel the same way: stone-faced and furious. But he couldn't muster
it. His mom had no car, almost no money, and no place to go. She'd

done something stupid, something careless and thoughtless, and it had backfired terribly, but he knew from the books he read that people could do much worse, and his heart felt brittle as he stood outside the motel, watching her pull her sweater around herself on that chilly Texas morning as if it might be enough to protect her from whatever was coming next.

"Say goodbye to your mother," their dad said, and they didn't understand then what the words meant, couldn't have known it would be the last time they'd see her, ever. If they had, maybe they would have done it differently; maybe they would have held her longer, hugged her tighter. Or maybe not.

Connor went first, stepping into her arms, his nose buried in her shoulder.

"Keep writing," she told him fiercely, her fists on his back. "Don't ever stop."

He nodded, his words lined up neatly in his throat. But he couldn't say them.

When it was Roddy's turn, she whispered to him too, and then Gemma, whom she hugged extra tightly, and finally Jude, who began to sob even before she threw herself into Frankie's arms. Frankie murmured softly for a long time while smoothing her younger daughter's hair.

And then that was it.

Years later, after Connor's editor had finished reading an early draft of *The Almost True Story of the Astonishing Atkinsons,* she took him out to lunch to tell him how much she loved it.

"There's just one thing I can't figure out," she said, her fork hovering over her Niçoise salad. "Why was the mom smoking pot in front of her daughter that night?"

Connor frowned. "What do you mean?"

"It just seems out of character," she said. "And maybe a little too convenient in terms of the fire, you know? There's no other place in the story where she does that."

Across the table, Connor wasn't thinking about the book. He was thinking of his mom, of Jude in the car that night, of the smoke and ash and the end of everything, and the smallest, faintest question mark planted itself somewhere deep in the back of his skull.

Roddy

North Dakota

2025

On the drive back to Portree, the kids fall asleep in the backseat. Roddy barely notices; he keeps his hands on the wheel, his shoulders stiff, focusing on the headlights sweeping the empty highway, which has thankfully been cleared of snow.

"Do you think," he asks, after they've been driving in silence for a little while, "that it's because of Mom that we're so bad at relationships?"

"Yes," Connor says without even taking a moment to consider it further. "Though Dad was completely checked out too, which probably didn't help. But we're all grown-ups now. We should probably be able to get our own shit together without blaming them at this point."

Roddy glances over at him. "Is that what you're doing with Annie? Trying to get your shit together?"

"No," he says with a smile. "I just really like her."

"That's nice," Roddy says, and Connor shakes his head.

"Look, I'm a writer, which means it's my job to observe things," he says, "and I can't help but observe that you're screwing everything up with Winston. And as someone who has screwed it all up before—

many times, in fact—I feel like I owe you some brotherly advice. Which is: get your head out of your ass. He's not asking you to pick between him and soccer. He's just asking that you consider him in the bargain."

"How do you know?"

Connor jabs a finger at Rosie, who is clutching her phone even in her sleep. "She's like a walking gossip magazine."

"I do consider him," Roddy says, his eyes on the road ahead.

"You don't," Connor says, but he says it gently. "You're so panicked about the end of your career that you can't even see what's really happening. I think you were so worried he wouldn't say yes, that he wouldn't agree you should go, that you didn't even give him a chance to rise to the occasion. But if Winston got the world's most amazing job offer in London and decided to go back without talking to you first, you'd feel pretty shitty too."

"Maybe," Roddy says, a little petulantly. "But I wouldn't fight him on it, if that's what he really wanted."

"Well, maybe that's your problem," Connor says, shifting his gaze back toward the window, the streaks of lights along the edges of the road as the world dims. "Maybe you should've been fighting for him more." There's a pause; then he adds: "Take it from someone who forgot how to fight altogether and now lives alone in a studio apartment in Nashville."

The car shudders as a truck passes them, kicking up flecks of salt. Above, the flat gray sky is completely empty, scooped clean by the storm. They pass an exit but keep driving, Hugh softly snoring in the backseat.

"It was his idea," Roddy says, gripping the steering wheel harder. "Taking a break."

"He didn't mean it," Rosie chimes in from the backseat, and they both half-turn in surprise. She leans forward, her face between the seats. "I heard him talking to Annie at the bar."

Roddy's heart leaps at the words, but he manages to shove it back down again. "Then why did he say it?"

"Because you told him you don't care about the relationship."

"I never said that," he says, sounding more panicked than indignant.

Rosie nods. "He said the wedding is a big deal, and you said it's just a party and it doesn't mean anything, and he said it does to him, and you said maybe you don't care about all of this as much as he does." She pauses, then adds: "Apparently."

Connor twists to look at his daughter, impressed. "Have you ever thought of becoming a reporter? Or a spy?"

"I didn't mean the *relationship*," Roddy says. "I just meant the wedding. I don't care as much about *the wedding* as he does."

"I don't think that helps your case quite as much as you think it does," Connor says, raising his eyebrows.

"Agreed," Rosie adds.

Roddy groans. "I want to marry him. I swear. I just don't care how or when. I'd marry him right here in North Dakota, for all it matters."

"Maybe you should," Connor says.

In spite of himself, Roddy laughs. "He'd hate that so much," he says, though his heart is beating fast now, because he can almost—almost—see a way forward.

When they stop for gas, Connor and the kids head into the mini-mart and Roddy pulls out his phone while he waits for the tank to fill. It takes only a second for his agent to pick up.

"Hey," Zack says. "Getting excited to head down to the Golden State?"

Roddy tucks the phone between his shoulder and his ear and shoves his chilly hands into his jacket pockets. "That's California. Florida is the Sunshine State."

Zack chuckles. "Even better."

"Listen," Roddy says, watching the numbers tick on the gas meter. "I need you to make a call for me . . ."

By the time the others emerge from the mini-mart with armfuls of snacks, Roddy has hung up. But as he pulls back out onto the highway, he keeps anxiously glancing at his phone where it's sitting in one of the cup holders.

"What's up with you?" Connor asks, popping a corn chip into his mouth.

"Nothing," Roddy mutters. "Just waiting to hear back from my agent on something."

"What's that guy's plan for you after Orlando, anyway?"

Roddy shrugs. "I don't know yet. I get a lot of requests for speaking gigs, soccer camps, sports commentating, stuff like that."

"Seriously? They're willing to put your ugly mug on TV?" Connor teases, and Roddy reaches over to punch his arm as, from the backseat, the kids—who are only half-listening as they pick through their bags of candy—squeal with laughter. "I'm only kidding. You'd be great."

Roddy shrugs. "Believe it or not, there was even some interest in a book."

"Dude," Connor says, shaking his head. "If you manage to write a book before I do, I swear I will never forgive you."

Roddy laughs. "Don't worry. I think I'll most likely end up coaching."

Connor glances over at him sharply. "Really?"

"Yeah, I've gotten some interest from D3 schools, and some bigger programs at the assistant level. But I'd probably wait till something came up around D.C."

"And that wouldn't..." Connor seems to be having trouble formulating the question. "That wouldn't feel like going backward?"

"Why would it?" Roddy asks, surprised. "You get to help other people improve at the thing you've always loved the most." He shrugs. "Sounds like a dream job to me."

Connor turns back toward the window. "I'm thinking about it too," he says after a moment.

"Thinking about what?"

"Teaching."

Roddy nods. "In Nashville?"

"No," Connor says. "You won't even believe where."

"Where?"

"Michigan."

Roddy laughs in surprise. "Wow. And they say you can't go home again."

"I guess they weren't talking about people with writer's block who could use a fresh start," he says with a rueful grin. "But they have a great MFA program. And it would only be one semester a year."

"So you could still write."

Connor sighs. "In theory. If I ever figure out what comes next."

"And you'd be in Nashville the rest of the time?"

"No." Connor glances back at the kids, who are busy arranging a candy trade, a complicated matter requiring small piles of sweets to be laid out on the seat between them. "New York. Feels like it's time to go home."

Rosie looks up from the candy. "You're coming back?"

Connor smiles at her. "For most of the year, yeah. I thought it would be fun to embarrass you in public on a more regular basis."

"Dad," Rosie says, rolling her eyes, but she looks elated as she returns to her piles of chocolate.

From the cup holder, Roddy's phone dings with a new text. He reaches for it automatically, but Connor picks it up instead. "It's from Zack Ramos."

Roddy's breath hitches in his chest. "What does it say?"

"*Three days,*" he says. "What does that mean?"

With a laugh, Roddy bangs a hand against the steering wheel. He doesn't bother to answer. Instead, he glances down at the map on the screen. "Ten miles to Portree," he says with a grin. "Let's fucking go."

By the time Roddy pulls up in front of the Portree Inn and throws the gearshift into park, he feels a little queasy. He trips as he gets out of the car, skidding on the icy pavement, and Connor—who is lifting a sleeping Hugh from the booster seat—gives him a strange look.

"You okay?"

"I think so," Roddy says, but it doesn't sound very convincing.

Just beyond the lobby of the inn, there's the entrance to a cozy pub, with tartan carpeting and rich green walls covered in old-timey photos of the town, which are hung haphazardly above the cracked leather booths. On the opposite side of the room, above the bar and the shelves of liquor, a giant moose head seems to follow Roddy with its eyes as he walks in.

The first person he sees is Gemma, and for a moment, the knot in his stomach unwinds itself. She grins when she spots him, and he hurries over to wrap her in an enormous hug before stepping back to make sure she's okay.

"It's fine," she says, her face lit with happiness. "I'm fine."

He gives her another hug, holding on even when she starts to break away. She laughs and pats his back. "Are you?"

"I think so," he says, his eyes searching the dimly lit pub. Connor appears at Roddy's side, now holding Hugh's hand, and Rosie is behind them, whispering something about Spencer Nolan being here, and Gemma is looking at Roddy like she already knows what he's about to do. He puts a hand on her shoulder. "I'm so happy for you. And I . . ."

He spots Winston in the corner booth, and his heart gives a great lurch. When Winston looks up, their eyes meet, and Roddy stumbles backward a step, flustered. He turns to Gemma. "I'll be right back," he says, then spins and rushes out to the lobby, hurrying past a family checking in with a mountain of suitcases, and back out into the frozen air.

Dusk has fallen, and the town is quiet. Roddy walks quickly, his head bent, his hands shoved into his pockets. As he gets closer to the tavern, he hears the sound of dinging, and his heart quickens, anxious and excited in equal measure. He hurries inside and straight over to the change machine.

Twenty minutes and thirty-three dollars later, he's tucking the stuffed diamond ring under his arm, feeling inordinately pleased with himself for managing to get it. He also has a smaller stuffed frog, which he snagged by accident, and he's hurrying out the door again, moving fast and full of purpose, when he crashes directly into Winston.

They both stumble backward a step, stunned.

"What are you doing here?" Roddy asks, stooping to pick up the stuffed ring, which he'd dropped in the collision. It's damp now, and a little muddy. He wipes it on his jacket.

"I was worried about you," Winston says, rubbing the elbow that had knocked directly into Roddy's rib cage. "I was—" His gaze drops to the stuffed ring. "Is that what you were doing?"

Roddy holds it up sheepishly. "I wanted to re-propose to you."

The frog is still on the ground between them, and Winston bends to pick it up, then studies it like it holds the key to something important. "I thought you didn't . . ."

"I do," Roddy says. "I'm sorry if I gave you the impression that I don't care about the wedding, or about our relationship, because I do. You have no idea how much." He feels a rush of adrenaline surging through him, the way it does when he sees a pocket of space between himself and the goal, the moment when everything clicks. "And you're right. This is a team sport, and this—you and me? It's the only team that really matters. I'm sorry I lost sight of that. I'm sorry I haven't been fighting for us. I'm sorry I didn't take you into consideration when I said yes, because this is your life too, and you're the best thing about *my* life by miles. And I promise—I *promise*—I'll do better if you'll still agree to marry me."

"Roddy . . ." Winston says, blinking at him. "Are you sure you—"

"I'm sure," he says with a grin. "I've never been so sure of anything. I'll even marry you right here and right now if you want."

Winston glances up and down the nearly empty street, then wrinkles his nose. "Here?"

"I knew you'd say that," Roddy says, laughing. He holds out the stuffed ring. "How about February fourteenth, then?"

"What do you mean?"

"I mean," Roddy says, unable to contain his smile, "will you marry me on Valentine's Day in D.C. like we always planned?"

"But . . . how?" Winston asks, shaking his head in bewilderment.

"You're the one who gave me the idea, actually," Roddy explains. "This whole time, I've been so anxious to keep playing that it felt like Orlando was doing me a favor by signing me. But I realized you're right. I'm doing them a favor too. And if they need the good press badly enough to sign a thirty-eight-year-old with a knee that's held together by tape and glue, it must mean I have at least *some* pull with them, right?"

Winston is staring at him. "Are you serious?"

"If I'm going to do this, I want to do it on my own terms. So I had Zack tell them I'd walk if they wouldn't give me a few days."

"Roddy, I—"

"I know it's not a lot, but it will be just enough time to marry you before I have to leave, which is all I want." He thrusts the stuffed ring into Winston's hands. "So what do you say?"

For a few long seconds, Winston is quiet. He just stares down at the ridiculous, oversized ring, which he holds in one hand, the googly-eyed frog in the other. Finally, he looks up at Roddy, his eyes wet behind his glasses, and hands him the frog. "All I want is to marry you too."

Roddy laughs and gives the little frog a squeeze. "I love you," he says, but before he can even get out the last word, Winston has stepped forward to kiss him, the ring and the frog pressed between them, and it feels different than it usually does. It feels like a new beginning.

"I love you too," Winston says when he steps back, "and I love everything about this plan. Except for one thing."

Roddy's heart bobbles in his chest.

"I think we should invite our families," Winston says, their swaying hands clasped in a knot between them. "I know it might be too late, and maybe nobody can make it at this point, but we should at least ask, don't you think?"

Roddy laughs. "Even after this weekend?"

"Even after this weekend," Winston says, but he can't help laughing too.

"You're on," Roddy says, and then he kisses him again.

Washington

2010

THE FIRST TIME RODDY SPOTTED THE BOOK, IT WAS IN THE
window of a small shop in Seattle. If he hadn't been on the phone
with Gemma at the time, he probably wouldn't have noticed it, but
he was, and so he stopped to take a closer look.

"*The Secret Garden,*" he said, peering at the cover through the rain-
streaked glass. "That was one of your favorites, right?"

"It still is," Gemma told him.

Roddy straightened up, adjusting his grip on the phone. "I remember you reading it on the beach back home."

She laughed. "I read it everywhere."

"I don't think I even know what it's about," he said, squinting up
at the gray sky and the spitting rain, hoping it would clear in time for
the match tomorrow.

"It's about a girl without parents who is miserable," Gemma said
on the other end of the phone, "then figures out a way to be happy."

Roddy glanced at the cover of the book again. "We had parents."

"Sometimes," Gemma said.

"And you weren't miserable."

"No," she agreed. "I wasn't miserable."

"How did she figure out how to be happy?"

"She found a garden," she said. "Something to tend to. And friends."

Roddy pulled his coat tighter around himself, thinking of those nights in Michigan after their mom left, when their dad wouldn't get home until after they were in bed. When it rained, Connor would make popcorn, and Gemma would turn on a movie, and they'd sit in a row on the couch, the light playing across their faces, the house warm as the wind whistled outside.

"So we were the garden?" he asked, still trying to understand.

"You were the friends," she said, and he could hear the smile in her voice.

Jude

North Dakota

2025

Later, after Roddy and Winston show up with matching smiles and a stuffed diamond ring, after Spencer answers about four thousand questions from Rosie ("Do you do all your own stunts?" "Do you have to practice before kissing scenes?" "Have you ever met Harry Styles?") and another thousand from Winston ("What kind of training do you do?" "How are your teeth so white?" "Are you ever in D.C.?"), after Hugh falls asleep in a booth and Connor disappears into a darkened corner of the bar with Annie, the two of them making out like teenagers, and Gemma and Rosie find a website of baby names to scroll through, laughing at some of the possibilities—after all of it, not just tonight, but the whole long weekend behind them and everything that came before it—Jude and Spencer sit at the end of the bar, their hands cupped around pint glasses as they talk.

The pub is all theirs now. Jude has no idea what time the place closes, only that the bartender seems more than happy to keep the food and drinks coming. It's partly the enormous tips she's been leaving and partly the way he's trying so hard not to look at Spencer. She knows Spencer has noticed too, and that later, as they close their tab, he'll offer to take a selfie with him to save the poor guy the embarrassment of asking, which is just another reason why she loves him. It's just another reason she's glad he's here.

"I'm sorry," she says when the bartender has left them another round and they're alone again. Across the bar, the rest of her family members are now gathered in a booth, and it clangs at something inside her, seeing them there like that, all together. She doesn't know whether this trip was a mistake or not, doesn't know whether the damage she did long ago is repairable. But she knows it was a good thing. To be together. To talk. To apologize.

And now she knows she has to do it again.

"I should've told you the truth," she tells Spencer, who is watching her with those deep blue eyes of his. "I should've trusted that you could handle it."

"Yes," he says, but then he shakes his head. "Actually, no. It's completely up to you when and how you want to share it. I'm sorry if I forced your hand. I was just worried."

"I appreciate that," Jude says.

"And honestly, I have no idea if I can handle it," he says a little sheepishly. "You're not wrong about me. I can be kind of immature. I've never had to deal with anything real or big or scary. And I don't even know what it is yet. How bad it is." He swallows hard, looking at her nervously. "But I do know that I love you. And I want to be the kind of guy who can be there for you. And I hope that counts for something."

She reaches over and takes his hand. "It counts for a lot. And for the record, I think you are that guy. I just didn't want to let myself believe it."

"Why not?"

"Because I can be really immature too," she admits. "And it's been easier to tell myself this isn't real. It's less risky, you know?" She leans a little closer. "I don't know if you realize this," she whispers with a grin, "but I have some slight abandonment issues." She twirls a finger behind her in the general direction of her siblings. "Runs in the family."

He smiles. "I'm not going anywhere."

"You still don't know how bad it is."

"It doesn't matter," he says, "because I love you."

"I love you too," she says. "And it's bad."

"Okay," he says, nodding a few times, trying to keep his face composed. He takes a deep breath. "Okay. What can I do?"

"For now?" she says. "You can stay and have a drink with me and my family."

He smiles. "That I can definitely do. Will you tell them, do you think?"

"I'm not sure," she says, glancing over at them: Roddy and Winston leaning against each other in a booth like two books on a shelf, Gemma glowing as she talks to Rosie over a shared plate of nachos, Hugh asleep with his head on Connor's lap. There are fairy lights in the windows of the pub, and an old Frank Sinatra song is playing softly from the speakers, and the coziness of it all makes time feel rubbery and immaterial; Jude remembers being here with her mother all those years ago on the last night of their trip, sitting together on these very same stools, in this very same spot.

"Do you wish you'd done things differently?" she'd asked, and Frankie—already hollow-eyed and much too thin—had smiled.

"If you haven't made at least a few big mistakes, you haven't really lived."

"What then?" Jude had pressed her.

Frankie was spinning her glass on the counter, maybe the same glass that Jude is holding now. "Let's not talk about the past," she said, and Jude thought: *That's all there is.*

"Were you happy?" she asked, though really she meant: *Was it worth it?* "At least tell me that."

"Most days," Frankie said. "Most days I was happy. Which is really all you can ask."

At the time, it had seemed to Jude a wildly insufficient answer. Now she's not so sure.

Frankie studied her carefully, reading her mind. "You want to know if it was worth it," she said, her eyes glittering. "You're too young to see it yet."

"See what?"

"How brilliant you'll be," she told her.

Back then, Jude was just a kid, eighteen years old and about to lose her mother for the third time. She was an above-average actor with a luminous, almost otherworldly quality that her teachers and directors couldn't quite figure out how to use. She assumed she'd be spending this fall the same way she'd spent the last one: at the middling college in Wisconsin where she had a partial theater scholarship. She couldn't have known that her whole life would change that summer. She couldn't have known that her mom was right, that the bet Frankie had made that night beside the burning car as sparks flew up into the sky would end up paying off. She couldn't have known how much she'd miss her when it did.

"I didn't do everything I wanted," Frankie said with a smile, "but I have a feeling you will."

Even now, Jude isn't sure exactly what she meant by that. Did she mean that Jude would do everything she herself dreamed of, or everything that Frankie had? And were they really all that different, in the end? That night, she couldn't have said what she wanted. Except for this: to be sitting in the late-night quiet of a nearly empty pub, the lights twinkling against the windows and the people she loves all around her, her heart somehow both achy and full.

"What do you think?" Frankie had asked her that night, their last ever together, smiling at her as she leaned an elbow on the bar. "Should we head up or stay a little longer?"

Now Jude pulls her gaze from her family back over to Spencer. "I think," she says, "I just want to stay in this moment a little longer."

He nods and takes her hand in his. "We'll stay as long as you'd like."

West Virginia

1994

ON THE VERY FIRST NIGHT OF THEIR VERY FIRST ROAD TRIP, the power went out at the motel. They'd made it as far as West Virginia, though it hadn't been explained to any of them whether this was the destination or just a place they'd stopped because Frankie was too tired to drive any farther. It didn't matter. They were too excited by her sudden return to their lives after months of increasingly sporadic bedtime phone calls and handwritten letters telling them about various auditions. She never mentioned whether she was getting the parts. Gemma said that meant she wasn't. But Jude didn't believe her.

When Frankie had pulled into the driveway, only their dad seemed unsurprised, and Jude knew then that this had all been arranged, and that they would be hers again, even if just for a little while. She felt spiky with happiness, a joy like a fever, her whole body aflame at the thought. She was the first to give her mom a hug. The first to run upstairs and pack her bag. The first to tumble into the car, where she rode in the backseat between her brothers, beaming the entire way.

That night, the power went out while Jude was brushing her teeth. She went galloping back into the room, where the rest of them were groaning. "Don't worry," she said, digging through her bag and emerging triumphantly with a flashlight she'd gotten for Christmas. She'd forgotten socks. And pajamas. But she'd packed a flashlight. And a box of crayons. And her two favorite stuffed animals.

For a while, they made shadow puppets on the walls, and then a fight broke out over the flashlight, and Frankie declared that they should save the batteries anyway, and they opened the curtains so the moonlight shone down into the room. Jude pulled out the stuffed lion and elephant.

"Let's have a puppet show," she said, and her mom—who had been lost to her for so many months, who had been traveling the country in search of a dream, who'd somehow come back again all the same—turned to her with a smile.

"*Yes,*" she said.

There were no other takers, so the two of them practiced for a while, and then they rigged a curtain out of the sheet from one of the beds, and Gemma and Connor and Roddy gathered on the other side to watch with a lack of enthusiasm that Jude was far too happy to notice.

But when it came time for the opening line, she lost her nerve. "I can't," she whispered to Frankie, thrusting the lion at her.

Frankie pushed it gently back toward Jude. "You can," she said firmly.

Jude looked down at the lion's regal face, ran a hand along his feathery mane. She was aware of Connor laughing softly on the other side of the sheet, of Roddy's restless sighs. "I don't want to go first," she said. "I'm too nervous."

To Jude's relief, Frankie nodded and reached for the elephant, though he wasn't due onstage until the second act. "Let's do it together then," she said, smiling at Jude through the dark. "It's always easier that way, don't you think?"

Jude did.

(She still does.)

Gemma

North Dakota

2025

For a while, they all sit around the enormous circular booth, trad-ing stories and memories. They'll be scattered again starting to-morrow; some combination of Jude's assistant, travel agent, and manager have already rebooked all their flights for the morning, to Los Angeles and Chicago, Nashville and D.C. and New York. But for now, they're still here, and Gemma can't remember the last time she's laughed this much, the last time she was this happy.

Eventually, as the clock ticks toward midnight, and the long day behind them makes itself felt, the others start to fall away. Annie is the first to excuse herself. Gemma had noticed that she and Connor were holding hands underneath the table, and Annie leans close to whisper something in his ear before unwinding her fingers from his and looking around at the rest of them.

"I think it's time for me to head home," she says. "But thanks for letting me be part of your weekend. It was . . . very memorable."

They all say their goodbyes, except for Connor, who hangs back with an uncertain smile while they thank her for driving, and apolo-gize for all the drama, and promise to give her a call if they're ever back in Portree, which makes her laugh.

"Or in New York," Connor says hopefully, and Annie looks over at him with such longing that Gemma can suddenly picture it, the two of them back in the city together, going out to dinners in tucked-away restaurants, walking along the Hudson River in the falling snow, finding places that will one day be theirs, getting to know each other for real.

It happens all the time, Gemma thinks. *So why not for them?*

Connor walks her out, and when he returns, looking a little lost, it's to find Hugh asleep again, this time with his head on the table. He once again lifts him—his arms limp and swaying, his cheek finding Connor's shoulder—but before he can turn to carry him upstairs, Rosie, who has been unable to stop yawning, admits she's ready to go up too.

"I'll be back," Connor promises, as they all say good night to the kids. "Just give me a few minutes."

Spencer, who is wedged into the booth beside Jude, an arm around her shoulders, gives Rosie a wave. "Good night, Rosie. It was really nice to meet you."

"You too, Spencer Nolan," Rosie says with a happy little sigh, and then she looks up at Connor with a grin. "Best trip ever."

Gemma's phone buzzes with a text from Mateo, who has been checking in practically every hour since the hospital: **How are you two doing?**

She puts a hand on her stomach and smiles, then types: **Can't wait to see you tomorrow.**

There's an immediate reply:

I'll be waiting at the airport. If you don't recognize me, I'll be the one jumping for joy.

Just then, the clerk from the lobby appears with a slightly sad-looking bunch of yellow tulips. "I'm sorry," he says, thrusting them at Jude. "But this is all I could find on short notice."

Jude—who is fairly accustomed to receiving flowers at random moments from nervous strangers—gives him a friendly nod, but then he adds, "They're from someone named Mateo?" and she laughs and hands them across to Gemma, whose chest floods with a strange kind of long-delayed happiness.

"Thank you," she says, burying her nose in them. "They're perfect."

Connor returns a few minutes later, and when he does, Winston stands up and stretches. "I'm knackered," he says, though they can all see that's not true. His eyes are shining as he glances down at Roddy, the stuffed ring clutched tight in his hands. But it's clear that he wants to give the four of them a chance to be alone.

Spencer takes his cue from Winston, looking to Jude, who nods and gives him a kiss that would've made Rosie's eyes pop, before he stands up too. "I'll see you all in the morning," he says, then turns to Gemma. "Congrats again. I'm so glad everything worked out."

She smiles at him. "Thanks for getting us there."

When they're down to four, the bartender wanders over to see if they need another round or some more food, though the table is still filled with an impressive collection of half-empty plates and glasses.

"We're not keeping you, are we?" Connor asks once they've ordered, and the guy—who isn't more than a kid really, probably nineteen or twenty, with freckles spilling across his pale face—flushes red. They wait for him to say he doesn't mind because of Jude, but instead he cuts his eyes over to Roddy.

"It's no problem," he says, then clears his throat. "I'm a huge fan."

"Of me?" Roddy asks, surprised—not because he doesn't have fans, but because he's so used to being eclipsed around Jude.

"Yeah, man," the bartender says, and even his ears are pink. "I have your jersey at home. Though I guess I'll have to get an Orlando one now. I'm glad you're still playing." He pauses, then adds: "It's nice to see someone out there who's like me."

Then, before Roddy can say anything more, the kid whisks away their empty glasses and hurries back over to the bar.

Roddy grins at the rest of them. "Damn, that feels good. I can't even play it cool."

"No need to," Jude says. "Not with us."

He leans forward, his elbows on the table, still beaming. "You guys should really come to a match this season. It's been a while."

"We'd love to," Jude says, but then her face shifts and she stands abruptly. "Sorry, I—I'll be right back."

They all sit there, watching her go. Then Gemma slides out of the booth to follow.

When she nudges open the door to the bathroom, Jude is standing at the mirror, her eyes shiny with tears. She moves to wipe them away, looking embarrassed.

"Hey," Jude says with forced casualness. "How are you feeling?"

Their eyes meet in the mirror.

"How are *you* feeling?" Gemma asks.

"What do you mean?"

"Jude, come on," she says in a gentle voice. "Talk to me."

Jude spins to face her, astonished. "How . . . ?"

"I'm your sister," Gemma says. "I know you."

Jude shakes her head, then turns back to the mirror. "I was planning to tell you," she says, meeting Gemma's eyes in the reflection. "I promise. But I just—I knew that would make it seem more real."

Gemma puts a hand on her sister's shoulder, feels the delicate curve of her bone.

"It's what Mom had," Jude says, and though Gemma didn't know this—couldn't have known this—it also feels like she did somehow, like she always has. She shivers, though she's standing right underneath a heat vent.

"Jude, I'm—"

"I don't want that," she says, turning back to look at Gemma with a watery smile. "Not yet. Okay? I just found you guys again. And Spencer. And I . . . I'm just not there yet. So none of that, okay?"

Gemma hadn't even known she was crying, but now she nods and swipes at her tears. "Okay. But Jude? I'm here for whatever you need. You know that, right? Don't disappear again. Don't do what Mom did. Promise me that."

Jude nods. Without quite meaning to, Gemma rests a hand on her belly, and she watches her sister's expression change.

"I really want to meet her," Jude says, and in spite of herself, Gemma laughs.

"How do you know it's a girl?"

Jude smiles. "I just know. And I'm going to try really hard to be there for her. The way you always were for me."

When Gemma opens her arms, Jude walks straight into them, and Gemma holds her tight, heart sinking like a weight in her chest. Jude is the one who has to untangle herself; if it were up to Gemma, she'd stay there like that forever.

They walk back out, arms intertwined, and Jude turns to Gemma just before they reach the bar. "Don't tell the boys yet, okay?"

Gemma looks at her in surprise. "I thought you were done with secrets."

"I just need a little more time on this one," she says, and though the words make Gemma want to cry again, she nods.

"Of course."

As they approach the table, Roddy and Connor look up nervously.

"Everything all right?" Roddy asks, and Jude and Gemma glance at each other, then flick their eyes away.

"Yes," Gemma says firmly.

"Because if this is about, you know, the fire and the car and keeping everything secret," Connor says, "we really do forgive you."

"How magnanimous," Gemma says, rolling her eyes. "Especially considering your own history."

"That was the opposite of keeping a secret," Connor tells her. "That was spilling secrets. Totally different thing."

Jude laughs as she slides into the booth. "Well, then we forgive you for that too."

"Just please don't write another book about us," Gemma says. "Or if you do, please don't make my character quite so boring."

Connor looks at her very seriously. "Trust me, if I ever write another one, you'll be the hero."

Gemma opens her mouth, then closes it again, suddenly emotional. It's the way they're all three looking at her, the way they're nodding in agreement. She blinks a few times, trying to hide her tears. "Well then," she says brusquely. "I better get to slay some dragons or something."

Connor laughs. "Don't get your hopes up. This is just a theoretical book."

"Aren't all your books theoretical these days?" Roddy asks with a grin.

"Hilarious," Connor says. "Especially coming from the guy who's about to be riding the bench all season."

"We can't all be Oscar nominees," Gemma chimes in, and they turn to look at Jude, who blushes.

"It's pretty amazing," Connor says earnestly.

Roddy nods. "Yeah, who would've thought?"

"Mom," Jude says with a smile. "Mom would've thought."

They're all quiet for a moment, thinking back. And then Connor shrugs.

"To be fair," he says, "she probably also thought *she* would get nominated at some point, so . . ."

"Fifty-fifty isn't terrible," Roddy says, and they laugh.

Later, as Gemma digs through her bag for her phone to text Mateo about the flowers, she finds the map she stole from the convenience store. "Oh," she says, surprised. She slides it across the table to Connor. "This was supposed to be for the kids."

He smiles. "They've already got one."

"They do?" Jude says, looking touched by this.

"Of course," says Connor; then he nudges it back across the table toward Gemma. "And a whole lot of thumbtacks. Save this one for yours."

Her eyes fill with tears again. "I will," she says, but instead of returning it to her bag, she unfolds it, and the others lean in. For a moment, she feels transported through time, flung back into their old kitchen in Michigan on the day the twins carted a different map home and she found a box of pushpins so they could mark off where they'd been.

"How many does everyone have now that we've added North Dakota?" Roddy asks, looking around as they tally up their new state totals.

"I think I'm at thirty-three," Connor says, and Jude rolls her eyes.

"That's impossible," she tells him. "We went to thirty-two as kids, which would mean you've basically been nowhere since then."

"I've gone places, just not new ones," he says. "Oh wait, I guess I did a reading in Portland a few years ago. Put me down for thirty-four."

"Keep counting," Jude tells him, then turns to Roddy. "What about you?"

He's studying the map and making notes on a napkin with a pen the bartender had happily given him. "I think forty-one."

"Not bad."

"It always made me feel better about those early morning flights to away games in random cities."

Gemma is still counting too. "I think we might be tied, Roddy."

"Last one to fifty is a rotten egg?" he says. "Not including Connor. He's been disqualified for having absolutely no memory of anywhere he's been."

"Wait, I think I went to a library conference once in New Mexico," Connor says, ignoring this. "That's where Albuquerque is, right?"

"Jeez," Gemma says. "Did they really give you a fancy book award?"

He waves this away and continues scanning the map.

"I've been to all fifty," Jude says quietly, and they look over at her.

"No way," says Roddy.

"I call bullshit," says Connor.

"Are you sure?" Gemma asks. "What about . . ."

"North Dakota?" Jude suggests with a wry smile. "Yes, I've kept track all these years. It was important to me. You guys know that."

Connor frowns. "Right, but . . . even, like, Mississippi?"

"Mississippi is lovely, actually," Jude says. "I highly recommend the mud pie."

"Utah?" asks Roddy.

"We did that one as kids."

"We did?" He looks back at his list, delighted. "Forty-two!"

"Minnesota?" Gemma asks.

"Believe it or not, I briefly dated a producer who was from St. Paul. He took me home to meet his parents. They loved me," she says. "Obviously."

"Missouri?"

"Yup." Jude nods. "I did a commercial in Kansas City once."

"That's in Kansas," Roddy points out.

"And Missouri."

"Oh."

Gemma pores over the map. "Montana?"

"Yeah," Jude says. "I went skiing there."

"Which slope?" Connor asks. "I went to Big Sky when I was researching the book."

"Sun Valley," she says.

"That's Idaho," Connor tells her, then glances down at his list. "Hey, I've been there too. Another one for me!"

"Wait, what's in Montana?" Jude asks, deep in thought. "I know I must've been there . . ."

"Missoula? Bozeman? Helena?"

Jude scowls at the map. "Shit," she says. "Did I somehow count this wrong? How did I screw this up?"

"In fairness," Roddy says sincerely, "there are a lot of states that start with *M*."

Jude lets out a surprised laugh, then looks over at Gemma. "Wow. I guess I've still got a bit more ground to cover then."

Gemma holds her gaze for a beat, then smiles. "I guess you do."

"How about we do another trip like this, but in Montana?" Jude suggests, and they all nod enthusiastically.

"As long as there's no snow," says Roddy.

"As long as we don't lose power," adds Connor.

Gemma looks around at the three of them. "As long as we're all there."

Jude nods solemnly. "Deal."

Michigan

2001

A WEEK AFTER THE FIRE, GEMMA FINALLY LEFT FOR COL-
lege. When they finished packing the car, she took turns hugging
each of the boys, then her dad, and then Liz.

"Where's Jude?" she asked, glancing around, and the rest of them
shrugged. Nobody ever knew where Jude was. This was no different.

Gemma held up a finger, then disappeared back into the house,
where she found her sister in her room, sitting cross-legged in front
of the map. It was leaning up against a bookshelf, bristling with
thumbtacks. Jude didn't look up, even as Gemma lowered herself
onto the floor beside her.

"What if we don't get to finish now?" she asked, her eyes trained
on the map.

"We will," Gemma said, though they both knew that wasn't true.
At least not in the way they'd started it. Not with their mom. Their
dad had made that much clear on the way home from Texas.

Jude reached out and traced a finger along the cornflower-blue
shore of Lake Michigan, coming to a stop where they were sitting
now, their home, the place where it had all started. She let her hand
fall away again and they both stared at it, a small dot on a big map.

"It won't be the same," she said, and Gemma shook her head.

"No, but you'll still travel. You can still see it all, if you want to." She reached over and squeezed her little sister's shoulder. "There's plenty of time."

Jude turned to face her, and Gemma saw that her eyes were bright with tears. "Is it weird that I miss it already?"

"What?"

"The four of us," she said, then leaned into Gemma, who kissed the side of her head.

One Year Later

Montana

2026

On a dude ranch outside of Bozeman, Gemma and Connor stand staring at a row of slightly swaybacked horses tied to a wooden post.

"This is so typical of Jude," Connor grumbles. "Who even likes horses?"

"I do," Rosie shouts cheerfully from atop a dappled-gray mare. She's riding in circles around a paddock, already steering as if she'd grown up here on the western plains, rather than in Brooklyn Heights.

Behind her, Hugh's little white pony stops to try to eat some grass, and he gives her a few ineffectual kicks before a ranch hand jogs over to help. "Hey, Dad?" he says as the horse begins to plod forward again. He's wearing an Orlando jersey, the name ENDICOTT printed on the back, not easy to find since Roddy announced his retirement and they began to sell out. "Can I be a cowboy when I grow up?"

"Sure," Connor says, grimacing as one of the ranch hands motions to him. "Why not."

Gemma leans against a fence post, watching with amusement as a guy in a cowboy hat helps her brother onto an enormous black horse.

Mateo appears at her side, and she feels that now-familiar burst of joy as her eyes land on the baby in his arms, who smiles back at her with his whole body.

"Are you sure you don't want to go too?" Mateo asks. "I could hang back."

Gemma winces. "You think I want to get on a horse six months after giving birth to this guy?" she says, reaching for the wriggling baby. "No, thank you." She holds him in front of her for a second, admiring his little face and inquisitive eyes, the way he always looks at her so expectantly, like she's about to tell him the very best joke he's ever heard. Then she shifts him onto her hip, and he rewards her with a toothy grin. "We'll meet you up there."

"I could come with you guys in the jeep . . ."

Gemma shakes her head. "You go ahead and giddy up. Get along, little dogie. Yee-haw and all that."

He grins and tips his baseball cap to her. "Yes, ma'am," he says; then he does a jokey, meet-me-at-high-noon sort of saunter toward the paddock, where the very first horse he approaches promptly sneezes all over him, splattering gunk across his Pelé jersey. He gives her a sheepish look, and Gemma laughs and brings her mouth close to the baby's ear. "Your dad is not much of a cowboy," she says, "but we still love him."

"Hey," Connor shouts from atop his horse, which is turning in small circles. "Where the hell are Roddy and Winston? How did they get out of this?"

Gemma is trying not to laugh at Connor's indignant expression as he clutches the pommel of his saddle. "I could ask the same of your girlfriend," she yells back.

The horse continues to turn in creaky circles as Connor perches there helplessly, tugging the reins back and forth. "She's two thousand miles away in some stuffy NYU office defending her dissertation," he says. "What's their excuse?"

"Our excuse," Roddy says with a grin as he and Winston walk up in matching cowboy hats, "is that we never got a honeymoon, so . . ."

"So . . . what?" Hugh asks with interest.

Winston laughs, and Roddy—blushing—points to the remaining horses. "Dibs on the polka-dotted one!"

"Not sure that guy will make it all the way up to the ridge," says one of the ranch hands. "He's retiring soon. Off to greener pastures."

"Just like you," Winston says, giving Roddy's shoulder a little pat.

Roddy smiles back at him from underneath the brim of his hat. "Just like me," he says, then turns to the ranch hand with alarm. "Unless that's a euphemism."

The guy laughs. "Don't worry. It's not."

When they're all mounted and ready to go, Gemma waves them off. "Have fun," she says as the horses walk past one by one, kicking up clouds of dust. "I'll see you up there."

"Thanks," says Roddy.

"Drive safe," says Winston.

"I hate you," says Connor.

Gemma navigates the dirt roads up to the ridge and parks the jeep where the ranch manager had suggested, then unbuckles the baby from his car seat and wrangles him into the carrier so that he's snug against her, his downy head tucked under her chin. As she makes her way slowly up the trail, she breathes in the smell of pine, listens to the sounds of birds all around her, the whistle of the wind, and she's happy to have an excuse to be here on her own, to wander through a place like this with only her thoughts.

At the top, she stops a few feet from the edge, her heart pounding and her throat tight. The sky is a startling shade of blue, crowded with huge, scudding clouds, and in the distance, jagged mountains are dusted with snow like something straight out of a painting. Beneath them are acres and acres of green grass parceled off by fence posts and dotted with oversized rolls of hay.

"I know you can't see it," she says to the baby, whose face is pressed against her chest, "but it's really something."

He sighs in his sleep, and Gemma looks up again, filling her lungs with air so clean it almost hurts to breathe. She watches a herd of horses move lazily down below, heads bent over the grass, and she swears she can almost hear their hoofbeats until she realizes the sound is coming from behind her. She whirls to see her group appear, the great barrel chests of the horses straining as they hurtle themselves up the steep trail.

Everyone greets her happily as the ranch hands help them off and then lead the horses back down the trail to get some water. The rest of them stumble in Gemma's direction, bowlegged and sunburned and full of stories from their ride. Mateo comes over to kiss the baby, and Winston and Roddy stare wide-eyed at the view in front of them, and Hugh and Rosie interrupt each other as they try to tell Gemma about the fox they saw on the trail.

Connor stands back, uncharacteristically quiet, watching them all with a sober expression. When his eyes meet Gemma's, a knot forms in her throat, because she knows it's time, has felt it moving closer all day. But she still doesn't feel ready. She wants to cry, but instead she blinks fast and presses her cheek against the baby's soft head, taking a moment to feel the flutter of his heartbeat against hers. And then she looks up at her brother and nods.

"Hey, so . . ." he begins, then trails off. But it's enough. They all know why they're here.

Connor pulls a tin from his pocket, and they gather around. They're careful, because of the wind. Each one cups their hands solemnly, taking a small amount of ash, and then one by one they sprinkle it on the ridge, taking it all in: the sky and the mountains and the never-ending green fields. If you'd asked Gemma before this, she would've guessed that they'd say something. That there would be speeches and tears. But the truth is, they've already said all that needs to be said. During the long months of Jude's illness—at first private and then surreally, inevitably public—and afterward too.

The world had mourned her loudly, even before she was gone. But for the three of them, it was quieter; they each flew out as often as they could, taking turns stretching out on the lounge chairs by her pool beneath a wash of stars, the air smelling of jasmine, the smoke from Jude's joint twisting into the sky as they laughed about their childhood adventures: the time Jude found a spider in the shower of some hotel and left it on Connor's pillow; the time Roddy decided to run away on his bike but finished all his snacks within hours so returned home for dinner; the time they planted seeds in the garden and a few days later were delighted to find an enormous watermelon had sprouted, only to learn years later that Gemma had been the one to put it there; the time Jude nearly drowned in the lake for real while trying to set a world record for how long she could hold her breath, and the other three flailed around with numb fingers and frantic hearts until they had her, until they dragged her back, the same way they found themselves trying to drag her back now, though this time they knew it was impossible.

They had a last summer road trip together, just the four of them, where they drove up the California coast. Jude's eyes never left the window, taking in the beaches and cliffs and the jagged blue ocean; they laughed and teased one another and fought over the music; they sat by the fire pit and roasted marshmallows at one hotel, and at another they snuck into the pool area after hours and went swimming beneath a bone-white moon. At night, Gemma would climb into bed beside Jude, her pregnant belly squeezed between them, and hold her little sister the way she used to when they were kids and she'd had a bad dream.

In September, they celebrated the twins' birthday, knowing it would be Jude's last. By then, Gemma was too pregnant to fly, so they all came to Chicago, and though they made plenty of plans—to take a boat tour on the river and go to a Cubs game and ride the carousel at Navy Pier—they ended up mostly sitting on Gemma's back porch, the sun warm on their faces, the city loud all around them, talking until late in the night. Thanksgiving and Christmas were starting to seem like too much to hope for, so they celebrated those too, with turkey and stuffing and tinsel and carols. But nobody exchanged gifts; what could they have possibly given each other that would've meant half as much as this?

Later, at the funeral—which was held in a small church in Michigan on the edge of the lake Jude had loved so much—they each talked about that wintry weekend in North Dakota, how it felt suspended in time, the snow pinging against the windows of the cozy cabin where they'd found one another again, where they'd started anew.

Still, it hadn't felt like a goodbye. None of it had. Not really.

But this does. And Gemma isn't ready for it.

As she opens her hand to let the wind carry away the ash, tears stream from the corners of her eyes. The baby shifts against her, and she thinks of the way Jude had looked at him when she first held him. The doctors had tried to tell her she was too sick to fly by then, but she was determined enough to ignore them. "I've been waiting for this," she said, and Gemma knew she meant it literally, that it was part of what had kept her going, the promise of this moment, when she took her nephew in her arms, gazing down at him, her eyes wet with tears.

"You better name him after me," she said, and Gemma had known she was joking, which made the next part even better.

"I already did," she told her, and that moment right there—the look of surprise on Jude's face, the way it melted so quickly into something more like awe, like tenderness, like love—is something Gemma will never forget.

When their hands are empty, they stand looking out at the sprawl of land below for what feels like a very long time.

Montana. Jude's very last state.

"So what happens next?" Connor asks eventually, and the question pokes a neat little hole in Gemma's heart, because she doesn't know. She still doesn't know.

"I guess," she says, "that we keep moving forward. Somehow."

Connor shakes his head. "I meant on the schedule."

They all turn to Gemma, who smiles ruefully, then pulls the itinerary from her pocket. Spencer had been the one to find it. He'd been helping to sort through Jude's things, calling whenever he stumbled across something he wasn't sure about or—more often—something he wanted to tell them, to share with the people who loved her too. "Do you know she kept her Oscar in the bathroom?" he'd say. "Not even the nicer guest bathroom, but in ours, right next to that globby old toothbrush of hers." Or: "Did you guys know she played chess? I've found three chessboards. Three!" Or: "Do you have any idea how many single socks she kept? I think it's because she was a romantic. She was always trying to reunite the pairs."

Now Gemma unfolds the stapled pieces of paper, filled with instructions for the trip: airline and rental car confirmation numbers, the information for the dude ranch—all of it prepaid, of course—and a detailed schedule of events. Today is their last day, and right after *lunch* and *trail ride*, at the very end of the page, it says, *time to say goodbye.*

Gemma swallows hard. "That's it," she says, and they all stare at her, looking as lost as she feels.

"That's it?" Roddy says,

Connor frowns. "No more instructions?"

Gemma flips over the page. "Oh, wait. It says we should go to the bar for drinks."

"Typical," Connor says, but he seems relieved. "And then?"

She looks up at them, her voice wobbling: "And then it says we have to do this again next year. And the year after. And the year after that."

They're all quiet for a moment, taking this in, imagining this future she set out for them, how it'll feel like poking at a bruise, doing this without her again and again, but how they'll be able to keep her with them in this way, to carry her forward, and they're standing there with heads bowed as they think about her when Connor breaks the silence to say, "Please don't tell me we have to come to a dude ranch in Montana every year for the rest of our lives."

Gemma laughs. "No, I think we just have to take a trip together."

"Wow," Roddy says, and the others nod.

"She's so bossy," Connor says, but he's smiling. They all are. "Even now."

Somewhere farther down the trail, one of the horses snorts, and Hugh's attention drifts in that direction. As he starts to wander back, Connor catches Rosie's eye, and she hurries after her little brother and grabs his hand, and the two of them walk side by side in a way that makes Gemma's heart ache.

Winston looks around, then gives Roddy a nod. "I'll go make sure they don't fall off a cliff or anything," he says, and Mateo squeezes Gemma's arm before following him.

The sun is starting to slip in the sky, and a hawk circles above as the remaining three linger there. *The remaining four,* Gemma is reminded as the baby makes a snuffling sound.

Gemma, Connor, Roddy.

And Jude.

Gemma kisses the top of his head, and he shifts and stretches and lets out a fearsome yowl. Connor laughs.

"You're going to be just as opinionated as she was," he says, coming around to Gemma's side to peek at the scrunched-up face, "aren't you?"

Gemma smiles. "He's got to live up to his name somehow."

"Jude," Roddy says, and the way he says it, so full of love, makes her heart feel both empty and full, both cracked and whole. He puts a hand on the baby's head, his eyes wet with tears, and then he says it again: "Jude."

For a moment, the three of them stand there like that, side by side, the world humming all around them as they watch this tiny baby, who carries his name so well already.

"Hey," Connor says, once again breaking the silence, "maybe we should put *this* Jude in charge of future trips so we don't end up at any more dude ranches."

"Not all of us are afraid of horses," Roddy teases him.

"I'm not *afraid* of them," he says. "I just don't like the way they look at me."

"Your uncle is afraid of horses," Gemma whispers to the baby, and Connor rolls his eyes.

"All I'm saying is that if we're going to do this, let's really do it."

"What did you have in mind?" she asks as they begin to walk, picking their way carefully along the trail, leaving the sun and the sky and the mountains behind. For a second, Gemma feels panicky at the thought of what else they've left, at the memory of all those ashes whirling through the too-big sky. But she knows that's just dust, that what's important will always be with them.

"Well, you know there's a whole big world out there, right?" Connor says. "That there's something beyond just the fifty states?"

"Wow," Roddy says with a grin. "Next you're gonna tell us the earth is round."

"All I'm saying is that there's more to see," he continues as the trail curves and the others appear: Mateo and Winston and Rosie and Hugh. Gemma glances at them, then over at her brothers, then down at the baby, who is looking up at her with those same blue eyes as his aunt, infinitely wise and gentle and true. She smiles at him.

"Then I suppose," she says, "we'll need a new map."

Acknowledgments

As always, this book wouldn't have been possible without so many wonderful people in my life. I'm incredibly lucky that my agent and editor are both dear friends and stalwart supporters of me and my work. Thank you doesn't seem like quite enough, but I'm enormously grateful to Jennifer Joel and Kara Cesare for all their help and encouragement along the way.

I'm so fortunate to be published by Ballantine, which is full of creative, passionate, fierce advocates for their books. A huge thank you to Kara Welsh, Jennifer Hershey, Kim Hovey, Jesse Shuman, Gabby Colangelo, Karen Fink, Taylor Noel, Megan Whalen, Katie Horn, Elena Giavaldi, Loren Noveck, Bonnie Thompson, Julie Ehlers, and Audrey Iocca for taking especially good care of this one.

I'm thankful to Jake Smith-Bosanquet, Josie Freedman, Paige Holtzman, Sindhu Vegesena, and Zara Shepherd-Brierly at CAA, as well as Stephanie Thwaites at Curtis Brown, for everything they do. Also to Cassie Browne, Kat Burdon, and the brilliant team at Quercus. And to Binky Urban for still looking out for me all these years later.

It's a huge gift to have great friends who are also great readers, and the early feedback from Robin Wasserman, Morgan Matson, Anna Carey, Lauren Graham, Sarah Mlynowski, and Adele Griffin was completely invaluable. I'm grateful to all of them—and to the whole Wednesday crew—for making this feel like a team sport.

A great big thank you to my family—Mom, Dad, Kelly, Errol, Andrew, and Jack—for always cheering me on. And to Edna, Maria, and Ana, who took such amazing care of my son while I worked on this novel; I quite literally couldn't have done it without them.

And lastly—mostly—for Declan. Anything that's good about this book is because of you. And anything that could be better is because you didn't sleep nearly enough while I was writing it. I love you so much!

About the Author

JENNIFER E. SMITH is the bestselling author of more than a dozen books, including *The Unsinkable Greta James* and the young adult novels *The Statistical Probability of Love at First Sight* and *Hello, Goodbye, and Everything in Between,* both of which have been adapted for film. She earned a master's degree in creative writing from the University of St. Andrews in Scotland, and her work has been translated into thirty-four languages. She lives in Los Angeles.

About the Type

This book was set in Legacy, a typeface family designed by Ronald Arnholm (b. 1939) and issued in digital form by ITC in 1992. Both its serifed and unserifed versions are based on an original type created by the French punchcutter Nicholas Jenson in the late fifteenth century. While Legacy tends to differ from Jenson's original in its proportions, it maintains much of the latter's characteristic modulations in stroke.